The proceeds from the sale of this book will be used to support the mission of Library of America, a nonprofit organization that champions the nation's cultural heritage by publishing America's greatest writing in authoritative new editions and providing resources for readers to explore this rich, living legacy.

THE FUTURE IS *FEMALE!*

VOLUME 2

THE FUTURE *IS FEMALE!*

MORE CLASSIC SCIENCE FICTION STORIES BY WOMEN
VOLUME TWO: THE 1970S

LISA YASZEK, EDITOR

A Library of America Special Publication

CONTENTS

Introduction

BY LISA YASZEK

I am delighted to write this introduction in 2022, which marks the fiftieth anniversary of the slogan that gave name to this anthology. "The Future Is Female" entered the American vocabulary in 1972 when Jane Lurie and Marizel Rios began selling merchandise bearing those words to support New York City's first feminist bookstore, Labyris Books. It was preserved for posterity when feminist photographer Liza Cowan took a picture of her girlfriend Alix Dobkin wearing a T-shirt emblazoned with the slogan for her 1975 slide show, "What the Well-Dressed Dyke Will Wear in the Future." Cowan remembers that the phrase first caught her imagination because it had "no precise meaning. We are asked to absorb two powerful archetypes, and to imagine them in relationship to each other. . . . [It is] a call to arms. . . . And an invocation. . . . A spell for the good of all."[1] I would argue that these two archetypes have fueled feminism for nearly 250 years, and that they are both very much at the heart of the classic 1970s science fiction stories you will encounter in this anthology.

It is a truth universally acknowledged that there are as many definitions of "feminism" and "science fiction" as there are people who identify as feminists and science fiction enthusiasts—in fact, that is part of what makes both of these communities attractive to many people. However, by 1981, science fiction author Joanna Russ could easily identify scores of women writing a specific kind of future-oriented fiction that celebrated female agency, community, and sexuality in reaction to "what [its] authors believe society . . . and/or women lack in the here and now."[2] For Russ, feminist science fiction authors were—much like their political counterparts—bound together by a shared set of goals, using their art to demonstrate the limits of patriarchal culture and articulate the possibility of more egalitarian alternatives for all.

Of course, the idea that women might use science fiction to comment on the relations of science and society and to stake claims for women in the future was nothing new. Margaret Cavendish's *The Blazing World* (1666) cast its author as a dimension-traveling philosopher-warrior queen who saves her homeland with an army of sentient alien animals. Meanwhile, Mary Shelley's *Frankenstein* (1818) dramatized the dangers of a male-centered science that excludes female intellect and morality, all while introducing modern audiences to some of science fiction's most enduring characters, including the mad scientist, the scientist's imperiled love-interest, and the misunderstood monster. At the turn of the twentieth century, feminists Charlotte Perkins Gilman, Pauline Hopkins, and Rokheya Sakhawat Hossain imagined techno-utopian futures in which women could become fully modern political and scientific subjects. Early and mid-twentieth-century science fiction writers like Leslie F. Stone, C. L. Moore, and Judith Merril helped build the genre by setting stories in living rooms and launchpads alike while exploring how science and technology might be deployed to literally reshape sex relations.[3]

Then, on or about 1970, women's science fiction changed—the date is approximate, but the evidence throughout the decade is palpable. This was not principally a matter of increased numbers; women had long comprised about 15 percent of science fiction professionals and while there were more women than ever writing in the 1970s, there were more men doing so as well, leading veteran author and agent Virginia Kidd to conclude that "the proportion of women writing . . . science fiction today may be exactly the same or, just possibly, a little bit larger" than in previous generations.[4] Suddenly, however, women were much more *visible* in the genre. Women writers earned accolades from fans and professionals alike, taking home a disproportionate share of Hugo and Nebula Awards over the course of the decade (19 percent and 25 percent, respectively) while leading professional organizations such as the Science Fiction and Fantasy Writers of America (SFWA, recently renamed the Science Fiction Writers Association), the Clarion West Writers Workshop, and the Science Fiction and Fantasy Poetry Association (SFPA). Women also made their mark as science fiction artists during this era. To offer just a few examples: Wendy Pini and Fara Shimbo (née Valenza) imagined futures populated by space-faring animals and females of all species for *Galaxy* (see figs. 1, 2); the Hugo and Caldecott award-winning wife-and-husband team Diane and Leo Dillon produced cover art for *The Magazine of Fantasy and Science Fiction* that staked claims for people of color in the future (see fig. 3); and Jeanne Gomoll helped lead the charge to create cons, fanzines, and even an amateur press association (APA) within feminist fandom (see Gomoll's artwork for *Janus*, fig. 4). Perhaps most important, no matter what corner of the genre they hailed from, for the first time ever women began to represent themselves as a politically and aesthetically coherent

Figure 1. Wendy Pini, artwork for *Galaxy*, June 1975.

group, creating a new mode of speculative art that would soon be known as feminist science fiction.

Like other forms of progressive politics, feminism enjoyed a resurgence in the 1960s and '70s. Activists associated with new political groups such as the National Organization for Women (NOW) carried on the work of their suffragist foremothers by lobbying for equal access to employment and economic opportunities, while artists and scholars transformed Americans' understanding of the past by recovering the *herstory* of strong-willed women who made their own present possible. Recognizing that "the personal is political," activists created grassroots groups dedicated to women's physical, mental, and sexual health issues and used new household technologies to redistribute domestic labor more equitably. As these latter examples suggest, science and technology were increasingly part of the feminist agenda in this historical moment. Social scientist Bernice Sandler led the legal battle that resulted in the Education Amendment Acts of 1972, which banned sex discrimination in all federally funded education programs; writers Gloria Steinem and Dorothy Pitman Hughes launched *Ms.* magazine, also in 1972, to amplify feminist voices in the U.S. media landscape; and cultural theorist Shulamith Firestone argued that women should use new fertility technologies to seize "control of reproduction" and redistribute childbearing and childrearing practices.[5]

At the same time, the science fiction genre at large was changing in ways that made it more relevant than ever to politically engaged artists. Blockbuster movies such as *Star Wars* (1977) and *Star Trek* (1979) and TV shows such as *Battlestar Galactica* (1978–79) and *The Six Million Dollar Man*

(1973–78) proved that science fiction had moved from the margins to the center of American popular culture, as did the use of science fiction motifs in the music and performances of rock stars Jimi Hendrix, Paul Kantner and Grace Slick of Jefferson Starship, and George Clinton of Parliament. Science fiction invaded the mainstream world of words as novels by Michael Crichton and Anne McCaffrey topped the *New York Times* Best Seller lists and literary authors Thomas Pynchon, Kurt Vonnegut, and Margaret Atwood borrowed elements of the genre in their critically acclaimed fiction. Even scholars got in on the action, establishing the first professional organizations, journals, and conferences dedicated to the serious study of science fiction across media.

While the literary establishment began to visit the strange new world of science fiction, a "New Wave" of authors and editors returned to the genre with elevated aesthetic expectations. Coined by P. Schuyler Miller in 1961 to describe the group of science fiction writers associated with the British publication *New Worlds* under the editorship of Michael Moorcock, the phrase was soon extended to include United States writers such as Harlan Ellison, Roger Zelazny, Samuel R. Delany, Joanna Russ, Ursula K. Le Guin, Robert Silverberg, and Thomas Disch. Diverse in tone and theme, New Wave authors were loosely bound together by a shared refusal of the naive techno-optimism characteristic of earlier American science fiction. Instead, they innovated both stylistically and thematically, borrowing social insights from the soft sciences to explore the impact of technology on the human psyche, map the limits of a "rapacious industrial culture," and speculate about the new science and societies that might replace our current ones.[6] Although magazines remained important venues for publication, authors of experimental science fiction usually placed their most groundbreaking work in the original anthology series that were quickly replacing magazines as the center of generic innovation due to their "high pay, perceived prestige, and selectivity."[7] Over the course of the decade, authors and editors associated with anthology series, including Damon Knight's *Orbit* (1965–80), Robert Silverberg's *New Dimensions* (1971–81), Terry Carr's *Universe* (1971–87), and Harlan Ellison's *Dangerous Visions* (1968 and 1972), earned a "remarkable number of Hugo and Nebula" nominations and wins.[8]

Feminist science fiction author and editor Pamela Sargent recalls that the "atmosphere of change" heralded by the New Wave attracted women to the genre because it suddenly seemed that their stories "were likely to find a more receptive audience, even if [they] violated some of the traditional canons."[9] These women, many of whom are featured in the present anthology, included old pros who had been involved in science fiction for decades, such as Miriam Allen deFord and Elinor Busby; rising stars associated with the New Wave experiments of the 1960s, including Joanna Russ, Ursula K. Le Guin, and Kate Wilhelm; and new authors who came to science fiction in the 1970s, such as Joan D. Vinge, Vonda N. McIntyre, Connie Willis, and Lisa Tuttle. Like their activist counterparts in the Women's Liberation Movement (and, for that matter, like their male counterparts in the science fiction community), the majority of feminist science fiction authors publishing in the 1970s identified as white, middle-class, heterosexual, and cisgender. Not surprisingly, many of their stories revolve around characters with similar identities and values. But, as in the larger feminist community, women science fiction writers of this era were indeed taking the first tentative steps toward exploring how sexuality and race might complicate some of America's most-dearly held beliefs about "Woman" as a universal, biologically-based category that encompasses the experience of all people who identify as female or femme.

The nascent feminist science fiction community was home to LGBTQ+ authors Joanna Russ, Vonda N. McIntyre, Alice Sheldon, and C. J. Cherryh, all of whom wrote stories exploring same-sex love and desire, as well as straight-identified authors such as Marta Randall and Kate Wilhelm, who imagined futures where homosexuality is an unremarkable part of everyday life. It was also home to pioneering BIPOC authors Joan D. Vinge, Marta Randall, and Octavia E. Butler (whose work is featured in a separate Library of America volume, *Octavia E. Butler: Kindred, Fledgling, Collected Stories*). From the start, Butler grappled with issues of race and racism in science fiction more directly than most of her counterparts, noting that the genre "has always been nearly all white, just as, until recently, it has been nearly all male" and that "science fiction, more than any other genre, deals with change. . . . But science fiction itself changes slowly, often under protest." ("Lost Races in Science Fiction").[10] Still, Butler was not entirely alone: at least a few other feminist authors of this era, including Randall and white-identified writers such as Miriam Allen deFord, took up Butler's challenge to "spread the burden" of representation in science fiction by casting women of color as their protagonists. Taken together, such authors paved the way for the rich and still-growing body of modern, intersectional feminist science fiction we enjoy today.

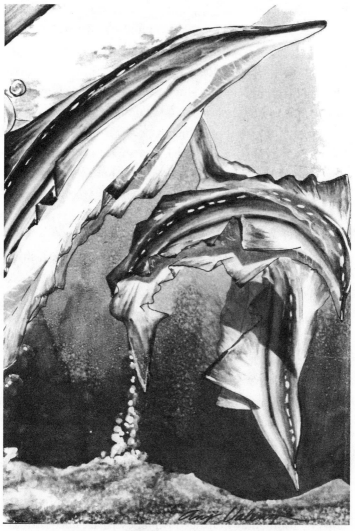

Figure 2. Fara Shimbo (née Valenza) for *Galaxy*,
December 1977–January 1978.

Like their male counterparts, feminist science fiction writers were often drawn to genre fiction by the vast canvas it provided for their imaginations. As Eleanor Arnason puts it, "I've always read science fiction and fantasy and murder mysteries. . . . My problem with realism is that a realistic novel about the psychological problems of middle-class people is a story which is very similar to the life I'm leading, and thus is not too interesting. Whereas the minute you throw in a dragon or global warming, it becomes very interesting. Internal thoughts become much less important, and you basically want to deal with the dragon."[11] For others, science fiction provided an escape from midcentury America's many constraints. Marta Randall turned to it for reassurance that "I wasn't going to be the one stuck at home baking cookies, I was going to be the one balancing on the raft in the lashing seas, gripping the mast with one hand while the other held on to the cookies somebody else had baked."[12] Still others embraced science fiction as teens and young adults because it promised, as Sargent puts it, "that just about everything could be other than it is."[13]

Several of the women you will encounter in this anthology directly attribute their careers to reading science fiction at a young age. Connie Willis recalls that Robert Heinlein's *Have Spacesuit—Will Travel* showed her the genre could be both "very literary and very funny," while Judith Merril's *Best of SF* anthologies revealed the "vast variety of things you could do" with the genre.[14] Upon reading Frank Herbert's politically and environmentally engaged *Dune*, Cynthia Felice realized that "this is the kind of thing I write!"[15] Other women writers were inspired by science fiction television, radio, and film.

Eleanor Arnason was "hooked" after seeing her very first episode of *Captain Video*, and C. J. Cherryh credits *Flash Gordon* as direct inspiration for her career. "When that went off the air, after about 5 complete runs, I had to write my own episodes," Cherryh recollects, "but I was so afraid of the plagiarism police (thank my 5th grade teacher) that I changed every fact and character to something opposite. And ended up with an original."[16, 17]

Many of the women associated with the founding of feminist science fiction were themselves from families of remarkable women. During the U.S.–Dakota War of 1862, Gayle Netzer's great-grandmother Adeline Foot single-handedly defended two families from a Dakota attack after the men with them were wounded; according to Foot's husband, white people never acknowledged her heroism but the Dakota honored her with the name "Brave Woman Who Defended Her House with Her Gun."[18] Miriam Allen deFord's dual career in socialist journalism and science fiction was inspired by her experiences with collective activism as a teenaged "soapbox suffragist."[19] Eleanor Arnason, niece to Molly Yard, Eleanor Roosevelt's personal assistant and the eighth president of NOW, attributes her interest in science fiction to growing up in an experimentally designed home surrounded by artists and activists, noting that "avant-gardists, like socialists, believe in the future."[20] These authors were often active in the revival of feminism and other progressive politics themselves: Netzer participated in the 1977 National Women's Conference; deFord was the subject of an oral history project called "The Suffragists: From Tea-Parties to Prison"; and Arnason, "coming from second-wave feminism," has worked for striking coal miners in Kentucky, served as an official in the National Writers Union, and engaged in Minnesota Democratic-Farmer-Labor Party politics.[21]

DeFord and Arnason are just a few of the authors you will meet in this book who credit their writing careers to feminism. Lisa Tuttle explains that "I was a feminist, formed by the Women's Liberation Movement that started in the USA when I was a high school student. I was hopeful, and expected to experience many more positive changes towards equality in my lifetime." She felt that science fiction was an ideal genre for feminists because "we did not have to be limited to the way things had been in the past! [We could imagine] a more egalitarian culture."[22] Similarly, Joan D. Vinge posits that "the girls and young women who are attracted to science fiction are frequently also attracted to feminism because the very nature of science fiction presents

Figure 3. Diane and Leo Dillon, cover art for *The Magazine of Fantasy and Science Fiction*, March, 1973.

you with possibilities that don't exist in daily life . . . myself included."[23] Joanna Russ cited the Cornell colloquium she took in college with feminists Betty Friedan and Kate Millet as a consciousness-raising catalyst for her, while Vonda N. McIntyre credited a host of earlier feminists in science fiction with inspiring her career: "people like Kate Wilhelm, and Ursula Le Guin, and Joanna Russ, and Andre Norton, and Anne McCaffrey, and Marion Zimmer Bradley kicked down doors in their generation that people in my generation got to walk through. I don't think I would have existed as the writer I am now if it weren't for those writers."[24, 25]

As has often been the case when new groups of women "invade" popular culture, the science fiction community's reactions to the first wave of self-proclaimed feminist authors were complex. Those who identified with classic traditions of engineering-oriented "hard" science fiction were sometimes skeptical about the aesthetic and political value of feminist genre writing. Powerhouse editor Judy-Lynn Del Rey disliked all forms of experimental science fiction, including its feminist variants, for "not telling a story," while publishers passed on Joanna Russ's *The Female Man* (1975) for four years because either they felt it was too "whiney" or they "had already printed one feminist novel."[26, 27] Even those who were sympathetic to feminist genre art were hesitant to publish it: when Pamela Sargent first proposed her all-female *Women of Wonder* anthology, ultimately published in 1975, "a few editors thought the idea was wonderful but decided not to do the book anyway. Some editors found the idea absurd, a couple doubted whether I could find enough good stories to fill the book, and one editor didn't think there was a large enough audience for such an anthology."[28] Feminist fans encountered similar gatekeeping on the con circuit, where "it was considered progressive for most conventions to schedule a single 'Women in SF' panel."[29]

On the whole, however, the science fiction establishment welcomed, even hailed, the accomplishments of this new generation of women: as author-critic Harlan Ellison put it, introducing Russ's story "When It Changed" in his 1972 anthology *Again, Dangerous Visions*, "the best writers in SF today are the women."[30] Lisa Tuttle recalls that her early writing partner George R. R. Martin was "happy" to follow her suggestion that they buck convention and center what would become their award-winning novella "The Storms of Windhaven" around a female protagonist, seeing it as "a good excuse to try different things."[31] Similarly positive encounters with male authors led Joan D. Vinge to feel "very proud of the science fiction field back in the 70s. It seemed to be socially forward-thinking as well as technologically forward-looking. [The field's] acceptance of women writers and women as equals seemed to be progressing so much faster than society at large. Even guys like Jerry Pournelle would try to write stories with female protagonists that were strong and tough, even though they kind of came off like men in skirts, smoking cigars."[32] And as Connie Willis notes, "I am a woman who worked my entire life in what was largely a man's field. But I also got advantages in that field, too. . . . [Editors] would be putting together an anthology and they'd say, 'Oh no. We don't have a woman.' And they'd call me. They were not calling fellow writers of my age and my friends who were guys . . . so I felt it all balanced out."[33]

The most intense debates over the meaning and value of feminist science fiction came from women within the science fiction community themselves. Willis remembers some female colleagues who "totally raked me over the coals because I was writing stories with housewives for heroines. They felt . . . I had an obligation to write about women's issues. And I was like, *every* issue is a goddamned woman's issue."[34] For others, the challenge required hard-fought personal reinvention: Ursula K. Le Guin described embracing feminist writing "slow and late. All my early fiction tended to be rather male-centered. . . . But I began coming up against certain discomforts. My first feminist text was *The Left Hand of Darkness*. . . . As a thought experiment [it] was messy." It was not until nearly a decade later that she realized "I didn't know how to write about women. I blundered around a while and then found some guidance in feminist theory. . . . I read *The Norton Book of Literature by Women* from cover to cover. It was a bible for me. It taught me that I didn't have to write like an honorary man anymore, that I could write like a woman and feel liberated in doing so."[35]

The women who wrote feminist science fiction in the 1970s changed the genre in three important ways—often with stories collected in this volume. First, they expanded the scope of science fiction by paying homage to the all-female separatist utopias written by women at the turn of the century and incorporating elements of those utopias into their own work. For example, Joanna Russ celebrated the fictional all-female societies of suffragists Mary Bradley Lane and Charlotte Perkins Gilman in her critical essay "Recent Feminist Utopias" and paid homage to them in her Nebula Award–winning story "When It Changed." The dream of a separate space for women outside the constraints of a culture where "men hog the good things" is central to many of the other stories you

Figure 4. Jeanne Gomoll, back cover for *Janus*,
Winter, 1977–78.

will encounter here as well, including Sonya Dorman Hess's "Bitching It" and Gayle N. Netzer's "Hey, Lilith!"; conversely, the marginalization and destruction of such communities—a threat that clouds the end of Russ's tale—provides the dystopian starting point for Lisa Tuttle's "Wives" and Kate Wilhelm's "The Funeral."[36]

Populating the new worlds inspired by earlier feminist utopias led to a second major transformation in science fiction, as authors reworked science fiction's usual "images of women [as] modest maidens, wicked temptresses, pretty schoolmarms, beautiful bitches, faithful wives, and so on" with mind-expanding stories about future females at every stage of life.[37] For instance, Chelsea Quinn Yarbro's "Frog Pond" replaces the passive maiden with the self-reliant mutant girl, while Kate Wilhelm's "The Funeral" and Connie Willis's "Daisy, in the Sun" immodestly speculate about the revolutionary and literally universe-stopping powers that might accompany a girl's first period. The happily unmarried women of Miriam Allen deFord's "A Way Out" and Dorman Hess's "Bitching It" engage in kinky sex, Ph.D. research, and galactic politics with equal gusto, while their alienated sisters in Doris Piserchia's "Pale Hands" and James Tiptree, Jr.'s "The Girl Who Was Plugged In" reveal the devastation wreaked by men's attempts to control female sexuality. In other stories such as Marta Randall's "A Scarab in the City of Time" and Cynthia Felice's "No One Said Forever," married women remain secure in the faith of their partners and children as they negotiate work challenges ranging from entrapment in a dome of high-tech white supremacists to inconvenient job transfers on the galactic frontier. Finally, feminist writers went where no man had gone before—into futures made by middle-aged, menopausal, and old women. Stories such as Kathleen Sky's "Lament of the Keeku Bird," Ursula K. Le Guin's "The Day Before the Revolution," and M. Lucie Chin's "The Best Is Yet to Be" insist on the most scandalous revelation of all: that life does not end, but might actually begin for women, at 40, 50, 60, or even 160.

As they introduced new stories and character types to science fiction, feminist authors revised the core themes of the genre to encompass new perspectives on science, society, and sexuality as well. This third contribution is particularly evident in Eleanor Arnason and Gayle N. Netzer's metafictional tales about women exploring the gendered boundaries of genre fiction. Other authors used their feminist fictions to question the belief that science will always, unproblematically, win us new and better futures. This suspicion imbues many of Alice Sheldon's stories written under the pseudonyms of James Tiptree, Jr., and Raccoona Sheldon; both of the Sheldon tales featured here, "The Girl Who Was Plugged In" and "The Screwfly Solution," insist that it does not matter if humans or aliens win the battle for the universe; either way, women will be sacrificed to the cause. Western science applied to military ends is also the implicit culprit behind the apocalyptic worlds of Arnason's "The Warlord of Saturn's Moons," C. J. Cherryh's "Cassandra," Elinor Busby's "Time to Kill," and Netzer's "Hey, Lilith!" With similar pessimism, Kathleen M. Sidney's "The Anthropologist" and Lisa Tuttle's "Wives" make evident the gendered assumptions driving the project of American empire, as Earthly conquistadors force hermaphroditic aliens into grotesque parodies of human sex roles. At the same time, feminist authors reworked such themes to imagine new scientific and social arrangements that might inspire real change: The astronaut in Joan D. Vinge's "View from a Height" transcends the sexist and ableist assumptions of her male colleagues and gains a universe of her own; the itinerant doctor of Vonda N. McIntyre's "Of Mist, and Grass, and Sand" uses witchy biotechnologies to heal the physical and psychic scars of her postapocalyptic world, thereby winning the love of a faithful man and the everywoman narrator of Netzer's "Hey, Lilith!" walks away from the smoking ruins of science—and science fiction—to join her newfound sisters in writing feminist futures beyond the end of civilization as we know it.

This anthology celebrates the pioneers of American feminist science fiction who paid homage to their foremothers by insisting that women have always been part of the future, and who opened the genre's truly global potential by multiplying our ideas about the many futures we might inhabit and the many different kinds of women who might build them. It is a time machine back to the decade in which it all began, an adventure in time and space through some of the wild, witty, angry, sexy, and seriously hopeful stories that showed an entire generation there were alternatives to inherited ideas about science and society—ideas that still marginalize so many Americans. It revisits authors who dared us to dream that we could win better futures for all with the tools of emotional intelligence, collaborative action, reverence for life, and the occasional dirty joke. I hope you enjoy the journey.

1. Charlotte Gush, "Casting Spells for a Female Future with '70s Lesbian Separatist Liza Cowan." First published in *i–D*, December 2015; reprinted at https://www.dykeaquarterly.com/venue-labyris-books/. Accessed January 24, 2022

2. Joanna Russ, "Recent Feminist Utopias," in *To Write Like a Woman: Essays in Feminism and Science Fiction* (Bloomington: Indiana University Press, 1995), 144.

3. See my anthology *The Future Is Female!: 25 Classic Science Fiction Stories by Women, from Pulp Pioneers to Ursula K. Le Guin* (New York: Library of America, 2018), predecessor of the present volume, for examples and discussion of these early and mid-twentieth-century innovators.

4. Jeffrey D. Smith, *Khatru Symposium: Women in Science Fiction* (Oakland, CA: James Tiptree Literary Council, 2009), 35. Originally published in 1975.

5. Shulamith Firestone, *The Dialectic of Sex: The Case for Feminist Revolution* (New York: William Morrow, 1970), 11.

6. Roger Luckhurst, *Science Fiction* (Cambridge, UK: Polity Press, 2005), 170.

7. Rich Horton, "The Original Anthology Series in SF: The Prolific 1970s" (1999), *SFSite.com,* accessed February 5, 2022, https://www.sfsite.com/columns/rich56.htm.

8. Peter Nicholls and David Langford, "Anthologies," in *The Science Fiction Encyclopedia,* accessed February 5, 2022, https://sf-encyclopedia.com/entry/anthologies.

9. Pamela Sargent, *Women of Wonder: The Classic Years* (New York: Harvest Books, 1995), 14.

10. Octavia E. Butler, "The Lost Races of Science Fiction," *Transmission,* Summer 1980, pp. 16–18.

11. Francesca Myman, "Eleanor Arnason: Unfolding," *Locus,* September 11, 2016, accessed February 6, 2022, https://locusmag.com/2016/09/eleanor-arnason-unfolding/.

12. Marta Randall, "Welcome!" *Marta Randall: Writer, Editor, Teacher,* accessed February 7, 2022, http://www.scripsit.com.

13. "Exclusive Interview: Pamela Sargent," *SciFiChick.com,* November 3, 2010, accessed February 7, 2022, https://scifichick.com/exclusive-interview-pamela-sargent/2010/11/03/.

14. Carrie S. "An Interview with Connie Willis, Part II," *Smart Bitches, Trashy Books,* August 8, 2013. https://smartbitchestrashybooks.com/2013/08/an-interview-with-connie-willis-part-ii/. Accessed February 7, 2022.

15. Scott Edelman, "Grab Lunch at the Watergate with My Unindicted Co-conspirator Cynthia Felice," *Eating the Fantastic,* May 17, 2017, accessed February 7, 2022, http://www.scottedelman.com/2017/05/17/grab-lunch-at-the-watergate-with-my-unindicted-co-conspirator-cynthia-felice-in-episode-37-of-eating-the-fantastic/.

16. Eleanor Arnason, "At the Edge of the Future: Eleanor Arnason Interviewed by Terry Bisson," in *Mammoths of the Great Plains* (Oakland, CA: PM Press, 2010), 108.

17. R. K. Troughton, "Interview with Award-Winning Author C. J. Cherryh," *Amazing Stories*, February 19, 2014.

18. Jessica Amanda Salmonson, *The Encyclopedia of Amazons: Women Warriors from Antiquity to the Modern Era* (New York: Open Road Media, 2015), 18–19.

19. Sherna Gluck, *The Suffragists: From Tea-Parties to Prison* (Suffragists Oral History Project, Regional Oral History Office, University of California, Berkeley, 1972–74), n.p., accessed February 7, 2022, http://texts.cdlib.org/view?docId=kt2h4n992z&query=&brand=calisphere.

19. Arnason, "At the Edge of the Future," 109.

20. Caroline M. Yoachim, "Interview: Eleanor Arnason," *Uncanny Magazine,* July 2021, accessed February 8, 2022, https://uncannymagazine.com/article/interview-eleanor-arnason/.

22. Arthur Maia, "Exclusive interview with Lisa Tuttle, co-author of *Windhaven*," *Gelo & Fogo*, July 23, 2018, accessed February 7, 2022, https://www.geloefogo.com/2018/07/exclusive-interview-with-lisa-tuttle-co-author-of-windhaven.html.

23. "Joan D. Vinge: 04-08-1981," SUNY Brockport Digital Repository, accessed February 7, 2022, https://dspace.sunyconnect.suny.edu/handle/1951/80438.

24. Ritch Calvin, "'This shapeless book': Reception and Joanna Russ's *The Female Man*," *Femspec* 10.2 (2010): 24–34, 130.

25. Josh Wimmer, "Feminism, Astronauts, and Riding Sidesaddle: Talking to *Dreamsnake*'s Vonda N. McIntyre," *Gizmodo*, October 24, 2010, accessed February 7, 2022, https://gizmodo.com/feminism-astronauts-and-riding-sidesaddle-talking-to-30859488.

26. Dave Truesdale, "An Interview with Lester and Judy-Lynn Lester del Rey." Originally published 1975; reprinted in *Tangent Online*. https://tangentonline.com/interviews-columnsmenu-166/interviews-columnsmenu-166-interviews-columnsmenu-166/classic-lester-a-judy-lynn-del-rey-interview/. Accessed February 4, 2022.

27. Quoted in Ritch Calvin, "This shapeless book": Reception and Joanna Russ's *The Female Man*," *Femspec* 10.2 (2010): 24–34, 130.

28. Sargent, *Women of Wonder*, 1.

29. "History." *WisCon*, 2016, accessed February 8, 2022, http://wiscon.net/about/history/.

30. Harlan Ellison, ed. *Again, Dangerous Visions* (Garden City: Doubleday & Company, 1972), 249.

31. Maia, "Exclusive interview with Lisa Tuttle, co-author of *Windhaven*."

32. Lydia Morehouse, "SFC Interview: Joan D. Vinge," *Science Fiction Chronicle* 22.11 (November 2001): 33, 51–54.

33. Lorraine Berry, "Connie Willis: Success Is the Best Revenge," *Talking Writing: Creating Meaning Through Personal Stories,* March 25, 2013, accessed February 7, 2022, http://talkingwriting.com /connie-willis-success-is-the-best-revenge.

34. Berry, "Connie Willis: Success Is the Best Revenge."

35. Jonathan White, "Ursula Le Guin: Coming Back from the Silence," in *Talking on the Water: Conversations About Nature and Creativity* (San Francisco: Sierra Club Books, 1994), 102.

36. Russ, "Recent Feminist Utopias," 140.

37. Joanna Russ, "The Image of Women in Science Fiction, " in *Images of Women in Fiction,* ed. Susan Koppleman Cornillon (Bowling Green, OH: Bowling Green University Popular Press, 1973), 81.

THE FUTURE IS *FEMALE!*

VOLUME 2

Bitching It

MY MULTI-LEVEL plastiplex windows dated back to the 1980's, and I was in a hurry to get the new curtains up before the rest of the gang came over. My Akita bitch, Tora, was mouthing the brass rings up to me one at a time as I stood on the ladder. Then Crotch came in, mean and stingy as he always is, the puke.

"How much did those cost?" he yelled, and kicked the ladder out from under me. As I went down I smashed him in the face with my elbow, and Tora got a grip on one of his buttocks, denim and all, until he yelled with pain. She was always irritable when in heat, not to mention it was a nuisance because she liked to sleep against the pale-yellow appliances, and when she got up the surfaces were splotched with the brown roses of her blood.

"Fifty credits a yard," I screamed from the floor where I was trying to untangle myself from the pink ruffles. It had taken me hours to trim each tier of ruffles with red fiberglass fringe and balls, so I was careful not to tear any of this handiwork. Aside from the fact it was difficult to pry an extra penny out of Crotch, I would no more spoil my own creative works than I would slash a Picasso canvas.

"You shit," I said to him, removing the last of the fringe from around my neck.

"Must be ten yards of nylon in those curtains; what do you think I'm made of, money?" Crotch said. He held the torn flap of his chlorine-pale dungarees against his left cheek to sop up the blood where Tora's front teeth had met.

"You bitch," he said to her. She growled an acknowledgement and lay down.

"Look! Look!" I commanded, shaking with rage. The ruffles were half torn from one curtain. When I think of the hours I spend, and my friends Rosa and Margie, and all of us, on curtains and bedspreads and throw rugs, all done by hand, with real art, while we talk about how many years we'll spend getting our respective Ph.D's, and Crotch comes in and in one minute tears everything apart.

I said to him, "What kind of shit are you to do a thing like that? You better get out. There isn't enough pie anyway because some of the gang are coming over." Pretty stupid of me to say that, but it's too late.

He lifted the pie down from the top of the fridge. I'd already eaten out a big wedge and Tora's fang marks were visible on the other side. He was such a sorehead, he threw the pie at me. I ducked. Tora jumped over me and hit the floor right beside the pie. She held the pan between her big front paws, growling between mouthfuls.

"This place is crummy," he said. "How can you invite anyone over to such a pigpen? You think new curtains cover the crap? I wouldn't have given you the money only you promised to clean up the place."

"You don't own me, Crotch. You think I got nothing better to do than scrub floors? After all, I'm going for my Ph.D and an educated creative woman has better to do than clean a house all day."

Tora picked up the empty pie tin and carried it across the kitchen; with an expert flip she tossed it into the sink where it clanged, and came to rest. She turned her head from right, me, to left, him, and licked her whiskers. Out in the yard, Betty's red setter dog came sniffing. He found the spot where Tora had pee'd in the morning and lifted one leg to cover each delicious drop with a few drops of his own. Possession is accomplished in a lot of different ways, but any way it's done, it sure is hateful.

Crotch looked at me possessively and I bristled with resentment. He'd spent the last few months trying to level me down to his across-the-town blocks where Industry was; the air-conditioned offices, banks of typing machines, computers, watercoolers, for-free women, dim-lit mahogany bars with rows of Martinis on the rocks sparkling like diamond juice. The little trains pulled in and ran out right on schedule, no time to oversleep or one more fuck or a second cup of coffee. Sometimes our gang stood on the girders above the train platform, safe in our ballet shoes, and hurled down jeers, beer cans, and other stuff at the hard black derbies below; especially at the well dressed sweetly smelling free women who did it in the name of "love" with all those men. Men, them and their whiskers, like shaving was something important, a good substitute for menstruation.

"Why don't you go back where you came from?" I asked him, putting the curtains in a neat pile on the table.

With his usual nauseating kindness he asked, "Don't you like to see me now and then?"

I could hear Mary and Annajane, with their bitches, on the way over. He hadn't heard them yet. His hearing had been impaired by the sound of sixty-cycle hums and little trains on straight tracks.

They were coming along the alleyway where the hollyhocks

had seeded themselves; pink, red, double white, and dusty maroon, they grew five feet tall against the picket fence. Indestructible. Like me, the wire lady: walk across me, I twang off your name and number before your footsteps have finished crossing. Twing, twang, the metal marvel sheathed in squashy flesh, that's what drew him here, the poor cock.

Annajane came in first, with her bird-dog bitch Duckeater. Crotch whirled, caught, too late to escape. Annajane squealed, "Oh Suki, you've made a surprise party," and she fell on him. He never had a chance. They rolled under the table and she had him unzipped and hard as a peppermint stick in a moment. Duckeater and Tora charged out the open door to meet Mary and her Chihuahua bitch Hairy. The red setter, who'd been patiently waiting out there, pounced on Tora, ramming it home half a dozen times before he caught, his penis swelled to four times its usual size. He stepped over, and tied her, back to back.

Tora pointed her black nose into the air and began to sing in a high, quavering wolf voice. After all, a dog's penis has a bone in it.

Under the kitchen table Annajane was astride Crotch, her head and shoulders hunched over because of the cramped space. A few cobwebs had caught in her hair and a spider was running furiously up and down her arm. They were galloping at such a rate the whole kitchen quivered.

"Oh Suki!" Mary said, "what a wonderful idea," and gazed down at them. Hairy the Chihuahua ran around under the table and tried to clean them.

"I'll help with the curtains, until it's my turn," Mary offered. "How'd you ever get Crotch over here?"

"Oh, he drops over now and then to see how the other half

lives. It's a miracle he gets through the guards on the Avenue. I guess Jeannie and Rosa went swimming today." I got up on the ladder and she handed the curtains and brass rings up to me. "How do you like them?" I asked.

But she was looking back over her shoulder to see if Annajane had finished and it was her turn yet, but it wasn't, yet. Out in the yard, the red setter was lying prone, panting and gasping, while Tora was scrunched up on one hindquarter, neatening up her vagina. Through the cracks in the fence, a bull terrier was eyeing her.

"Oh oh oh oh," Annajane said from her new position, and slid off, massaging a cramp in her thigh. Though breathless, Crotch was about to get up and escape. Mary lunged for him. Unfortunately, the Chihuahua had already thrown herself on Crotch; that little bitch had a passion for cleaning everything up. She yelled shrilly when Mary landed on her, and Crotch roared when the bitch bit him. The kitchen began to quiver again, and one curtain rod slipped and hung down, dropping my new pink curtains, brass ring by brass ring, in folds onto the floor. Trying to keep my temper, I began to put them back up again, though by now they were getting dusty and spotted. It was Crotch's fault, damn him.

Hairy crawled out whimpering from between Mary and Crotch, and I reminded her, "Just once, Mary. Because I haven't had a chance at him either, and he isn't getting any younger or more vibrant."

"Just once, just once," Mary gasped twice.

While they were resting, or at any rate, he was, I took a bowl of jello (Lemon Flavor) out of the fridge. After all, the pie was a total loss, and I had to serve something or lose status. I squeezed a ring of whipped topping on the jello, sprinkled chocolate bits over that, and stuck in some maraschino cherries all around, until it looked very pretty. The curtains looked okay, too, now they were up. I needn't hang my head in shame before the rest of the gang.

Annajane took a bucket of water out into the yard, for the dogs, who were pretty thirsty, except the bull terrier, who had tied Duckeater.

"I didn't know she was in heat," I said.

"It's crazy, she comes in every two months," Annajane said. "I can't give the puppies away any more."

"Puppies!" I shrieked. "Aren't you giving her some of your pills?"

Tora and I always shared the bottle of pills. Fair's fair, after all; a nursing bitch isn't much of a fighter and who wants all those lousy puppies anyway?

Annajane blushed. "I was getting low on the pills so I skipped her a few days."

"Multiple births! what a rotten thing to do," I said. "Now she's going to have bull terrier pups. I think that's shitty. People like you shouldn't have a bitch."

"Don't be so righteous," Annajane said, giving one curtain a mean little yank which made the curtain rod groan. "It won't hurt her to have a little fun."

"Fun is fun and puppies are puppies," I said. "Mary, isn't it time you got up? The dessert is ready."

"I'll serve the coffee while you have him," Annajane said. She was a good friend, in spite of our occasional disagreements.

"Watch out!" I yelled at Mary who was crawling out from under the table. "He's leaving us. And penniless."

Mary pulled him by the belt, backward, as I grabbed him

from the front. He hit his head on the edge of the table as he fell, and lay there like the dead.

We stood around looking down at him. Mary felt his pulse, which was normal. Annajane put a cold sponge on his brow, and his eyelids quivered, but he wasn't conscious. I unzipped him, but he was a goner. Though ordinarily it was pretty good, just pretty good isn't good enough. No matter how big and busy a penis is, it's not good at all if it hasn't got a big fat wallet on the other end of it.

"Try ice cubes," Mary suggested.

"Ice cubes, you're outta your skull," Annajane said.

"Try it," Mary insisted. "I heard it works sometimes, I heard it's called a Roth Bath, or something, and it works."

"That's not ice cubes, that's whiskey," Annajane said.

While I thought over their advice, I took the credit chips from his wallet and we shared them around, though I got the biggest share, naturally, since he had come across through the dangers of the Avenue to see me.

Finally, we tried the whiskey, though we hated to waste it. We dripped it on with a teaspoon, and took turns. It really worked. He groaned a few times, opened his eyes, then opened his mouth to say something, probably a protest, so I poured in a slug of whiskey and he woke wide awake. Mary and Annajane pulled chairs up to the table and began to drink coffee and eat the dessert, while Crotch and I screwed under the table, first me on top, then him on top, then both of us sideways, and my head stuck out so Mary reached down spoon by spoon and fed me some jello.

He was a good sport, after all, and we let him have a cup of coffee before we took our bitches out of the yard to escort him back to the Avenue. His own territory lay on the other side, unpatrolled. Rosa and Jeannie had come back from swimming and were on guard with their bitches. Crotch tried to run for it, but the bitches brought him down, and by the time the guards called them off he was crawling, bloody and wretched, on his hands and knees across the Avenue. Just a poor slob of a masochist, like most of them.

We went home to finish the dessert and have a talk. While we were having second cups of coffee, Tora tried mounting Duckeater but she was so small she collapsed under the big bitch's weight and just lay there, panting. This scene aroused Hairy, all five inches of her, and she tried mounting Tora, which caused so much resentment that Tora nipped her on the nose.

"Put her out in the yard where the dogs can find her," I suggested, but it was too late. Squeaking, Hairy ran away, Tora pursuing her. Both curtain rods got jolted and there were my new curtains in a heap, except one, which fell over Hairy and eclipsed her entirely. My curtains began to run around the kitchen, barking. Tora snatched the curtain off the Chihuahua and bit her again. The bull terrier came in right through the screen door and tried to mount Duckeater, who just lay there, panting, while he pumped at her head. He was a very young bull terrier.

I decided I'd never get those damn curtains up in one piece. But we'd had a great morning, and we planned that the next time Crotch came over, we'd have the rest of the gang in, too. Before he got any older. By that time I could repair the curtains and get them up.

1971

CHELSEA QUINN YARBRO

Frog Pond

NO MATTER what Mr. Thompson said, it was a good day for frogging and fishing. The morning sun had that bright double halo that meant the whole day would be clear. I got up before Mom, took some old pie from where she hid it last night, grabbed my wading shoes and net and lit out for the creek. I had to leave real quiet. I'm not supposed to be going down to the creek any more. They say it's dangerous down there.

But the creek ain't dangerous if you know what you're doing. You just have to stay away from the pink water spots and you're safe all the way.

I took the long way around the Baxter place. I think Pop was right about them; something's wrong there. Dr. Baxter ain't been at Town Meeting for a long time—Pop thinks that maybe some sick people moved in on the Baxters.

So I walked through the brambles on the edge of the woods where the new trees are growing. It was sunny and fine and the breeze came in nice and sweet from the north. No cities up that way, not for hundreds of miles.

Caught some crickets along the way, the big kind with the long wings. They make good bait for the stickery fish in the shallows. All I got to do is tangle them up in the net and put it down in the water. The stickery fish go right for 'em. Mr. Thompson, he says that it ain't safe to eat 'em, which just shows you how much he knows. I eat 'em all the time.

I headed right for Rotten Log Hollow. There's a nice big hole in there and a gravel bar and you can catch lots of frogs there if you're careful. They like to hide under that old broken pipe, under the foam. I got maybe a dozen there, last time out.

First I walked along the bank, looking down into the water to see what was there, you know. It was still and there wasn't a lot of foam piling up. There wasn't any fish either, so I sat down in the warm gravel, ate my pie and pulled on my wading shoes. They've got high tops that Pop always tells me to pull all the way up, but I ain't bothered with that for years. Heck, a little water can't kill me.

After a little while I went into the water real cautious—careful not to scare the frogs. I worked my way out into midstream and started peering around for frogs. I had my net in my belt but I don't use it much—not for frogs.

So there I was in the creek, careful as could be, when all of a sudden this bunch of rocks and grass comes rolling down the bank and this city fellow comes down after it, trying to grab hold of bushes on the way. He hit the pipe and it stopped him, but he sure messed up the water.

A couple of minutes went by and he started to get up. He had a heck of a time doing it. He kept flailing his arms around and pulling himself back onto the pipe.

I was mad because he'd scared the frogs, so I yelled out, "Hey, mister, don't do that!"

Boy, did he look up fast. You'd of thought I was a C.D. man or something the way he snapped around. His eyes got wild and he shook all over. Before he could fall again I called out. "It's just me, mister, down in the creek."

He turned around, grabbing the pipe for balance. I waited

till he'd steadied himself and then I said, "You're scaring the frogs."

"Scaring the frogs?" he yelled back, sounding like frogs were monsters.

"Yeah. I'm trying to catch some. Can you just sit there a minute?"

I could see he was thinking this over. Finally he sat back on the pipe like he was worn out and said real quiet, "Why not?" And he leaned his head back and closed his eyes.

I got three frogs while he was sleeping there. They were big and fat. I put a stick through their throats and let 'em dangle in the creek to keep fresh. I almost had the fourth one when the city guy woke up.

"Listen," he called to me. "Where am I?"

"Rotten Log Hollow."

"Where is that?"

I sure couldn't see the point in yelling all the time, so I told him to come closer and we could talk. "Talk makes less noise. Maybe I can still catch some frogs if we're just talking."

He hustled off the pipe and scrambled along the shore, splashing dirt and stones into the water.

"Hi," I said when he got closer.

"Hello." He was still awful nervous and had that funny white look around his eyes, sort of like turtle skin. "What's your name?"

He was really trying to be friendly and even if Mr. Thompson says in that spooly voice of his that there ain't any friendly strangers, well, this guy wasn't anything I couldn't handle.

"My name is Althea," I told him, polite like Mom tells me to be. "But mostly my friends call me Thorny. Who are you?"

"Uh—" He looked around, then back. "Stanl—Stan—just call me Stan."

You could see that he was lying. He wasn't even good at it. So I said, sure, his name was Stan. Then I waited for him to say something.

"You like this place?" he asked.

"Yeah. I come here lots of times."

"You live around here, then?"

A dumb question. He was really all city. Maybe he thought we had subways out here in the country. He kept looking around like he expected a whole herd of people to come running out of the pipe.

"Yeah. I live at the Baxter place." It was a lie but he'd told me one—and besides, Pop said I wasn't to tell people where we live, just in case.

"Where's that?" He said it like he wasn't really interested, like he didn't give a damn where the Baxter place was. He just wanted to talk to someone. I pointed back toward the Baxter place and told him it was about a mile along the road.

"Do a lot of people live there, at the Baxter place?"

"Not too many. About six or seven. You planning on moving in, mister?"

He laughed at that. It was one of those high laughs that sounds like crying. My brother Davey cries like that a lot. It ain't right a six-year-old kid should cry like that. About this Stan—or whoever—I didn't know.

"What's funny, mister?" I would have gone and left him there, but I saw that he was standing almost in some green gunk that comes out of the pipe and washes on shore so I said to him a little louder, "And you better get away from there."

He stopped laughing. "From where? Why?"

Wow, he was nervous.

"From that." I pointed so he would get panicked again. "That stuff is bad for you. It can give you burns if you're not used to it." That isn't quite right. Some people can't get used to it, but it never burned me, not even the first time. Mr. Thompson says that means selective mutations are adapting to the new demands of the environment. Mr. Thompson thinks that just because he's a geneticist he knows everything.

Stan leaped away from the green stuff like it was about to bite him.

"What is it?"

"I don't know. Just stuff that comes out of the pipe. When the Santa Rosa pumping station got blown up a couple of years back this broke and started dripping that green stuff." I shrugged. "It won't hurt you if you don't touch it." Stan looked like he was going to start laughing again, so I said, real quick, "I bet you're from Santa Rosa, huh?"

"Santa Rosa? What makes you think that?" He sure got jumpy if you asked him anything.

"Nothing. Santa Rosa's the first big city south of here. I just figured you probably had to come from there. Or maybe Sonoma or Napa, but those ain't too likely."

"Why do you say that?" He was real close now and his hands were balling into fists.

"Simple," I said, trying to keep my eyes off his fists. He must have been sick or something, the way he kept tightening and loosening his fingers. "The big highway north is still open, but not the one between Sonoma and Santa Rosa."

He wobbled his head up and down at that. "Yes, yes of

course. That would be why." He looked at me, letting his hands open up again. I was glad to see that. "Sorry, Thorny. I guess I'm jumpier than I thought."

"That's okay," I told him. I didn't want to set him off again.

So Stan stood back and watched me while I looked for frogs.

After a while he asked me, "Is there anyone needing some help on their farms around here? Anyone you know of?"

I said no.

"Maybe there's a school somewhere that needs a teacher. Unless I miss my guess I could teach a few things. You kids probably don't have too many good teachers."

What a spooly thing to say. "My Pop teaches at the high school. Maybe he could help you find work." We didn't need teachers, but if Stan knew about teaching maybe one of the other towns could use him.

"Were you born around here?" Stan was looking around the hollow like anyone's having been born here was real special and unlikely.

"Nope. Over at Davis." That was where Pop had been doing the research into plant viruses, before he and the Baxters and the Thompsons and the Wainwrights and the Aumendsens and the Leventhals bought this place here.

"On a farm?"

"Sort of."

His voice sounded like being born on a farm was something great like saving the seaweed or maybe going back to the moon some day.

"I've always wanted to live in the country. Maybe now I can." He stumbled along the bank to the sandy spot opposite the gravel bar and sat down. Boy, he was really dumb.

"There's snakes there," I said, real gentle. Sure enough, up he shot, squealing like Mrs. Wainwright's pig.

"They won't hurt you. Just watch out for them. They only bite if you hurt 'em or scare 'em."

And with him jumping up and down I wasn't going to get any more frogs, that was for sure. So I decided to settle just for conversation.

"Is any place safe in this bank?" he asked.

"Sure," I said with a smile. "Right where you were sitting. Just keep an eye out for the snakes. They're about two feet long and sort of red. About the color of those pine needles." I pointed up the bank. "Like that."

"Dear God. How long have the pine needles been that way?"

I slogged over into the deep water. "About the last five, six years. The smog does it."

"Smog?" He gave me a real blank look. "There isn't any smog here."

"Can't see it or even smell it. Mr. Thompson says there's too much of it everywhere so we can't tell it's there any more. But the trees know it. That's why they turn that color."

"But they'll die," he said. He sounded real upset.

"Maybe. Maybe they'll change."

"How can they? This is terrible."

"Well, the pines are holding up. Most of the redwoods south of the Navarro River died years ago. Lots of them are still standing," I explained, seeing him go blank again. "But they aren't alive any more. But the pines here, they haven't died yet and maybe they aren't going to." A real sharp shine was coming into his eyes and I knew I had said more than I should have. I tried to cover up as best I could. "We learn about this in school. They say we'll have to find ways to handle all the trouble when we grow up. Mr. Thompson tells us about biology." That last part was true, at least.

"Biology. At your age."

That kind of talk can still make me mad. "Look, mister, I'm fifteen years old, and that's plenty old to know about biology. And chemistry, too. Just because this is a long way from Santa Rosa, don't think we can't read or like that."

I was really angry. I know I'm little, but, heck, lots of people are small now.

"I didn't mean anything. I was just surprised that you have such good schools here." Boy, that Stan really couldn't lie at all.

"What do they teach where you come from?" I knew that might make him jumpy again, but I wanted to get back at him for that.

"Nothing important. They teach history and language and art with no emphasis on survival. Why, when some of the students last semester requested that the administration include courses in things like forestry, basket making and plant grafting, they called out the C.D. and there was a riot. One of the C.D.—" Stan licked his lips in an odd way—"was ambushed and left hanging from a lamppost by his heels."

"That's bad," I said. It was, too. That was the first time I found out how bad it had got in the cities. Stan was still smiling when he told me what had been done to the C.D. It wasn't nice to hear. He kept trying to make it better by calling it gelding. He said that the last time they did it was during the black-white trouble.

And that guy wanted to teach in our schools. He said that he knew what it was really like with people all over and could contribute to our system. I could see Pop's face getting real set and hard at what Stan was saying. But Stan insisted he thought that it was very important for people to understand "The System"—like it was a religious thing. You know? I was beginning to get scared.

"Fifteen is too old," he went on. "Do you have any brothers or sisters younger than yourself?"

I was pretty cautious about answering him. "Yes. I got two brothers. And one sister." I didn't tell him that Jamie was already doing research work or that Davey didn't do anything. Or that Lisa was getting ready to board in the next town so that we could keep the families from interbreeding too much.

"Older or younger?"

"Mostly older." So I lied again. At least I was good at it. He didn't think to ask anything more about them.

"Too bad. We are going to have to change what's been happening. Martial law, searches without warrants, confiscations. It's terrible, Thorny, terrible."

He must have thought that living out here we didn't hear anything or see anything. He kept telling me how bad it was to have soldiers everywhere and how they were doing awful things. I knew about that and a lot of other things, too. And I knew about how there were gangs that killed people and robbed them—and murder clubs that just killed people for fun. Heck, Jules Leventhal used to be a clinical psychologist and he taught us a lot about the way mobs act and how too many people make problems for everybody.

"How are things north of here?" Stan was asking.

"Not too bad. Humboldt County is doing pretty good and there are more people around the Klamath River now." I sure didn't want a guy like him staying with us. I figured that maybe telling him about conditions in the north might encourage him to move on. But he just looked tense and nodded, like that crazy preacher who wanted us all to die for god, a couple of years back. "Of course, that's redwood country so they might have trouble there in a few years."

He looked at me real hard. "Thorny, do you think you could tell me how to get to Humboldt county?"

Dumb, dumb, I told you. All he had to do is keep going up old 101 and there it would be. That crazy guy hadn't even looked at a map. Or else he had and was trying to trap me, but I ain't easy to trap.

"You can keep going up the main highway," I said, talking real sincere-like. "But there might be C.D. men up ahead, you know, near Ukiah. Or Willits. The best way is to cut over to the coast and just follow it up."

There, I thought. That ought to get him; he was jumpy enough before.

"Yes, yes, that would work. And Eureka is a port—there would be the ocean for access—"

He went on like that for about five minutes. He wanted to launch some kind of attack against The System, to protect the People, but for another System. He kept talking about rights and saying how he knew what the People really wanted and he would change things so that they could have it. He said he knew what was best for them. Wow, I wish Mr. Leventhal could have heard him.

"And what about you? You should be in school, right?"

"Nope," I said. "We have school just two days in the week. The rest of the time is free."

I wondered if that much had been all right to tell. We weren't supposed to let out much about our school.

"But it's a waste, don't you see?" Stan crouched down on the bank, looking like a huge skinny rabbit squatting there. "This is the time when you must learn political philosophy. You should be learning about how society works. It's terribly important."

"I know how society works," I said.

Heck, all the kids who learned from Mr. Wainwright know about that. After all, one of the reasons the Wainwrights came along with the rest of us was that the politicians in Sacramento didn't like what he was teaching about the way *they* worked. And they were society.

"Not this society," he said in a real haughty way, like Mr. Thompson when he's crossed. "Society in the cities, in the population centers."

He was going on that way when I saw a couple of frogs moving on the bottom. I watched where they were going and then I reached down for them, holding my breath as my face hit the water. I dragged one of them out but the other got away.

"Spending your time catching frogs," Stan spat.

"Sure. They taste real good. Mom fixes 'em up with batter and fries 'em."

"You mean you eat them?" he squeaked, looking gray.

"Of course. They're meat ain't they?" I waded over to the other frogs on the stick and stuck the new one on, too. He wiggled and jerked for a bit and then stopped.

"But frogs? How can you eat frogs?"

"Easy." I didn't think he was going to get over it, that we eat frogs. Just to be sure, I reached over and grabbed the stick with the frogs on it. "See? This one," I put my thumb on one's belly, "is the fattest. It'll taste real good."

"And do you really chase after them without seeing them?"

I turned around and looked at him. He was standing up on the other bank and the frightened look was back in his eye. "No. You got to see what you're after."

"But in that water—"

"Oh, I don't open my eyes like you do," I said, real casual-like. "I go after them with these." And I slid up the membranes.

Stan looked like he'd swallowed a salamander. "What was that?" he demanded, looking more scared than ever.

"Nictating membranes—I was engineered for it," I said.

"Mutants," he gibbered. "Already!"

He started trying to back up the bank watching me like he thought I was a werewolf or something. He slipped and stumbled until he got to the top and then he ran away—I would hear him crashing through the brush making more noise than a herd of deer.

By the time he left the whole hole was filled with leaves and sticks and rocks and I knew that there wouldn't be any more frogs or fish that day, so I took the frogs on the stick, got off my wading shoes and started back for the house. I knew Mom would be mad but I was hoping that the frogs would help her get over it. I guessed I had to tell them about Stan. They didn't like people coming here.

They were real mad about it. The funny thing is that they were maddest about my having shown my eyes. But cripes, that was just one little flap of skin that Mr. Thompson got us to breed. Just one lousy bit of extra skin near the eye.

But to hear him tell it, you'd think he'd changed the whole world.

1971

KATE WILHELM

The Funeral

NO ONE could say exactly how old Madam Westfall was when she finally died. At least one hundred twenty, it was estimated. At the very least. For twenty years Madam Westfall had been a shell containing the very latest products of advances made in gerontology, and now she was dead. What lay on the viewing dais was merely a painted, funereally garbed husk.

"She isn't real," Carla said to herself. "It's a doll, or something. It isn't really Madam Westfall." She kept her head bowed, and didn't move her lips, but she said the words over and over. She was afraid to look at a dead person. *The second time they slaughtered all those who bore arms, unguided, mindless now, but lethal with the arms caches that they used indiscriminately.* Carla felt goose bumps along her arms and legs. She wondered if anyone else had been hearing the old Teacher's words.

The line moved slowly, all the girls in their long gray skirts had their heads bowed, their hands clasped. The only sound down the corridor was the sush-sush of slippers on plastic flooring, the occasional rustle of a skirt.

The Viewing Room had a pale green, plastic floor, frosted-green plastic walls, and floor to ceiling windows that were now slits of brilliant light from a westering sun. All the furniture had been taken from the room, all the ornamentation. There were no flowers, nothing but the dais, and the bedlike

23

box covered by a transparent shield. And the Teachers. Two at the dais, others between the light strips, at the doors. Their white hands clasped against black garb, heads bowed, hair slicked against each head, straight parts emphasizing bilateral symmetry. The Teachers didn't move, didn't look at the dais, at the girls parading past it.

Carla kept her head bowed, her chin tucked almost inside the V of her collarbone. The serpentine line moved steadily, very slowly. "She isn't real," Carla said to herself, desperately now.

She crossed the line that was the cue to raise her head; it felt too heavy to lift, her neck seemed paralyzed. When she did move, she heard a joint crack, and although her jaws suddenly ached, she couldn't relax.

The second green line. She turned her eyes to the right and looked at the incredibly shrunken, hardly human mummy. She felt her stomach lurch and for a moment she thought she was going to vomit. "She isn't real. It's a doll. She isn't real!" The third line. She bowed her head, pressed her chin hard against her collarbone, making it hurt. She couldn't swallow now, could hardly breathe. The line proceeded to the South Door and through it into the corridor.

She turned left at the South Door, and with her eyes downcast, started the walk back to her genetics class. She looked neither right nor left, but she could hear others moving in the same direction, slippers on plastic, the swish of a skirt, and when she passed by the door to the garden she heard laughter of some Ladies who had come to observe the viewing. She slowed down.

She felt the late sun hot on her skin at the open door and with a sideways glance, not moving her head, she looked quickly into the glaring greenery, but could not see them. Their laughter sounded like music as she went past the opening.

"That one, the one with the blue eyes and straw-colored hair. Stand up, girl."

Carla didn't move, didn't realize she was being addressed until a Teacher pulled her from her seat.

"Don't hurt her! Turn around, girl. Raise your skirts, higher. Look at me, child. Look up, let me see your face . . ."

"She's too young for choosing," said the Teacher, examining Carla's bracelet. "Another year, Lady."

"A pity. She'll coarsen in a year's time. The fuzz is so soft right now, the flesh so tender. Oh, well . . ." She moved away, flicking a red skirt about her thighs, her red-clad legs narrowing to tiny ankles, flashing silver slippers with heels that were like icicles. She smelled . . . Carla didn't know any words to describe how she smelled. She drank in the fragrance hungrily.

"Look at me, child. Look up, let me see your face . . ." The words sang through her mind over and over. At night, falling asleep she thought of the face, drawing it up from the deep black, trying to hold it in focus: white skin, pink cheek ridges, silver eyelids, black lashes longer than she had known lashes could be, silver-pink lips, three silver spots—one at the corner of her left eye, another at the corner of her mouth, the third like a dimple in the satiny cheek. Silver hair that was loose, in waves about her face, that rippled with life of its own when she moved. If only she had been allowed to touch the hair, to run her finger over that cheek . . . The dream that began with the music of the Lady's laughter, ended with the nightmare of her other words: "She'll coarsen in a year's time . . ."

After that Carla had watched the changes take place on and within her body, and she understood what the Lady had meant. Her once smooth legs began to develop hair; it grew under her arms, and, most shameful, it sprouted as a dark, coarse bush under her belly. She wept. She tried to pull the hairs out, but it hurt too much, and made her skin sore and raw. Then she started to bleed, and she lay down and waited to die, and was happy that she would die. Instead, she was ordered to the infirmary and was forced to attend a lecture on feminine hygiene. She watched in stony-faced silence while the Doctor added the new information to her bracelet. The Doctor's face was smooth and pink, her eyebrows pale, her lashes so colorless and stubby that they were almost invisible. On her chin was a brown mole with two long hairs. She wore a straight blue-gray gown that hung from her shoulders to the floor. Her drab hair was pulled back tightly from her face, fastened in a hard bun at the back of her neck. Carla hated her. She hated the Teachers. Most of all she hated herself. She yearned for maturity.

Madam Westfall had written: Maturity brings grace, beauty, wisdom, happiness. Immaturity means ugliness, unfinished beings with potential only, wholly dependent upon and subservient to the mature citizens.

There was a True-False quiz on the master screen in front of the classroom. Carla took her place quickly and touch-typed her ID number on the small screen of her machine.

She scanned the questions, and saw that they were all simple declarative statements of truth. Her stylus ran down the True column of her answer screen and it was done. She wondered why they were killing time like this, what they were waiting for. Madam Westfall's death had thrown everything off schedule.

Paperlike brown skin, wrinkled and hard, with lines crossing lines, vertical, horizontal, diagonal, leaving little islands of flesh, hardly enough to coat the bones. Cracked voice, incomprehensible: *they took away the music from the air . . . voices from the skies . . . erased pictures that move . . . boxes that sing and sob . . .* Crazy talk. And, *. . . only one left that knows. Only one.*

Madam Trudeau entered the classroom and Carla understood why the class had been personalized that period. The Teacher had been waiting for Madam Trudeau's appearance. The girls rose hurriedly. Madam Trudeau motioned for them to be seated once more.

"The following girls attended Madam Westfall during the past five years." She read from a list. Carla's name was included on her list. On finishing it, she asked, "Is there anyone who attended Madam Westfall whose name I did not read?"

There was a rustle from behind Carla. She kept her gaze fastened on Madam Trudeau. "Name?" the Teacher asked.

"Luella, Madam."

"You attended Madam Westfall? When?"

"Two years ago, Madam. I was a relief for Sonya, who became ill suddenly."

"Very well." Madam Trudeau added Luella's name to her list. "You will all report to my office at 8 A.M. tomorrow morning. You will be excused from classes and duties at that time. Dismissed." With a bow she excused herself to the class Teacher and left the room.

Carla's legs twitched and ached. Her swim class was at eight each morning and she had missed it, had been sitting on the straight chair for almost two hours, when finally she was told to go into Madam Trudeau's office. None of the other waiting girls looked up when she rose and followed the attendant from the anteroom. Madam Trudeau was seated at an oversized desk that was completely bare, with a mirrorlike finish. Carla stood before it with her eyes downcast, and she could see Madam Trudeau's face reflected from the surface of the desk. Madam Trudeau was looking at a point over Carla's head, unaware that the girl was examining her features.

"You attended Madam Westfall altogether seven times during the past four years, is that correct?"

"I think it is, Madam."

"You aren't certain?"

"I . . . I don't remember, Madam."

"I see. Do you recall if Madam Westfall spoke to you during any of those times?"

"Yes, Madam."

"Carla, you are shaking. Are you frightened?"

"No, Madam."

"Look at me, Carla."

Carla's hands tightened, and she could feel her fingernails cutting into her hands. She thought of the pain, and stopped shaking. Madam Trudeau had pasty, white skin, with peaked black eyebrows, sharp black eyes, black hair. Her mouth was wide and full, her nose long and narrow. As she studied the girl before her, it seemed to Carla that something changed in her expression, but she couldn't say what it was, or how it now differed from what it had been a moment earlier. A new intensity perhaps, a new interest.

"Carla, I've been looking over your records. Now that you are fourteen it is time to decide on your future. I shall propose your name for the Teachers' Academy on the completion of your current courses. As my protégé, you will quit the quarters you now occupy and attend me in my chambers . . ." She narrowed her eyes, "What is the matter with you, girl? Are you ill?"

"No, Madam. I . . . I had hoped . . . I mean, I designated my choice last month. I thought . . ."

Madam Trudeau looked to the side of her desk where a records screen was lighted. She scanned the report, and her lips curled derisively. "A Lady. You would be a Lady!" Carla felt a blush fire her face, and suddenly her palms were wet with sweat. Madam Trudeau laughed, a sharp barking sound. She said, "The girls who attended Madam Westfall in life, shall attend her in death. You will be on duty in the Viewing Room for two hours each day, and when the procession starts for the burial services in Scranton, you will be part of the entourage. Meanwhile, each day for an additional two hours immediately following your attendance in the Viewing Room you will meditate on the words of wisdom you have heard from Madam Westfall, and you will write down every word she ever spoke in your presence. For this purpose there will be placed a notebook and a pen in your cubicle, which you will use for no other reason. You will discuss this with no one except me. You, Carla, will prepare to move to my quarters immediately, where a learning cubicle will be awaiting you. Dismissed."

Her voice became sharper as she spoke, and when she finished the words were staccato. Carla bowed and turned to leave.

"Carla, you will find that there are certain rewards in being chosen as a Teacher."

Carla didn't know if she should turn and bow again, or stop where she was, or continue. When she hesitated, the voice came again, shorter, raspish. "Go. Return to your cubicle."

The first time, they slaughtered only the leaders, the rous-ers, . . . would be enough to defuse the bomb, leave the rest silent and powerless and malleable . . .

Carla looked at the floor before her, trying to control the trembling in her legs. Madam Westfall hadn't moved, hadn't spoken. She was dead gone. The only sound was the sush, sush of slippers. The green plastic floor was a glare that hurt her eyes. The air was heavy and smelled of death. Smelled the Lady, drank in the fragrance, longed to touch her. Pale, silvery-pink lips, soft, shiny, with two high peaks on the upper lip. The Lady stroked her face with fingers that were soft and cool and gentle. . . . *when their eyes become soft with unspeakable desires and their bodies show signs of woman-hood, then let them have their duties chosen for them, some to bear the young for the society, some to become Teachers, some Nurses, Doctors, some to be taken as Lovers by the citizens, some to be . . .*

Carla couldn't control the sudden start that turned her head to look at the mummy. The room seemed to waver, then steadied again. The tremor in her legs became stronger, harder to stop. She pressed her knees together hard, hurting them where bone dug into flesh and skin. Fingers plucking at the coverlet. Plucking bones, brown bones with horny nails.

Water. Girl, give me water. Pretty, pretty. You would have been killed, you would have. Pretty. The last time they left no one over ten. No one at all. Ten to twenty-five.

Pretty. Carla said it to herself. Pretty. She visualized it as p-r-i-t-y. Pity with an r. Scanning the dictionary for p-r-i-t-y. Nothing. Pretty. *Afraid of shiny, pretty faces. Young, pretty faces.*

The trembling was all through Carla. Two hours. Eternity.

She had stood here forever, would die here, unmoving, trembling, aching. A sigh and the sound of a body falling softly to the floor. Soft body crumbling so easily. Carla didn't turn her head. It must be Luella. So frightened of the mummy. She'd had nightmares every night since Madam Westfall's death. What made a body stay upright, when it fell so easily? Take it out, the thing that held it together, and down, down. Just to let go, to know what to take out and allow the body to fall like that into sleep. Teachers moved across her field of vision, two of them in their black gowns. Sush-sush. Returned with Luella, or someone, between them. No sound. Sush-sush.

The new learning cubicle was an exact duplicate of the old one. Cot, learning machine, chair, partitioned-off commode and washbasin. And new, the notebook and pen. Carla had never had a notebook and pen before. There was the stylus that was attached to the learning machine, and the lighted square in which to write, that then vanished into the machine. She turned the blank pages of the notebook, felt the paper between her fingers, tore a tiny corner off one of the back pages, examined it closely, the jagged edge, the texture of the fragment; she tasted it. She studied the pen just as minutely; it had a pointed, smooth end, and it wrote black. She made a line, stopped to admire it, and crossed it with another line. She wrote very slowly, "Carla," started to put down her number, the one on her bracelet, then stopped in confusion. She never had considered it before, but she had no last name, none that she knew. She drew three heavy lines over the two digits she had put down.

At the end of the two hours of meditation she had written her name a number of times, had filled three pages with it, in fact, and had written one of the things that she could remember hearing from the gray lips of Madam Westfall: "Non-citizens are the property of the state."

The next day the citizens started to file past the dais. Carla breathed deeply, trying to sniff the fragrance of the passing Ladies, but they were too distant. She watched their feet, clad in shoes of rainbow colors: pointed toes, stiletto heels; rounded toes, carved heels; satin, sequinned slippers . . . And just before her duty ended for the day, the Males started to enter the room.

She heard a gasp, Luella again. She didn't faint this time, merely gasped once. Carla saw the feet and legs at the same time and she looked up to see a male citizen. He was very tall and thick, and was dressed in the blue and white clothing of a Doctor of Law. He moved into the sunlight and there was a glitter from gold at his wrists, and his neck, and the gleam of a smooth polished head. He turned past the dais and his eyes met Carla's. She felt herself go light-headed and hurriedly she ducked her head and clenched her hands. She thought he was standing still, looking at her, and she could feel her heart thumping hard. Her relief arrived then and she crossed the room as fast as she could without appearing indecorous.

Carla wrote: "Why did he scare me so much? Why have I never seen a Male before? Why does everyone else wear colors while the girls and the Teachers wear black and gray?"

She drew a wavering line-figure of a man, and stared at it, and then Xed it out. Then she looked at the sheet of paper with dismay. Now she had four ruined sheets of paper to dispose of.

Had she angered him by staring? Nervously she tapped

on the paper and tried to remember what his face had been like. Had he been frowning? She couldn't remember. Why couldn't she think of anything to write for Madam Trudeau? She bit the end of the pen and then wrote slowly, very carefully: *Society may dispose of its property as it chooses, following discussion with at least three members, and following permission which is not to be arbitrarily denied.*

Had Madam Westfall ever said that? She didn't know, but she had to write something, and that was the sort of thing that Madam Westfall had quoted at great length. She threw herself down on the cot and stared at the ceiling. For three days she had kept hearing the Madam's dead voice, but now when she needed to hear her again, nothing.

Sitting in the straight chair, alert for any change in the position of the ancient one, watchful, afraid of the old Teacher. Cramped, tired and sleepy. Half listening to mutterings, murmurings of exhaled and inhaled breaths that sounded like words that made no sense. . . . *Mama said hide child, hide don't move and Stevie wanted a razor for his birthday and Mama said you're too young, you're only nine and he said no Mama I'm thirteen don't you remember and Mama said hide child hide don't move at all and they came in hating pretty faces . . .*

Carla sat up and picked up the pen again, then stopped. When she heard the words, they were so clear in her head, but as soon as they ended, they faded away. She wrote: "hating pretty faces. . . . hide child. . . . only nine." She stared at the words and drew a line through them.

Pretty faces. Madam Westfall had called her pretty, pretty.

The chimes for social hour were repeated three times and finally Carla opened the door of her cubicle and took a step into the anteroom where the other protégés already had gathered. There were five. Carla didn't know any of them, but she had seen all of them from time to time in and around the school grounds. Madam Trudeau was sitting on a high-backed chair that was covered with black. She blended into it, so that only her hands and her face seemed apart from the chair, dead white hands and face. Carla bowed to her and stood uncertainly at her own door.

"Come in, Carla. It is social hour. Relax. This is Wanda, Louise, Stephanie, Mary, Dorothy." Each girl inclined her head slightly as her name was mentioned. Carla couldn't tell afterward which name went with which girl. Two of them wore the black-striped overskirt that meant they were in the Teacher's Academy. The other three still wore the gray of the lower school, as did Carla, with black bordering the hems.

"Carla doesn't want to be a Teacher," Madam Trudeau said drily. "She prefers the paint box of a Lady." She smiled with her mouth only. One of the academy girls laughed. "Carla, you are not the first to envy the paint box and the bright clothes of the Ladies. I have something to show you. Wanda, the film."

The girl who had laughed touched a button on a small table and on one of the walls a picture was projected. Carla caught her breath. It was a Lady, all gold and white, gold hair, gold eyelids, filmy white gown that ended just above her knees. She turned and smiled, holding out both hands, flashing jeweled fingers, long, gleaming nails that came to points. Then she reached up and took off her hair.

Carla felt that she would faint when the golden hair came

off in the Lady's hands, leaving short, straight brown hair. She placed the gold hair on a ball, and then, one by one, stripped off the long gleaming nails, leaving her hands just hands, bony and ugly. The Lady peeled off her eyelashes and brows, and then patted a brown, thick coating of something on her face, and, with its removal, revealed pale skin with wrinkles about her eyes, with hard, deep lines aside her nose down to her mouth that had also changed, had become small and mean. Carla wanted to shut her eyes, turn away and go back to her cubicle, but she didn't dare move. She could feel Madam Trudeau's stare, and the gaze seemed to burn.

The Lady took off the swirling gown, and under it was a garment Carla never had seen before that covered her from her breasts to her thighs. The stubby fingers worked at fasteners, and finally got the garment off, and there was her stomach, bigger, bulging, with cruel red lines where the garment had pinched and squeezed her. Her breasts drooped almost to her waist. Carla couldn't stop her eyes, couldn't make them not see, couldn't make herself not look at the rest of the repulsive body.

Madam Trudeau stood up and went to her door. "Show Carla the other two films." She looked at Carla then and said, I order you to watch. I shall quiz you on the contents." She left the room.

The other two films showed the same Lady at work. First with a protégé, then with a male citizen. When they were over Carla stumbled back to her cubicle and vomited repeatedly until she was exhausted. She had nightmares that night.

How many days, she wondered, have I been here now? She no longer trembled, but became detached almost as soon as she took her place between two of the tall windows. She didn't try to catch a whiff of the fragrance of the Ladies, or try to get a glimpse of the Males. She had chosen one particular spot in the floor on which to concentrate, and she didn't shift her gaze from it.

They were old and full of hate, and they said, let us remake them in our image, and they did.

Madam Trudeau hated her, despised her. Old and full of hate . . .

"Why were you not chosen to become a Woman to bear young?"

"I am not fit, Madam. I am weak and timid."

"Look at your hips, thin, like a Male's hips. And your breasts, small and hard." Madam Trudeau turned away in disgust. "Why were you not chosen to become a Professional, a Doctor, or a Technician?"

"I am not intelligent enough, Madam. I require many hours of study to grasp the mathematics."

"So. Weak, frail, not too bright. Why do you weep?"

"I don't know, Madam. I am sorry."

"Go to your cubicle. You disgust me."

Staring at a flaw in the floor, a place where an indentation distorted the light, creating one very small oval shadow, wondering when the ordeal would end, wondering why she couldn't fill the notebook with the many things that Madam Westfall had said, things that she could remember here, and could not remember when she was in her cubicle with pen poised over the notebook.

Sometimes Carla forgot where she was, found herself in the chamber of Madam Westfall, watching the ancient one struggle to stay alive, forcing breaths in and out, refusing to admit death. Watching the incomprehensible dials and tubes and bottles of fluids with lowering levels, watching needles that vanished into flesh, tubes that disappeared under the bedclothes, that seemed to writhe now and again with a secret life, listening to the mumbling voice, the groans and sighs, the meaningless words.

Three times they rose against the children and three times slew them until there were none left none at all because the contagion had spread and all over ten were infected and carried radios . . .

Radios? A disease? Infected with radios, spreading it among young people?

And Mama said hide child hide and don't move and put this in the cave too and don't touch it.

Carla's relief came and numbly she walked from the Viewing Room. She watched the movement of the black border of her skirt as she walked and it seemed that the blackness crept up her legs, enveloped her middle, climbed her front until it reached her neck, and then it strangled her. She clamped her jaws hard and continued to walk her measured pace.

The girls who had attended Madam Westfall in life were on duty throughout the school ceremonies after the viewing. They were required to stand in a line behind the dais. There were eulogies to the patience and firmness of the first Teacher. Eulogies to her wisdom in setting up the rules of the school. Carla tried to keep her attention on the speakers, but she was so tired and drowsy that she heard only snatches. Then she was jolted into awareness. Madam Trudeau was talking.

". . . a book that will be the guide to all future Teachers, showing them the way through personal tribulations and trials to achieve the serenity that was Madam Westfall's. I am honored by this privilege, in choosing me and my apprentices to accomplish this end . . ."

Carla thought of the gibberish that she had been putting down in her notebook and she blinked back tears of shame. Madam Trudeau should have told them why she wanted the information. She would have to go back over it all and destroy all the nonsense that she had written down.

Late that afternoon the entourage formed that would accompany Madam Westfall to her final ceremony in Scranton, her native city, where her burial would return her to her family.

Madam Trudeau had an interview with Carla before departure. "You will be in charge of the other girls," she said. "I expect you to maintain order. You will report any disturbance, or any infringement of rules immediately, and if that is not possible, if I am occupied, you will personally impose order in my name."

"Yes, Madam."

"Very well. During the journey the girls will travel together in a compartment of the tube. Talking will be permitted, but no laughter, no childish play. When we arrive at the Scranton home, you will be given rooms with cots. Again you will all comport yourselves with the dignity of the office which you are ordered to fulfill at this time."

Carla felt excitement mount within her as the girls lined up to take their places along the sides of the casket. They went with it to a closed limousine where they sat knee to knee, unspeaking, hot, to be taken over smooth highways for an hour to the tube. Madam Westfall had refused to fly in life, and was granted the same rights in death, so her body was to be transported from Wilmington to Scranton by the rocket tube. As soon as the girls had accompanied the casket to its car, and were directed to their own compartment, their voices raised in a babble. It was the first time any of them had left the schoolgrounds since entering them at the age of five.

Ruthie was going to work in the infants' wards, and she turned faintly pink and soft looking when she talked about it. Luella was a music apprentice already, having shown skill on the piano at an early age. Lorette preened herself slightly and announced that she had been chosen as a Lover by a Gentleman. She would become a Lady one day. Carla stared at her curiously, wondering at her pleased look, wondering if she had not been shown the films yet. Lorette was blue-eyed, with pale hair, much the same build as Carla. Looking at her, Carla could imagine her in soft dresses, with her mouth painted, her hair covered by the other hair that was cloud soft and shiny . . . She looked at the girl's cheeks flushed with excitement at the thought of her future, and she knew that with or without the paint box, Lorette would be a Lady whose skin would be smooth, whose mouth would be soft . . .

"The fuzz is so soft now, the flesh so tender." She remembered the scent, the softness of the Lady's hands, the way her skirt moved about her red-clad thighs.

She bit her lip. But she didn't want to be a Lady. She couldn't even think of them again without loathing and disgust. She was chosen to be a Teacher.

They said it is the duty of society to prepare its non-citizens for citizenship but it is recognized that there are those who will not meet the requirements and society itself is not to be blamed for those occasional failures that must accrue.

She took out her notebook and wrote the words in it.

"Did you just remember something else she said?" Lisa asked. She was the youngest of the girls, only ten, and had attended Madam Westfall one time. She seemed to be very tired.

Carla looked over what she had written, and then read it aloud. "It's from the school rules book," she said. "Maybe changed a little, but the same meaning. You'll study it in a year or two."

Lisa nodded. "You know what she said to me? She said I should go hide in the cave, and never lose my birth certificate. She said I should never tell anyone where the radio is." She frowned. "Do you know what a cave is? And a radio?"

"You wrote it down, didn't you? In the notebook?"

Lisa ducked her head. "I forgot again. I remembered it once and then forgot again until now." She searched through her cloth travel bag for her notebook and when she didn't find it, she dumped the contents on the floor to search more carefully. The notebook was not there.

"Lisa, when did you have it last?"

"I don't know. A few days ago. I don't remember."

"When Madam Trudeau talked to you the last time, did you have it then?"

"No. I couldn't find it. She said if I didn't have it the next time I was called for an interview, she'd whip me. But I can't find it!" She broke into tears and threw herself down on her small heap of belongings. She beat her fists on them and sobbed. "She's going to whip me and I can't find it. I can't. It's gone."

Carla stared at her. She shook her head. "Lisa, stop that crying. You couldn't have lost it. Where? There's no place to lose it. You didn't take it from your cubicle, did you?"

The girl sobbed louder. "No. No. No. I don't know where it is."

Carla kneeled by her and pulled the child up from the floor to a squatting position. "Lisa, what did you put in the notebook? Did you play with it?"

Lisa turned chalky white and her eyes became very large, then she closed them, no longer weeping.

"So you used it for other things? Is that it? What sort of things?"

Lisa shook her head. "I don't know. Just things."

"All of it? The whole notebook?"

"I couldn't help it. I didn't know what to write down. Madam Westfall said too much. I couldn't write it all. She wanted to touch me and I was afraid of her and I hid under the chair and she kept calling me, 'Child, come here don't hide, I'm not one of them. Go to the cave and take it with you.' And she kept reaching for me with her hands. I . . . they were like chicken claws. She would have ripped me apart with them. She hated me. She said she hated me. She said I should have been killed with the others, why wasn't I killed with the others."

Carla, her hands hard on the child's shoulders, turned away from the fear and despair she saw on the girl's face. Ruthie pushed past her and hugged the child.

"Hush, hush, Lisa. Don't cry now. Hush. There, there."

Carla stood up and backed away. "Lisa, what sort of things did you put in the notebook?"

"Just things that I like. Snowflakes and flowers and designs."

"All right. Pick up your belongings and sit down. We must be nearly there. It seems like the tube is stopping."

Again they were shown from a closed compartment to a closed limousine and whisked over countryside that remained invisible to them. There was a drizzly rain falling when they stopped and got out of the car.

The Westfall house was a three-storied, pseudo-Victorian wooden building, with balconies and cupolas, and many chimneys. There was scaffolding about it, and one of the three porches had been torn away and was being replaced as restoration of the house, turning it into a national monument, progressed. The girls accompanied the casket to a gloomy, large room where the air was chilly and damp, and scant lighting cast deep shadows. After the casket had been positioned on the dais which also had accompanied it, the girls followed Madam Trudeau through narrow corridors, up narrow steps, to the third floor where two large rooms had been prepared for them, each containing seven cots.

Madam Trudeau showed them the bathroom that would serve their needs, told them good-night, and motioned Carla to follow her. They descended the stairs to a second floor room that had black, massive furniture: a desk, two straight chairs, a bureau with a wavery mirror over it, and a large canopied bed.

Madam Trudeau paced the black floor silently for several minutes without speaking, then she swung around and said, "Carla, I heard every word that silly little girl said this afternoon. She drew pictures in her notebook! This is the third time the word cave has come up in reports of Madam Westfall's mutterings. Did she speak to you of caves?"

Carla's mind was whirling. How had she heard what they had said? Did maturity also bestow magical abilities? She said, "Yes, Madam, she spoke of hiding in a cave."

"Where is the cave, Carla? Where is it?"

"I don't know, Madam. She didn't say."

Madam Trudeau started to pace once more. Her pale face was drawn in lines of concentration that carved deeply into her flesh, two furrows straight up from the inner brows, other lines at the sides of her nose, straight to her chin, her mouth tight and hard. Suddenly she sat down and leaned back in the chair. "Carla, in the last four or five years Madam Westfall became childishly senile; she was no longer living in the present most of the time, but was reliving incidents in her past. Do you understand what I mean?"

Carla nodded, then said hastily, "Yes, Madam."

"Yes. Well it doesn't matter. You know that I have been commissioned to write the biography of Madam Westfall, to immortalize her writings and her utterances. But there is a gap, Carla. A large gap in our knowledge, and until recently it seemed that the gap never would be filled in. When Madam Westfall was found as a child, wandering in a dazed condition, undernourished, almost dead from exposure, she did not know who she was, where she was from, anything about her past at all. Someone had put an identification bracelet on her arm, a steel bracelet that she could not remove, and that was the only clue there was about her origins. For ten years she received the best medical care and education available, and her intellect sparkled brilliantly, but she never regained her memory."

Madam Trudeau shifted to look at Carla. A trick of the lighting made her eyes glitter like jewels. "You have studied how she started her first school with eight students, and over the next century developed her teaching methods to the point of perfection that we now employ throughout the nation, in the Males' school as well as the Females'. Through her efforts Teachers have become the most respected of all citizens and the schools the most powerful of all institutions." A mirthless smile crossed her face, gone almost as quickly as it formed, leaving the deep shadows, lines, and the glittering eyes. "I honored you more than you yet realize when I chose you for my protégé."

The air in the room was too close and dank, smelled of moldering wood and unopened places. Carla continued to watch Madam Trudeau, but she was feeling light-headed and exhausted and the words seemed interminable to her. The glittering eyes held her gaze and she said nothing. The thought occurred to her that Madam Trudeau would take Madam Westfall's place as head of the school now.

"Encourage the girls to talk, Carla. Let them go on as much as they want about what Madam Westfall said, lead them into it if they stray from the point. Written reports have been sadly deficient." She stopped and looked questioningly at the girl. "Yes? What is it?"

"Then . . . I mean after they talk, are they to write . . . ? Or should I try to remember and write it all down?"

"There will be no need for that," Madam Trudeau said. "Simply let them talk as much as they want."

"Yes, Madam."

"Very well. Here is a schedule for the coming days. Two girls on duty in the Viewing Room at all times from dawn until dark, yard exercise in the enclosed garden behind the building if the weather permits, kitchen duty and so on. Study it, and direct the girls to their duties. On Saturday afternoon everyone will attend the burial, and on Sunday we return to the school. Now go."

Carla bowed, and turned to leave. Madam Trudeau's voice stopped her once more. "Wait, Carla. Come here. You may brush my hair before you leave."

Carla took the brush in numb fingers and walked obediently behind Madam Trudeau who was loosening hair clasps that restrained her heavy black hair. It fell down her back like a dead snake, uncoiling slowly. Carla started to brush it.

"Harder, girl. Are you so weak that you can't brush hair?"

She plied the brush harder until her arm became heavy and then Madam Trudeau said, "Enough. You are a clumsy girl, awkward and stupid. Must I teach you everything, even how to brush one's hair properly?" She yanked the brush from Carla's hand and now there were two spots of color on her cheeks and her eyes were flashing. "Get out! Go! Leave me! On Saturday immediately following the funeral you will administer punishment to Lisa for scribbling in her notebook. Afterward report to me. And now get out of here!"

Carla snatched up the schedule and backed across the room, terrified of the Teacher who seemed demoniacal suddenly. She bumped into the other chair and nearly fell down. Madam Trudeau laughed shortly and cried, "Clumsy, awkward! You would be a Lady! You?"

Carla groped behind her for the doorknob and finally escaped into the hallway, where she leaned against the wall trembling too hard to move on. Something crashed into the door behind her and she stifled a scream and ran. The brush. Madam had thrown the brush against the door.

Madam Westfall's ghost roamed all night, chasing shadows in and out of rooms, making the floors creak with her passage, echoes of her voice drifting in and out of the dorm where Carla tossed restlessly. Twice she sat upright in fear, listening intently, not knowing why. Once Lisa cried out and she went to her and held her hand until the child quieted again. When dawn lighted the room Carla was awake and standing at the windows looking at the ring of mountains that encircled the city. Black shadows against the lesser black of the sky, they darkened, and suddenly caught fire from the sun striking their tips. The fire spread downward, went out and became merely light on the leaves that were turning red and gold. Carla turned from the view, unable to explain the pain that filled her. She awakened the first two girls who were to be on duty with Madam Westfall and after their quiet departure, returned to the window. The sun was all the way up now, but its morning light was soft; there were no hard outlines anywhere. The trees were a blend of colors with no individual boundaries, and rocks and earth melted together and were one. Birds were singing with the desperation of summer's end and winter's approach.

"Carla?" Lisa touched her arm and looked up at her with wide, fearful eyes. "Is she going to whip me?"

"You will be punished after the funeral," Carla said, stiffly. "And I should report you for touching me, you know."

The child drew back, looking down at the black border on Carla's skirt. "I forgot." She hung her head. "I'm . . . I'm so scared."

"It's time for breakfast, and after that we'll have a walk in the gardens. You'll feel better after you get out in the sunshine and fresh air."

"Chrysanthemums, dahlias, marigolds. No, the small ones there, with the brown fringes . . ." Luella pointed out the various flowers to the other girls. Carla walked in the rear, hardly listening, trying to keep her eye on Lisa, who also trailed behind. She was worried about the child. She had not slept well, had eaten no breakfast, and was so pale and wan that she didn't look strong enough to take the short garden walk with them.

Eminent personages came and went in the gloomy old house and huddled together to speak in lowered voices. Carla paid little attention to them. "I can change it after I have some authority," she said to a still inner self who listened and made no reply. "What can I do now? I'm property. I belong to the state, to Madam Trudeau and the school. What good if I disobey and am also whipped? Would that help any? I won't hit her hard." The inner self said nothing, but she thought she could hear a mocking laugh come from the mummy that was being honored.

They had all those empty schools, miles and miles of school halls where no feet walked, desks where no students sat, books that no students scribbled up, and they put the children in them and they could see immediately who couldn't keep up, couldn't learn the new ways and they got rid of them. Smart. Smart of them. They were smart and had the goods and the money and the hatred. My God, they hated. That's who wins, who hates most. And is more afraid. Every time.

Carla forced her arms not to move, her hands to remain locked before her, forced her head to stay bowed. The voice now went on and on and she couldn't get away from it.

. . . rained every day, cold freezing rain and Daddy didn't come back and Mama said, hide child, hide in the cave where it's warm, and don't move no matter what happens,

don't move. Let me put it on your arm, don't take it off, never take it off show it to them if they find you show them make them look. . . .

Her relief came and Carla left. In the wide hallway that led to the back steps she was stopped by a rough hand on her arm. "Damme, here's a likely one. Come here, girl. Let's have a look at you." She was spun around and the hand grasped her chin and lifted her head. "Did I say it! I could spot her all the way down the hall, now couldn't I. Can't hide what she's got with long skirts and that skinny hairdo, now can you? Didn't I spot her!" He laughed and turned Carla's head to the side and looked at her in profile, then laughed even louder.

She could see only that he was red faced, with bushy eyebrows and thick gray hair. His hand holding her chin hurt, digging into her jaws at each side of her neck.

"Victor, turn her loose," the cool voice of a female said then. "She's been chosen already. An apprentice Teacher."

He pushed Carla from him, still holding her chin, and he looked down at the skirts with the broad black band at the bottom. He gave her a shove that sent her into the opposite wall. She clutched at it for support.

"Whose pet is she?" he said darkly.

"Trudeau's."

He turned and stamped away, not looking at Carla again. He wore the blue and white of a Doctor of Law. The female was a Lady in pink and black.

"Carla. Go upstairs." Madam Trudeau moved from an open doorway and stood before Carla. She looked up and down the shaking girl. "Now do you understand why I apprenticed you before this trip? For your own protection."

They walked to the cemetery on Saturday, a bright, warm

day with golden light and the odor of burning leaves. Speeches were made, Madam Westfall's favorite music was played, and the services ended. Carla dreaded returning to the dormitory. She kept a close watch on Lisa who seemed but a shadow of herself. Three times during the night she had held the girl until her nightmares subsided, and each time she had stroked her fine hair and soft cheeks and murmured to her quieting words, and she knew it was only her own cowardice that prevented her saying that it was she who would administer the whipping. The first shovelful of earth was thrown on top the casket and everyone turned to leave the place, when suddenly the air was filled with raucous laughter, obscene chants, and wild music. It ended almost as quickly as it started, but the group was frozen until the mountain air became unnaturally still. Not even the birds were making a sound following the maniacal outburst.

Carla had been unable to stop the involuntary look that she cast about her at the woods that circled the cemetery. Who? Who would dare? Only a leaf or two stirred, floating downward on the gentle air effortlessly. Far in the distance a bird began to sing again, as if the evil spirits that had flown past were now gone.

"Madam Trudeau sent this up for you," Luella said nervously, handing Carla the rod. It was plastic, three feet long, thin, flexible. Carla looked at it and turned slowly to Lisa. The girl seemed to be swaying back and forth.

"I am to administer the whipping," Carla said. "You will undress now."

Lisa stared at her in disbelief, and then suddenly she ran across the room and threw herself on Carla, hugging her hard, sobbing. "Thank you, Carla. Thank you so much. I was so afraid, you don't know how afraid. Thank you. How did you make her let you do it? Will you be punished too? I love you so much, Carla." She was incoherent in her relief and she flung off her gown and underwear and turned around.

Her skin was pale and soft, rounded buttocks, dimpled just above the fullness. She had no waist yet, no breasts, no hair on her baby body. Like a baby she had whimpered in the night, clinging tightly to Carla, burying her head in the curve of Carla's breasts.

Carla raised the rod and brought it down, as easily as she could. Anything was too hard. There was a red welt. The girl bowed her head lower, but didn't whimper. She was holding the back of a chair and it jerked when the rod struck.

It would be worse if Madam Trudeau was doing it, Carla thought. She would try to hurt, would draw blood. Why? Why? The rod was hanging limply, and she knew it would be harder on both of them if she didn't finish it quickly. She raised it and again felt the rod bite into flesh, sending the vibration into her arm, through her body.

Again. The girl cried out, and a spot of blood appeared on her back. Carla stared at it in fascination and despair. She couldn't help it. Her arm wielded the rod too hard, and she couldn't help it. She closed her eyes a moment, raised the rod and struck again. Better. But the vibrations that had begun with the first blow increased, and she felt dizzy, and couldn't keep her eyes off the spot of blood that was trailing down the girl's back. Lisa was weeping now, her body was shaking. Carla felt a responsive tremor start within her.

Eight, nine. The excitement that stirred her was unnameable, unknowable, never before felt like this. Suddenly she thought of the Lady who had chosen her once, and scenes of the film she had been forced to watch flashed through her mind. . . . *remake them in our image.* She looked about in that moment frozen in time, and she saw the excitement on some of the faces, on others fear, disgust and revulsion. Her gaze stopped on Helga, who had her eyes closed, whose body was moving rhythmically. She raised the rod and brought it down as hard as she could, hitting the chair with a noise that brought everyone out of her own kind of trance. A sharp, cracking noise that was a finish.

"Ten!" she cried and threw the rod across the room.

Lisa turned and through brimming eyes, red, swollen, ugly with crying, said, "Thank you, Carla. It wasn't so bad."

Looking at her Carla knew hatred. It burned through her, distorted the image of what she saw. Inside her body the excitement found no outlet, and it flushed her face, made her hands numb, and filled her with hatred. She turned and fled.

Before Madam Trudeau's door, she stopped a moment, took a deep breath, and knocked. After several moments the door opened and Madam Trudeau came out. Her eyes were glittering more than ever, and there were two spots of color on her pasty cheeks.

"It is done? Let me look at you." Her fingers were cold and moist when she lifted Carla's chin. "Yes, I see. I see. I am busy now. Come back in half an hour. You will tell me all about it. Half an hour." Carla never had seen a genuine smile on the Teacher's face before, and now when it came, it was more frightening than her frown was. Carla didn't move, but she felt as if every cell in her body had tried to pull back.

She bowed and turned to leave. Madam Trudeau followed her a step and said in a low vibrant voice, "You felt it, didn't you? You know now, don't you?"

"Madam Trudeau, are you coming back?" The door behind her opened, and one of the Doctors of Law appeared there.

"Yes, of course." She turned and went back to the room.

Carla let herself into the small enclosed area between the second and third floor, then stopped. She could hear the voices of girls coming down the stairs, going on duty in the kitchen, or outside for evening exercises. She stopped to wait for them to pass, and she leaned against the wall tiredly. This space was two and a half feet square perhaps. It was very dank and hot. From here she could hear every sound made by the girls on the stairs. Probably that was why the second door had been added, to muffle the noise of those going up and down. The girls had stopped on the steps and were discussing the laughter and obscenities they had heard in the cemetery.

Carla knew that it was her duty to confront them, to order them to their duties, to impose proper silence on them in public places, but she closed her eyes and pressed her hand hard on the wood behind her for support and wished they would finish their childish prattle and go on. The wood behind her started to slide.

She jerked away. A sliding door? She felt it and ran her finger along the smooth paneling to the edge where there was now a six-inch opening as high as she could reach down to the floor. She pushed the door again and it slid easily, going between the two walls. When the opening was wide enough she stepped through it. The cave! She knew it was the cave that Madam Westfall had talked about incessantly.

The space was no more than two feet wide, and very dark. She felt the inside door and there was a knob on it, low enough for children to reach. The door slid as smoothly from the inside as it had from the outside. She slid it almost closed and the voices were cut off, but she could hear other voices, from the room on the other side of the passage. They were not clear. She felt her way farther, and almost fell over a box. She held her breath as she realized that she was hearing Madam Trudeau's voice:

". . . be there. Too many independent reports of the old fool's babbling about it for there not to be something to it. Your men are incompetent."

"Trudeau, shut up. You scare the living hell out of the kids, but you don't scare me. Just shut up and accept the report. We've been over every inch of the hills for miles, and there's no cave. It was over a hundred years ago. Maybe there was one that the kids played in, but it's gone now. Probably collapsed."

"We have to be certain, absolutely certain."

"What's so important about it anyway? Maybe if you would give us more to go on we could make more progress."

"The reports state that when the militia came here, they found only Martha Westfall. They executed her on the spot without questioning her first. Fools! When they searched the house, they discovered that it was stripped. No jewels, no silver, diaries, papers. Nothing. Steve Westfall was dead. Dr. Westfall dead. Martha. No one has ever found the articles that were hidden, and when the child again appeared, she had true amnesia that never yielded to attempts to penetrate it."

"So, a few records, diaries. What are they to you?" There

was silence, then he laughed. "The money! He took all his money out of the bank, didn't he."

"Don't be ridiculous. I want records, that's all. There's a complete ham radio, complete. Dr. Westfall was an electronics engineer as well as a teacher. No one could begin to guess how much equipment he hid before he was killed."

Carla ran her hand over the box, felt behind it. More boxes.

"Yeah, yeah. I read the reports, too. All the more reason to keep the search nearby. For a year before the end a close watch was kept on the house. They had to walk to wherever they hid the stuff. And I can just say again that there's no cave around here. It fell in."

"I hope so," Madam Trudeau said.

Someone knocked on the door, and Madam Trudeau called, "Come in."

"Yes, what is it? Speak up, girl."

"It is my duty to report, Madam, that Carla did not administer the full punishment ordered by you."

Carla's fists clenched hard. Helga.

"Explain," Madam Trudeau said sharply.

"She only struck Lisa nine times, Madam. The last time she hit the chair."

"I see. Return to your room."

The man laughed when the girl closed the door once more. "Carla is the golden one, Trudeau? The one who wears a single black band?"

"The one you manhandled earlier, yes."

"Insubordination in the ranks, Trudeau? Tut, tut. And your reports all state that you never have any rebellion. Never."

Very slowly Madam Trudeau said, "I have never had a student who didn't abandon any thoughts of rebellion under my guidance. Carla will be obedient. And one day she will be an excellent Teacher. I know the signs."

Carla stood before the Teacher with her head bowed and her hands clasped together. Madam Trudeau walked around her without touching her, then sat down and said, "You will whip Lisa every day for a week, beginning tomorrow."

Carla didn't reply.

"Don't stand mute before me, Carla. Signify your obedience immediately."

"I . . . I can't, Madam."

"Carla, any day that you do not whip Lisa, I will. And I will also whip you double her allotment. Do you understand?"

"Yes, Madam."

"You will inform Lisa that she is to be whipped every day, by one or the other of us. Immediately."

"Madam, please . . ."

"You speak out of turn, Carla!"

"I, Madam, please don't do this. Don't make me do this. She is too weak . . ."

"She will beg you to do it, won't she, Carla. Beg you with tears flowing to be the one, not me. And you will feel the excitement and the hate and every day you will feel it grow strong. You will want to hurt her, want to see blood spot her bare back. And your hate will grow until you won't be able to look at her without being blinded by your own hatred. You see, I know, Carla. I know all of it."

Carla stared at her in horror. "I won't do it. I won't."

"I will."

They were old and full of hatred for the shiny young faces, the bright hair, the straight backs and strong legs and arms. They said: let us remake them in our image and they did.

Carla repeated Madam Trudeau's words to the girls gathered in the two sleeping rooms on the third floor. Lisa swayed and was supported by Ruthie. Helga smiled.

That evening Ruthie tried to run away and was caught by two of the the blue-clad Males. The girls were lined up and watched as Ruthie was stoned. They buried her without a service on the hill where she had been caught.

After dark, lying on the cot open-eyed, tense, Carla heard Lisa's whisper close to her ear. "I don't care if you hit me, Carla. It won't hurt like it does when she hits me."

"Go to bed, Lisa. Go to sleep."

"I can't sleep. I keep seeing Ruthie. I should have gone with her. I wanted to, but she wouldn't let me. She was afraid there would be Males on the hill watching. She said if she didn't get caught, then I should try to follow her at night." The child's voice was flat, as if shock had dulled her sensibilities.

Carla kept seeing Ruthie too. Over and over she repeated to herself: I should have tried it. I'm cleverer than she was. I might have escaped. I should have been the one. She knew it was too late now. They would be watching too closely.

An eternity later she crept from her bed and dressed quietly. Soundlessly she gathered her own belongings, and then collected the notebooks of the other girls, and the pens, and she left the room. There were dim lights on throughout the house as she made her way silently down stairs and through corridors. She left a pen by one of the outside doors, and very cautiously made her way back to the tiny space between the floors. She slid the door open and deposited everything else she carried inside the cave. She tried to get to the kitchen for food, but stopped when she saw one of the Officers of Law. She returned soundlessly to the attic rooms and tiptoed among the beds to Lisa's cot. She placed one hand over the girl's mouth and shook her awake with the other.

Lisa bolted upright, terrified, her body stiffened convulsively. With her mouth against the girl's ear Carla whispered, "Don't make a sound. Come on." She half-led, half-carried the girl to the doorway, down the stairs and into the cave and closed the door.

"You can't talk here, either," she whispered. "They can hear." She spread out the extra garments she had collected and they lay down together, her arms tight about the girl's shoulders. "Try to sleep," she whispered. "I don't think they'll find us here. And after they leave, we'll creep out and live in the woods. We'll eat nuts and berries . . ."

The first day they were jubilant at their success and they giggled and muffled the noise with their skirts. They could hear all the orders being issued by Madam Trudeau: guards in all the halls, on the stairs, at the door to the dorm to keep other girls from trying to escape also. They could hear all the interrogations, of the girls, the guards who had not seen the escapees. They heard the mocking voice of the Doctor of Law deriding Madam Trudeau's boasts of absolute control.

The second day Carla tried to steal food for them, and, more important, water. There were blue-clad Males everywhere. She returned empty-handed. During the night Lisa whimpered in her sleep and Carla had to stay awake to quiet the child who was slightly feverish.

"You won't let her get me, will you?" she begged over and over.

The third day Lisa became too quiet. She didn't want Carla to move from her side at all. She held Carla's hand in her hot, dry hand and now and then tried to raise it to her face, but she was too weak now. Carla stroked her forehead.

When the child slept Carla wrote in the notebooks, in the dark, not knowing if she wrote over other words, or on blank pages. She wrote her life story, and then made up other things to say. She wrote her name over and over, and wept because she had no last name. She wrote nonsense words and rhymed them with other nonsense words. She wrote of the savages who had laughed at the funeral and she hoped they wouldn't all die over the winter months. She thought that probably they would. She wrote of the golden light through green-black pine trees and of birds' songs and moss underfoot. She wrote of Lisa lying peacefully now at the far end of the cave amidst riches that neither of them could ever have comprehended. When she could no longer write, she drifted in and out of the golden light in the forest, listening to the birds' songs, hearing the raucous laughter that now sounded so beautiful.

1972

JOANNA RUSS

When It Changed

KATY DRIVES like a maniac; we must have been doing over 120 km/hr on those turns. She's good, though, extremely good, and I've seen her take the whole car apart and put it together again in a day. My birthplace on Whileaway was largely given to farm machinery and I refuse to wrestle with a five-gear shift at unholy speeds, not having been brought up to it, but even on those turns in the middle of the night, on a country road as bad as only our district can make them, Katy's driving didn't scare me. The funny thing about my wife, though: she will not handle guns. She has even gone hiking in the forests above the 48th parallel without firearms, for days at a time. And that *does* scare me.

Katy and I have three children between us, one of hers and two of mine. Yuriko, my eldest, was asleep in the back seat, dreaming twelve-year-old dreams of love and war: running away to sea, hunting in the North, dreams of strangely beautiful people in strangely beautiful places, all the wonderful guff you think up when you're turning twelve and the glands start going. Some day soon, like all of them, she will disappear for weeks on end to come back grimy and proud, having knifed her first cougar or shot her first bear, dragging some abominably dangerous dead beastie behind her, which I will never forgive for what it might have done to my daughter. Yuriko says Katy's driving puts her to sleep.

For someone who has fought three duels, I am afraid of far, far too much. I'm getting old. I told this to my wife.

"You're thirty-four," she said. Laconic to the point of silence, that one. She flipped the lights on, on the dash—three km. to go and the road getting worse all the time. Far out in the country. Electric-green trees rushed into our headlights and around the car. I reached down next to me where we bolt the carrier panel to the door and eased my rifle into my lap. Yuriko stirred in the back. My height but Katy's eyes, Katy's face. The car engine is so quiet, Katy says, that you can hear breathing in the back seat. Yuki had been alone in the car when the message came, enthusiastically decoding her dot-dashes (silly to mount a wide-frequency transceiver near an I.C. engine, but most of Whileaway is on steam). She had thrown herself out of the car, my gangly and gaudy offspring, shouting at the top of her lungs, so of course she had had to come along. We've been intellectually prepared for this ever since the Colony was founded, ever since it was abandoned, but this is different. This is awful.

"Men!" Yuki had screamed, leaping over the car door. "They've come back! Real Earth men!"

We met them in the kitchen of the farmhouse near the place where they had landed; the windows were open, the night air very mild. We had passed all sorts of transportation when we parked outside, steam tractors, trucks, an I.C. flatbed, even a bicycle. Lydia, the district biologist, had come out of her Northern taciturnity long enough to take blood and urine samples and was sitting in a corner of the kitchen shaking her head in astonishment over the results; she even forced herself (very big, very fair, very shy, always painfully blushing) to dig up the old language manuals—though I can talk the old tongues in my sleep. And do. Lydia is uneasy with us; we're Southerners and too flamboyant. I counted twenty people in that kitchen, all the brains of North Continent. Phyllis Spet, I think, had come in by glider. Yuki was the only child there.

Then I saw the four of them.

They are bigger than we are. They are bigger and broader. Two were taller than me, and I am extremely tall, 1m, 80cm in my bare feet. They are obviously of our species but *off*, indescribably off, and as my eyes could not and still cannot quite comprehend the lines of those alien bodies, I could not, then, bring myself to touch them, though the one who spoke Russian—what voices they have!—wanted to "shake hands," a custom from the past, I imagine. I can only say they were apes with human faces. He seemed to mean well, but I found myself shuddering back almost the length of the kitchen—and then I laughed apologetically—and then to set a good example (*interstellar amity*, I thought) did "shake hands" finally. A hard, hard hand. They are heavy as draft horses. Blurred, deep voices. Yuriko had sneaked in between the adults and was gazing at *the men* with her mouth open.

He turned *his* head—those words have not been in our language for six hundred years—and said, in bad Russian:

"Who's that?"

"My daughter," I said, and added (with that irrational attention to good manners we sometimes employ in moments of insanity), "My daughter, Yuriko Janetson. We use the patronymic. You would say matronymic."

He laughed, involuntarily. Yuki exclaimed, "I thought they would be *good-looking*!" greatly disappointed at this reception of herself. Phyllis Helgason Spet, whom someday I shall kill, gave me across the room a cold, level, venomous look, as if to say: *Watch what you say. You know what I can do.* It's true that I have little formal status, but Madam President will get herself in serious trouble with both me and her own staff if she continues to consider industrial espionage good clean fun. Wars and rumors of wars, as it says in one of our ancestors' books. I translated Yuki's words into *the man's* dog-Russian, once our *lingua franca*, and *the man* laughed again.

"Where are all your people?" he said conversationally.

I translated again and watched the faces around the room; Lydia embarrassed (as usual), Spet narrowing her eyes with some damned scheme, Katy very pale.

"This is Whileaway," I said.

He continued to look unenlightened.

"Whileaway," I said. "Do you remember? Do you have records? There was a plague on Whileaway."

He looked moderately interested. Heads turned in the back of the room, and I caught a glimpse of the local professions-parliament delegate; by morning every town meeting, every district caucus, would be in full session.

"Plague?" he said. "That's most unfortunate."

"Yes," I said. "Most unfortunate. We lost half our population in one generation."

He looked properly impressed.

"Whileaway was lucky," I said. "We had a big initial gene pool, we had been chosen for extreme intelligence, we had a high technology and a large remaining population in which every adult was two-or-three experts in one. The soil is good. The climate is blessedly easy. There are thirty millions of us now. Things are beginning to snowball in industry—do you understand?—give us seventy years and we'll have more than one real city, more than a few industrial centers, full-time professions, full-time radio operators, full-time machinists, give us seventy years and not everyone will have to spend three quarters of a lifetime on the farm." And I tried to explain how hard it is when artists can practice full-time only in old age, when there are so few, so very few who can be free, like Katy and myself. I tried also to outline our government, the two houses, the one by professions and the geographic one; I told him the district caucuses handled problems too big for the individual towns. And that population control was not a political issue, not yet, though give us time and it would be. This was a delicate point in our history; give us time. There was no need to sacrifice the quality of life for an insane rush into industrialization. Let us go our own pace. Give us time.

"Where are all the people?" said that monomaniac.

I realized then that he did not mean people, he meant *men*, and he was giving the word the meaning it had not had on Whileaway for six centuries.

"They died," I said. "Thirty generations ago."

I thought we had poleaxed him. He caught his breath. He made as if to get out of the chair he was sitting in; he put his hand to his chest; he looked around at us with the strangest blend of awe and sentimental tenderness. Then he said, solemnly and earnestly:

"A great tragedy."

I waited, not quite understanding.

"Yes," he said, catching his breath again with that queer smile, that adult-to-child smile that tells you something is being hidden and will be presently produced with cries of encouragement and joy, "a great tragedy. But it's over." And

again he looked around at all of us with the strangest deference. As if we were invalids.

"You've adapted amazingly," he said.

"To what?" I said. He looked embarrassed. He looked
inane. Finally he said, "Where I come from, the women don't
dress so plainly."

"Like you?" I said. "Like a bride?" for the men were wearing
silver from head to foot. I had never seen anything so gaudy.
He made as if to answer and then apparently thought better
of it; he laughed at me again. With an odd exhilaration—as
if we were something childish and something wonderful, as
if he were doing us an enormous favor—he took one shaky
breath and said, "Well, we're here."

I looked at Spet, Spet looked at Lydia, Lydia looked at Amalia, who is the head of the local town meeting, Amalia looked
at I don't know who. My throat was raw. I cannot stand local
beer, which the farmers swill as if their stomachs had irid-
ium linings, but I took it anyway, from Amalia (it was her
bicycle we had seen outside as we parked), and swallowed it
all. This was going to take a long time. I said, "Yes, here you
are," and smiled (feeling like a fool), and wondered seriously
if male Earth people's minds worked so very differently from
female Earth people's minds, but that couldn't be so or the
race would have died out long ago. The radio network had got
the news around-planet by now and we had another Russian
speaker, flown in from Varna; I decided to cut out when *the
man* passed around pictures of his wife, who looked like the
priestess of some arcane cult. He proposed to question Yuki,
so I barreled her into a back room in spite of her furious pro-
tests, and went out on the front porch. As I left, Lydia was
explaining the difference between parthenogenesis (which is

so easy that anyone can practice it) and what we do, which is the merging of ova. That is why Katy's baby looks like me. Lydia went on to the Ansky Process and Katy Ansky, our one full-polymath genius and the great-great-I don't know how many times great-grandmother of my own Katharina.

A dot-dash transmitter in one of the outbuildings chattered faintly to itself: operators flirting and passing jokes down the line.

There was a man on the porch. The other tall man. I watched him for a few minutes—I can move very quietly when I want to—and when I allowed him to see me, he stopped talking into the little machine hung around his neck. Then he said calmly, in excellent Russian, "Did you know that sexual equality has been re-established on Earth?"

"You're the real one," I said, "aren't you? The other one's for show." It was a great relief to get things cleared up. He nodded affably.

"As a people, we are not very bright," he said. "There's been too much genetic damage in the last few centuries. Radiation. Drugs. We can use Whileaway's genes, Janet." Strangers do not call strangers by the first name.

"You can have cells enough to drown in," I said. "Breed your own."

He smiled. "That's not the way we want to do it." Behind him I saw Katy come into the square of light that was the screened-in door. He went on, low and urbane, not mocking me, I think, but with the self-confidence of someone who has always had money and strength to spare, who doesn't know what it is to be second-class or provincial. Which is very odd, because the day before, I would have said that was an exact description of me.

"I'm talking to you, Janet," he said, "because I suspect you have more popular influence than anyone else here. You know as well as I do that parthenogenetic culture has all sorts of inherent defects, and we do not—if we can help it—mean to use you for anything of the sort. Pardon me; I should not have said 'use.' But surely you can see that this kind of society is unnatural."

"Humanity is unnatural," said Katy. She had my rifle under her left arm. The top of that silky head does not quite come up to my collar-bone, but she is as tough as steel; he began to move, again with that queer smiling deference (which his fellow had showed to me but he had not) and the gun slid into Katy's grip as if she had shot with it all her life.

"I agree," said the man. "Humanity is unnatural. I should know. I have metal in my teeth and metal pins here." He touched his shoulder. "Seals are harem animals," he added, "and so are men; apes are promiscuous and so are men; doves are monogamous and so are men; there are even celibate men and homosexual men. There are homosexual cows, I believe. But Whileaway is still missing something." He gave a dry chuckle. I will give him the credit of believing that it had something to do with nerves.

"I miss nothing," said Katy, "except that life isn't endless."

"You are—?" said the man, nodding from me to her.

"Wives," said Katy. "We're married." Again the dry chuckle.

"A good economic arrangement," he said, "for working and taking care of the children. And as good an arrangement as any for randomizing heredity, if your reproduction is made to follow the same pattern. But think, Katharina Michaela-son, if there isn't something better that you might secure for your daughters. I believe in instincts, even in Man, and I can't think that the two of you—a machinist, are you? and I gather you are some sort of chief of police—don't feel somehow what even you must miss. You know it intellectually, of course. There is only half a species here. Men must come back to Whileaway."

Katy said nothing.

"I should think, Katharina Michaelason," said the man gently, "that you, of all people, would benefit most from such a change," and he walked past Katy's rifle into the square of light coming from the door. I think it was then that he noticed my scar, which really does not show unless the light is from the side: a fine line that runs from temple to chin. Most people don't even know about it.

"Where did you get that?" he said, and I answered with an involuntary grin, "In my last duel." We stood there bristling at each other for several seconds (this is absurd but true) until he went inside and shut the screen door behind him. Katy said in a brittle voice, "You damned fool, don't you know when we've been insulted?" and swung up the rifle to shoot him through the screen, but I got to her before she could fire and knocked the rifle out of aim; it burned a hole through the porch floor. Katy was shaking. She kept whispering over and over, "That's why I never touched it, because I knew I'd kill someone, I knew I'd kill someone." The first man—the one I'd spoken with first—was still talking inside the house, something about the grand movement to re-colonize and rediscover all that Earth had lost. He stressed the advantages to Whileaway: trade, exchange of ideas, education. He too said that sexual equality had been re-established on Earth.

Katy was right, of course; we should have burned them down where they stood. Men are coming to Whileaway.

When one culture has the big guns and the other has none, there is a certain predictability about the outcome. Maybe men would have come eventually in any case. I like to think that a hundred years from now my great-grandchildren could have stood them off or fought them to a standstill, but even that's no odds; I will remember all my life those four people I first met who were muscled like bulls and who made me—if only for a moment—feel small. A neurotic reaction, Katy says. I remember everything that happened that night; I remember Yuki's excitement in the car, I remember Katy's sobbing when we got home as if her heart would break, I remember her lovemaking, a little peremptory as always, but wonderfully soothing and comforting. I remember prowling restlessly around the house after Katy fell asleep with one bare arm flung into a patch of light from the hall. The muscles of her forearms are like metal bars from all that driving and testing of her machines. Sometimes I dream about Katy's arms. I remember wandering into the nursery and picking up my wife's baby, dozing for a while with the poignant, amazing warmth of an infant in my lap, and finally returning to the kitchen to find Yuriko fixing herself a late snack. My daughter eats like a Great Dane.

"Yuki," I said, "do you think you could fall in love with a man?" and she whooped derisively. "With a ten-foot toad!" said my tactful child.

But men are coming to Whileaway. Lately I sit up nights and worry about the men who will come to this planet, about my two daughters and Betta Katharinason, about what will happen to Katy, to me, to my life. Our ancestors' journals are one long cry of pain and I suppose I ought to be glad now but one can't throw away six centuries, or even (as I have lately discovered) thirty-four years. Sometimes I laugh at the question those four men hedged about all evening and never quite dared to ask, looking at the lot of us, hicks in over-alls, farmers in canvas pants and plain shirts: *Which of you plays the role of the man?* As if we had to produce a carbon copy of their mistakes! I doubt very much that sexual equality has been re-established on Earth. I do not like to think of myself mocked, of Katy deferred to as if she were weak, of Yuki made to feel unimportant or silly, of my other children cheated of their full humanity or turned into strangers. And I'm afraid that my own achievements will dwindle from what they were—or what I thought they were—to the not-very-interesting curiosa of the human race, the oddities you read about in the back of the book, things to laugh at some-times because they are so exotic, quaint but not impressive, charming but not useful. I find this more painful than I can say. You will agree that for a woman who has fought three duels, all of them kills, indulging in such fears is ludicrous. But what's around the corner now is a duel so big that I don't think I have the guts for it; in Faust's words: *Verweile doch, du bist so schoen!* Keep it as it is. Don't change.

Sometimes at night I remember the original name of this planet, changed by the first generation of our ancestors, those curious women for whom, I suppose, the real name was too painful a reminder after the men died. I find it amusing, in a grim way, to see it all so completely turned around. This too shall pass. All good things must come to an end.

Take my life but don't take away the meaning of my life.
For-A-While.

1972

KATHLEEN SKY

Lament of the Keeku Bird

MY THROBBING womb is stuffed with bloody sand instead of the new cub I should have had this year. It burns as if I had crawled on my belly through the firepits. Uuuh, the sand inside me scrapes at my wombskin, eating my hide as I crawl over mountains of ripping, tearing sand. Each speck of grit is lying in wait for me so that it can avenge itself on my body for the sin of dragging this torn, bleeding carcass over it. One piece of sand is so small I can hardly see it, but, oh gods, there are such a lot of them!

Why did they not tell me it would hurt so, or that I would leave a me-wide trail of scraps of skin and bloody sand stretching back to the horizon? My hide is being worn away, ground off between heaps of sand within and without.

My womb! It's rubbed thin as a mandus leaf, a burning mandus leaf flaming in my belly.

They took me trembling and pleading to the edge of the desert, the Old Ones did. They said I must crawl like a beast on my belly to the Long Rock if I wanted to live.

"You must not lift your belly from the sand," they said.

"Do not turn back on your way to the Long Rock," they said.

"Crawl to the Long Rock."

"On your belly to the Long Rock."

"Do not stop on the way to the Long Rock."
"Find the Long Rock."

Die on your way to the Long Rock! No, they did not tell me that; they did not tell me how much it would pain me, this Long Rock story of the Old Ones . . .

I haven't stopped crawling, but I did pause once to snap my jaws together. My teeth are turning green, they wobble loosely in their sockets—I have not tightened them in warm flesh for more time than I can count. They rub against the ridges of my jaw and rattle together like the bones of the dead after the keeku have gone. Aaah, for a bite, just a small bite of warm meat!

My eyes are rimmed with itching salt crystals—tears? They burn like the sand I crawl over, the sand that crawls in me. The lash ridges have gummed themselves together, and they pulled at my eyes when I blink. My eyes are so dry even a keeku would not want them.

There is nothing but sand for as far as my eyes see. I was called "Keen-eyed" in my youth, now my eyes only blur and dry up in their sockets, and I can see but a few measures in any direction.

What if I miss the Long Rock? It might be off to either side of me, hidden by the tall drifts of sand or lost because of my failing eyes. I saw a dust dream out there yesterday, a rock that shimmered in the sun, and then vanished. It was a rock, very long, and crawling like me with its belly to the sand. What if it wasn't a dust dream? My eyes are so very bad I can not tell the real from the unreal . . .

I *have* missed the Long Rock.

They told me if I crawled in a straight line I would most certainly find the Long Rock—they did not say how far I must crawl, but surely I have passed it by now.

Am I still even moving in the right direction, I wonder? Or is my body simply chasing its own tail? I can't turn my head far enough to see if my trail is straight. To do so I must be facing the way I came and that is forbidden by the Old Ones.

They said I could not turn back—to do so was to die. But I am dying! I can feel the blood on my womb lining as it rubs between the sand inside and that which I slide over, but the damp sand is easier to crawl on, even if it is my blood dampening it down . . .

There isn't so much as a beetle in all this sand. I would eat even a zanthu now, even though the bush toad is forbidden to my people. It would taste good I'm sure, and would serve to tighten my teeth. Anything which I might find to eat would taste good—aaah, even a keeku, even a keeku!

I did see a small swift-crawler once, but it went too fast and was behind me before I could even think on the meaning of its hopping so bravely over my foreclaws. It would have tasted good if I had caught it. I might have snapped it so quickly in my jaws, the bones—little bones!—crunching and warm, blood and flesh; my teeth tightening hard in warm flesh.

My womb screams as my hide is ripped off in strips by the sand, and the ache in my gut is tying itself in knots around my soul, strangling it. I did not know this horror could exist—

this grinding, grinding in my belly, and the blood leaking drop by drop into the thirsty sand. I did not know this was how the Old Ones got their maturity scars—I did not know this was how I would become an Old One. . . .

I crawled like a beast, crawling on my belly—I have never cried so loudly, even in the pain of the birthing hut—aaah, pain, pa-a-a-i-n!

My guts are twisted, tightening against this never-ending rub, rub of sand in my belly. Do the Old Ones mean me to lose the rest of myself to the sand once my womb is worn away?

WHERE IS THE LONG ROCK!

Do I still have my milk dugs? Oh, how they clustered like ripe fruit at the mouth of my womb. Rosy pink, gorged with rich milk; soft, spurting with warmth, my dugs filled the mouths of many cubs. No one had such beautiful warm love-teats as I; they were flames at the mating times, fires, beckoning the hands of my lovers—aaah, warm and grasping, caressing his womb hands—warm and lovely, pulsating as he rubbed his quickening seed deep into my womb! AAAH, deep, deeply he rubs his womb hands into me! His eyes are bright, water drips from his open mouth—aaah, his hands grow glowing warm, throbbing in my womb, aaah . . .

I am not sure I *want* to be an Old One.

I can feel the ribbons of flesh from my underside catching in my tail. It tangles itself in the loose strips, and they tear at the tender underskin of my back legs. There is no water in all this sand. Nothing for me to drink; nothing to wash my bloody hide in—oh, how I loved the swift river that ran below the cliffs of my village! Cold it was, clean it was, shining swift, bubbling, dancing over the rocks, falling sweetly into the bathingpool of the village.

Aaah, to drink all the water my belly could hold—to catch the swift water in my mouth—the swift water, the little water beasts that swam all unknowingly into my waiting jaws. Crunch! Cold, cold water, warm, warm flesh, and I, I with my sleek hide glowing like the river as the water slipped from my shining back!

I am glad there is water in my body which I can drink, but there is no river to clean my dusty hide, nor is there any meat for my teeth to crunch. Would that I might store the swift small water creatures in my bones as I do the stale water which trickles so slowly up into my mouth. Up, up into my jaws the water would come—up, up would swim the little water beasts—aaah, to crunch the cold and the warm again!

Why can I not eat myself? I drink the water from my body, little as it does for my thirst—why not eat the strips of this bloody flesh which the sand rips from me? I am losing large chunks of my hide, wasted, going only to feed the rapacious sand; surely it does not need my flesh—why could my body not feed me instead?

I was never told it was forbidden to eat one's own hide, but to reach the bits of me which are ripped off my belly I must stop crawling, lift my body off the sand, and twist my head until I am facing the way I came. I can't, I can't, the Old Ones said I could only stop if I was dying or dead!

Aaah, how you torment me, you Old Ones . . .

Ho, there is a bit of loose skin working its way off of my right foreclaw. I can pull myself along on one foot, and not stop crawling; I can stretch my leg up to my mouth—almost —a little more—there!

Uuuuh, my mouth is filled with burning sand and the bitter taste of carrion; the dead, dank taste of my hide mingles with the bile which climbs my throat to fill my aching jaws. Swirling slop in my mouth reminding me of my shame; grit, poisonous things never found in warm flesh fill me—bile, my body revolts at such food. I can not swallow this, it drips from my jaws into the waiting sand whose feast it was meant to be—uuuh, will my mouth never be free of this carrion swill? I am not meant to eat my own skin—why did the Old Ones not tell me so?

There is a piece of grit caught in one of my forward fangs. It grinds at my gums each time the fang shifts its position in my sore jaws. Why are my teeth so loose, why, why is there nothing to eat that will tighten my teeth?

My claws are too blunted with all this crawling to pick out the sand, and my dry, swollen tongue will not fit into the crack below the tooth. What I would give for a small twig to poke my teeth with—aaah, would that there was a small bit of meat stuck in my teeth instead of only tasteless sand!

At festival times when I was a child, we used to roast a whole sleam carcass in the firepits. Aaah, how big it was! It took so many of our males to lift such a large beast into the pits, and it was hard work for them. The sleam's fur would turn crisp and black in the heat of the pit, and we shrilled with joy at the first smell of hot flesh. Uuuh, but the sleam are harder to catch now, and the earth gods grow impotent with age so that there are not so many firepits.

The festivals of my cub days, aaah, such firepits we had! Hot, filled with jagged grey rocks of an earth god's body; aaah, the leaping womb hands of the god! Flaming fingers burning blue, orange and yellow, rising out of the body of an earth god to make warm our food. How I wished we might use the pits every day to heat our meat, but the Old Ones—always the Old Ones—they said we must make do with warmth of fresh kills and the crunch of unbaked bones; the gods would leave us if we came to use their warmth too often; their fireseed was not created just for us to use for warming food—it was needed for the making of new gods and more firepits. The god-seed must replenish itself and wait, bursting and ripe, until the times when the earth god's womb hands rose to quicken the body of his mate.

Perhaps we had too many festivals, or took too much of the seed at matingtime, but we do not have so many gods now, nor enough firepits. I wish we had so much of gods, and fire, sleam and festivals—I wish I were still a cub eating hot meat which was a gift of the gods—I remember being so greedy for the warm flesh that I would grab it hot and smoking from the flames and stuff my jaws with it; crunch! Oh, how often I burned my mouth with my greediness! My old dam, her jaws rattling with anger, she would cuff me, sending me rolling belly over back in the dust. I remember the warmth of the meat; aaah, how good it was, even with a burnt mouth . . .

My feet sink deeply into the dry sand, puffing little spurts of dust up over my skin. I can't even tell what color I am anymore; not that it matters much, but am I green, grey, or the bright blue of the river? It is not so important to me now, but there was a time when I enjoyed the changing colors of my hide very much. But you can not eat the shades of your own hide, nor lick the dust away with a cracked and drying tongue.

Aaaah, how my great purple-blue father loved the river! He taught me to sport in the ripples, taught me to catch the cold and the warm, taught me what joy there was in the clear cold of the river. My father, greenish and blue, showed me how to float the *chroci* blossoms in the small, still pools at the edge of the river, showed me how to float beside them, gentle, like a flower in the water.

We could swim, he and I, for more measures at a time than anyone else in our village. We swam, my great blue-green father and I, so clean and strong in the water, and we ate, ah, so many water creatures! Swift in the river they swam, but not as swift as we were.

My father was young—oh, so young! He never made this crawl to the Long Rock. He had no maturity scars on his fine sleek belly; he still had his—womb hands—and the pouch which held them.

I never really saw his womb hands—such things are forbidden—but I know they were kept snug, tucked sweetly into his belly pouch. . . .

No! I must not think of my father in that way!

SHAME.

I MUST NOT!

IT'S WRONG!

He died, he died, the great purple-green of him. The fevers which come creeping into our village in the cold season caught him in their warm embrace, hugging his body to them until he died. I miss him, my father . . .

I do not feel the pain as much. Is it really less, or has my mind refused to accept it any longer? Aaah, I am no longer bleeding—I think. My hide feels dry, it's thickly covered in hard sand, and the pain has become a pale dust dream of itself. I wonder why there is no more blood. Have I nothing left to give to the sand which sucks at my body?—or perhaps even its monumental thirst is at last quenched. I hope it is so, and not just another trick of the Old Ones.

Ho, the pain is back! The sand-covering of my belly has been scraped away by the grit I crawl over, and my raw skin rubs itself like a lover into the womb of the waiting sand. My gut is laced with fire. I pull, tugging upward, at my sagging belly muscles, lifting internal parts away from the aching walls of my body. I am meant to lose even my guts to this sand of a sand of a sand!

Old Ones, hear me! I can not stand much more of this crawling; you may keep your Long Rock tale, and may you die of it as I am dying—do you hear me?

I curse the Old Ones, but I continue to crawl. I am a fool. I did not need to come here; there are tales of those who did not submit, those who live in the hills toward the far edge of the world. They have still an unscarred belly, and no Old Ones among them—I am a fool; I am a fool . . .

The sand is sticking in dry patches to my skinned belly, but since there is less blood it does not coat me as it has before; little matter—if there was such a coating, the sand would only wear it away again. I can feel the sand sliding along the bottom of my jaw, down my belly, over the entrance to my—

My womb is gone.

I am strangely smooth from head to tail, one large, sand-smeared curve from snout to anus, unmarked by the milk-dugged opening to my womb. Is my hide really as smooth as it seems or is that only the dry slickness of my own blood I feel? No, I am not bleeding, and I am smooth—strange, this nothingness of my belly and the pain which slides on and off of my body like a virgin lover unsure of himself.

Which is worse, Old Ones, the pain of the fires which raged through my belly as my womb was scraped to oblivion on the sand, or this new pain which fills my pitiful soul as my mind screams as the thought of never having another cub races through my head?

There will be no more cubs. No pleasuring together with a handsome male as he rubs his seed deep into my eager womb, quickening it with life—no more—no more!

May your afterlife be filled with such pain as mine, you Old Ones . . .

They should not have let this happen to me—I should not have let this happen to me—I produced many cubs for the village. I deserved a year—two—three, of trying to get once more with young. You have stolen all my pleasures; now I can not even pretend I may yet have a cub—you have taken away my dreams, you Old Ones. I have now no place to receive seed, nowhere to shelter a growing cub, and no way to feed it once it is born—damned be you, Old Ones, damned be you!

Splayfoot was my first—then Greeneyed—no, he was eaten in his first year by a marauding sleam. I had Cubmaker next, or was it that strange red cub which everyone laughed at? I loved him well, even though at last I had to kill him because of his strangeness. It is not good to be unlike one's own people. He was so slow to learn; he would not play with the other cubs, he would not eat as he should, catching the cold and the warm, nor would he learn the ways of the people—he had to die, that peculiar cub of mine.

Then there was Thruster, or was it that year I had the girl child? I was pleased with the girl; there was much her father could teach her, just as mine taught me. Swisher came after the girl, then, then—

I gave birth to twins.

Aaaah, even after so many years my mind rebels against the thought of so shameful a thing as my—my *twins*.

The village was very still after the Old One who had been with me in the birthing hut had walked slowly, so slowly around the perimeter stones proclaiming disaster, terror, and the enmity of the gods. I was weak from the—the double birthing, and wanted nothing so much as to die there in the stuffy, blood-soaked hut—why did I not die then instead of living only to be sent out here to this wasteland?

The Old Ones came and took them from beside me. They were so small, still wet from my womb; my mind still pulls away from the thought that they were anything more than ordinary cubs. The only problem was that there were *two* of them, not one. They took them, my cubs, and impaled their twitching bodies on the sharpened stakes that lined the entrance to our village. I followed after, dragging my sore body

along the ground, even as I do now, to see what would become of my young.

They were so small, dark with my blood, and the Old Ones
had not broken their womb skins, nor opened their eyes. I lay
beside the stakes, my tail wrapped around the tall poles; my
cubs bled, dripping red streams down the stakes and onto my
sweat-soaked hide. I wept, both from fear and for my shame
in birthing them. I covered my eyes with my foreclaws as I
waited for the Old Ones to lift me up and thrust my body
down onto the sharp-pointed stakes. I shivered in my fear—
waiting . . .

The Old Ones left me alone.

My cubs, my small wet-from-the-womb cubs! I lay so still
beside them and I listened to their cries as they shat blood
and died, writhing on the sharp sticks.

It was so quiet in the village; only the sound of my cubs
crying, then no sound, and finally the searching cry of the
keeku:

Kee? keee, ke-e-e-e?

The Old Ones chased the keeku away; the birds were not
allowed to weep for *my* young. No tears, only the sharp
stakes for my two cubs. They left us alone for many days, my
cubs and I. They would not let the keeku come, they would
not take down my dead cubs. I ate nothing and my teeth grew
loose in my head. My cubs began to stink, and still the keeku
were not allowed to weep over them.

Then, after many days, the Old Ones returned. They came
to take away my cubs from the village entrance; they would
not let the keeku weep for them.

It was my sin in having them—why didn't they kill me as

well? Why did they make me suffer such shame? Why did they wait to kill me now, slowly and with this crawling over sand, no food—no Long Rock?

I gave the people many cubs after that—why would they not let me continue to try to give more? Eight, ten? There must have been more young of mine than that—I did have more cubs . . .

Sometimes the Old One in the birthing hut is not watchful, and birthing is a hungry-making thing—

New cubs taste very good.

I should have eaten my twins when they were new. But the Old One was watchful—I was so tired from the birthing, I did not think of eating then.

I was very big with the cubs; they must have known it might be twins. They suspected me—they were watchful— they knew! They let me eat my cubs outside the burning birthing hut—they *made* me eat my dead cubs.

New cubs are good, sweet and warm—crunch! Dead cubs, many-day-dead cubs are not good; cold they were, soft and slimy they were, a sickness in the belly they were. It is a hard thing to eat one's own shame.

Keeku?

I thought I heard one at suns-up. The stiff-winged rattle of its flight is quite distinct early in the day before other noises can drown it out. They fly with the Dawn, their Lord, as he rises out of the firepits beyond the far hills. The keeku are servants of Dawn, glorying in his victory over Night, which each evening pushes him deep, deep into the far hills. He sits in the firepits, He warms his flesh in the firepits; He rises strong, bright, to battle. The keeku cry victory! The keeku welcome him:

Kee—oo, kee—oo, kee-o-o-o-o!

There are no sounds out here but the wind blowing dust over my hide, the scuff, scuff, scuff of my crawling body, and my sucking at a fang to pull out a bit of useless sand.

But I do hear a keeku!

Kee? keee, ke-e-e-e? The black-winged bird is searching for me. Kee? keee, ke-e-e-e?

A Keeku?

I *know* the keeku, I remember them well; they travel in packs looking for the dead or dying. A dead body attracts them—I wonder how they know it is dead? The keeku fly very high, searching—the keeku fly in packs—the keeku come for the dead. Why only one keeku?

I first saw them when they came for my father. The keeku wept a long time for him. They gathered around his body so closely that he was covered by their outstretched wings, and the dust of their coming fell on them until he was black as they were. The keeku wept, they walked slow, so slowly around my father, circling his rotting body. They stroked him with their wings, wiping his body free of the dust. Oh, how they cried for him! Wailing their deathsong:

Oooo-uh, oooo-uh, O-O-O-O-O-a-a-a-h!

The keeku tears made his carcass shine as if he had been sporting himself in the river awhile instead of wasting his time with dying.

The keeku wept for him, a long time they wept:

Oooo-uh, oooo-uh, O-O-O-O-O-a-a-a-h!

I did not know a bird could have so much water in its eyes, but then there were so many keeku for him—

Hundreds of them came to walk around his darkening body, and wail for him. After a time one keeku came close to his head, leaping onto his snout; then daintily, on the edge of its claws, it tip-toed up his long face to stand balanced on his massive eyeridges. Then, with the delicacy of a healer, the keeku lifted back my father's eyelid, popped out the death-clouded eye with his sharp beak, and devoured it. The other keeku cried loudly, and began to feed.

Kee? keee, ke-e-e-e?

I hear only *one* keeku. He cries kee? keee, ke-e-e-e? A searching song—kee? keee, ke-e-e-e?

Am I so skimpy a carcass that they think I'll not feed more than one bird? Perhaps this place is so barren it has but one keeku.

Kee? keee, ke-e-e-e?

Soon I will die, and the keeku will weep for me; he will walk beside me and cry:

Oooo-uh, oooo-uh, O-O-O-O-O-a-a-a-h!

How will I taste to a keeku? Ooo-uh, I am bitter, will it care? Oooo-uh, how does it know when I am dead? Can it smell death from so high in the air? O-O-O-O-O-a-a-a-h!

I am worthy of only one keeku because I was too stupid to find the Long Rock. I did not believe the Old Ones, I did not find the Long Rock—thank the gods, they at least allow me *one* keeku.

How will it feel to be eaten by a hungry keeku?

How—how does a *keeku* taste?

It flies over me quite low. I can feel its wings brush the air over my spine, the sand swirls on my hide at the motion of its wings, and I smell the carrion warmth of its breath. I wonder how big it is? Are they made mostly of feathers, or is there much thick flesh hidden beneath those dust-colored pinions? My teeth would tighten, were they to crunch deeply into its warm, food-covered bones—

How can I catch a keeku?

I might roll onto my back and grab it in my claws as it flies over me. No, I cannot lift my belly off of the sand. I could rise up on my hind legs—no.

My tail.

Slashing at it does no good. I can't see what I am trying to strike, and I can't turn around to watch my tail.

The keeku is gone. I frightened it away.

The keeku is back, or another one has come; I'm not sure which is the truth—it does not matter, there is a keeku on the sand in front of me—a warm keeku, a dead keeku, with blood flowing from my claw marks on its neck . . .

Dust dream—no keeku.

I am dying at last. I have covered no more than three lengths of my body since dawn, and the late-day sun is beating on my dry hide. The land is getting greener here; there is a small twig with several leaves on it caught in my claw. I haven't the strength to pull it out—anyway, it looks so bright, that bit of green waving in the wind of my breath. It is alive, and I am dying. The sand is harder, rocks push up through the loose soil, making crawling much more difficult, even if I could crawl.

I wish I could eat this green stuff around me, but plants are not for eating—I am—was—a meat eater. I did swallow a leaf or two at dawn; it did nothing good or ill for me—my teeth are still too loose. They will never taste warm flesh again—never.

I lie here in the sand as it slowly covers me. The wind blows and sand falls on my hide like rain. The leaves in my claw are sprinkled with sand; I blow on them, and it goes away. I could not crawl any further, my body will not move; my claws sink into the sand, they pull, but my body will not move. I am sorry, Old Ones, I cannot crawl any more. I will not find the Long Rock—if there is a Long Rock . . .

I lie in the sand and watch the little green things grow; I listen to the thoughts spinning in my head. Odd, I had not noticed so many thoughts there before; only food and my womb concerned me—such thoughts were so big they crowded out all the others. The Old Ones do not have wombs, nor do they eat as much as the rest of the people. Perhaps I had to get my snout out of my womb and my jaws away from meat before I could think so much—is this how I become an Old One? If so, I will have very little use for it; there is no one out here for whom I can be an Old One . . .

I came here because I was afraid to do anything else; I did not believe the Old Ones—I did not even believe much in the tales of the far caves where the people who would not become Old Ones went. No one told me anything that would help me; I was shoved out into the desert and told to crawl—I crawled.

I can not lift my belly off the sand, Old Ones; I have no strength left for such a task. I can't turn around either; see how well I obey you, Old Ones!

I am dead—I think. I died back at the edge of the desert where it touches the wall of my village. The Old Ones must have killed me there, and this is my afterlife. I am dead.

We were told by the Old Ones that we would have an afterlife most suited to our past conduct in the village. I deserved this afterlife. I had the twins, I cursed the Old Ones and did not always obey them—I took a lover who was my aunt's cub, I—I dreamed of my father's womb hands touching my womb; aaah, too many sins to ever hope for a sweet afterlife. I deserve this sand.

The Long Rock is the afterlife I should have had, but I was too evil for it—there was too much wrong with me, far too much . . .

The keeku is back! I can not be dead yet, the keeku does not sing my deathsong—I am still alive, I hear a keeku:

Kee? keee, ke-e-e-e?

It does not fly over me any more, but walks on the sand beside me, just out of my reach.

Kee? keee, Ke-e-e-e?

If I were dead the keeku would come close to me and weep. It would come very close and climb my face. It would touch my teeth with its sharp claws as it climbed my face; its claws are sharp, but so are mine—I must catch the keeku.

I would be strong with the keeku's flesh in my body; I could crawl if I had the keeku's meat—I could find the Long Rock.

Kee? keee, ke-e-e-e?

The keeku does not sing of death, but he must, for until he thinks I am dead he will not come near me. I must seem to be dead for the keeku.

How does "dead" look to a keeku?

My claws are drifted with sand and there is grit in my snout. I must not sneeze. My eyes are half closed, and I lie as still as I can—I am dead, keeku, I *am* dead!

Is the keeku still there?

It is walking around me as a keeku would about a dead body, but it does not weep. I can see it from the slits of my eyes. It preens its feathers and walks slowly, so very slowly around me. Come closer, keeku, come closer and sing of my death.

The keeku is still too far away, I can not grab at it until it is much closer; if I snatch at it now I will miss it, and the keeku will know I am not dead. Come closer, keeku, and water my dusty hide with your tears—I am waiting for you, keeku—my teeth are waiting, too.

Kee? keee, ke-e-e-e?

He measures my bones with his eyes and walks around me, but far, too far away—why is there only one keeku? If there were more of them I could reach in all directions and fill my arms with keeku—why did *I* deserve only one keeku?

Kee? keee, Ke-e-e-e?

The keeku nested not far from me through the night; at dawn he flew away to welcome his Lord:

Kee—oo, kee—oo, kee-o-o-o-o!

He came back as the sun climbed above me. He had welcomed the dawn, and I welcomed him back to me by being very dead, lying so still on the sand; but he only called a searching cry and landed on the sand beside my body and began to walk around me like an Old One admiring the biggest sleam carcass on a festival day.

Kee? Keee, Ke-e-e-e?

The keeku will not believe I am dead until I really am; by that time it will not matter very much to me how close the keeku comes—I *am* dead, keeku!

I feel much stronger because I rested, but not strong enough to go on; for strength to crawl I need the warm flesh of a keeku. Why doesn't he believe I am dead?

Aaah, the leaves that tangled themselves in my claws are dead. I thought they would live far longer than I would, but here they are, brown and dry in my claws—all of the life-green is gone. My father was such a green before the fevers caught him, a beautiful green for a leaf—or a father. Poor green leaves; aaah, poor green father too. I miss him; I will miss the brightness of the brave little twig in my claws.

Do the leaves, too, have an afterlife?

These leaves may know all the answers for which I know only questions; odd, to think a leaf might know far more than our oldest Old One—leaf, I envy you.

My tears drip from my eyes, and the keeku knows I still live. He has stopped his walking, and now I fear he will leave me because I take so much time with my dying. Stay with me, keeku, stay with me and wail for a small green twig that is dead—weep with me, for you too do not know if you have an afterlife.

Is that why the keeku weeps? Because he too wonders about what comes after this life? Is it the not knowing that you weep for, keeku, my brother? . . .

My tears fall onto the leaves and they shine as if they had been pulled from the river; my tears make them shine, but they will not make the leaves green again. The tears of the keeku will not bring back the dead either . . .

The keeku stands and watches me, his head is tilted to one side, and his bright shining eyes move back and forth as he looks first at me, then at the leaves—they *are* dead, keeku! Come and see . . .

Oooo-uh, oooo-uh, O-O-O-O-O-a-a-a-h!

I weep for the leaves, I cry like a keeku, I cry the keeku deathsong, and I watch the keeku. He watches the leaves and he watches me:

Oooo-uh, oooo-uh, O-O-O-O-O-a-a-a-h!

The keeku walks slowly closer, he listens to me weep, and he walks around my arms, staring at the leaves—he does not weep.

Oooo-uh, oooo-uh, O-O-O-O-O-a-a-a-h!

My voice cracks with pain; it is hard to cry, but the leaves are dead. I will soon be dead, and the keeku does not believe me—damned be you, keeku, damned be you! I weep and no one answers. Aaah, leaf, mourn with me:

Oooo-uh, oooo-uh, O-O-O-O-O-a-a-a-h!

Kee? Oooo-uh? Oooo-uh, oooo-uh, O-O-O-O-O-a-a-a-h!

The keeku weeps with me!

He comes closer, he weeps, his tears water the sand as he weeps with me—aaah, keeku, weep with me!

Come closer, water the leaves with your tears, make them shine, keeku, make them gleam like the river, my keeku. Do not mind my claw, I only wish to touch your feathers; do not mind my open jaws, I only wish to wail louder—come, keeku, come closer to me—CRUNCH!

The keeku lies between my claws; he is only a heap of tat-tered feathers, but there is thick meat on his bones; I felt it as my jaws closed over his struggling body. I felt his warm blood trickle down my throat; I felt my teeth tighten deep, deeply in his warm, warm flesh. Aaaah, dear keeku, dear, dear keeku!

My joy in the keeku is not that of joy in the kill. We wept together, the keeku and I; we wept together for death and because we did not know what there would be for us after our deaths. We wept, the keeku and I; we will go on together to the Long Rock, the keeku and I.

My tears water the feathers of the keeku and he shines like the river. I weep for what I do not understand; I weep for the keeku:

Oooo-uh, oooo-uh, O-O-O-O-O-a-a-a-h!

1973

MIRIAM ALLEN DEFORD

A Way Out

MARPELM HAD to go where he was sent and to stay there until his term of office ended. But he didn't have to like it. He would never get used to this appalling place and the creatures inhabiting it.

When he presented his credentials to the President General of the United Planets, she (it was one of their females) actually grabbed a sensitive tentacle and shook it! No sacrifice, no present of a slave, no ritual whatever. If anyone had tried that sort of thing at home in Kyria he would, of course, have killed him or her instantly. As it was, he managed as he left to start a small fire, which he understood spread quite a bit. After all, he had his honor.

Old Gomforb, who was his predecessor here, should have warned him. But naturally he wouldn't; their families had had a hereditary feud for ages. How he was going to stick it out for five sun-cycles was beyond him. He really couldn't see the sense of sending a delegate to their United Planets at all. Kyria was not "united" with them and never would be. But he supposed it was a matter of dignity; they couldn't allow themselves to be ignored.

One of this planet's chroniclers—he called himself a reporter—did something he described as "interviewing" Marpelm for tridimens. He asked a lot of impertinent questions, and it was amazing that the new delegate managed to "keep his cool," as they put it. The chronicler seemed to find the normal, civilized customs of Kyria amusing.

Here, their world was divided into small sections called nations, and their wars were between these nations or combinations of nations. The "reporter" couldn't understand the system of total, permanent war, in which Kyrians were always engaged except for Truce Year every five sun-cycles. And he couldn't see the clean beauty of that system, where the conquered automatically became slaves of the conquerors. In that way the free always had a large stockpile of workers to produce everything needed by the victors of the past five years' battles, while the victors could devote themselves solely to cultivating their military art and sharpening their intellects in general.

"But these are your own people who become slaves of your state, aren't they?" he wanted to know. "People just like you except that they lost a battle."

"Certainly," Marpelm told him. "They are often our own close relatives. I have two uncles who are slaves, and one of my former sex-mates."

"And they stay that way for the rest of their lives?"

"Well, yes; there's no way to reverse a victory. But their children are free, and may in turn enslave ours. Besides, no male or female is any citizen's personal slave. I believe that in the history of your planet many of your 'nations' did have slaves who were the private property of their owners. We should consider that atrocious."

The reporter just looked confused. Marpelm felt like reminding him that on *this* planet they'd hunted nearly all their wild animals practically out of existence; that seemed to him much worse than the Kyrian fair and honorable system of Perpetual Warfare. He kept a tight rein on himself, but he couldn't help his conditioned recollection of the Sacred Writings, which every Kyrian breathed in from earliest childhood. Tears welled up in his eye at the memory of himself, with all the others of his hatching season, imbibing the Holy Words, which guided all Kyrians forever—righteous, unchangeable, unbreakable. He turned his head away to hide from this alien his nostalgic weakness. He couldn't stand much more of this. He summoned all his self-control.

"Sorry," he said, "but I have a committee meeting coming up." He stalked out of the room in which the reporter had trapped him, as the interviewer reluctantly packed up his equipment.

But there are limits to restraint. The bland, smug arrogance of this meddler had to be avenged somehow, or Marpelm's honor would be tarnished. At the door he paused long enough to smear the knob the reporter would have to touch with a glob of *cacu*—to him a delicious stimulant every Kyrian kept about him for chewing, but which to his amusement acted as a blistering irritant on the skins of these weaklings. A small revenge, but better than none at all.

He did not, of course, have to attend any committee meeting. He never did; he evaded all attempts to appoint him. They could make him come here, and stay here, but he wouldn't participate in the UP nonsense. Gomforb had done the same. They had no choice in the matter; both had been given strict orders to stay off committees. No Kyrian could like having an alien chairman put over him.

But five sun-cycles of it! "Oh, holy forebears, help me to endure it!" he muttered as he escaped from the hated building.

There was no surcease to be found in the utterly unsuitable lodging provided for him. Even getting decent rest and edible food was a problem.

But the worst trial of all was not the lack of a comfortable moist nest or the scramble for digestible provender, but the enforced celibacy. No female of his own kind nearer than a thousand light-years away—and the mere thought of the disgusting sex practices of this place made him feel like vomiting.

Oh, he had tried! He learned early that one could not go up to any female and simply ask, "Are you satisfactorily sex-mated?" She would probably slap his face—or worse, call the police. Then he had learned there were professional sex-mates here, known as call girls. He was lavishly provided with their means of commercial exchange, so he inquired as to the method of securing such a partner. He video'd one. She seemed no more repulsive than any other of their females (though for some incomprehensible reason seemingly reluctant to date him), so he summoned her and she came to his apartment.

He ignored the multicolored paint bedizening her face and the necessity to have her strip before she became available. But incredibly, the creature was sexless: she had no attachment plate!

His own plate throbbing, Marpelm thrust the sum she had demanded into her ugly hand and bade her dress and depart. He was furious at himself for having made such a concession to one of these lower beings, but under the circumstances he dared not simply kill her to insure her silence. He could not even smear *cacu* on her undergarments. "One-eyed octopus—freak!" she sneered vindictively as she left.

He made no further attempt to end his enforced chastity.

As for decent rest and edible provender—!

He dragged the mattress off its ridiculous high frame and dumped it on the floor. Every night he doused it with water, though even so it was only a crude approximation of a cozy nest. He saw an advertisement for a thing called a water bed, and went eagerly to the supplier. "Will it leak?" he asked hopefully. "Positively not," the salesman answered. He walked out disappointed, leaving for some reason a puzzled expression on the man's face.

Then the tenants below him complained of water dripping through their ceiling. Doubtless Marpelm would have been evicted except for his high diplomatic status. As it was, the superintendent sprayed the whole floor with a liquid plastic that dried to seal the floor—and was hard on his sensitive feet.

As for food, the place abounded in it—nourishing products they called grass and leaves. But the imbeciles kept them as a sort of decoration instead of eating them, and when he pulled up a clump of succulent grass to appease his hunger, some groundskeeper or other official was sure to interfere. He was too proud to become surreptitious; he was obliged to resort to the markets they called florists' shops, and then the leaves (there was never any delicious, delicate grass) were stale and bitter by the time he ate them.

It was too much. He had been here now for less than half a sun-cycle. Somehow he must find a way out. Perhaps old Gomforb could go the course, but he was too young, and he knew he couldn't. And to think that this had been given him as an honor, a reward for services rendered to the state! His eye filled again.

So since there is always a way to find how to do what absolutely must be done, a possible means of escape finally came to him.

It might mean reproach at home. He might never again receive any civic honors, or titles or decorations. His nest-siblings and his own nestlings would show contempt for him—or, worse, make him the butt of their humor. So be it: anything was better than this.

He must commit some deed that this planet considered a crime—preferably a crime involving moral turpitude—and be expelled and deported. There was no chance that he could see of his being called home honorably before his term was up.

From his reading of historical microbooks he had learned that there was no lack of choice—practically every sensible action, from a Kyrian viewpoint, was considered immoral or illegal here. There were physical obstacles, naturally—crimes he could not commit because he had not the bodily equipment for them. But that still left plenty to choose from.

He could easily kill any of the creatures, of course. That, for some strange reason, was thought to be a crime here, though it was the most normal response to any opposition or affront on Kyria. But they were so soft and squishy, not pleasingly chitinous like respectable people, and having to get his tentacles slimy with their insides made him feel queasy.

They valued a lot of useless property, including (believe it or not) shiny stones they dug out of the earth. Steal some of these from the nearest possessor? But what would he do with them? He had no place to keep such trash. And if he threw it away, how would they find and catch and punish him?

Rape, their third great "crime," was of course physically

impossible—even if the mere idea hadn't nauseated him. All other so-called crimes were either in the same category or too repugnant to attempt. He certainly had no expertise in or occasion for forgery or counterfeiting or embezzlement.

Then he began trying to think of crimes in his own world. What were they? Well, cowardice, treason, weak concession to an enemy, undue concern for others at the expense of one's own nest's well-being. With the exception of treason, these were, if not exactly virtues here, at least not subject to legal punishment; and how could an alien commit treason against a foreign world?

Then it came to him—the ideal crime: kidnapping.

That seemed to be a major felony here, but unheard of on Kyria: what would be the point of abducting anybody there? The abducted would be given up by his own nest-siblings at once, nobody would dream of paying ransom, he or she would be either enslaved—and there were plenty of slaves from Perpetual Warfare—or killed, in which case the abductor would have the corpse to dispose of.

So—whom to kidnap?

And there again, the ideal victim—the President General of the United Planets.

And how wonderfully it worked into Marpelm's scheme that the current President General was a female—and on this planet females were clearly differentiated from males and received some very peculiar special considerations—and also what they called a black (though actually, to Marpelm's sight, a light beige in color)—and there was a strange sensibility here about what they called race. Their double eyes were of a different hue, and so was the skin-excrescence they called hair, but these they considered of no importance; only the color of the skin itself mattered. From it they derived a special half-guilty sensibility.

And the ransom?

He played with that for a while, bringing forth several ideas. What he wanted, of course, was to be relieved of his office and sent home, but he could hardly offer that in the form of a ransom demand. Moreover, naturally, he would never collect any tangible ransom; all he wanted was to be caught (though not before the kidnapping had been successfully undertaken), the rescue of the abducted person (since these maudlin sentimentalists would scarcely let her stay under threat of imminent death), and no punishment except deportation.

That was one of the two thorniest problems to solve. Suppose they locked him up in one of their prisons before or instead of deporting him? He would certainly die quickly in that case—and that was distinctly not part of his brilliant plan.

The other problem, naturally, was just how to accomplish the kidnapping.

For one thing, he must change his tactics as a UP delegate, and begin not only serving actively (though with extreme caution; after all they had told him to avoid such things) on all committees to which he might be appointed and where there might be an opportunity to approach the President General, but also he must begin attending the excruciating social functions, the dinners and parties and so on, at which she was present, which he had scrupulously avoided so far by the valid excuse that he could not eat their food or drink their stimulants.

Marpelm spent a sleepless night working out the details

of his strategy. He was impatient to begin and to get it over with.

It was a difficult problem because these beings had so many strange laws and customs, beyond (or beneath) the understanding of a sensible civilized person like a Kyrian. For example, official representatives of other planets or even parts of their own planet possessed a thing called "diplomatic immunity," which meant that if they broke the local law they were subject only to the discipline of their own home territory. But did this extend to the serious local crimes they called felonies? He would have to find out.

Despite her exalted position, the President General *was* both black and a female, giving her a claim on her planetmates, who felt shame at the memory of past discrimination and persecution. An evocation of those memories would therefore be an excellent means of insuring efforts to ransom her. (Her name, he must remember, was Sharon Chester VI; they set great store by their individual names.)

But still another thing he had to solve: how could one approach the President General informally? ("Ugh!" he exclaimed, remembering his squeezed tentacle.) Was she always surrounded by security guards? Even so, Marpelm felt he could manage it, but the technique would have to be different.

He discovered soon that it would be impossible to isolate her during the conduct of UP business. So it would have to be a social occasion. He made his plans.

She was an official, but she was also a not very old female of this planet. Could he disguise his repugnance for their distasteful sexual habits enough to make her think he was enamored of her? He could try. Then if he could achieve a state of sentimental attachment, it might be possible to lure her into meeting him alone. From then on it would be only a matter of providing a safe hiding place and making his bid to the UP authorities.

What would appeal more to her—points of likeness or the fascination of the complete alien? Would their physical differences intrigue or disturb her? Color wouldn't matter, of course, but how about tentacles? Or chitin? He studied the subject as if he were solving a mathematical problem.

Social invitations had always been plentiful—after all, he was the delegate from a great planet, and therefore a target of social interest—and now he accepted all at which she was likely to be present. And whenever she was, he stifled his boredom and managed, if only for a minute, to have some kind of communication with her.

He was succeeding. Each time, he felt he was greeted with a little more warmth, a little closer approach to a personal relation. The President General was obviously fascinated by him. The intellectual effort of solving his problem even made his discontent and impatience easier to bear. Then an opportunity arrived that he felt must be the one to be seized.

She herself issued invitations to a party for all the delegates. As her own home, though within commuting distance to UP headquarters, was not large enough, the party was to be held in a local hotel. For this occasion, Marpelm felt sure, there would be a minimum of security guards, if any at all.

He was right. After everybody except himself (he could go to the affairs, but he couldn't assimilate their food and particularly their stimulants), including the hostess, had had three or four rounds of the proffered drinks, people broke up into little groups, intent on socializing plus politics, and the most frequently changing group was that around Sharon Chester VI. Casually Marpelm, after exchanging greetings and small talk with sundry of his colleagues, drifted into one of these groups. When it scattered, he remained.

She was most amiable, and made it rather clear that she considered this guest the highlight of the occasion. Marpelm exerted all the charm that had cursed him by suggesting him for this unwanted assignment to UP. After another—birdtail, he believed they called them—he took advantage of a moment when they were alone together to suggest a bit of fresh air, if it could be found near by and unnoticed. Chatting lightly, he steered her toward a selected door.

He was as usual wearing a long dark cloak, since his chitinous exterior seemed to repel most of these soft creatures. Sharon Chester VI was small and slight. With his far greater strength, there was no question that he could wrap the cloak about her and overpower her if that became necessary.

He had—what did their criminals call it?—"cased the joint" before. The banquet hall in which the party was being held opened by a rear door onto the long flat roof of the hotel's annex, which also served as a port for helicabs and private copters. His own little buzzwagon (learning to steer which had been one of his first tasks as a delegate) was parked there. Looking quickly around to make sure they were alone, he hurried her to it.

The President General did not resist, she giggled. He reached his copter, picked her up and thrust her into it, jumped into the pilot's seat, and was off. A hundred miles straight ahead was the cabin he had rented (in the name of

his alien secretary) in the Hunting Reserve of a Mountain
Public Wilderness.

"Oh, this is exciting!" his victim cried. "I do get so bored!
But we must get back before I'm missed; after all, I'm the
hostess."

Marpelm was aghast. He had been prepared to combat
cold indignation or hot fury, but not flirtatiousness. Instead
of being frightened, this outré creature was flattered! Great
Stars Above, did she think they were eloping? He lost his
aplomb.

"Bu—but Your Excellency," he began stiffly.

"Oh, do call me Sharon!"

He ignored that. "What I mean—I mean I'm *kidnapping*
you."

"Kidnapping!" She laughed aloud. "How quaint! Nobody
has carried out a real abduction since the Chaotic Age. I remember reading about such things in historical microbooks
when I was in school. And what ransom are you asking?" she
inquired coyly.

A cold chill ran through him. In a stifled voice he said, "But
isn't kidnapping a felony any more?"

"Do you *want* it to be?"

Marpelm panicked.

Struggling to regain control, he blurted, "I want to have
you alone with me."

And that outrageous female cried, "Oh, darling, I never
dreamed—"

What could he do? There was no way out but going ahead
with it.

These aliens stretched their mouths to express amiability.
He could not do that, but he could achieve a caressing tone

of voice. His insides churning, he managed to say placatingly, "Why do you think I am doing this? I can't endure resisting your attraction any longer."

If she had the delusion that she had conquered the heart of a proud Kyrian, he must change his tactics. It worked— beyond his wish.

"Oh, Marpelm," she sighed. "Never mind about the party— let them think what they want. Where are you taking me?"

Where but to the cabin?

For the rest of his life he preferred to forget the awful day he spent there with her, still more the awful night.

No attachment plate, and she looked at his, glowing red, with complete lack of understanding. He disdained to explain. Clumsily he did what he could—though once, at least, he had to excuse himself, rush outside, and be sick. But the alien actually seemed to be enjoying it. She took his poor, sensitive tentacles and used them for purposes he could not fathom. By the time she told him that they would *have* to be getting back to civilization, she had reduced Marpelm to a quivering hulk. Fortunately, she interpreted the quivers as being induced by passion.

Marpelm flew her back to the city in silence; conversation only would have added to his misery. As she alit from his buzzwagon in front of her home, she turned back to him, closed one of her double eyes for a second, and said, "That was fun, Marpelm. We really must do it again soon."

Even the lowliest drudge-slave on Kyria couldn't have felt more miserable than he did as he returned to his own apartment. Not only had his plan failed to work, it had backfired; now the President General was enamored of him. His eye filled from self-pity. He was doomed. He knew that down to the tips of his tentacles. Doomed to spend five abstinent sun-cycles on this lunatic world, a thousand light-years away from all that was normal and good. Had his enemies wished to destroy him completely, they could have found no better method than to send him to this horrid place as an "honor."

His directional ray-communicator was ringing as he entered his apartment. He answered it hastily.

Of all people, it was his predecessor and hereditary enemy, Gomforb.

"Where have you been?" Gomforb asked belligerently. "I've tried to get hold of you since day before yesterday, and the ray couldn't find you."

"I'm sorry," Marpelm said smoothly. "I was in the country, trying to snatch a moment's rest from the strain of my post here."

Gomforb laughed meanly.

"Strain, eh?" he said. "Well, you needn't bear it any longer. Did you think we're so stupid we have no secret agents at the United Planets? I've got incontrovertible evidence that you've been serving actively on committees—just what you were warned not to do, as you very well know . . . I've sent a ship for you, Marpelm—actually to find out where you were, but now I know that, the autopilot has instructions to take you on board and return you to Kyria. In fact, your successor is a passenger, so all you need do is surrender your credentials and any documents you have. Don't leave where you are till he arrives . . . Believe me, you'll never get an honor like this again."

He rang off without even saying goodbye.

But what did Marpelm care for that? He needn't ever see the President General again, or have to spend another disgusting interlude with her. He packed immediately, his heart singing. Oh, come quickly, he mentally implored his successor-savior—quickly, before she could catch him!

Away forever from these nauseating aliens and their ghastly planet! Home to his own dear nest! Home to his nest-siblings! Home to his sex-mates and their hatchings!

Home!

1973

VONDA N. MCINTYRE

Of Mist, and Grass, and Sand

THE LITTLE boy was frightened. Gently, Snake touched his hot forehead. Behind her, three adults stood close together, watching, suspicious, afraid to show their concern with more than narrow lines around their eyes. They feared Snake as much as they feared their only child's death. In the dimness of the tent, the flickering lamplights gave no reassurance.

The child watched with eyes so dark the pupils were not visible, so dull that Snake herself feared for his life. She stroked his hair. It was long and very pale, a striking color against his dark skin, dry and irregular for several inches near the scalp. Had Snake been with these people months ago, she would have known the child was growing ill.

"Bring my case, please," Snake said.

The child's parents started at her soft voice. Perhaps they had expected the screech of a bright jay, or the hissing of a shining serpent. This was the first time Snake had spoken in their presence. She had only watched, when the three of them had come to observe her from a distance and whisper about her occupation and her youth; she had only listened, and then nodded, when finally they came to ask her help. Perhaps they had thought she was mute.

The fair-haired younger man lifted her leather case from the felt floor. He held the satchel away from his body, lean-ing to hand it to her, breathing shallowly with nostrils flared against the faint smell of musk in the dry desert air. Snake had almost accustomed herself to the kind of uneasiness he showed; she had already seen it often.

When Snake reached out, the young man jerked back and dropped the case. Snake lunged and barely caught it, set it gently down, and glanced at him with reproach. His husband and his wife came forward and touched him to ease his fear. "He was bitten once," the dark and handsome woman said. "He almost died." Her tone was not of apology, but of justification.

"I'm sorry," the younger man said. "It's—" He gestured toward her; he was trembling, and trying visibly to control the reactions of his fear. Snake glanced down, to her shoulder, where she had been unconsciously aware of the slight weight and movement. A tiny serpent, thin as the finger of a baby, slid himself around behind her neck to show his narrow head below her short black curls. He probed the air with his trident tongue, in a leisurely manner, out, up and down, in, to savor the taste of the smells.

"It's only Grass," Snake said. "He cannot harm you."

If he were bigger, he might frighten; his color was pale green, but the scales around his mouth were red, as if he had just feasted as a mammal eats, by tearing. He was, in fact, much neater.

The child whimpered. He cut off the sound of pain; perhaps he had been told that Snake, too, would be offended by crying. She only felt sorry that his people refused themselves such a simple way of easing fear. She turned from the adults, regretting their terror of her, but unwilling to spend the time it would take to convince them their reactions were unjustified. "It's all right," she said to the little boy. "Grass is smooth, and dry, and soft, and if I left him to guard you, even death could not reach your bedside." Grass poured himself into her narrow, dirty hand, and she extended him toward the child. "Gently." He reached out and touched the sleek scales with one fingertip. Snake could sense the effort of even such a simple motion, yet the boy almost smiled.

"What are you called?"

He looked quickly toward his parents, and finally they nodded. "Stavin," he whispered. He had no strength or breath for speaking.

"I am Snake, Stavin, and in a little while, in the morning, I must hurt you. You may feel a quick pain, and your body will ache for several days, but you will be better afterwards."

He stared at her solemnly. Snake saw that though he understood and feared what she might do, he was less afraid than if she had lied to him. The pain must have increased greatly as his illness became more apparent, but it seemed that others had only reassured him, and hoped the disease would disappear or kill him quickly.

Snake put Grass on the boy's pillow and pulled her case nearer. The lock opened at her touch. The adults still could only fear her; they had had neither time nor reason to discover any trust. The wife was old enough that they might never have another child, and Snake could tell by their eyes, their covert touching, their concern, that they loved this one very much. They must, to come to Snake in this country.

It was night, and cooling. Sluggish, Sand slid out of the case, moving his head, moving his tongue, smelling, tasting, detecting the warmth of bodies.

"Is that—?" The older husband's voice was low, and wise, but terrified, and Sand sensed the fear. He drew back into striking position, and sounded his rattle softly. Snake spoke to him and extended her arm. The pit viper relaxed and flowed around and around her slender wrist to form black and tan bracelets. "No," she said. "Your child is too ill for Sand to help. I know it is hard, but please try to be calm. This is a fearful thing for you, but it is all I can do."

She had to annoy Mist to make her come out. Snake rapped on the bag, and finally poked her twice. Snake felt the vibration of sliding scales, and suddenly the albino cobra flung herself into the tent. She moved quickly, yet there seemed to be no end to her. She reared back and up. Her breath rushed out in a hiss. Her head rose well over a meter above the floor. She flared her wide hood. Behind her, the adults gasped, as if physically assaulted by the gaze of the tan spectacle design on the back of Mist's hood. Snake ignored the people and spoke to the great cobra in a singsong voice. "Ah, thou. Furious creature. Lie down; 'tis time for thee to earn thy piglet. Speak to this child, and touch him. He is called Stavin." Slowly, Mist relaxed her hood, and allowed Snake to touch her. Snake grasped her firmly behind the head, and held her so she looked at Stavin. The cobra's silver eyes picked up the yellow of the lamplight. "Stavin," Snake said, "Mist will only meet you now. I promise that this time she will touch you gently."

Still, Stavin shivered when Mist touched his thin chest. Snake did not release the serpent's head, but allowed her body to slide against the boy's. The cobra was four times longer than Stavin was tall. She curved herself in stark white loops across Stavin's swollen abdomen, extending herself, forcing her head toward the boy's face, straining against Snake's hands. Mist met Stavin's frightened stare with the gaze of lidless eyes. Snake allowed her a little closer.

Mist flicked out her tongue to taste the child.

The younger husband made a small, cut-off, frightened sound. Stavin flinched at it, and Mist drew back, opening her mouth, exposing her fangs, audibly thrusting her breath through her throat. Snake sat back on her heels, letting out her own breath. Sometimes, in other places, the kinfolk could stay while she worked. "You must leave," she said gently. "It's dangerous to frighten Mist."

"I won't—"

"I'm sorry. You must wait outside."

Perhaps the younger husband, perhaps even the wife, would have made the indefensible objections and asked the answerable questions, but the older man turned them and took their hands and led them away.

"I need a small animal," Snake said as the man lifted the tent-flap. "It must have fur, and it must be alive."

"One will be found," he said, and the three parents went into the glowing night. Snake could hear their footsteps in the sand outside.

Snake supported Mist in her lap, and soothed her. The cobra wrapped herself around Snake's narrow waist, taking in her warmth. Hunger made her even more nervous than usual, and she was hungry, as was Snake. Coming across the black sand desert, they had found sufficient water, but Snake's traps were unsuccessful. The season was summer, the weather was hot, and many of the furry tidbits Sand and Mist preferred were estivating. When the serpents missed their regular meal, Snake began a fast as well.

She saw with regret that Stavin was more frightened now. "I am sorry to send your parents away," she said. "They can come back soon."

His eyes glistened, but he held back the tears. "They said to do what you told me."

"I would have you cry, if you are able," Snake said. "It isn't such a terrible thing." But Stavin seemed not to understand, and Snake did not press him; she knew that his people taught themselves to resist a difficult land by refusing to cry, refusing to mourn, refusing to laugh. They denied themselves grief, and allowed themselves little joy, but they survived.

Mist had calmed to sullenness. Snake unwrapped her from her waist and placed her on the pallet next to Stavin. As the cobra moved, Snake guided her head, feeling the tension of the striking muscles. "She will touch you with her tongue," she told Stavin. "It might tickle, but it will not hurt. She smells with it, as you do with your nose."

"With her tongue?"

Snake nodded, smiling, and Mist flicked out her tongue to caress Stavin's cheek. Stavin did not flinch; he watched, his child's delight in knowledge briefly overcoming pain. He lay perfectly still as Mist's long tongue brushed his cheeks, his eyes, his mouth. "She tastes the sickness," Snake said. Mist stopped fighting the restraint of her grasp, and drew back her head. Snake sat on her heels and released the cobra, who spiraled up her arm and laid herself across her shoulders.

"Go to sleep, Stavin," Snake said. "Try to trust me, and try not to fear the morning."

Stavin gazed at her for a few seconds, searching for truth in Snake's pale eyes. "Will Grass watch?"

The question startled her, or, rather, the acceptance behind the question. She brushed his hair from his forehead and smiled a smile that was tears just beneath the surface. "Of course." She picked Grass up. "Thou wilt watch this child, and guard him." The snake lay quiet in her hand, and his eyes glittered black. She laid him gently on Stavin's pillow.

"Now sleep."

Stavin closed his eyes, and the life seemed to flow out of him. The alteration was so great that Snake reached out to touch him, then saw that he was breathing, slowly, shallowly. She tucked a blanket around him and stood up. The abrupt change in position dizzied her; she staggered and caught herself. Across her shoulders, Mist tensed.

Snake's eyes stung and her vision was over-sharp, fever-clear. The sound she imagined she heard swooped in closer. She steadied herself against hunger and exhaustion, bent slowly, and picked up the leather case. Mist touched her cheek with the tip of her tongue.

She pushed aside the tent-flap and felt relief that it was still night. She could stand the heat, but the brightness of the sun curled through her, burning. The moon must be full; though the clouds obscured everything, they diffused the light so the sky appeared gray from horizon to horizon. Beyond the tents, groups of formless shadows projected from the ground. Here, near the edge of the desert, enough water existed so clumps and patches of bush grew, providing shelter and sustenance for all manner of creatures. The black sand, which sparkled and blinded in the sunlight, at night was like a layer of soft soot. Snake stepped out of the tent, and the illusion of softness disappeared; her boots slid crunching into the sharp hard grains.

Stavin's family waited, sitting close together between the dark tents that clustered in a patch of sand from which the bushes had been ripped and burned. They looked at her silently, hoping with their eyes, showing no expression in their faces. A woman somewhat younger than Stavin's mother sat with them. She was dressed, as they were, in a long loose robe, but she wore the only adornment Snake had seen among these people: a leader's circle, hanging around her neck on a leather thong. She and the older husband were marked close kin by their similarities: sharp-cut planes of face, high cheekbones, his hair white and hers graying early from deep black, their eyes the dark brown best suited for survival in the sun. On the ground by their feet a small black animal jerked sporadically against a net, and infrequently gave a shrill weak cry.

"Stavin is asleep," Snake said. "Do not disturb him, but go to him if he wakes."

The wife and young husband rose and went inside, but the older man stopped before her. "Can you help him?"

"I hope we may. The tumor is advanced, but it seems solid." Her own voice sounded removed, slightly hollow, as if she were lying. "Mist will be ready in the morning." She still felt the need to give him reassurance, but she could think of none.

"My sister wished to speak with you," he said, and left them alone, without introduction, without elevating himself by saying that the tall woman was the leader of this group. Snake glanced back, but the tent flap fell shut. She was feeling her exhaustion more deeply, and across her shoulders Mist was, for the first time, a weight she thought heavy.

"Are you all right?"

Snake turned. The woman moved toward her with a natural elegance made slightly awkward by advanced pregnancy.

Snake had to look up to meet her gaze. She had small fine lines at the corners of her eyes, as if she laughed, sometimes, in secret. She smiled, but with concern. "You seem very tired. Shall I have someone make you a bed?"

"Not now," Snake said, "not yet. I won't sleep until afterwards."

The leader searched her face, and Snake felt a kinship with her, in their shared responsibility.

"I understand, I think. Is there anything we can give you? Do you need aid with your preparations?"

Snake found herself having to deal with the questions as if they were complex problems. She turned them in her tired mind, examined them, dissected them, and finally grasped their meanings. "My pony needs food and water—"

"It is taken care of."

"And I need someone to help me with Mist. Someone strong. But it's more important that he is not afraid."

The leader nodded. "I would help you," she said, and smiled again, a little. "But I am a bit clumsy of late. I will find someone."

"Thank you."

Somber again, the older woman inclined her head and moved slowly toward a small group of tents. Snake watched her go, admiring her grace. She felt small and young and grubby in comparison.

Sand began to unwrap himself from her wrist. Feeling the anticipatory slide of scales on her skin, she caught him before he could drop to the ground. Sand lifted the upper half of his body from her hands. He flicked out his tongue, peering toward the little animal, feeling its body heat, smelling its fear.

"I know thou art hungry," Snake said, "but that creature is not for thee." She put Sand in the case, lifted Mist from her shoulder, and let her coil herself in her dark compartment.

The small animal shrieked and struggled again when Snake's diffuse shadow passed over it. She bent and picked it up. The rapid series of terrified cries slowed and diminished and finally stopped as she stroked it. Finally it lay still, breathing hard, exhausted, staring up at her with yellow eyes. It had long hind legs and wide pointed ears, and its nose twitched at the serpent smell. Its soft black fur was marked off in skewed squares by the cords of the net.

"I am sorry to take your life," Snake told it. "But there will be no more fear, and I will not hurt you." She closed her hand gently around it, and, stroking it, grasped its spine at the base of its skull. She pulled, once, quickly. It seemed to struggle, briefly, but it was already dead. It convulsed; its legs drew up against its body, and its toes curled and quivered. It seemed to stare up at her, even now. She freed its body from the net.

Snake chose a small vial from her belt pouch, pried open the animal's clenched jaws, and let a single drop of the vial's cloudy preparation fall into its mouth. Quickly she opened the satchel again, and called Mist out. She came slowly, slipping over the edge, hood closed, sliding in the sharp-grained sand. Her milky scales caught the thin light. She smelled the animal, flowed to it, touched it with her tongue. For a moment Snake was afraid she would refuse dead meat, but the body was still warm, still twitching reflexively, and she was very hungry. "A tidbit for thee," Snake said. "To whet thy appetite." Mist nosed it, reared back, and struck, sinking her short fixed fangs into the tiny body, biting again, pumping out her store of poison. She released it, took a better grip, and began to work her jaws around it; it would hardly distend her throat. When Mist lay quiet, digesting the small meal, Snake sat beside her and held her, waiting.

She heard footsteps in the coarse sand.

"I'm sent to help you."

He was a young man, despite a scatter of white in his dark hair. He was taller than Snake, and not unattractive. His eyes were dark, and the sharp planes of his face were further hard-ened because his hair was pulled straight back and tied. His expression was neutral.

"Are you afraid?"

"I will do as you tell me."

Though his body was obscured by his robe, his long fine hands showed strength.

"Then hold her body, and don't let her surprise you." Mist was beginning to twitch from the effects of the drugs Snake had put in the small animal's body. The cobra's eyes stared, unseeing.

"If it bites—"

"Hold, quickly!"

The young man reached, but he had hesitated too long. Mist writhed, lashing out, striking him in the face with her tail. He staggered back, at least as surprised as hurt. Snake kept a close grip behind Mist's jaws, and struggled to catch the rest of her as well. Mist was no constrictor, but she was smooth and strong and fast. Thrashing, she forced out her breath in a long hiss. She would have bitten anything she could reach. As Snake fought with her, she managed to squeeze the poison glands and force out the last drops of venom. They hung from Mist's fangs for a moment, catching light as jewels would; the force of the serpent's convulsions flung them away into the darkness. Snake struggled with the cobra, speaking softly, aided for once by the sand, on which Mist could get no purchase. Snake felt the young man behind her, grabbing for Mist's body and tail. The seizure stopped abruptly, and Mist lay limp in their hands.

"I am sorry—"

"Hold her," Snake said. "We have the night to go."

During Mist's second convulsion, the young man held her firmly and was of some real help. Afterward, Snake answered his interrupted question. "If she were making poison and she bit you, you would probably die. Even now her bite would make you ill. But unless you do something foolish, if she manages to bite, she will bite me."

"You would benefit my cousin little, if you were dead or dying."

"You misunderstand. Mist cannot kill me." She held out her hand, so he could see the white scars of slashes and punctures. He stared at them, and looked into her eyes for a long moment, then looked away.

The bright spot in the clouds from which the light radiated moved westward in the sky; they held the cobra like a child. Snake found herself half-dozing, but Mist moved her head, dully attempting to evade restraint, and Snake woke herself abruptly. "I must not sleep," she said to the young man. "Talk to me. What are you called?"

As Stavin had, the young man hesitated. He seemed afraid of her, or of something. "My people," he said, "think it unwise to speak our names to strangers."

"If you consider me a witch you should not have asked my

aid. I know no magic, and I claim none. I can't learn all the customs of all the people on this earth, so I keep my own. My custom is to address those I work with by name."

"It's not a superstition," he said. "Not as you might think. We're not afraid of being bewitched."

Snake waited, watching him, trying to decipher his expression in the dim light.

"Our families know our names, and we exchange names with those we would marry."

Snake considered that custom, and thought it would fit badly on her. "No one else? Ever?"

"Well . . . a friend might know one's name."

"Ah," Snake said. "I see. I am still a stranger, and perhaps an enemy."

"A *friend* would know my name," the young man said again. "I would not offend you, but now you misunderstand. An acquaintance is not a friend. We value friendship highly."

"In this land one should be able to tell quickly if a person is worth calling 'friend'."

"We make friends seldom. Friendship is a commitment."

"It sounds like something to be feared."

He considered that possibility. "Perhaps it's the betrayal of friendship we fear. That is a very painful thing."

"Has anyone ever betrayed you?"

He glanced at her sharply, as if she had exceeded the limits of propriety. "No," he said, and his voice was as hard as his face. "No friend. I have no one I call friend."

His reaction startled Snake. "That's very sad," she said, and grew silent, trying to comprehend the deep stresses that could close people off so far, comparing her loneliness of necessity and theirs of choice. "Call me Snake," she said finally, "if you can bring yourself to pronounce it. Speaking my name binds you to nothing."

The young man seemed about to speak; perhaps he thought again that he had offended her, perhaps he felt he should further defend his customs. But Mist began to twist in their hands, and they had to hold her to keep her from injuring herself. The cobra was slender for her length, but powerful, and the convulsions she went through were more severe than any she had ever had before. She thrashed in Snake's grasp, and almost pulled away. She tried to spread her hood, but Snake held her too tightly. She opened her mouth and hissed, but no poison dripped from her fangs.

She wrapped her tail around the young man's waist. He began to pull her and turn, to extricate himself from her coils.

"She's not a constrictor," Snake said. "She won't hurt you. Leave her—"

But it was too late; Mist relaxed suddenly and the young man lost his balance. Mist whipped herself away and lashed figures in the sand. Snake wrestled with her alone while the young man tried to hold her, but she curled herself around Snake and used the grip for leverage. She started to pull herself from Snake's hands. Snake threw them both backward into the sand; Mist rose above her, open-mouthed, furious, hissing. The young man lunged and grabbed her just beneath her hood. Mist struck at him, but Snake, somehow, held her back. Together they deprived Mist of her hold, and regained control of her. Snake struggled up, but Mist suddenly went quite still and lay almost rigid between them. They were both sweating; the young man was pale under his tan, and even Snake was trembling.

"We have a little while to rest," Snake said. She glanced at him and noticed the dark line on his cheek where, earlier, Mist's tail had slashed him. She reached up and touched it. "You'll have a bruise, no more," she said. "It will not scar."

"If it were true that serpents sting with their tails, you would be restraining both the fangs and the stinger, and I'd be of little use."

"Tonight I'd need someone to keep me awake, whether or not he helped me with Mist." Fighting the cobra had produced adrenaline, but now it ebbed, and her exhaustion and hunger were returning, stronger.

"Snake . . ."

"Yes?"

He smiled, quickly, half-embarrassed. "I was trying the pronunciation."

"Good enough."

"How long did it take you to cross the desert?"

"Not very long. Too long. Six days."

"How did you live?"

"There is water. We traveled at night, except yesterday, when I could find no shade."

"You carried all your food?"

She shrugged. "A little." And wished he would not speak of food.

"What's on the other side?"

"More sand, more bush, a little more water. A few groups of people, traders, the station I grew up and took my training in. And farther on, a mountain with a city inside."

"I would like to see a city. Someday."

"The desert can be crossed."

He said nothing, but Snake's memories of leaving home were recent enough that she could imagine his thoughts.

The next set of convulsions came, much sooner than Snake had expected. By their severity, she gauged something of the stage of Stavin's illness, and wished it were morning. If she were to lose him, she would have it done, and grieve, and try to forget. The cobra would have battered herself to death against the sand if Snake and the young man had not been holding her. She suddenly went completely rigid, with her mouth clamped shut and her forked tongue dangling.

She stopped breathing.

"Hold her," Snake said. "Hold her head. Quickly, take her, and if she gets away, run. Take her! She won't strike at you now, she could only slash you by accident."

He hesitated only a moment, then grasped Mist behind the head. Snake ran, slipping in the deep sand, from the edge of the circle of tents to a place where bushes still grew. She broke off dry thorny branches that tore her scarred hands. Peripherally she noticed a mass of horned vipers, so ugly they seemed deformed, nesting beneath the clump of desiccated vegetation; they hissed at her: she ignored them. She found a narrow hollow stem and carried it back. Her hands bled from deep scratches.

Kneeling by Mist's head, she forced open the cobra's mouth and pushed the tube deep into her throat, through the air passage at the base of Mist's tongue. She bent close, took the tube in her mouth, and breathed gently into Mist's lungs.

She noticed: the young man's hands, holding the cobra as she had asked; his breathing, first a sharp gasp of surprise, then ragged; the sand scraping her elbows where she leaned; the cloying smell of the fluid seeping from Mist's fangs; her own dizziness, she thought from exhaustion, which she forced away by necessity and will.

Snake breathed, and breathed again, paused, and repeated, until Mist caught the rhythm and continued it unaided.

Snake sat back on her heels. "I think she'll be all right," she said. "I hope she will." She brushed the back of her hand across her forehead. The touch sparked pain: she jerked her hand down and agony slid along her bones, up her arm, across her shoulder, through her chest, enveloping her heart. Her balance turned on its edge. She fell, tried to catch herself but moved too slowly, fought nausea and vertigo and almost succeeded, until the pull of the earth seemed to slip away in pain and she was lost in darkness with nothing to take a bearing by.

She felt sand where it had scraped her cheek and her palms, but it was soft. "Snake, can I let go?" She thought the question must be for someone else, while at the same time she knew there was no one else to answer it, no one else to reply to her name. She felt hands on her, and they were gentle; she wanted to respond to them, but she was too tired. She needed sleep more, so she pushed them away. But they held her head and put dry leather to her lips and poured water into her throat. She coughed and choked and spat it out.

She pushed herself up on one elbow. As her sight cleared, she realized she was shaking. She felt as she had the first time she was snake-bit, before her immunities had completely developed. The young man knelt over her, his water flask in his hand. Mist, beyond him, crawled toward the darkness. Snake forgot the throbbing pain. "Mist!"

The young man flinched and turned, frightened; the serpent reared up, her head nearly at Snake's standing eye level, her hood spread, swaying, watching, angry, ready to strike. She formed a wavering white line against black. Snake forced herself to rise, feeling as though she were fumbling with the control of some unfamiliar body. She almost fell again, but held herself steady. "Thou must not go to hunt now," she said. "There is work for thee to do." She held out her right hand, to the side, a decoy, to draw Mist if she struck. Her hand was heavy with pain. Snake feared, not being bitten, but the loss of the contents of Mist's poison sacs. "Come here," she said. "Come here, and stay thy anger." She noticed blood flowing down between her fingers, and the fear she felt for Stavin was intensified. "Didst thou bite me, creature?" But the pain was wrong: poison would numb her, and the new serum only sting . . .

"No," the young man whispered, from behind her.

Mist struck. The reflexes of long training took over. Snake's right hand jerked away, her left grabbed Mist as she brought her head back. The cobra writhed a moment, and relaxed. "Devious beast," Snake said. "For shame." She turned, and let Mist crawl up her arm and over her shoulder, where she lay like the outline of an invisible cape and dragged her tail like the edge of a train.

"She did not bite me?"

"No," the young man said. His contained voice was touched with awe. "You should be dying. You should be curled around the agony, and your arm swollen purple. When you came back—" He gestured toward her hand. "It must have been a bush viper."

Snake remembered the coil of reptiles beneath the branches, and touched the blood on her hand. She wiped it away, revealing the double puncture of a snakebite among the scratches of the thorns. The wound was slightly swollen. "It needs cleaning," she said. "I shame myself by falling to it." The pain of it washed in gentle waves up her arm, burning no longer. She stood looking at the young man, looking around her, watching the landscape shift and change as her tired eyes tried to cope with the low light of setting moon and false dawn. "You held Mist well, and bravely," she said to the young man. "Thank you."

He lowered his gaze, almost bowing to her. He rose, and approached her. Snake put her hand gently on Mist's neck so she would not be alarmed.

"I would be honored," the young man said, "if you would call me Arevin."

"I would be pleased to."

Snake knelt down and held the winding white loops as Mist crawled slowly into her compartment. In a little while, when Mist had stabilized, by dawn, they could go to Stavin.

The tip of Mist's white tail slid out of sight. Snake closed the case and would have risen, but she could not stand. She had not yet quite shaken off the effects of the new venom. The flesh around the wound was red and tender, but the hemorrhaging would not spread. She stayed where she was, slumped, staring at her hand, creeping slowly in her mind toward what she needed to do, this time for herself.

"Let me help you. Please."

He touched her shoulder and helped her stand. "I'm sorry," she said. "I'm so in need of rest . . ."

"Let me wash your hand," Arevin said. "And then you can sleep. Tell me when to waken you—"

"No. I can't sleep yet." She pulled together the skeins of her nerves, collected herself, straightened, tossed the damp curls of her short hair off her forehead. "I'm all right now. Have you any water?"

Arevin loosened his outer robe. Beneath it he wore a loin-cloth and a leather belt that carried several leather flasks and pouches. The color of his skin was slightly lighter than the sun-darkened brown of his face. He brought out his water flask, closed his robe around his lean body, and reached for Snake's hand.

"No, Arevin. If the poison gets in any small scratch you might have, it could infect."

She sat down and sluiced lukewarm water over her hand. The water dripped pink to the ground and disappeared, leaving not even a damp spot visible. The wound bled a little more, but now it only ached. The poison was almost inactivated.

"I don't understand," Arevin said, "how it is that you're unhurt. My younger sister was bitten by a bush viper." He could not speak as uncaringly as he might have wished. "We could do nothing to save her—nothing we had would even lessen her pain."

Snake gave him his flask and rubbed salve from a vial in her belt pouch across the closing punctures. "It's a part of our preparation," she said. "We work with many kinds of serpents, so we must be immune to as many as possible." She shrugged. "The process is tedious and somewhat painful." She clenched her fist; the film held, and she was steady. She leaned toward Arevin and touched his abraded cheek again. "Yes . . ." She spread a thin layer of the salve across it. "That will help it heal."

"If you cannot sleep," Arevin said, "can you at least rest?"

"Yes," she said. "For a little while."

Snake sat next to Arevin, leaning against him, and they watched the sun turn the clouds to gold and flame and amber.

The simple physical contact with another human being gave Snake pleasure, though she found it unsatisfying. Another time, another place, she might do something more, but not here, not now.

When the lower edge of the sun's bright smear rose above the horizon, Snake rose and teased Mist out of the case. She came slowly, weakly, and crawled across Snake's shoulders. Snake picked up the satchel, and she and Arevin walked together back to the small group of tents.

Stavin's parents waited, watching for her, just outside the entrance of their tent. They stood in a tight, defensive, silent group. For a moment Snake thought they had decided to send her away. Then, with regret and fear like hot iron in her mouth, she asked if Stavin had died. They shook their heads, and allowed her to enter.

Stavin lay as she had left him, still asleep. The adults followed her with their stares, and she could smell fear. Mist flicked out her tongue, growing nervous from the implied danger.

"I know you would stay," Snake said. "I know you would help, if you could, but there is nothing to be done by any person but me. Please go back outside."

They glanced at each other, and at Arevin, and she thought for a moment that they would refuse. Snake wanted to fall into the silence and sleep. "Come, cousins," Arevin said. "We are in her hands." He opened the tent flap and motioned them out. Snake thanked him with nothing more than a glance, and he might almost have smiled. She turned toward Stavin, and knelt beside him. "Stavin—" She touched his forehead;

it was very hot. She noticed that her hand was less steady than before. The slight touch awakened the child. "It's time," Snake said.

He blinked, coming out of some child's dream, seeing her, slowly recognizing her. He did not look frightened. For that Snake was glad; for some other reason she could not identify she was uneasy.

"Will it hurt?"

"Does it hurt now?"

He hesitated, looked away, looked back. "Yes."

"It might hurt a little more. I hope not. Are you ready?"

"Can Grass stay?"

"Of course," she said.

And realized what was wrong.

"I'll come back in a moment." Her voice changed so much, she had pulled it so tight, that she could not help but frighten him. She left the tent, walking slowly, calmly, restraining herself. Outside, the parents told her by their faces what they feared.

"Where is Grass?" Arevin, his back to her, started at her tone. The younger husband made a small grieving sound, and could look at her no longer.

"We were afraid," the older husband said. "We thought it would bite the child."

"I thought it would. It was I. It crawled over his face, I could see its fangs—" The wife put her hands on the younger husband's shoulders, and he said no more.

"Where is he?" She wanted to scream; she did not.

They brought her a small open box. Snake took it, and looked inside.

Grass lay cut almost in two, his entrails oozing from his

body, half turned over, and as she watched, shaking, he writhed once, and flicked his tongue out once, and in. Snake made some sound, too low in her throat to be a cry. She hoped his motions were only reflex, but she picked him up as gently as she could. She leaned down and touched her lips to the smooth green scales behind his head. She bit him quickly, sharply, at the base of the skull. His blood flowed cool and salty in her mouth. If he were not dead, she had killed him instantly.

She looked at the parents, and at Arevin; they were all pale, but she had no sympathy for their fear, and cared nothing for shared grief. "Such a small creature," she said. "Such a small creature, who could only give pleasure and dreams." She watched them for a moment more, then turned toward the tent again.

"Wait—" She heard the older husband move up close behind her. He touched her shoulder; she shrugged away his hand. "We will give you anything you want," he said, "but leave the child alone."

She spun on him in a fury. "Should I kill Stavin for your stupidity?" He seemed about to try to hold her back. She jammed her shoulder hard into his stomach, and flung herself past the tent flap. Inside, she kicked over the satchel. Abruptly awakened, and angry, Sand crawled out and coiled himself. When the younger husband and the wife tried to enter, Sand hissed and rattled with a violence Snake had never heard him use before. She did not even bother to look behind her. She ducked her head and wiped her tears on her sleeve before Stavin could see them. She knelt beside him.

"What's the matter?" He could not help but hear the voices outside the tent, and the running.

"Nothing, Stavin," Snake said. "Did you know we came across the desert?"

"No," he said, with wonder.

"It was very hot, and none of us had anything to eat. Grass is hunting now. He was very hungry. Will you forgive him and let me begin? I will be here all the time."

He seemed so tired; he was disappointed, but he had no strength for arguing. "All right." His voice rustled like sand slipping through the fingers.

Snake lifted Mist from her shoulders, and pulled the blanket from Stavin's small body. The tumor pressed up beneath his rib cage, distorting his form, squeezing his vital organs, sucking nourishment from him for its own growth. Holding Mist's head, Snake let her flow across him, touching and tasting him. She had to restrain the cobra to keep her from striking; the excitement had agitated her. When Sand used his rattle, she flinched. Snake spoke to her softly, soothing her; trained and bred-in responses began to return, overcoming the natural instincts. Mist paused when her tongue flicked the skin above the tumor, and Snake released her.

The cobra reared, and struck, and bit as cobras bite, sinking her fangs their short length once, releasing, instantly biting again for a better purchase, holding on, chewing at her prey. Stavin cried out, but he did not move against Snake's restraining hands.

Mist expended the contents of her venom sacs into the child, and released him. She reared up, peered around, folded her hood, and slid across the mats in a perfectly straight line toward her dark, close compartment.

"It is all finished, Stavin."

"Will I die now?"

"No," Snake said. "Not now. Not for many years, I hope."
She took a vial of powder from her belt pouch. "Open your
mouth." He complied, and she sprinkled the powder across
his tongue. "That will help the ache." She spread a pad of
cloth across the series of shallow puncture wounds, without
wiping off the blood.

She turned from him.

"Snake? Are you going away?"

"I will not leave without saying good-bye. I promise."

The child lay back, closed his eyes, and let the drug take
him.

Sand coiled quiescently on the dark matting. Snake called
him. He moved toward her, and suffered himself to be replaced in the satchel. Snake closed it, and lifted it, and it still
felt empty. She heard noises outside the tent. Stavin's parents
and the people who had come to help them pulled open the
tent flap and peered inside, thrusting sticks in even before
they looked.

Snake set down her leather case. "It's done."

They entered. Arevin was with them too; only he was
empty-handed. "Snake—" He spoke through grief, pity, confusion, and Snake could not tell what he believed. He looked
back. Stavin's mother was just behind him. He took her by
the shoulder. "He would have died without her. Whatever
has happened now, he would have died."

The woman shook his hand away. "He might have lived. It
might have gone away. We—" She could not speak for hiding
tears.

Snake felt the people moving, surrounding her. Arevin
took one step toward her and stopped, and she could see he
wanted her to defend herself. "Can any of you cry?" she said.

"Can any of you cry for me and my despair, or for them and their guilt, or for small things and their pain?" She felt tears slip down her cheeks.

They did not understand her; they were offended by her crying. They stood back, still afraid of her, but gathering themselves. She no longer needed the pose of calmness she had used to deceive the child. "Ah, you fools." Her voice sounded brittle. "Stavin—"

Light from the entrance struck them. "Let me pass." The people in front of Snake moved aside for their leader. She stopped in front of Snake, ignoring the satchel her foot almost touched. "Will Stavin live?" Her voice was quiet, calm, gentle.

"I cannot be certain," Snake said, "but I feel that he will."

"Leave us." The people understood Snake's words before they did their leader's; they looked around and lowered their weapons, and finally, one by one, they moved out of the tent. Arevin remained. Snake felt the strength that came from danger seeping from her. Her knees collapsed. She bent over the satchel with her face in her hands. The older woman knelt in front of her, before Snake could notice or prevent her. "Thank you," she said. "Thank you. I am so sorry . . ." She put her arms around Snake, and drew her toward her, and Arevin knelt beside them, and he embraced Snake too. Snake began to tremble again, and they held her while she cried.

Later she slept, exhausted, alone in the tent with Stavin, holding his hand. They had given her food, and small animals for Sand and Mist, and supplies for her journey, and sufficient water for her to bathe, though that must have strained their resources. About that, Snake no longer cared.

When she awakened, she felt the tumor, and found that it had begun to dissolve and shrivel, dying, as Mist's changed poison affected it. Snake felt little joy. She smoothed Stavin's pale hair back from his face. "I would not lie to you again, little one," she said, "but I must leave soon. I cannot stay here." She wanted another three days' sleep, to finish fighting off the effects of the bush viper's poison, but she would sleep somewhere else. "Stavin?"

He half woke, slowly. "It doesn't hurt any more," he said.

"I am glad."

"Thank you . . ."

"Good-bye, Stavin. Will you remember later on that you woke up, and that I did stay to say good-bye?"

"Good-bye," he said, drifting off again. "Good-bye, Snake. Good-bye, Grass." He closed his eyes, and Snake picked up the satchel and left the tent. Dusk cast long indistinct shadows; the camp was quiet. She found her tiger-striped pony, tethered with food and water. New, full water-skins lay on the ground next to the saddle. The tiger pony whickered at her when she approached. She scratched his striped ears, saddled him, and strapped the case on his back. Leading him, she started west, the way she had come.

"Snake—"

She took a breath, and turned back to Arevin. He faced the sun, and it turned his skin ruddy and his robe scarlet. His streaked hair flowed loose to his shoulders, gentling his face. "You will not stay?"

"I cannot."

"I had hoped . . ."

"If things were different, I might have stayed."

"They were frightened. Can't you forgive them?"

"I can't face their guilt. What they did was my fault. I said he could not hurt them, but they saw his fangs and they didn't know his bite only gave dreams and eased dying. They couldn't know; I didn't understand them until too late."

"You said it yourself, you can't know all the customs and all the fears."

"I'm crippled," she said. "Without Grass, if I cannot heal a person, I cannot help at all. I must go home. Perhaps my teachers will forgive me my stupidity, but I am afraid to face them. They seldom give the name I bear, but they gave it to me, and they'll be disappointed."

"Let me come with you."

She wanted to; she hesitated, and cursed herself for that weakness. "They may cast me out, and you would be cast out too. Stay here, Arevin."

"It wouldn't matter."

"It would. After a while, we would hate each other. I don't know you, and you don't know me. We need calmness, and quiet, and time to understand each other."

He came toward her, and put his arms around her, and they stood together for a moment. When he raised his head, he was crying. "Please come back," he said. "Whatever happens, please come back."

"I will try," Snake said. "Next spring, when the winds stop, look for me. And the spring after that, if I do not come, forget me. Wherever I am, if I live, I will forget you."

"I will look for you," Arevin said, and he would promise no more.

Snake picked up the pony's lead, and started across the desert.

1973

JAMES TIPTREE, JR.

The Girl Who Was Plugged In

LISTEN, ZOMBIE. Believe me. What I could tell you—you with your silly hands leaking sweat on your growth-stocks portfolio. One-ten lousy hacks of AT&T on twenty-percent margin and you think you're Evel Knievel. AT&T . . . You doubleknit dummy, how I'd love to show you something.

Look, dead daddy, I'd say. See for instance that rotten girl?

In the crowd over there, that one gaping at her gods. One rotten girl in the city of the future. (That's what I said.) Watch.

She's jammed among bodies, craning and peering with her soul yearning out of her eyeballs. Love! Oo-ooh, love them! Her gods are coming out of a store called Body East. Three youngbloods, larking along loverly. Dressed like simple streetpeople but . . . smashing. See their great eyes swivel above their nose-filters, their hands lift shyly, their inhumanly tender lips melt? The crowd moans. Love! This whole boiling megacity, this whole fun future world loves its gods.

You don't believe gods, dad? Wait. Whatever turns you on, there's a god in the future for you, custom-made. Listen to this mob. "I touched his foot! Ow-oow, I TOUCHED Him!"

Even the people in the GTX tower up there love the gods—in their own way and for their own reasons.

The funky girl on the street, she just loves. Grooving on their beautiful lives, their mysterioso problems. No one ever told her about mortals who love a god and end up as a tree

135

or a sighing sound. In a million years it'd never occur to her that her gods might love her back.

She's squashed against the wall now as the godlings come by. They move in a clear space. A holocam bobs above but its shadow never falls on them. The store display screens are magically clear of bodies as the gods glance in and a beggar underfoot is suddenly alone. They give him a token. "Aaaaah!" goes the crowd.

Now one of them flashes some wild new kind of timer and they all trot to catch a shuttle, just like people. The shuttle stops for them—more magic. The crowd sighs, closing back. The gods are gone.

(In a room far from—but not unconnected to—the GTX tower a molecular flipflop closes too, and three account tapes spin.)

Our girl is still stuck by the wall while guards and holocam equipment pull away. The adoration's fading from her face. That's good, because now you can see she's the ugly of the world. A tall monument to pituitary dystrophy. No surgeon would touch her. When she smiles, her jaw—it's half purple—almost bites her left eye out. She's also quite young, but who could care?

The crowd is pushing her along now, treating you to glimpses of her jumbled torso, her mismatched legs. At the corner she strains to send one last fond spasm after the god-lings' shuttle. Then her face reverts to its usual expression of dim pain and she lurches onto the moving walkway, stumbling into people. The walkway junctions with another. She crosses, trips and collides with the casualty rail. Finally she comes out into a little place called a park. The sportshow is working, a basketball game in 3-di is going on right overhead. But all she does is squeeze onto a bench and huddle there while a ghostly free-throw goes by her ear.

After that nothing at all happens except a few furtive hand-mouth gestures which don't even interest her benchmates.

But you're curious about the city? So ordinary after all, in the FUTURE?

Ah, there's plenty to swing with here—and it's not all that *far* in the future, dad. But pass up the sci-fi stuff for now, like for instance the holovision technology that's put TV and radio in museums. Or the worldwide carrier field bouncing down from satellites, controlling communication and trans-port systems all over the globe. That was a spin-off from as-teroid mining, pass it by. We're watching that girl.

I'll give you just one goodie. Maybe you noticed on the sportshow or the streets? No commercials. No ads.

That's right. NO ADS. An eyeballer for you.

Look around. Not a billboard, sign, slogan, jingle, skywrite, blurb, sublimflash, in this whole fun world. Brand names? Only in those ticky little peep-screens on the stores and you could hardly call that advertising. How does that finger you?

Think about it. That girl is still sitting there.

She's parked right under the base of the GTX tower as a matter of fact. Look up and you can see the sparkles from the bubble on top, up there among the domes of godland. Inside that bubble is a boardroom. Neat bronze shield on the door: Global Transmissions Corporation—not that that means anything.

I happen to know there's six people in that room. Five of them technically male, and the sixth isn't easily thought of as a mother. *They are absolutely unremarkable.* Those faces were seen once at their nuptials and will show again in their obituaries and impress nobody either time. If you're looking for the secret Big Blue Meanies of the world, forget it. I know. Zen, do I know! Flesh? Power? Glory? You'd horrify them.

What they do like up there is to have things orderly, especially their communications. You could say they've dedicated their lives to that, to freeing the world from garble. Their nightmares are about hemorrhages of information: channels screwed up, plans misimplemented, garble creeping in. Their vast wealth only worries them, it keeps opening new vistas of disorder. Luxury? They wear what their tailors put on them, eat what their cooks serve them. See that old boy there—his name is Isham—he's sipping water and frowning as he listens to a databall. The water was prescribed by his medistaff. It tastes awful. The databall also contains a disquieting message about his son, Paul.

But it's time to go back down, far below to our girl. Look! She's toppled over sprawling on the ground.

A tepid commotion ensues among the bystanders. The consensus is she's dead, which she disproves by bubbling a little. And presently she's taken away by one of the superb ambulances of the future, which are a real improvement over ours when one happens to be around.

At the local bellevue the usual things are done by the usual team of clowns aided by a saintly mop-pusher. Our girl revives enough to answer the questionnaire without which you can't die, even in the future. Finally she's cast up, a pumped-out hulk on a cot in the long, dim ward.

Again nothing happens for a while except that her eyes leak a little from the understandable disappointment of finding herself still alive.

But somewhere one GTX computer has been tickling another, and toward midnight something does happen. First comes an attendant who pulls screens around her. Then a man in a business doublet comes daintily down the ward. He motions the attendant to strip off the sheet and go.

The groggy girl-brute heaves up, big hands clutching at body-parts you'd pay not to see.

"Burke? P. Burke, is that your name?"

"Y-yes." Croak. "Are you . . . policeman?"

"No. They'll be along shortly, I expect. Public suicide's a felony."

". . . I'm sorry."

He has a 'corder in his hand. "No family, right?"

"No."

"You're seventeen. One year city college. What did you study?"

"La—languages."

"H'm. Say something."

Unintelligible rasp.

He studies her. Seen close, he's not so elegant. Errand-boy type.

"Why did you try to kill yourself?"

She stares at him with dead-rat dignity, hauling up the gray sheet. Give him a point, he doesn't ask twice.

"Tell me, did you see Breath this afternoon?"

Dead as she nearly is, that ghastly love-look wells up. Breath is the three young gods, a loser's cult. Give the man another point, he interprets her expression.

"How would you like to meet them?"

The girl's eyes bug out unequally.

"I have a job for someone like you. It's hard work. If you did well you'd be meeting Breath and stars like that all the time."

Is he insane? She's deciding she really did die.

"But it means you never see anybody you know again. Never, *ever*. You will be legally dead. Even the police won't know. Do you want to try?"

It all has to be repeated while her great jaw slowly sets. *Show me the fire I walk through.* Finally P. Burke's prints are in his 'corder, the man holding up the rancid girl-body without a sign of distaste. It makes you wonder what else he does.

And then—THE MAGIC. Sudden silent trot of litterbearers tucking P. Burke into something quite different from a bellevue stretcher, the oiled slide into the daddy of all luxury ambulances—real flowers in that holder!—and the long jarless rush to nowhere. Nowhere is warm and gleaming and kind with nurses. (Where did you hear that money can't buy genuine kindness?) And clean clouds folding P. Burke into bewildered sleep.

. . . Sleep which merges into feedings and washings and more sleeps, into drowsy moments of afternoon where midnight should be, and gentle businesslike voices and friendly (but very few) faces, and endless painless hyposprays and peculiar numbnesses . . . and later comes the steadying rhythm of days and nights, and a quickening which P. Burke doesn't identify as health, but only knows that the fungus place in her armpit is gone . . . and then she's up and following those few new faces with growing trust, first tottering, then walking strongly, all better now—clumping down the short hall to the tests, tests, tests, and the other things.

And here is our girl, looking—

If possible, worse than before. (You thought this was Cinderella transistorized?)

The disimprovement in her looks comes from the electrode jacks peeping out of her sparse hair, and there are other meldings of flesh and metal. On the other hand, that collar and spinal plate are really an asset; you won't miss seeing that neck.

P. Burke is ready for training in her new job.

The training takes place in her suite, and is exactly what you'd call a charm course. How to walk, sit, eat, speak, blow her nose, how to stumble, to urinate, to hiccup—DELICIOUSLY. How to make each nose-blow or shrug delightfully, subtly different from any ever spooled before. As the man said, it's hard work.

But P. Burke proves apt. Somewhere in that horrible body is a gazelle, a houri who would have been buried forever without this crazy chance. See the ugly duckling go!

Only it isn't precisely P. Burke who's stepping, laughing, shaking out her shining hair. How could it be? P. Burke is doing it all right, but she's doing it through something. The something is to all appearances a live girl. (You were warned, this is the FUTURE.)

When they first open the big cryocase and show her her new body she says just one word. Staring, gulping, "How?"

Simple, really. Watch P. Burke in her sack and scuffs stump down the hall beside Joe, the man who supervises the technical part of her training. Joe doesn't mind P. Burke's looks, he hasn't noticed them. To Joe system matrices are beautiful.

They go into a dim room containing a huge cabinet like a one-man sauna and a console for Joe. The room has a glass wall that's all dark now. And just for your information, the whole shebang is five hundred feet underground near what used to be Carbondale, Pa.

Joe opens the sauna-cabinet like a big clamshell standing on end with a lot of funny business inside. Our girl shucks her shift and walks into it bare, totally unembarrassed. *Eager.* She settles in face-forward, butting jacks into sockets. Joe closes it carefully onto her humpback. Clunk. She can't see in there or hear or move. She hates this minute. But how she loves what comes next!

Joe's at his console and the lights on the other side of the glass wall come up. A room is on the other side, all fluff and kicky bits, a girly bedroom. In the bed is a small mound of silk with a rope of yellow hair hanging out.

The sheet stirs and gets whammed back flat.

Sitting up in the bed is the darlingest girl child you've EVER seen. She quivers—porno for angels. She sticks both her little arms straight up, flips her hair, looks around full of sleepy pazazz. Then she can't resist rubbing her hands down over her minibreasts and belly. Because, you see, it's the godawful P. Burke who is sitting there hugging her perfect girl-body, looking at you out of delighted eyes.

Then the kitten hops out of bed and crashes flat on the floor.

From the sauna in the dim room comes a strangled noise. P. Burke, trying to rub her wired-up elbow, is suddenly smothered in *two* bodies, electrodes jerking in her flesh. Joe juggles inputs, crooning into his mike. The flurry passes; it's all right.

In the lighted room the elf gets up, casts a cute glare at the glass wall and goes into a transparent cubicle. A bathroom, what else? She's a live girl, and live girls have to go to the bathroom after a night's sleep even if their brains are in a sauna cabinet in the next room. And P. Burke isn't in that cabinet, she's in the bathroom. Perfectly simple, if you have the glue for that closed training circuit that's letting her run her neural system by remote control.

Now let's get one thing clear. P. Burke does not *feel* her brain is in the next room, she feels it's in that sweet little body. When you wash your hands, do you feel the water is running on your brain? Of course not. You feel the water on your hand, although the "feeling" is actually a potential-pattern flickering over the electrochemical jelly between your ears. And it's delivered there via the long circuits from your hands. Just so, P. Burke's brain in the cabinet feels the water on her hands in the bathroom. The fact that the signals have jumped across space on the way in makes no difference at all. If you want the jargon, it's known as eccentric projection or sensory reference and you've done it all your life. Clear?

Time to leave the honey-pot to her toilet training—she's made a booboo with the toothbrush, because P. Burke can't get used to what she sees in the mirror—

But wait, you say. Where did that girl-body come from?

P. Burke asks that too, dragging out the words.

"They grow 'em," Joe tells her. He couldn't care less about the flesh department. "PDs. Placental decanters. Modified embryos, see? Fit the control implants in later. Without a Remote Operator it's just a vegetable. Look at the feet—no callus at all." (He knows because they told him.)

"Oh . . . oh, she's incredible . . ."

"Yeah, a neat job. Want to try walking-talking mode today? You're coming on fast."

And she is. Joe's reports and the reports from the nurse and the doctor and style man go to a bushy man upstairs who is some kind of medical cybertech but mostly a project administrator. His reports in turn go—to the GTX boardroom? Certainly not, did you think this is a *big* thing? His reports just go up. The point is, they're green, very green. P. Burke promises well.

So the bushy man—Doctor Tesla—has procedures to initiate. The little kitten's dossier in the Central Data Bank, for instance. Purely routine. And the phase-in schedule which will put her on the scene. This is simple: a small exposure in an off-network holoshow.

Next he has to line out the event which will fund and target her. That takes budget meetings, clearances, coordinations. The Burke project begins to recruit and grow. And there's the messy business of the name, which always gives Doctor Tesla an acute pain in the bush.

The name comes out weird, when it's suddenly discovered that Burke's "P." stands for *Philadelphia*. Philadelphia? The astrologer grooves on it. Joe thinks it would help identification. The semantics girl references *brotherly love*, *Liberty-Bell*, *main-line*, *low teratogenesis*, blah-blah. Nicknames—Philly? Pala? Pooty? Delphi? Is it good, bad? Finally *Delphi* is gingerly declared goodo. ("Burke" is replaced by something nobody remembers.)

Coming along now. We're at the official checkout down in the underground suite, which is as far as the training circuits reach. The bushy Doctor Tesla is there, braced by two budgetary types and a quiet fatherly man whom he handles like hot plasma.

Joe swings the door wide and she steps shyly in.

Their little Delphi, fifteen and flawless.

Tesla introduces her around. She's child-solemn, a beautiful baby to whom something so wonderful has happened you can feel the tingles. She doesn't smile, she . . . brims. That brimming joy is all that shows of P. Burke, the forgotten hulk in the sauna next door. But P. Burke doesn't know she's alive—it's Delphi who lives, every warm inch of her.

One of the budget types lets go a libidinous snuffle and freezes. The fatherly man, whose name is Mr. Cantle, clears his throat.

"Well, young lady, are you ready to go to work?"

"Yes sir," gravely from the elf.

"We'll see. Has anybody told you what you're going to do for us?"

"No, sir." Joe and Tesla exhale quietly.

"Good." He eyes her, probing for the blind brain in the room next door.

"Do you know what *advertising* is?"

He's talking dirty, hitting to shock. Delphi's eyes widen and her little chin goes up. Joe is in ecstasy at the complex expressions P. Burke is getting through. Mr. Cantle waits.

"It's, well, it's when they used to tell people to buy things." She swallows. "It's not allowed."

"That's right." Mr. Cantle leans back, grave. "Advertising as it used to be is against the law. *A display other than the legitimate use of the product, intended to promote its sale.* In former times every manufacturer was free to tout his wares any way, place or time he could afford. All the media and most of the landscape was taken up with extravagant competing displays. The thing became uneconomic. The public rebelled. Since the so-called Huckster Act, sellers have been restrained to, I quote, 'displays in or on the product itself, visible during its legitimate use or in on-premise sales.'" Mr.

Cantle leans forward. "Now tell me, Delphi, why do people buy one product rather than another?"

"Well . . ." Enchanting puzzlement from Delphi. "They, um, they see them and like them, or they hear about them from somebody?" (Touch of P. Burke there; she didn't say, from a friend.)

"Partly. Why did *you* buy your particular body-lift?"

"I never had a body-lift, sir."

Mr. Cantle frowns; what gutters did they drag for these Remotes?

"Well, what brand of water do you drink?"

"Just what was in the faucet, sir," says Delphi humbly. "I—I did try to boil it—"

"Good God." He scowls; Tesla stiffens. "Well, what did you boil it in? A cooker?"

The shining yellow head nods.

"What *brand* of cooker did you buy?"

"I didn't buy it, sir," says frightened P. Burke through Delphi's lips. "But—I know the best kind! Ananga has a Burnbabi, I saw the name when she—"

"*Exactly!*" Cantle's fatherly beam comes back strong; the Burnbabi account is a strong one, too. "You saw Ananga using one so you thought it must be good, eh? And it is good or a great human being like Ananga wouldn't be using it. Absolutely right. And now, Delphi, you know what you're going to be doing for us. You're going to show some products. Doesn't sound very hard, does it?"

"Oh, no, sir . . ." Baffled child's stare; Joe gloats.

"And you must never, *never* tell anyone what you're doing." Cantle's eyes bore for the brain behind this seductive child.

"You're wondering why we ask you to do this, naturally.

There's a very serious reason. All those products people use, foods and healthaids and cookers and cleaners and clothes and car—they're all made by *people*. Somebody put in years of hard work designing and making them. A man comes up with a fine new idea for a better product. He has to get a factory and machinery, and hire workmen. Now. What happens if people have no way of hearing about his product? Word-of-mouth is far too slow and unreliable. Nobody might ever stumble onto his new product or find out how good it was, right? And then he and all the people who worked for him—they'd go bankrupt, right? So, Delphi, there has to be *some way* that large numbers of people can get a look at a good new product, right? How? By letting people see you using it. You're *giving that man a chance.*"

Delphi's little head is nodding in happy relief.

"Yes, sir, I do see now—but sir, it seems so sensible, why don't they let you—"

Cantle smiles sadly.

"It's an overreaction, my dear. History goes by swings. People overreact and pass harsh unrealistic laws which attempt to stamp out an essential social process. When this happens, the people who understand have to carry on as best they can until the pendulum swings back." He sighs. "The Huckster Laws are bad, inhuman laws, Delphi, despite their good intent. If they were strictly observed they would wreak havoc. Our economy, our society would be cruelly destroyed. We'd be back in caves!" (His inner fire is showing; if the Huckster Laws were strictly enforced he'd be back punching a databank.)

"It's our duty, Delphi. Our solemn social duty. Nor are we breaking the law. You will be using the product. But people wouldn't understand, if they knew. They would become upset, just as you did. So you must be very, very careful not to mention any of this to anybody."

(And somebody will be very, very carefully monitoring Delphi's speech circuits.)

"Now we're all straight, aren't we? Little Delphi here"— He is speaking to the invisible creature next door—"Little Delphi is going to live a wonderful, exciting life. She's going to be a girl people watch. And she's going to be using fine products people will be glad to know about and helping the good people who make them. Yours will be a genuine social contribution." He keys up his pitch; the creature in there must be older.

Delphi digests this with ravishing gravity.

"But sir, how do I—?"

"Don't worry about a thing. You'll have people behind you whose job it is to select the most worthy products for you to use. Your job is just to do as they say. They'll show you what outfits to wear to parties, what suncars and viewers to buy and so on. That's all you have to do."

Parties—clothes—suncars! Delphi's pink mouth opens. In P. Burke's starved seventeen-year-old head the ethics of product sponsorship float far away.

"Now tell me in your own words what your job is, Delphi."

"Yes sir. I—I'm to go to parties and buy things and use them as they tell me, to help the people who work in factories."

"And what did I say was so important?"

"Oh—I shouldn't let anybody know, about the things."

"Right." Mr. Cantle has another paragraph he uses when the subject shows, well, immaturity. But he can sense only eagerness here. Good. He doesn't really enjoy the other speech.

"It's a lucky girl who can have all the fun she wants while doing good for others, isn't it?" He beams around. There's a prompt shuffling of chairs. Clearly this one is go.

Joe leads her out, grinning. The poor fool thinks they're admiring her coordination.

It's out into the world for Delphi now, and at this point the up-channels get used. On the administrative side account schedules are opened, subprojects activated. On the technical side the reserved bandwidth is cleared. (That carrier field, remember?) A new name is waiting for Delphi, a name she'll never hear. It's a long string of binaries which have been quietly cycling in a GTX tank ever since a certain Beautiful Person didn't wake up.

The name winks out of cycle, dances from pulses into modulations of modulations, whizzes through phasing, and shoots into a giga-band beam racing up to a synchronous satellite poised over Guatemala. From there the beam pours twenty thousand miles back to earth again, forming an all-pervasive field of structured energics supplying tuned demand-points all over the CanAm quadrant.

With that field, if you have the right credit rating you can sit at a GTX console and operate a tuned ore-extractor in Brazil. Or—if you have some simple credentials like being able to walk on water—you could shoot a spool into the network holocam shows running day and night in every home and dorm. Or you could create a continentwide traffic jam. Is it any wonder GTX guards those inputs like a sacred trust?

Delphi's "name" appears as a tiny analyzable nonredundancy in the flux, and she'd be very proud if she knew about it. It would strike P. Burke as magic; P. Burke never even understood robotcars. But Delphi is in no sense a robot. Call her a waldo if you must. The fact is she's just a girl, a real live girl with her brain in an unusual place. A simple real-time on-line system with plenty of bit-rate—even as you and you.

The point of all this hardware, which isn't very much hardware in this society, is so Delphi can walk out of that underground suite, a mobile demand-point draining an omnipresent fieldform. And she does—eighty-nine pounds of tender girl flesh and blood with a few metallic components, stepping out into the sunlight to be taken to her new life. A girl with everything going for her including a meditech escort. Walking lovely, stopping to widen her eyes at the big antennae system overhead.

The mere fact that something called P. Burke is left behind down underground has no bearing at all. P. Burke is totally un-self-aware and happy as a clam in its shell. (Her bed has been moved into the waldo cabinet room now.) And P. Burke isn't in the cabinet; P. Burke is climbing out of an airvan in a fabulous Colorado beef preserve and her name is Delphi. Delphi is looking at live Charlais steers and live cottonwoods and aspens gold against the blue smog and stepping over live grass to be welcomed by the reserve super's wife.

The super's wife is looking forward to a visit from Delphi and her friends and by a happy coincidence there's a holocam outfit here doing a piece for the nature nuts.

You could write the script yourself now while Delphi learns a few rules about structural interferences and how to handle the tiny time lag which results from the new forty-thousand-mile parenthesis in her nervous system. That's right—the people with the leased holocam rig naturally find the gold aspen shadows look a lot better on Delphi's flank than they do on a steer. And Delphi's face improves the mountains too, when you can see them. But the nature freaks aren't quite as joyful as you'd expect.

"See you in Barcelona, kitten," the head man says sourly as they pack up.

"Barcelona?" echoes Delphi with that charming little subliminal lag. She sees where his hand is and steps back.

"Cool, it's not her fault," another man says wearily. He knocks back his grizzled hair. "Maybe they'll leave in some of the gut."

Delphi watches them go off to load the spools on the GTX transport for processing. Her hand roves over the breast the man had touched. Back under Carbondale, P. Burke has discovered something new about her Delphi-body.

About the difference between Delphi and her own grim carcass.

She's always known Delphi has almost no sense of taste or smell. They explained about that: Only so much bandwidth. You don't have to taste a suncar, do you? And the slight overall dimness of Delphi's sense of touch—she's familiar with that, too. Fabrics that would prickle P. Burke's own hide feel like a cool plastic film to Delphi.

But the blank spots. It took her a while to notice them. Delphi doesn't have much privacy; investments of her size don't. So she's slow about discovering there's certain definite places where her beastly P. Burke body *feels* things that Delphi's dainty flesh does not. H'mm! Channel space again, she thinks—and forgets it in the pure bliss of being Delphi.

You ask how a girl could forget a thing like that? Look. P. Burke is about as far as you can get from the concept *girl*. She's a female, yes—but for her, sex is a four-letter word spelled P-A-I-N. She isn't quite a virgin; you don't want the details. She'd been about twelve and the freak-lovers were bombed blind. When they came down they threw her out with a small hole in her anatomy and a mortal one elsewhere. She dragged off to buy her first and last shot and she can still hear the clerk's incredulous guffaws.

Do you see why Delphi grins, stretching her delicious little numb body in the sun she faintly feels? Beams, saying, "Please, I'm ready now."

Ready for what? For Barcelona like the sour man said, where his nature-thing is now making it strong in the amateur section of the Festival. A winner! Like he also said, a lot of strip-mines and dead fish have been scrubbed but who cares with Delphi's darling face so visible?

So it's time for Delphi's face and her other delectabilities to show on Barcelona's Playa Neuva. Which means switching her channel to the EurAf synchsat.

They ship her at night so the nanosecond transfer isn't even noticed by that insignificant part of Delphi that lives five hundred feet under Carbondale, so excited the nurse has to make sure she eats. The circuit switches while Delphi "sleeps," that is while P. Burke is out of the waldo cabinet. The next time she plugs in to open Delphi's eyes it's no different—do you notice which relay boards your calls go through?

And now for the event that turns the sugarcube from Colorado into the PRINCESS.

Literally true, he's a prince, or rather an Infante of an old Spanish line that got shined up in the Neomonarchy. He's also eighty-one, with a passion for birds—the kind you see in zoos. Now it suddenly turns out that he isn't poor at all. Quite the reverse; his old sister laughs in their tax lawyer's face and starts restoring the family hacienda while the Infante totters out to court Delphi. And little Delphi begins to live the life of the gods.

What do gods do? Well, everything beautiful. But (remember Mr. Cantle?) the main point is Things. Ever see a god empty-handed? You can't be a god without at least a magic girdle or an eight-legged horse. But in the old days some stone tablets or winged sandals or a chariot drawn by virgins would do a god for life. No more! Gods make it on novelty now. By Delphi's time the hunt for new god-gear is turning the earth and seas inside-out and sending frantic fingers to the stars. And what gods have, mortals desire.

So Delphi starts on a Euromarket shopping spree squired by her old Infante, thereby doing her bit to stave off social collapse.

Social what? Didn't you get it, when Mr. Cantle talked about a world where advertising is banned and fifteen billion consumers are glued to their holocam shows? One capricious self-powered god can wreck you.

Take the nose-filter massacre. Years, the industry worked years to achieve an almost invisible enzymatic filter. So a couple of pop-gods show up wearing nose-filters like *big purple bats.* By the end of the week the world market is screaming for purple bats. Then it switched to bird-heads and skulls. By the time the industry retooled the crazies had dropped bird-heads and gone to injection globes. Blood!

Multiply that by every consumer industry and you can see why it's economic to have a few controllable gods. Especially with the beautiful hunk of space R&D the Peace Department laid out for, and which the taxpayers are only too glad to have taken off their hands by an outfit like GTX which everybody knows is almost a public trust.

And so you—or rather, GTX—find a creature like P. Burke and give her Delphi. And Delphi helps keep things *orderly*, she does what you tell her to. Why? . . . That's right, Mr. Cantle never finished his speech.

But here come the tests of Delphi's button-nose twinkling in the torrent of news and entertainment. And she's noticed. The feedback shows a flock of viewers turning up the amps when this country baby gets tangled in her new colloidal body-jewels. She registers at a couple of major scenes, too, and when the Infante gives her a suncar, little Delphi trying out suncars is a tiger. There's a solid response in high-credit country. Mr. Cantle is humming his happy tune as he cancels a Benelux subnet option to guest her on a nude cook-show called Wok Venus.

And now for the superposh old-world wedding! The hacienda has Moorish baths and six-foot silver candelabras and real black horses and the Spanish Vatican blesses them. The final event is a grand gaucho ball with the old prince and his little Infanta on a bowered balcony. She's a spectacular doll of silver lace, wildly launching toy doves at her new friends whirling by below.

The Infante beams, twitches his old nose to the scent of her sweet excitement. His doctor has been very helpful. Surely now, after he has been so patient with the suncars and all the nonsense—

The child looks up at him, saying something incomprehensible about "breath." He makes out that she's complaining about the three singers she had begged for.

"They've changed!" she marvels. "Haven't they changed? They're so dreary. I'm so happy now!"

And Delphi falls fainting against a gothic vargueno.

Her American duenna rushes up, calls help. Delphi's eyes are open, but Delphi isn't there. The duenna pokes among Delphi's hair, slaps her. The old prince grimaces. He has no idea what she is beyond an excellent solution to his tax problems, but he had been a falconer in his youth. There comes to his mind the small pinioned birds which were flung up to stimulate the hawks. He pockets the veined claw to which he had promised certain indulgences and departs to design his new aviary.

And Delphi also departs with her retinue to the Infante's newly discovered yacht. The trouble isn't serious. It's only that five thousand miles away and five hundred feet down P. Burke has been doing it too well.

They've always known she has terrific aptitude. Joe says he never saw a Remote take over so fast. No disorientations, no rejections. The psychomed talks about self-alienation. She's going into Delphi like a salmon to the sea.

She isn't eating or sleeping, they can't keep her out of the body-cabinet to get her blood moving, there are necroses under her grisly sit-down. Crisis!

So Delphi gets a long "sleep" on the yacht and P. Burke gets it pounded through her perforated head that she's endangering Delphi. (Nurse Fleming thinks of that, thus alienating the psychomed.)

They rig a pool down there (Nurse Fleming again) and chase P. Burke back and forth. And she loves it. So naturally when they let her plug in again Delphi loves it too. Every noon beside the yacht's hydrofoils darling Delphi clips along in the blue sea they've warned her not to drink. And every night around the shoulder of the world an ill-shaped thing in a dark barrow beats its way across a sterile pool.

So presently the yacht stands up on its foils and carries Delphi to the program Mr. Cantle has waiting. It's long-range; she's scheduled for at least two decades' product life. Phase One calls for her to connect with a flock of young ultra-riches who are romping loose between Brioni and Djakarta where a competitor named PEV could pick them off.

A routine luxgear op see; no politics, no policy angles, and the main budget items are the title and the yacht, which was idle anyway. The storyline is that Delphi goes to accept some rare birds for her prince—who cares? The *point* is that the Haiti area is no longer radioactive and look!—the gods are there. And so are several new Carib West Happy Isles which can afford GTX rates, in fact two of them are GTX subsids.

But you don't want to get the idea that all these newsworthy people are wired-up robbies, for pity's sake. You don't need many if they're placed right. Delphi asks Joe about that when he comes down to Baranquilla to check her over. (P. Burke's own mouth hasn't said much for a while.)

"Are there many like me?"

"Nobody's like you, buttons. Look, are you still getting that Van Allen warble?"

"I mean, like Davy. Is he a Remote?"

(Davy is the lad who is helping her collect the birds. A sincere redhead who needs a little more exposure.)

"Davy? He's one of Matt's boys. Some psychojob. They haven't any channel."

"What about the real ones? Djuma van O, or Ali, or Jim Ten?"

"Djuma was born with a pile of GTX basic where her brain should be, she's nothing but a pain. Jimsy does what his astrologer tells him. Look, peanut, where do you get the idea you aren't real? You're the realest. Aren't you having joy?"

"Oh, Joe!" Flinging her little arms around him and his analyzer grids. "Oh, *me gusto mucho, muchissimo!*"

"Hey, hey." He pets her yellow head, folding the analyzer.

Four thousand miles north and five hundred feet down a forgotten hulk in a body-waldo glows.

And is she having joy. To waken out of the nightmare of being P. Burke and find herself a peri, a star-girl? On a yacht in paradise with no more to do than adorn herself and play with toys and attend revels and greet her friends—her, P. Burke, having friends!—and turn the right way for the holocams? Joy!

And it shows. One look at Delphi and the viewers know: DREAMS CAN COME TRUE.

Look at her riding pillion on Davy's sea-bike, carrying an apoplectic macaw in a silver hoop. *Oh, Morton, let's go there this winter!* Or learning the Japanese chinchona from that Kobe group, in a dress that looks like a blowtorch rising from one knee, and which should sell big in Texas. *Morton, is that real fire?* Happy, happy little girl!

And Davy. He's her pet and her baby and she loves to help him fix his red-gold hair. (P. Burke marveling, running Delphi's fingers through the curls.) Of course Davy is one of Matt's boys—not impotent exactly, but very *very* low drive. (Nobody knows exactly what Matt does with his bitty budget but the boys are useful and one or two have made names.) He's perfect for Delphi; in fact the psychomed lets her take him to bed like two kittens in a basket. Davy doesn't mind the

fact that Delphi "sleeps" like the dead. That's when P. Burke
is out of the body-waldo up at Carbondale, attending to her
own depressing needs.

A funny thing about that. Most of her sleepy-time Delphi's
just a gently ticking lush little vegetable waiting for P. Burke
to get back on the controls. But now and again Delphi all by
herself smiles a bit or stirs in her "sleep." Once she breathed
a sound: "Yes."

Under Carbondale P. Burke knows nothing. She's asleep
too, dreaming of Delphi, what else? But if the bushy Dr. Tesla
had heard that single syllable his bush would have turned
snow-white. Because Delphi is TURNED OFF.

He doesn't. Davy is too dim to notice and Delphi's staff
boss, Hopkins, wasn't monitoring.

And they've all got something else to think about now, because the cold-fire dress sells half a million copies, and not
only in Texas. The GTX computers already know it. When
they correlate a minor demand for macaws in Alaska the
problem comes to human attention: Delphi is something
special.

It's a problem, see, because Delphi is targeted on a limited
consumer bracket. Now it turns out she has mass-pop potential—those macaws in *Fairbanks*, man!—it's like trying to
shoot mice with an ABM. A whole new ball game. Dr. Tesla
and the fatherly Mr. Cantle start going around in headquarters circles and buddy-lunching together when they can get
away from a seventh-level weasel boy who scares them both.

In the end it's decided to ship Delphi down to the GTX
holocam enclave in Chile to try a spot on one of the mainstream shows. (Never mind why an Infanta takes up act-
ing.) The holocam complex occupies a couple of mountains

where an observatory once used the clear air. Holocam total-environment shells are very expensive and electronically super-stable. Inside them actors can move freely without going off-register and the whole scene or any selected part will show up in the viewer's home in complete 3-di, so real you can look up their noses and much denser than you get from mobile rigs. You can blow a tit ten feet tall when there's no molecular skiffle around.

The enclave looks—well, take everything you know about Hollywood-Burbank and throw it away. What Delphi sees coming down is a neat giant mushroom-farm, domes of all sizes up to monsters for the big games and stuff. It's orderly. The idea that art thrives on creative flamboyance has long been torpedoed by proof that what art needs is computers. Because this showbiz has something TV and Hollywood never had—*automated inbuilt viewer feedback*. Samples, ratings, critics, polls? Forget it. With that carrier field you can get real-time response-sensor from every receiver in the world, served up at your console. That started as a thingie to give the public more influence on content.

Yes.

Try it, man. You're at the console. Slice to the sex-age-educ-econ-ethno-cetera audience of your choice and start. You can't miss. Where the feedback warms up, give 'em more of that. Warm—warmer—*hot!* You've hit it—the secret itch under those hides, the dream in those hearts. You don't need to know its name. With your hand controlling all the input and your eye reading all the response you can make them a god . . . and somebody'll do the same for you.

But Delphi just sees rainbows, when she gets through the degaussing ports and the field relay and takes her first look at the insides of those shells. The next thing she sees is a team of shapers and technicians descending on her, and millisecond timers everywhere. The tropical leisure is finished. She's in gigabuck mainstream now, at the funnel maw of the unceasing hose that's pumping the sight and sound and flesh and blood and sobs and laughs and dreams of *reality* into the world's happy head. Little Delphi is going plonk into a zillion homes in prime time and nothing is left to chance. Work!

And again Delphi proves apt. Of course it's really P. Burke down under Carbondale who's doing it, but who remembers that carcass? Certainly not P. Burke, she hasn't spoken through her own mouth for months. Delphi doesn't even recall dreaming of her when she wakes up.

As for the show itself, don't bother. It's gone on so long no living soul could unscramble the plotline. Delphi's trial spot has something to do with a widow and her dead husband's brother's amnesia.

The bother comes after Delphi's spots begin to flash out along the world-hose and the feedback appears. You've guessed it, of course. Sensational! As you'd say, they IDENTIFY.

The report actually says something like InskinEmp with a string of percentages meaning that Delphi not only has it for anybody with a y-chromosome, but also for women and every thing in between. It's the sweet supernatural jackpot, the million-to-one.

Remember your Harlow? A sexpot, sure. But why did bitter hausfraus in Gary and Memphis know that the vanilla-ice-cream goddess with the white hair and crazy eyebrows was *their baby girl*? And write loving letters to Jean warning her that their husbands weren't good enough for her? Why?

The GTX analysts don't know either, but they know what to do with it when it happens.

(Back in his bird sanctuary the old Infante spots it without benefit of computers and gazes thoughtfully at his bride in widow's weeds. It might, he feels, be well to accelerate the completion of his studies.)

The excitement reaches down to the burrow under Carbondale where P. Burke gets two medical exams in a week and a chronically inflamed electrode is replaced. Nurse Fleming also gets an assistant who doesn't do much nursing but is very interested in access doors and identity tabs.

And in Chile little Delphi is promoted to a new home up among the stars' residential spreads and a private jitney to carry her to work. For Hopkins there's a new computer terminal and a full-time schedule man. What is the schedule crowded with?

Things.

And here begins the trouble. You probably saw that coming too.

"What does she think she is, a goddam *consumer rep*?" Mr. Cantle's fatherly face in Carbondale contorts.

"The girl's upset," Miss Fleming says stubbornly. "She *believes* that, what you told her about helping people and good new products."

"They are good products," Mr. Cantle snaps automatically, but his anger is under control. He hasn't got where he is by irrelevant reactions.

"She says the plastic gave her a rash and the glo-pills made her dizzy."

"Good god, she shouldn't swallow them," Doctor Tesla puts in agitatedly.

"You told her she'd use them," persists Miss Fleming. Mr. Cantle is busy figuring how to ease this problem to the weasel-faced young man. What, was it a goose that lays golden eggs?

Whatever he says to level Seven, down in Chile the offending products vanish. And a symbol goes into Delphi's tank matrix, one that means roughly *Balance unit resistance against PR index*. This means that Delphi's complaints will be endured as long as her Pop Response stays above a certain level. (What happens when it sinks need not concern us.) And to compensate, the price of her exposure-time rises again. She's a regular on the show now and response is still climbing.

See her under the sizzling lasers, in a holocam shell set up as a walkway accident. (The show is guesting an acupuncture school expert.)

"I don't think this new body-lift is safe," Delphi's saying. "It's made a funny blue spot on me—look, Mr. Vere."

She wiggles to show where the mini-grav pak that imparts a delicious sense of weightlessness is attached.

"So don't leave it *on*, Dee. With your meat—watch that deck-spot, it's starting to synch."

"But if I don't wear it it isn't honest. They should insulate it more or something, don't you see?"

The show's beloved old father, who is the casualty, gives a senile snigger.

"I'll tell them," Mr. Vere mutters. "Look now, as you step back bend like this so it just shows, see? And hold two beats."

Obediently Delphi turns, and through the dazzle her eyes connect with a pair of strange dark ones. She squints. A quite young man is lounging alone by the port, apparently waiting to use the chamber.

Delphi's used by now to young men looking at her with many peculiar expressions, but she isn't used to what she gets here. A jolt of something somber and knowing. *Secrets.*

"Eyes! Eyes, Dee!"

She moves through the routine, stealing peeks at the stranger. He stares back. He knows something.

When they let her go she comes shyly to him.

"Living wild, kitten." Cool voice, hot underneath.

"What do you mean?"

"Dumping on the product. You trying to get dead?"

"But it isn't right," she tells him. "They don't know, but I do, I've been wearing it."

His cool is jolted.

"You're out of your head."

"Oh, they'll see I'm right when they check it," she explains. "They're just so busy. When I tell them—"

He is staring down at little flower-face. His mouth opens, closes. "What are you doing in this sewer anyway? Who are you?"

Bewilderedly she says, "I'm Delphi."

"Holy Zen."

"What's wrong? Who are you, please?"

Her people are moving her out now, nodding at him.

"Sorry we ran over, Mister Uhunh," the script girl says.

He mutters something, but it's lost as her convoy bustles her toward the flower-decked jitney.

(Hear the click of an invisible ignition-train being armed?)

"Who was he?" Delphi asks her hair man.

The hair man is bending up and down from his knees as he works.

"Paul. Isham. Three," he says and puts a comb in his mouth.

"Who's that? I can't see."

He mumbles around the comb, meaning "Are you jiving?" Because she has to be, in the middle of the GTX enclave.

Next day there's a darkly smoldering face under a turban-towel when Delphi and the show's paraplegic go to use the carbonated pool.

She looks.

He looks.

And the next day, too.

(Hear that automatic sequencer cutting in? The system couples, the fuels begin to travel.)

Poor old Isham senior. You have to feel sorry for a man who values order: when he begets young, genetic information is still transmitted in the old ape way. One minute it's a happy midget with a rubber duck—look around and here's this huge healthy stranger, opaquely emotional, running with God knows who. Questions are heard where there's nothing to question, and eruptions claiming to be moral outrage. When this is called to Papa's attention—it may take time, in that boardroom—Papa does what he can, but without immortality-juice the problem is worrisome.

And young Paul Isham is a bear. He's bright and articulate and tender-souled and incessantly active and he and his friends are choking with appallment at the world their fathers made. And it hasn't taken Paul long to discover that *his* father's house has many mansions and even the GTX computers can't relate everything to everything else. He noses out a decaying project which adds up to something like Sponsoring Marginal Creativity (the free-lance team that "discovered" Delphi was one such grantee). And from there it turns out that an agile lad named Isham can get his hands on a viable packet of GTX holocam facilities.

So here he is with his little band, way down the mushroom-farm mountain, busily spooling a show which has no relation to Delphi's. It's built on bizarre techniques and unsettling distortions pregnant with social protest. An *underground* expression to you.

All this isn't unknown to his father, of course, but so far it has done nothing more than deepen Isham senior's apprehensive frown.

Until Paul connects with Delphi.

And by the time Papa learns this, those invisible hypergolics have exploded, the energy-shells are rushing out. For Paul, you see, is the genuine article. He's serious. He dreams. He even reads—for example, *Green Mansions*—and he wept fiercely when those fiends burned Rima alive.

When he hears that some new GTX pussy is making it big he sneers and forgets it. He's busy. He never connects the name with this little girl making her idiotic, doomed protest in the holocam chamber. This strangely simple little girl.

And she comes and looks up at him and he sees Rima, lost Rima the enchanted bird girl, and his unwired human heart goes twang.

And Rima turns out to be Delphi.

Do you need a map? The angry puzzlement. The rejection of the dissonance Rima-hustling-for-GTX-My-Father. Garbage, cannot be. The loitering around the pool to confirm the swindle . . . dark eyes hitting on blue wonder, jerky words exchanged in a peculiar stillness . . . the dreadful reorganization of the image into Rima-Delphi *in My Father's tentacles*—

You don't need a map.

Nor for Delphi either, the girl who loved her gods. She's seen their divine flesh close now, heard their unamplified voices call her name. She's played their god-games, worn their garlands. She's even become a goddess herself, though she doesn't believe it. She's not disenchanted, don't think that. She's still full of love. It's just that some crazy kind of *hope* isn't—

Really you can skip all this, when the loving little girl on the yellow-brick road meets a Man. A real human male burning with angry compassion and grandly concerned with human justice, who reaches for her with real male arms and—boom! She loves him back with all her heart.

A happy trip, see?

Except.

Except that it's really P. Burke four thousand miles away who loves Paul. P. Burke the monster, down in a dungeon smelling of electrode-paste. A caricature of a woman burning, melting, obsessed with true love. Trying over twenty-double-thousand miles of hard vacuum to reach her beloved through girl-flesh numbed by an invisible film. Feeling his arms around the body he thinks is hers, fighting through shadows to give herself to him. Trying to taste and smell him through beautiful dead nostrils, to love him back with a body that goes dead in the heart of the fire.

Perhaps you get P. Burke's state of mind?

She has phases. The trying, first. And the shame. The SHAME. *I am not what thou lovest.* And the fiercer trying. And the realization that there is no, no way, none. Never. *Never. . . .* A bit delayed, isn't it, her understanding that the bargain she made was forever? P. Burke should have noticed those stories about mortals who end up as grasshoppers.

You see the outcome—the funneling of all this agony into one dumb protoplasmic drive to fuse with Delphi. To leave, to close out the beast she is chained to. *To become Delphi.*

Of course it's impossible.

However, her torments have an effect on Paul. Delphi-as-Rima is a potent enough love object, and liberating Delphi's mind requires hours of deeply satisfying instruction in the rottenness of it all. Add in Delphi's body worshipping his flesh, burning in the fire of P. Burke's savage heart—do you wonder Paul is involved?

That's not all.

By now they're spending every spare moment together and some that aren't so spare.

"Mister Isham, would you mind staying out of this sports sequence? The script calls for Davy here."

(Davy's still around, the exposure did him good.)

"What's the difference?" Paul yawns. "It's just an ad. I'm not blocking that thing."

Shocked silence at his two-letter word. The script girl swallows bravely.

"I'm sorry, sir, our directive is to do the *social sequence* exactly as scripted. We're having to respool the segments we did last week, Mister Hopkins is very angry with me."

"Who the hell is Hopkins? Where is he?"

"Oh, please, Paul. *Please.*"

Paul unwraps himself, saunters back. The holocam crew nervously check their angles. The GTX boardroom has a foible about having things *pointed* at them and theirs. Cold shivers, when the image of an Isham nearly went onto the world beam beside that Dialadinner.

Worse yet. Paul has no respect for the sacred schedules which are now a full-time job for ferret boy up at headquarters. Paul keeps forgetting to bring her back on time and poor Hopkins can't cope.

So pretty soon the boardroom data-ball has an urgent personal action-tab for Mr. Isham senior. They do it the gentle way, at first.

"I can't today, Paul."

"Why not?"

"They say I have to, it's *very* important."

He strokes the faint gold down on her narrow back. Under Carbondale, Pa., a blind mole-woman shivers.

"Important. Their importance. Making more gold. Can't you see? To them you're just a thing to get scratch with. A *huckster*. Are you going to let them screw you, Dee? Are you?"

"Oh, Paul—"

He doesn't know it but he's seeing a weirdie; Remotes aren't hooked up to make much tears.

"Just say no, Dee. No. Integrity. You have to."

"But they say, it's my job—"

"Don't you believe I can take care of you, Dee? Baby, baby, you're letting them rip us. You have to choose. Tell them, no."

"Paul . . . I w-will . . ."

And she does. Brave little Delphi (insane P. Burke). Saying "No, please, I promised, Paul."

They try some more, still gently.

"Paul, Mr. Hopkins told me the reason they don't want us to be together so much. It's because of who you are, your father."

She thinks his father is like Mr. Cantle, maybe.

"Oh great. Hopkins. I'll fix him. Listen, I can't think about Hopkins now. Ken came back today, he found out something."

They are lying on the high Andes meadow watching his friends dive their singing kites.

"Would you believe, on the coast the police have *electrodes in their heads*?"

She stiffens in his arms.

"Yeah, weird. I thought they only used PPs on criminals and the army. Don't you see, Dee—something has to be going on. Some movement. Maybe somebody's organizing. How can we find out?" He pounds the ground behind her. "We should make *contact*! If we could only find anything."

"The, the news . . . ?" she asks distractedly.

"The news." He laughs. "There's nothing in the news except what they want people to know. Half the country could burn up and nobody would know it if they didn't want. Dee, can't you take what I'm explaining to you? They've got the whole world programmed! Total control of communication. They've got everybody's minds wired in to think what they show them and want what they give them and they give them what they're programmed to want—you can't break in or out of it, you can't *get hold* of it anywhere. I don't think they even have a plan except to keep things going round and round—and God knows what's happening to the people or the earth or the other planets, maybe. One great big vortex of lies and garbage pouring round and round getting bigger and bigger and nothing can ever change. If people don't wake up soon we're through!"

He pounds her stomach softly.

"*You* have to break out, Dee."

"I'll try, Paul, I will—"

"You're mine. They can't have you."

And he goes to see Hopkins, who is indeed cowed.

But that night up under Carbondale the fatherly Mr. Cantle goes to see P. Burke.

P. Burke? On a cot in a utility robe like a dead camel in a tent, she cannot at first comprehend that he is telling *her* to break it off with Paul. P. Burke has never seen Paul. *Delphi* sees Paul. The fact is, P. Burke can no longer clearly recall that she exists apart from Delphi.

Mr. Cantle can scarcely believe it either but he tries.

He points out the futility, the potential embarrassment for Paul. That gets a dim stare from the bulk on the bed. Then he goes into her duty to GTX, her job, isn't she grateful for the opportunity, etcetera. He's very persuasive.

The cobwebby mouth of P. Burke opens and croaks.

"No."

Nothing more seems to be forthcoming.

Mr. Cantle isn't dense, he knows an immovable obstacle when he bumps one. He also knows an irresistible force: GTX. The simple solution is to lock the waldo-cabinet until Paul gets tired of waiting for Delphi to wake up. But the cost, the schedules! And there's something odd here . . . he eyes the corporate asset hulking on the bed and his hunch-sense prickles.

You see, Remotes don't love. They don't have real sex, the circuits designed that out from the start. So it's been assumed that it's *Paul* who is diverting himself or something with the pretty little body in Chile. P. Burke can only be doing what comes natural to any ambitious gutter-meat. It hasn't occurred to anyone that they're dealing with the real hairy thing whose shadow is blasting out of every holoshow on earth.

Love?

Mr. Cantle frowns. The idea is grotesque. But his instinct for the fuzzy line is strong; he will recommend flexibility.

And so, in Chile:

"Darling, I don't have to work tonight! And Friday too— isn't that right, Mr. Hopkins?"

"Oh, great. When does she come up for parole?"

"Mr. Isham, please be reasonable. Our schedule—surely your own production people must be needing you?"

This happens to be true. Paul goes away. Hopkins stares after him wondering distastefully why an Isham wants to ball a waldo. (How sound are those boardroom belly-fears— garble creeps, creeps in!) It never occurs to Hopkins that an Isham might not know what Delphi is.

Especially with Davy crying because Paul has kicked him out of Delphi's bed.

Delphi's bed is under a real window.

"Stars," Paul says sleepily. He rolls over, pulling Delphi on top. "Are you aware that this is one of the last places on earth where people can see the stars? Tibet, too, maybe . . ."

"Paul . . ."

"Go to sleep. I want to see you sleep."

"Paul, I . . . I sleep so *hard*, I mean, it's a joke how hard I am to wake up. Do you mind?"

"Yes."

But finally, fearfully, she must let go. So that four thousand miles north a crazy spent creature can crawl out to gulp concentrates and fall on her cot. But not for long. It's pink dawn when Delphi's eyes open to find Paul's arms around her, his voice saying rude, tender things. He's been kept awake. The nerveless little statue that was her Delphi-body nuzzled him in the night.

Insane hope rises, is fed a couple of nights later when he tells her she called his name in her sleep.

And that day Paul's arms keep her from work and Hopkins' wails go up to headquarters where the sharp-faced lad is working his sharp tailbone off packing Delphi's program. Mr. Cantle defuses that one. But next week it happens again, to a major client. And ferret-face has connections on the technical side.

Now you can see that when you have a field of complexly heterodyned energy modulations tuned to a demand-point like Delphi there are many problems of standwaves and lashback and skiffle of all sorts which are normally balanced out with ease by the technology of the future. By the same token they can be delicately unbalanced too, in ways that feed back into the waldo operator with striking results.

"Darling—what the hell! What's wrong? DELPHI!"

Helpless shrieks, writhings. Then the Rima-bird is lying wet and limp in his arms, her eyes enormous.

"I . . . I wasn't supposed to . . ." she gasps faintly. "They told me not to . . ."

"Oh my god . . . *Delphi*."

And his hard fingers are digging in her thick yellow hair. Electronically knowledgeable fingers. They freeze.

"You're a *doll*! You're one of those. PP implants. They control you. I should have known. Oh God, I should have known."

"No, Paul," she's sobbing. "No, no, no—"

"Damn them. Damn them, what they've done—you're not *you*—"

He's shaking her, crouching over her in the bed and jerking her back and forth, glaring at the pitiful beauty.

"No!" She pleads (it's not true, that dark bad dream back there). "I'm Delphi!"

"My father. Filth, pigs—damn them, damn them, damn them."

"No, no," she babbles. "They were good to me—" P. Burke underground mouthing, "They were good to me—AAH-AAAAH!"

Another agony skewers her. Up north the sharp young man wants to make sure this so-tiny interference works. Paul can scarcely hang onto her, he's crying too. "I'll kill them."

His Delphi, a wired-up slave! Spikes in her brain, electronic shackles in his bird's heart. Remember when those savages burned Rima alive?

"I'll *kill* the man that's doing this to you."

He's still saying it afterward but she doesn't hear. She's sure he hates her now, all she wants is to die. When she finally understands that the fierceness is tenderness she thinks it's a miracle. *He knows—and he still loves!*

How can she guess that he's got it a little bit wrong?

You can't blame Paul—give him credit that he's even heard about pleasure-pain implants and snoops, which by their nature aren't mentioned much by those who know them most intimately. That's what he thinks is being used on Delphi, something to *control* her. And to listen—he burns at the unknown ears in their bed.

Of waldo-bodies and objects like P. Burke he has heard nothing.

So it never crosses his mind as he looks down at his violated bird, sick with fury and love, that he isn't holding *all* of her. Do you need to be told the mad resolve jelling in him now?

To free Delphi.

How? Well, he is after all Paul Isham III. And he even has an idea where the GTX neurolab is. In Carbondale.

But first things have to be done for Delphi, and for his own stomach. So he gives her back to Hopkins and departs in a restrained and discreet way. And the Chile staff is grateful and do not understand that his teeth don't normally show so much.

And a week passes in which Delphi is a very good, docile little ghost. They let her have the load of wildflowers Paul sends and the bland loving notes. (He's playing it coony.) And up in headquarters weasel boy feels that *his* destiny has clicked a notch onward floats the word up that he's handy with little problems.

And no one knows what P. Burke thinks in any way whatever, except that Miss Fleming catches her flushing her food down the can and next night she faints in the pool. They haul her out and stick her with IVs. Miss Fleming frets, she's seen expressions like that before. But she wasn't around when crazies who called themselves Followers of the Fish looked through flames to life everlasting. P. Burke is seeing Heaven on the far side of death too. Heaven is spelled P-a-u-l, but the idea's the same. *I will die and be born again in Delphi.*

Garbage, electronically speaking. No way.

Another week and Paul's madness has become a plan. (Remember, he does have friends.) He smolders, watching his love paraded by her masters. He turns out a scorching sequence for his own show. And finally, politely, he requests from Hopkins a morsel of his bird's free time, which duly arrives.

"—I thought you didn't want me any more," she's repeating as they wing over mountain flanks in Paul's suncar. "Now you *know*—"

"Look at me!"

His hand covers her mouth and he's showing her a lettered card.

DON'T TALK THEY CAN HEAR EVERYTHING WE SAY. I'M TAKING YOU AWAY NOW.

She kisses his hand. He nods urgently, flipping the card.

DON'T BE AFRAID. I CAN STOP THE PAIN IF THEY TRY TO HURT YOU.

With his free hand he shakes out a silvery scrambler-mesh on a power pack. She is dumfounded.

THIS WILL CUT THE SIGNALS AND PROTECT YOU DARLING.

She's staring at him, her head going vaguely from side to side, No.

"Yes!" He grins triumphantly. "Yes!"

For a moment she . . . wonders. That powered mesh will cut off the field, all right. It will also cut off Delphi. But he is *Paul*. Paul is kissing her, she can only seek him hungrily as he sweeps the suncar through a pass.

Ahead is an old jet ramp with a shiny bullet waiting to go. (Paul also has credits and a Name.) The little GTX patrol courier is built for nothing but speed. Paul and Delphi wedge in behind the pilot's extra fuel tank and there's no more talking when the torches start to scream.

They're screaming high over Quito before Hopkins starts to worry. He wastes another hour tracking the beeper on Paul's suncar. The suncar is sailing a pattern out to sea. By the time they're sure it's empty and Hopkins gets on the hot flue to headquarters the fugitives are a sourceless howl above Carib West.

Up at headquarters weasel boy gets the squeal. His first impulse is to repeat his previous play but then his brain snaps to. This one is too hot. Because, see, although in the long run they can make P. Burke do anything at all except maybe *live*, instant emergencies can be tricky. And—Paul Isham III.

"Can't you order her back?"

They're all in the GTX tower monitor station, Mr. Cantle and ferret-face and Joe and a very neat man who is Mr. Isham senior's personal eyes and ears.

"No sir," Joe says doggedly. "We can read channels, particularly speech, but we can't interpolate organized pattern. It takes the waldo op to send one-to-one—"

"What are they saying?"

"Nothing at the moment, sir." The console jockey's eyes are closed. "I believe they are, ah, embracing."

"They're not answering," a traffic monitor says. "Still heading zero zero three zero—due north, sir."

"You're certain Kennedy is alerted not to fire on them?" the neat man asks anxiously.

"Yes sir."

"Can't you just turn her off?" The sharp-faced lad is angry. "Pull that beast out of the controls!"

"If you cut the transmission cold you'll kill the Remote," Joe explains for the third time. "Withdrawal has to be phased right, you have to fade over to the Remote's own autonomics. Heart, breathing, cerebellum would go blooey. If you pull Burke out you'll probably finish her too. It's a fantastic cyber-system, you don't want to do that."

"The investment." Mr. Cantle shudders.

Weasel boy puts his hand on the console jock's shoulder, it's the contact who arranged the No-no effect for him.

"We can at least give them a warning signal, sir." He licks his lips, gives the neat man his sweet ferret smile. "We know that does no damage."

Joe frowns, Mr. Cantle sighs. The neat man is murmuring into his wrist. He looks up. "I am authorized," he says reverently, "I am authorized to, ah, direct a signal. If this is the only course. But minimal, minimal."

Sharp-face squeezes his man's shoulder.

In the silver bullet shrieking over Charleston Paul feels Delphi arch in his arms. He reaches for the mesh, hot for action. She thrashes, pushing at his hands, her eyes roll. She's afraid of that mesh despite the agony. (And she's right.) Frantically Paul fights her in the cramped space, gets it over her head. As he turns the power up she burrows free under his arm and the spasm fades.

"They're calling you again, Mister Isham!" the pilot yells.

"Don't answer. Darling, keep this over your head damn it how can I—"

An AX90 barrels over their nose, there's a flash.

"Mister Isham! Those are Air Force jets!"

"Forget it," Paul shouts back. "They won't fire. Darling, don't be afraid."

Another AX90 rocks them.

"Would you mind pointing your pistol at my head where they can see it, sir?" the pilot howls.

Paul does so. The AX90s take up escort formation around them. The pilot goes back to figuring how he can collect from GTX, too, and after Goldsboro AB the escort peels away.

"Holding the same course," Traffic is reporting to the group around the monitor. "Apparently they've taken on enough fuel to bring them to towerport here."

"In that case it's just a question of waiting for them to dock." Mr. Cantle's fatherly manner revives a bit.

"Why can't they cut off that damn freak's life-support," the sharp young man fumes. "It's ridiculous."

"They're working on it," Cantle assures him.

What they're doing, down under Carbondale, is arguing.

Miss Fleming's watchdog has summoned the bushy man to the waldo room.

"Miss Fleming, you will obey orders."

"You'll kill her if you try that, sir. I can't believe you meant it, that's why I didn't. We've already fed her enough sedative to affect heart action; if you cut any more oxygen she'll die in there."

The bushy man grimaces. "Get Doctor Quine here fast."

They wait, staring at the cabinet in which a drugged, ugly madwoman fights for consciousness, fights to hold Delphi's eyes open.

High over Richmond the silver pod starts a turn. Delphi is sagged into Paul's arm, her eyes swim up to him.

"Starting down now, baby. It'll be over soon, all you have to do is stay alive, Dee."

". . . Stay alive . . ."

The traffic monitor has caught them. "Sir! They've turned off for Carbondale—Control has contact—"

"Let's go."

But the headquarters posse is too late to intercept the courier wailing into Carbondale. And Paul's friends have come through again. The fugitives are out through the freight dock and into the neurolab admin port before the guard gets organized. At the elevator Paul's face plus his handgun get them in.

"I want Doctor—what's his name, Dee? Dee!"

". . . Tesla . . ." She's reeling on her feet.

"Doctor Tesla. Take me down to Tesla, fast."

Intercoms are squalling around them as they whoosh down, Paul's pistol in the guard's back. When the door slides open the bushy man is there.

"I'm Tesla."

"I'm Paul Isham. *Isham.* You're going to take your flaming implants out of this girl—now. Move!"

"*What?*"

"You heard me. Where's your operating room? Go!"

"But—"

"Move! Do I have to burn somebody?"

Paul waves the weapon at Dr. Quine, who has just appeared.

"No, no," says Tesla hurriedly. "But I can't, you know. It's impossible, there'll be nothing left."

"You screaming well can, right now. You mess up and I'll kill you," says Paul murderously. "Where is it, there? And wipe the creep that's on her circuits now."

He's backing them down the hall, Delphi heavy on his arm.

"Is this the place, baby? Where they did it to you?"

"Yes," she whispers, blinking at a door. "Yes . . ."

Because it is, see. Behind that door is the very suite where she was born.

Paul herds them through it into a gleaming hall. An inner door opens and a nurse and a gray man rush out. And freeze.

Paul sees there's something special about that inner door. He crowds them past it and pushes it open and looks in.

Inside is a big mean-looking cabinet with its front door panels ajar.

And inside that cabinet is a poisoned carcass to whom something wonderful, unspeakable, is happening. Inside is P. Burke the real living woman who knows that HE is there, coming closer—Paul whom she had fought to reach through forty thousand miles of ice—PAUL is here!—is yanking at the waldo doors—

The doors tear open and a monster rises up.

"Paul darling!" croaks the voice of love and the arms of love reach for him.

And he responds.

Wouldn't you, if a gaunt she-golem flab-naked and spouting wires and blood came at you—clawing you with metal-studded paws—

"*Get away!*" He knocks wires.

It doesn't much matter which wires, P. Burke has so to speak her nervous system hanging out. Imagine somebody jerking a handful of your medulla—

She crashes onto the floor at his feet, flopping and roaring *PAUL-PAUL-PAUL* in rictus.

It's doubtful he recognizes his name or sees her life coming out of her eyes at him. And at the last it doesn't go to him. The eyes find Delphi, fainting by the doorway, and die.

Now of course Delphi is dead, too.

There's total silence as Paul steps away from the thing by his foot.

"You killed her," Tesla says. "That was her."

"Your control." Paul is furious, the thought of that monster fastened into little Delphi's brain nauseates him. He sees her crumpling and holds out his arms. Not knowing she is dead.

And Delphi comes to him.

One foot before the other, not moving very well—but moving. Her darling face turns up. Paul is distracted by the terrible quiet, and when he looks down he sees only her tender little neck.

"Now you get the implants out," he warns them. Nobody moves.

"But, but she's dead," Miss Fleming whispers wildly.

Paul feels Delphi's life under his hand, they're talking about their monster. He aims his pistol at the gray man.

"You. If we aren't in your surgery when I count three I'm burning off this man's leg."

"Mr. Isham," Tesla says desperately, "you have just killed the person who animated the body you call Delphi. Delphi herself is dead. If you release your arm you'll see what I say is true."

The tone gets through. Slowly Paul opens his arm, looks down.

"*Delphi?*"

She totters, sways, stays upright. Her face comes slowly up.

"Paul . . ." Tiny voice.

"Your crotty tricks," Paul snarls at them. "Move!"

"Look at her eyes," Dr. Quine croaks.

They look. One of Delphi's pupils fills the iris, her lips writhe weirdly.

"Shock." Paul grabs her to him. "Fix her!" He yells at them, aiming at Tesla.

"For God's sake . . . bring it in the lab." Tesla quavers.

"Goodbye-bye," says Delphi clearly. They lurch down the hall, Paul carrying her, and meet a wave of people.

Headquarters has arrived.

Joe takes one look and dives for the waldo room, running into Paul's gun.

"Oh no, you don't."

Everybody is yelling. The little thing in his arm stirs, says plaintively, "I'm Delphi."

And all through the ensuing jabber and ranting she hangs on, keeps it up, the ghost of P. Burke or whatever whispering crazily "Paul . . . Paul . . . Please, I'm Delphi . . . Paul?"

"I'm here, darling, I'm here." He's holding her in the nursing bed. Tesla talks, talks, talks unheard.

"Paul . . . don't sleep . . ." the ghost-voice whispers. Paul is in agony, he will not accept, WILL NOT believe. Tesla runs down.

And then near midnight Delphi says roughly, "Ag-ag-ag—" and slips onto the floor, making a rough noise like a seal.

Paul screams. There's more of the *ag-ag* business and more gruesome convulsive disintegrations, until by two in the morning Delphi is nothing but a warm little bundle of vegetative functions hitched to some expensive hardware— the same that sustained her before her life began. Joe finally persuades Paul to let him at the waldo-cabinet. Paul stays by her long enough to see her face change in a dreadfully alien and coldly convincing way, and then he stumbles out bleakly through the group in Tesla's office.

Behind him Joe is working wet-faced, sweating to reintegrate the fantastic complex of circulation, respiration, endocrines, mid-brain homeostasis, the patterned flux that was a human being—it's like saving an orchestra abandoned in midair. Joe is also crying a little; he alone had truly loved P. Burke. P. Burke, now a dead pile on a table, was the greatest cybersystem he has ever known, and he never forgets her.

The end, really.

You're curious? Sure, Delphi lives again. Next year she's back on the yacht getting sympathy for her tragic breakdown. But there's a different chick in Chile, because while Delphi's new operator is competent, you don't get two P. Burkes in a row—for which GTX is duly grateful.

The real belly-bomb of course is Paul. He was *young*, see. Fighting abstract wrong. Now life has clawed into him and he goes through gut rage and grief and grows in human wisdom and resolve. So much so that you won't be surprised, some time later, to find him—where?

In the GTX boardroom, dummy. Using the advantage of his birth to radicalize the system. You'd call it "boring from within."

That's how he put it, and his friends couldn't agree more. It gives them a warm, confident feeling to know that Paul is up there. Sometimes one of them that is still around runs into him and gets a big hello.

And the sharp-faced lad?

Oh, he matures too. He learns fast, believe it. For instance, he's the first to learn that an obscure GTX research unit is actually getting something with their loopy temporal anomal-izer project. True, he doesn't have a physics background, and he's bugged quite a few people. But he doesn't really learn about that until the day he stands where somebody points him during a test run—

—and wakes up lying on a newspaper headlined NIXON UNVEILS PHASE TWO.

Lucky he's a fast learner.

Believe it, zombie. When I say *growth* I mean growth. Capital appreciation. You can stop sweating. There's a great future there.

1973

PAMELA SARGENT

If Ever I Should Leave You

WHEN YURI walked away from the Time Station for the last time, his face was pale marble, his body only bones barely held together by skin and the weak muscles he had left. I hurried to him and grasped his arm, oblivious to the people who passed us in the street. He resisted my touch at first, embarrassed in front of the others; then he gave in and leaned against me as we began to walk home.

I knew that he was too weak to go to the Time Station again. His body, resting against mine, seemed almost weightless. I guided him through the park toward our home. Halfway there, he tugged at my arm and we rested against one of the crystalline trees surrounding the small lake in the center of the park.

Yuri had aged rapidly in the last six months, transformed from a young man into an aged creature hardly able to walk by himself. I had expected it. One cannot hold off old age indefinitely, even now. But I could not accept it. I knew that his death could be no more than days away.

You can't leave me now, not after all this time, I wanted to scream. Instead, I helped him sit on the ground next to the tree, then sat at his side.

His blue eyes, once clear and bright, now watery with age and surrounded by tiny lines, watched me. He reached inside his shirt and fumbled for something. I had always teased Yuri about his shirts: sooner or later he would tear them along the shoulder seams while flexing the muscles of his broad back and sturdy arms. Now the shirt, like his skin, hung on his bones in wrinkles and folds. At last he pulled out a piece of paper and pressed it into my hand with trembling fingers.

"Take care of this," he whispered to me. "Copy it down in several places so you won't lose it. All the coordinates are there, all the places and times I went to these past months. When you're lonely, when you need me, go to the Time Station and I'll be waiting on the other side." He was trying to comfort me. Because of his concern, he had gone to the Time Station every day for the past six months and had traveled to various points in the past. I could travel to any of those points and be with him at those times. It suddenly struck me as a mad idea, an insane and desperate thing.

"What happens to me?" I asked, clutching the paper. "What am I like when I see you? You've already seen me at all those times. What do I do, what happens to me?"

"I can't tell you, you know that. You have to decide for yourself. Anything I say might affect what you do."

I looked away from him and toward the lake. Two golden swans glided by, the water barely rippling in their wake. Their shapes blurred and I realized I was crying silently. Yuri's blue-veined hand rested on my shoulder.

"Don't cry. Please. You make it harder for me."

At last the tears stopped. I reached over and stroked his hair, once thick and blond, now thin and white. Only a year before we had come to this same tree, our bodies shiny with lake water after a moonlight swim, and made love in the darkness. We were as young as everyone else, confident that we would live forever, forgetting that our bodies could not be rejuvenated indefinitely.

"I'm not really leaving you," Yuri said. His arms held me firmly and for a moment I thought his strength had returned. "I'll be at the other side of the Time Station, any time you need me. Think of it that way."

"All right," I said, trying to smile. "All right." I nestled against him, my head on his chest, listening to his once-strong heart as it thumped against my ear.

Yuri died that night, only a few hours after we returned home.

The relationships among our friends had been an elaborate web, always changing, couples breaking up and recombining in a new pattern. We were all eternally young and time seemed to stretch ahead of us with no end. Throughout all of this, Yuri and I stayed together, the strands of our love becoming stronger instead of more tenuous. I was a shy, frightened girl when I met Yuri and was attracted in part by his boldness; he had appeared at my door one day, introduced himself and told me a friend of his had made him promise he would meet me. I could not have looked very appealing with my slouched, bony body, the thick black hair that would not stay out of my face, my long legs marked with bruises by my clumsiness. But Yuri had loved me almost on sight and I discovered, in time, that his boldness was the protective covering of a serious and intense young man.

Our lives became intertwined so tightly that, after a while, they were one life. It was inconceivable that anything could separate us, even though our relationship may have lacked the excitement of others' lives. With almost three centuries to live at the full height of our physical and mental powers, and the freedom to live several different kinds of lives, changing our professions and pursuits every twenty or thirty years, we know how rarely anyone chooses to stay with the same person throughout. Yet Yuri and I had, even through our changes, fallen in love with each other over and over again. We were lucky, I thought.

We were fools, I told myself when Yuri was gone. I had half a life after his death. I was a ghost myself, wandering from friend to friend seeking consolation, then isolating myself in my house for days, unwilling to see anyone.

But Yuri had not really left me. I had only to walk down to the Time Station, give them the coordinates he had given me, and I would be with him again, at least for a little while. Yet during those first days alone I could not bring myself to go there. He's gone, I told myself angrily; you must learn to live without him. And then I would whisper, Why? You have no life alone, you are an empty shell. Go to him.

I began to wander past the Time Station, testing my resolve. I would walk almost to the door, within sight of the technicians, then retreat, racing home, my hands shaking. *Yuri.*

I would make the time and trouble he took useless. He had wanted to be with me when I needed him, but he had also wanted to see my future self, what I would become after his death. The Time Station could not penetrate the future, that unformed mass of possibilities. I would be denying Yuri the chance to see it through my eyes, and the chance to see what became of me.

At last I walked to the Time Station and through its glassy door into the empty hall. Time Portals surrounded me on all sides, silvery cubicles into which people would step, then disappear. A technician approached me, silently offering assistance. I motioned her away and went over to one of the unoccupied cubicles. I fumbled for the piece of paper in my pocket, then pulled it out and stared at the first set of coordinates. I stepped inside the cubicle, reciting the coordinates aloud—time, place, duration of my stay.

Suddenly I felt as though my body were being thrown through space, that my limbs were being torn from my torso. The walls around me had vanished. The feeling lasted only an instant. I was now standing next to a small, clear pool of water shadowed by palm trees.

I turned from the pool. In front of me stretched a desolate waste, a rocky desert bleached almost white by the sun. I retreated farther into the shade of the oasis, and knelt by the pool.

"Yuri," I whispered as I dipped my hand into the coolness of the water. A pebble suddenly danced across the silvery surface before me, and the ripples it made mingled with those my hand had created.

I looked around. Yuri stood only a few feet away. He had barely begun to age. His face was still young, his skin drawn tightly across high cheekbones, and his hair was only lightly speckled with silver.

"Yuri," I whispered again, and then I was running to him.

After we swam, we sat next to each other by the small pool with our feet in the water. I was intoxicated, my mind whirling from one thing to another with nothing needing to be said. Yuri smiled at me and skipped pebbles across the pool. Some of my thoughts seemed to skip with them, while another part of me whispered, He's alive, he's here with me, and he'll be with me at a hundred other places in a hundred other times.

Yuri started to whistle a simple tune, one that I had heard for as long as I knew him. I pursed my lips and tried to whistle along but failed, as I always had.

"You'll never learn to whistle now," he said. "You've had two and a half centuries to learn and you still haven't figured it out."

"I will," I replied. "I've done everything else I ever wanted to do and I can't believe that a simple thing like whistling is going to defeat me."

"You'll never learn."

"I will."

"You won't."

I raised my feet, then lowered them forcefully, splashing us both. Yuri let out a yell, and I scrambled to my feet, stumbled and tried to run. He grabbed me by the arm.

"You *still* won't learn how," he said again, laughing.

I looked into his eyes, level with my own.

I pursed my lips again, and Yuri disappeared. My time was up and I was being thrown and torn at again. I was in the cubicle once more. I left the Time Station and walked home alone.

I became a spendthrift, visiting the Time Station several times a week, seeing Yuri as often as I wanted. We met on the steps of a deserted Mayan pyramid and argued about the mathematical theories of his friend Alney, while jungle birds shrieked around us. I packed a few of his favorite foods and wines and found him in Hawaii, still awaiting the arrival of its first inhabitants. We sat together on a high rocky cliff in

Africa, while far below us apelike creatures with primitive weapons hunted for food.

I became busy again, and began work with a group who was designing dwelling places inside the huge trees that surrounded the city. The biologists who had created the trees hundreds of years before had left the trunks hollow. I would hurry to the Time Station with my sketches of various designs, anxious to ask Yuri for advice or suggestions.

Yet during this time I had to watch Yuri grow old again. Each time I saw him he was a little older, a little weaker. I began to realize that I was watching him die all over again, and our visits took on a tone of panic and desperation. He grew more cautious in his choice of times and sites, and I was soon meeting him on deserted island beaches or inside empty summer homes in the twentieth century. Our talks with each other grew more muted, as I was afraid of arguing too vigorously with him and thus wasting the little time we had left. Yuri noticed this and understood what it meant.

"Maybe I was wrong," he said to me after I showed him the final plans for the tree dwellings. I had been overly animated, trying to be cheerful, ignoring the signs of age that reminded me of his death. I couldn't fool him. "I wanted to make it easier for you to live without me, but I might have made things worse. If I hadn't planned these visits, maybe you would have recovered by now, maybe—"

"Don't," I whispered. We were sitting near a sunny stretch of beach in southern France, hiding ourselves behind a large rock from the family picnicking below us. "Don't worry about me, please."

"You've got to face it. I can't make too many more of these journeys. I'm growing weaker."

I tried to say something but my vocal cords were locked, frozen inside my throat. The voices of the family on the beach were piercing. I wondered, idly, how many of them would die in their coming world war.

Yuri held my hand, opened his lips to say something else, then vanished. I clutched at the empty air in desperation. "No!" I screamed. "Not yet! Come back!"

I found myself, once again, at the Time Station.

I had been a spendthrift. Now I became a miser, going to the Time Station only two or three times a month, trying not to waste the few remaining visits I had with Yuri. I was no longer working on the tree dwellings. We had finished our designs and now those who enjoyed working with their hands had begun construction.

A paralysis seized me. I spent days alone in my house, unable even to clothe myself, wandering from room to room. I would sleep fitfully, then rise and, after sitting for a few hours alone, would sleep again.

Once, I forced myself to walk to the Slumber House and asked them to put me to sleep for a month. I felt the same after awakening, but at least I had been able to pass that lonely month in unconsciousness. I went to the Time Station, visited Yuri, and went back to the Slumber House to ask for another month of oblivion. When I awoke the second time, two men were standing over me, shaking their heads. They told me I would have to see a Counselor before they would put me to sleep again.

I had been a Counselor once myself, and I knew all their tricks. Instead, I went home and waited out the time between my visits to the Time Station.

This could not go on indefinitely. The list of remaining co-ordinates grew shorter until there was only one set left, and I knew I would see Yuri for the last time.

We met by a large wooden summer home that overlooked a small lake. It was autumn there and Yuri began to shiver in the cool air. I managed to open the back door of the house and we went inside, careful not to disturb anything.

Yuri lay on one of the couches, his head on my lap. Outside, the thick wooded area that surrounded the house was bright with colors, orange, red, yellow. A half-grown fawn with white spots on its back peered in the window at the other end of the room, then disappeared among the trees.

"Do you regret anything?" Yuri suddenly asked. I stroked his white hair and managed a smile.

"No, nothing."

"You're sure."

"Yes," I said, trying to keep my voice from quavering.

"I have one regret, that I didn't meet you sooner. But I wouldn't have met you at all, except for that promise I made."

"I know," I said. We had talked about our meeting at least a thousand times. The conversation had become a ritual, yet I wanted to go over it again. "You were so blatant, Yuri, coming to my door like that, out of nowhere. I thought you were a little crazy."

He smiled up at me and repeated what he had said then. "Hello, I'm Yuri Malenkov. I know this is a little strange, but I promised a friend of mine I met today I'd see you. Do you mind if I come in for a little while?"

"And I was so surprised I let you in."

"And I never left."

"I know, and you're still around." Tears stung my eyes.

"You were the only person aside from that friend that I could talk to honestly right away."

By then tears were running down my cheeks. "You never told me anything about your friend," I said abruptly, breaking the ritual.

"An acquaintance, really. I never saw that person again after that."

"Oh, Yuri, what will I do now? You can't leave me. I can't let you die again."

"Don't," he murmured. "You don't have much longer. Can't you see what's happening to you?"

"No."

"Get up and look in the mirror over the fireplace."

I rose, wandered over to the mirror, and looked. The signs were unmistakable. My once jet-black hair was lightly sprinkled with silver and tiny lines were etched into the skin around my eyes.

"I'm dying," I said. "My body isn't rejuvenating itself anymore." I felt a sudden rush of panic; then the fear vanished as quickly as it came, replaced by calm. I hurried back to Yuri's side.

"It won't be long," he said. "Try to do something meaningful with those last months. We'll be together again soon, just keep thinking of that."

"All right, Yuri," I whispered. Then I kissed him for the last time.

I did not fear death and do not fear it now. I became calmer, consoled by the fact that I would not be alone much longer.

How ironic it would be if my many recent uses of the Time

Station had caused my sudden aging, if Yuri's gift to me had condemned me instead. Yet I knew this was not so. We all imagine that we'll have our full three centuries; most of us do, after all. But not everyone, and not I. The irony is part of life itself. It was the work not of any Time Station, but of the final timekeeper, Death, who had decided to come for me a few decades early.

What was I to do with the time left to me? I had trained as a Counselor many years ago and had worked as one before choosing a new profession. I decided to use my old experience in helping those who, like me, had to face death.

The dying began to come to me, unable to accept their fate. They were used to their youthfulness and their full lives, feeling invulnerable to anything except an accident. The suddenness with which old age had descended on them drove some to hysteria, and they would concoct wild schemes to bring about the return of their youth. One man, a biologist, spoke to me and then decided to spend his last months involved in the elusive search for immortality. Another man, who had recently fallen in love with a young girl, cried on my shoulder and I didn't know whether to weep for him or for the young woman he was leaving behind. A woman came to me, only seventy and already aging, deprived of what should have been her normal life span.

I began to forget about myself in talking with these people. Occasionally I would walk through the city and visit old friends. My mind was aging too, and on these walks I found myself lost in memories of the past, clearer to me than more recent events. As I passed the Time Station, I would contemplate a visit to my past and then shake my head, knowing that was impossible.

I might have gone on that way if I had not passed the Time Station one warm evening while sorting through my thoughts. As I walked by, I saw Onel Lialla, dressed as a technician, looking almost exactly the same as when I had known him.

An idea occurred to me. Within seconds it had formed itself in my mind and become an obsession. I can do it, I thought. Onel will help me.

Onel had been a mathematician. He had left the city some time before and I had heard nothing about him. I hurried over to his side.

"Onel," I said, and waited. His large black eyes watched me uncertainly and anxiety crossed his classically handsome face. Then he recognized me.

He clasped my arms. He said nothing at first, perhaps embarrassed by the overt signs of my approaching death. "Your eyes haven't changed," he said finally.

We walked toward the park, talking of old times. I was surprised at how little he had changed. He was still courtly, still fancied himself the young knight in shining armor. His dark eyes still paid me homage, in spite of my being an old gray-haired woman. Blinded perhaps by his innate romanticism, Onel saw only what he wished to see.

Years before, while barely more than a boy, Onel had fallen in love with me. It had not taken me long to realize that Onel, being a romantic, did not really wish to obtain the object of his affections and had unconsciously settled on me because I was so deeply involved with Yuri. He would follow me almost everywhere, pouring out his heart. I tried to be kind, not wanting to make him bitter, and spent as much time as I could in conversation with him about his feelings. Onel had finally left the city, and I let him go, knowing he would forget and realizing that this, too, was part of his romantic game.

Onel remembered all this. We sat in the park under one of the crystalline willows and he paid court again. "I never forgot your kindness," he said to me. "I swore I would repay it someday. If there's anything I can do for you now, I will." He sighed dramatically at this point.

"There is," I replied.

"What is it?"

The opportunity had fallen into my lap with no effort. "I want you," I went on, "to come to the Time Station with me and send me back to this park two hundred and forty years in the past. I want to see the scenes of my youth one last time."

Onel seemed stunned. "You know I can't," he said. "The Portal can't send you to any time you've already lived through. We'd have people bumping into themselves, or going back to give their earlier selves advice. It's impossible."

"The Portal can be overridden for emergencies," I said. "You can override it, you know how. Send me through."

"I can't."

"Onel, I don't want to change anything. I don't even want to talk to anybody."

"If you changed the past—"

"I won't. It would already have happened then, wouldn't it? Besides, why should I? I had a happy life, Onel. I'll go back to a day when I wasn't in the park. It would just give me a little pleasure before I die to see things as they were. Is that asking too much?"

"I can't," he said. "Don't ask this of me."

In the end he gave in, as I knew he would. We went to the Station. Onel, his hands shaking, adjusted a Portal for me and sent me through.

Onel had given me four hours. I appeared in the park behind a large refreshment tent. Inside the tent, people sat at small round tables enjoying delicacies and occasionally rising to sample the pink wine that flowed from a fountain in the center. As a girl I had worked as a cook in that tent, removing raw foodstuffs from the transformer in the back and spending hours in the small kitchen making desserts, which were my specialty. I had almost forgotten the tents, which had been replaced later on by more elaborate structures.

I walked past the red tent toward the lake. It too was as I remembered it, surrounded by oaks and a few weeping willows. Biologists had not yet developed the silvery vines and glittering crystal trees that would be planted later. A peacock strutted past me as I headed for a nearby bench. I wanted only to sit for a while near the lake, then perhaps visit one of the tents before I had to return to my own time.

I watched my feet as I walked, being careful not to stumble. Most of those in the park ignored me rather pointedly, perhaps annoyed by an old woman who reminded them of their eventual fate. I had been the same, I thought, avoiding those who would so obviously be dead soon, uncomfortable around those who were dying when I had everything ahead of me.

Suddenly a blurred face was in front of me and I collided with a muscular young body. Unable to retain my balance, I fell.

A hand was held out to me and I grasped it as I struggled to my feet. "I'm terribly sorry," said a voice, a voice I had come to know so well, and I looked up at the face with its wide cheekbones and clear blue eyes.

"Yuri," I said.

He was startled. "Yuri Malenkov," I said, trying to recover.

"Do I know you?" he asked.

"I attended one of your lectures," I said quickly, "on holographic art."

He seemed to relax a bit. "I've only given one," he said. "Last week. I'm surprised you remember my name."

"Do you think," I said, anxious now to hang on to him for at least a few minutes, "you could help me over to that bench?"

"Certainly."

I hobbled over to it, clinging to his arm. By the time we sat down, he was already expanding on points he had covered in the lecture. He was apparently unconcerned about my obvious aging and seemed happy to talk to me.

A thought struck me forcefully. I suddenly realized that Yuri had not yet met my past self. I had never attended that first lecture, having met him just before he was to do his second. Desperately, I tried to recall the date I had given Onel, what day it was in the past.

I had not counted on this. I was jumpy, worried that I *would* change something, that by meeting Yuri in the park like this I might somehow prevent his meeting me. I shuddered. I knew little of the circumstances that had brought him to my door. I could somehow be interfering with them.

Yuri finished what he had to say and waited for my reaction. "You certainly have some interesting insights," I said. "I'm looking forward to your next lecture." I smiled and nodded, hoping that he would now leave and go about his business.

Instead he looked at me thoughtfully. "I don't know if I'll give any more lectures."

My stomach turned over. I knew he had given ten more. "Why not?" I asked as calmly as I could.

He shrugged. "A lot of reasons."

"Maybe," I said in desperation, "you should talk about it with somebody, it might help." Hurriedly I dredged up all the techniques I had learned as a Counselor, carefully questioning him, until at last he opened up and flooded me with his sorrows and worries.

He became the Yuri I remembered, an intense person who concealed his emotions under a cold, business-like exterior. He had grown tired of the city's superficiality, uncomfortable with those who grew annoyed at his seriousness and penetration. He was unsuited to the gaiety and playfulness that surrounded him, wanting to pursue whatever he did with single-minded devotion.

He looked embarrassed after telling me all this and began once more to withdraw behind his shield. "I have some tentative plans," he said calmly, regaining control. "I may be leaving here in a couple of days with one of the scientific expeditions for Mars. I prefer the company of serious people and have been offered a place on the ship."

My hands trembled. Neither of us had gone with an expedition until five years after our meeting. "I'm sorry for bothering you with my problems," he went on. "I don't usually do that to strangers, or anyone else for that matter. I'd better be on my way."

"You're not bothering me."

"Anyway, I have a lot of things to do. I appreciate the time you took to listen to me."

He stood up and prepared to walk away. No, I thought, you can't, I can't lose you like this. But then I realized something and was shocked that I hadn't thought of it before. I knew what I had to do.

"Wait!" I said. "Wait a minute. Do you think you could humor an old lady, maybe take some advice? It'll only be an hour or so of your time."

"It depends," he said stiffly.

"Before you go on that expedition, do you think you could visit a person I think might enjoy talking to you?"

He smiled. "I suppose," he said. "But I don't see what difference it makes."

"She's a lot like you. I think you'd find her sympathetic." And I told him where I lived and gave him my name. "But don't tell her an old woman sent you, she'll think I'm meddling. Just tell her it was a friend."

"I promise." He turned to leave. "Thank you, friend." I watched him as he ambled down the pebbled path that would lead him to my home.

1974/77

DORIS PISERCHIA

Pale Hands

Whom do you lead on Rapture's roadway, far,
Before you agonize them in farewell?

2021, AND what had we to show for it? Overpopulation, for
one thing. What did people see in each other? I read por-
nography by the pile, thinking I might find the answer there,
but I didn't. It cost me a great deal, that erotica, because it
was forbidden. The only way to get it was from pushers who
charged according to how expensively a buyer was dressed.
I always wore my oldest dress whenever I went on the hunt
for porno.

Everyone spent their first six years of life in the Conditioning Center in Illinois. I didn't remember what I learned there,
and no matter how much I questioned my friends, they told
me nothing about their memories or their personal lives. It
made me feel ignorant.

I cleaned masturbation stalls for a living. There must have
been millions of them. One side of Fifth Avenue was my territory, the other side belonged to Lydon. I didn't know his last
name. He came after Pisby died. Pisby was a dirty old man
who spent too much time in the stalls. With that bad heart of
his, he shouldn't have pumped his beef so much.

My best friend was Permilia. She worked in a jewelry
store on the corner of Fifth, and she always used one of my
stalls whenever she got the urge to do it. The thing that fas-

cinated me about Permilia was her hands. I mean, why make a fetish of hands? I thought about it and finally decided she removed all her rings and bracelets before getting down to business. Crude way of putting it? No cruder than saying people used to bang their heads off until they got the world so crowded it was like a can of beans. Banging. Why did they call it that? Why did some people always smear mud on the beautiful things? Wasn't it beautiful to make love? But how did they determine if they were in love or merely in a state of randiness?

Oh, well, it didn't affect me personally. I wasn't interested in sex, and as for masturbation, the stalls were just places I cleaned. Once a week I painted the walls. Every day I scoured them with ammonia, dragged the stools out onto the sidewalk and hosed them down. That was my life.

I had a one-room pad just off Fifth, a comfortable place I called home. Stall maids earned fairly good pay, so I had some modern conveniences, though not as many as Permilia. Jewelry was a very popular commodity.

Poor Pisby. He had something wrong in his head. That was where his trouble lay. His body was a pawn of his mind, and he couldn't control that, so he died. Maybe he was sick both in body and mind. Why didn't he simply quit doing it, or why didn't he find a girl? It made no sense. After all, he was nearly fifty, and nobody that age had an intense sexual urge. Had they? I couldn't say, being young and inexperienced and dead as a doornail in the beef department.

Fifth Avenue wasn't exactly crawling with queers, but now and then one ambled by. They were particularly vulnerable to the stalls, so they ought to have stayed on the few streets where there were none. For instance, a queer walks by, takes a gander at a stall and breaks his neck getting inside. According to the erotica I read, such people used to frequent park toilets, which may have been a good deal like the stalls in appearance. Anyway, I sympathized with the queers, as they were made randy as hell by their botched hormones.

Lydon. What did I think of him? He took over for Pisby, showed up one rainy day when the stink of the stalls was ruining the air. I described him to Permilia, and she laughed and said he was a virgin, like me. How could she tell? Because he didn't make a fetish of his hands. Later I recalled how she frowned and stiffened after she said that, exactly as if she had suddenly experienced a sharp pain. I asked her what she meant by the hand-fetish business, but she didn't answer, broke her neck getting away from me, and it was a week before I saw her again.

No one could live together; no roommates; no girls together, no men together, and, of course, a male and female were not permitted to share a pad. The population had to be kept down.

Permilia said Lydon must be dead in the beef department because males almost always took to the stalls in their early teens. Their bodies were too exposed to stimulation, and this made them vulnerable. Women were a step behind them. Permilia laughed as she added, "But it's a short step."

Lydon. The first time I laid eyes on him, I thought, "What a grubby little thing; but interesting."

He had a red face, and it wasn't until I got close to him that I realized the redness was acne. It wasn't bad, except at his jawline. It was unfortunate, because his face was sweetly formed. He had dark eyes and a small nose and mouth. His body was square, but too small. Well, not too small, at that. Looked at as a package of man, he wasn't unattractive.

We got off on the wrong foot right from the start. "This isn't fit work for a fellow," I said, and he took offense.

"It's what I like to do, and who says one job is for a man while another isn't?"

Plunging through the crowds, I went back to my own side of the street and figured to stay there. Tension I could do without. This man had a burr up his tail because he had a few pimples. How dumb could you get?

"You going to vote today?" he yelled at me the next morning. It was early and the sidewalks were empty.

"Nope."

Approaching the curb, he stood with his hands on his hips and scowled. "Why?"

"For what purpose should I do a dumb thing like that? You think votes make any difference? It's a con game, and I don't intend to add to the farce."

"What kind of government would we have if everyone felt that way?"

"Same kind we already got," I said.

That was all we had to say to each other that day. Toward evening, he washed up in the outdoor sink and walked away toward the voting booths. I had to laugh behind my hand. With his ass tucked in and his shoulders shoved up in the air, he looked like a stubborn little chicken. For sure, he knew I was watching him, and, for sure, his face was the color of raw mutton. One funny fellow. Except there was something sad about seeing him outlined against the dirty buildings. One leg forward, then the other leg, and his arms didn't swing too much, and he kept moving farther away from me, and for some reason I continued watching until long after he was out of sight. Lydon. I should find out his last name.

Permilia came by the next day. "What kind of men are you attracted to?" I said to her, and she gave me an odd look. "Of course, it's none of my business," I said. "I know people don't like personal questions. Only I never see you with your boyfriend. In fact, I never see any couples anywhere. Can't figure it out. Everybody is banging their head off, but I wonder where they're doing it."

"You're feeling smutty today," she said. "Could the gonads be stirring at last?"

"There are too many things I don't understand, is all. Used to be it didn't bother me, but now, well, what kind of world do we live in? I never been anywhere since Conditioning Center, other than in the orphanage. Been to fifth grade, like most people, and once in a while I take a bus to the Rally Field and listen to the election baloney, but that's hardly any experience."

"You're asking the wrong person, love. I never been anywhere, either."

"Don't you ever get curious about what's out of sight?"

"Only when I get desperate," said Permilia, and laughed.

Since I couldn't think of a response to that, I changed the subject. "Did you vote?"

"Sure."

"Who for?"

This time she merely smiled. "Sydney Lummet."

"You're kidding."

"Dammit, Vega, when are you going to grow up?"

"Why didn't you vote for Sebastian?"

"That virgin."

This was a subject I was interested in. "Lummet has something wrong with him. I mean, he's weird. I saw him once on TV, and that was too often. Let me tell you about it. First thing that happened after the screen lighted up was a close shot of his hands; nothing but his hands. He had colored noodles strung on them like Christmas ornaments. Next thing that showed was his teeth, growing big as saws, and then the next thing you knew, he started eating those damned noodles off his fingers, one at a time. Never witnessed anything like it in my life. If that business draws votes for him, I'll eat my hat."

Keeping a straight face, Permilia said, "Vega, you're the dearest friend I have. You're so innocent and stupid and sweet. Why don't you lay off subjects you don't understand? If you don't like Sydney Lummet, vote for Sebastian or don't vote at all."

She started to walk away, and I called after her. "Were you ever innocent and stupid and sweet?"

She whirled and gave me an angry stare. Suddenly her face softened, crumpled. My surprise increased as I watched her eyes glisten with quick tears. Then she hurried away from me so fast she almost ran. I lost sight of her as she shouldered her way into the crowds.

That scene made me brood for a solid week. Somehow I had hurt Permilia, and I wanted to punish myself for having done it. More, I wanted to know how and why it had happened.

I had some words with Lydon. "My name is Vega, not that you're all that interested, but since we work close together, I'm not about to go on yelling, 'Hey, you.'"

One leg to hold him up, red face, stammering; the man was bright but he was also dumb. "I wondered what it was."

"Why didn't you just ask me?"

"Wasn't wondering that much." His fingers rambled up to his face and worried a pimple.

"Don't do that," I said. "Your hands are filthy from cleaning stalls and you shouldn't be pawing your face with them. If you stopped doing—"

"Why don't you mind your own business?"

"It's obvious you can't stand me, but I may as well tell you I couldn't care less. It's only that we work almost side by side—"

"I didn't mean to say it."

"In that case, I want to ask you a question; about older women. You think maybe their nerves go with age? I have this friend—"

"I don't know anything about women."

"Aren't men pretty much the same?"

He got redder by the second. "I can't answer that."

"Why not?"

"I just told you. I don't know anything about women."

"Then I'll change the subject. Take these stalls. Why do you figure so many people use them? My clientele are regular as clockwork; two, three times a day most of them come by, and some more often than that. I can't figure out the attraction, can you?"

Lydon stiffened up like a board. When he left me and stalked into his resting booth, he was more statue than human. I tried to get another glimpse of him, but some people walked by and blocked him from my view.

I knew. He was embarrassed about sex. Shy. Set me to

wondering how old he was. He hadn't any beard to speak of, but then his hair wasn't too dark, which may have accounted for that. Probably he was my age. Two dunderheads.

Slept terribly that night, dreamed of a skeleton that had no flesh on it except in a crazy place. It kept following me around and I kept telling it to go away and leave me alone because I was dead as a doornail in the beef department. The skeleton laughed, and when I looked at its teeth I recognized it as Sydney Lummet. Instead of ordinary equipment between his legs, he had colored noodles.

The next day, Lydon brought me an eggbeater. "It's a present."

"What for?"

"Know you don't have one. They're dear on the market."

"And eggs aren't even on the market," I said.

He spoke very seriously. "You never know when one will turn up."

He went back to his side of the street, and I spent the morning alternately smiling and frowning. Permilia came by to use a stall, but she didn't speak to me.

Finished with my cleaning, I sat and snatched glimpses of Lydon between passersby. It was uncanny, but each day he seemed to be growing better-looking. How could that be? I heard first impressions were the only true ones, and when I first laid eyes on Lydon he was a grubby little mutt. Today he was no worse-looking than any of the fancy fellows who used my stalls.

Couldn't watch him in the afternoon because he sat on the curb and watched me. That pleased me. I passed time by examining the hands of my customers. The women preferred heavy jewelry; the men liked crepe streamers or thin chains that dangled free or were wrapped around the fingers. One fellow, a kook, had a thing about handcuffs. Once a day, every day, he came bursting through the mobs, stopped at the first stall, burst into tears, unlocked the cuffs on his wrists and darted inside.

"I'm sick and tired of your feeling sorry for me," I said to Permilia. It had been a week since I'd spoken to her. "You act like I'm a lamb about to be led to the slaughter. Kindly tell me what in hell is wrong with you."

"Memory. There's a piece of brain in my head that won't be laid to rest."

"You're different. Don't you like me anymore? If you don't you can be frank about it. You don't have to use my stalls out of politeness."

"You fool."

"That's easy to say. Everyone is a fool."

Quick as a wink, she changed the subject, or I thought she did. "There's a clinic on Eighth does a lot of operations free of charge."

"What kind of operations?"

"They'll lop off your beef if you ask them."

"Holy crow."

"Takes three minutes; no pain, no fuss."

"Permilia, what in the world—"

"Go over there and get it done. Right away. Today."

"There's another clinic on Ninth," I said. "It's for nuts, and you'd better get over there fast."

"Do it, sweetie," she said, and her eyes were full of tears.

"Go away. You're scaring me."

Lydon. He makes me miserable. Do I make him miserable? I hope so. There is a kind of sweetness like no other, and it only comes riding on the person of another. This sweetness worries me. It makes me despair. A pair of pants is nothing but a pair of pants. Shoulders, smelly old feet, hands, sweaty neck, hair in need of a shampoo, common face. Ordinary things. He comes out of his resting booth and everything which I am grows alert, like hair that suddenly stands on end. He looks across the street to see if I'm there, and naturally I am, and where else does he think I'd be? I'm never sick, so why look to see if I went somewhere?

The stink of the stalls saturates the air. The crowds have gone home. It is raining. I like the stink and the moans and the rain. He's over there where I can see him. The sweetness is as the steam rising from the sidewalks. Unhappy am I because it's almost quitting time, and he'll lock up his booth and walk away without saying good-bye. This business is making me sick. He sits over there, watching me all day, but seldom does he smile or say good-bye. I mean, if I'm fit to look at all day, aren't I fit for more?

"Permilia, I have a problem."

"You're alive."

"That isn't the problem."

"I'm in a hurry."

"You're getting to hate me, and I don't know what I did."

She replied, but not to me; to herself maybe. "I should have grown a shell around me, like a clam. What do I care about a dumb kid? So she'll grow up, the same as everybody else, and I should laugh. I told her to go to that clinic, but she wants to keep her button. Why? Because without the goddam thing she might as well be dead. But she'll be dead if she keeps it. What kind of a world is this?"

Sydney Lummet won the election. We had a new President

and everybody was happy. I was happy too. That old Lydon, that dumbbell, he brought me a present; a camera. I took his picture, he took mine.

"Did you vote for Lummet?" I said.

"Sebastian. I'm sorry the way the election turned out. I don't think Lummet can handle the economic crisis. Already we got too many people starving. He's an egotist. Besides, he leans too heavy toward psychology. You can't run a country on speculation, which is all psychology is."

I wasn't paying any attention to what he said. From the corner of my eye, I stared at his throat. The sun made it pink; it glistened like baby skin. Probably he looked that way all over. Next I examined his face. Common, ordinary man, except that he gave me a bellyache.

He was smiling at me. "Do you like to read?"

It was my turn to get red. "You won't laugh?"

"Of course not."

"I don't know enough to get along. You know. I'm not backward as far as brains go, but nobody ever tells me anything. How can I learn about life unless I read? So I read porno."

The smile left his face as if someone had smacked it off. His eyes grew small and narrow, and his mouth went thin. "Both of us are in the same boat. I read it too."

At noon he came over to my side of the street. We sat on the curb and had lunch together.

"What do you want to do with your life?" he said. "What is it that you have to have? I mean, what's your main interest?"

"I don't know yet."

"Me, either. I guess I'm just waiting for life to come and get me. Doesn't it work that way? We wait for death. I guess we wait for life too."

"I guess."

Permilia and I were both out of sorts. My trouble was a mystery to me. As for my friend, I planned to tell her to see a doctor, that is if I could get close enough to her. Suddenly I had the plague or something. Regular, she came to use the stalls, and regular, she kept out of my reach. From what I could see from a distance, she was steadily losing weight. Her skin looked bad. In fact, her whole appearance was haggard. Maybe she had gotten hooked on dope. I'd ask her, first chance I got.

My trouble. Awake at three every morning with my brain clicking away at the same old subject. Lydon. Why didn't he go away? So he didn't show up at work for three days. I didn't know if he had been sick. For some reason I was afraid to cross the street and ask him. Why didn't he come over and tell me where he had been? He sat in his resting booth, after he returned, and he looked as white as a sheet. Damn you, Lydon, what's wrong? Why don't you like me anymore?

Tuesday. As soon as I got to my resting booth, I knew I was in for a bellyache. I hadn't slept hardly any. The sidewalks were wet and hot, people were all over the place, the sun was a furnace, I was already sweaty, the stalls stunk to high heaven, my belly was killing me. Back in my mind, some idiot said over and over again, "Lydon, Lydon, Lydon."

"Why don't you go to hell?" I yelled.

He came out of his booth, walked to the curb, stopped. I walked to my curb, stopped. We stared across the wet street at each other. All I could see were his eyes. They went all the way down into my soul and back out again, taking my guts with them. He smiled. My belly turned over. I smiled. How serious were we that morning, two dunderheads glaring at each other as if the life we were waiting for had suddenly materialized between us. A yearning in my throat, I said, "Lydon."

"Vega." He was hurting. So was I. Neither of us knew the truth. There wasn't anyone else in the world. The planet was ours, and our togetherness tore both of us to tatters, and it was the most glorious pain there could be. I wanted to be a worm clinging to his skin. That way he couldn't leave me. I'd be hanging onto him, secretly, and he'd take me with him wherever he went.

The sun was hot between us. I had a headache.

"Vega."

The way he said it made me smile again, but my face felt as if it were going to crack. I was so happy I wanted to cry, and then I did cry a few minutes later, because Lydon didn't come across the street to me. He started to; I know that was what he intended, but he never made it. His smile was like mine, simply there to dress up a naked face, and he put one foot down onto the street, with the other foot ready to follow. His hands were stretched out toward me.

All of a sudden his face turned purple. His feet stopped moving. His body froze. His expression deadened. He turned and walked over to one of the stalls. He slammed through the door.

I bawled my eyes out. I sat on the curb and waited for him to come out so that he would see my rage. I wanted to kill him with my anger. He didn't see it. After the longest time, he popped out of the stall and ran down the street at high speed.

At three in the morning I woke up in my one-room home. Dry-eyed, I didn't fight the chunk of my brain that had developed during the past weeks. Some gift. It was a chunk of a man named Lydon. Consider him. Monster. Nothing but a beef pumper, same as everybody. Rather do that than . . . what?

What if Lydon had no mind? Say he was just a man with no will, and he was with me alone somewhere, and I could do anything to him that I wanted? Consider it. Lydon, you were so sweet. What would I do to you? You wear too many clothes. How can I see you that way? You're skin all over, and I want to look at all of it. I take off your shirt. Just as I thought; you give me a bellyache. Common, ordinary back and chest. Let me put my lips between your shoulderblades. They aren't common if they make me want to do that. Now, Lydon, puppet man, take off your pants. Not too fast, as I'm getting ill. Wait a minute, let me kiss your mouth, because I may never get around to it later. There he is, Lydon is naked as a jaybird, and since I read all that porno I know all about men.

I have made a mistake. All I intended to do was look at him.

It was four in the morning, and I came stumbling from one of my stalls. I didn't remember getting out of bed and going there, didn't remember walking through the rain. But I knew what I had done inside the stall. The first time, and now I was really sick. It had taken about fifty seconds to do the job, and I hated it. I was a monster like everyone else.

Someone came out of a stall across the street. It was Lydon. He saw me and ran away. I sat down on the curb and cried. The past came back to me, haunted me. Now I remembered what they had done to me in the Conditioning Center.

"When you hear the sound of the bell, your physical desire will be focused. You will step inside a stall and bring yourself to orgasm. You are promised a rich, full sexual life. No urge must be ignored. Sexual activity in private quarters is evil. Desire is unfocused. Sexual activity between two people is evil. Desire is unfocused. The masturbation stalls are public facilities built for your use. You have nothing to hide. Your neighbors can see that you have nothing to hide. Sex and the stalls are united in your mind. There cannot be the first without the second. First comes desire. Without the sound of the bell, desire remains unfocused. You will not be deprived of pleasure, as the sound of the bell can be heard when you pass the stalls. First comes desire. Remember that it is un-focused without the sound of the bell. Remember that the sound comes from the stalls. You must go to the stalls. When you hear the sound of the bell . . . desire is focused . . . evil is sex with another . . . no such thing as private love or sex, as you can't be trusted to obey if you are hidden away from the eyes of the world . . . someone might be with you and you might be tempted . . . rich, full life . . . many orgasms mean lack of tension and happiness . . . sex like stepping into public toilet . . . so sorry, but you've such a ravenous appetite . . . you won't be able to talk about it because your head will hurt . . . sound of bell in your head . . . not real . . . your id clamoring . . . oh, how I need a good one, or, it's a nice day and I feel energetic and mellow, oops, there goes the bell, better hop inside and enjoy my rich, full . . . that man I saw, he makes my id clamor, oops, where's the bell, where's the bell, where's the . . . he does me like no other, and all my life there will be men who send me speeding to the stalls, why don't they just cut out our eyes . . . one day I saw a human being who had the average complement of qualities, except that God meant for him to be meaningful to me, and my hands and my mind reached out for him and when I grasped him because I had to I found not him but a bell and it rang not in my hands but in my head and I wanted to scream because . . ."

It was true that the bell sounded only in my head, because never in my life did I ever hear it ring.

Sunup and I came out of a stall, and there was Permilia walking toward me. She had an axe in her hand. She went inside a stall. I heard a strange sound, and she walked outside and let the blood from the stump of her wrist leak into the gutter. Across the street, Lydon stood on the curb, crying.

"I love you, Vega," he said and went into a stall.

"I love you, Lydon," I said and went into a stall.

1974

URSULA K. LE GUIN

The Day Before the Revolution

THE SPEAKER'S voice was as loud as empty beer-trucks in a stone street, and the people at the meeting were jammed up close, cobblestones, that great voice booming over them. Taviri was somewhere on the other side of the hall. She had to get to him. She wormed and pushed her way among the dark-clothed, close-packed people. She did not hear the words, nor see the faces: only the booming, and the bodies pressed one behind the other. She could not see Taviri, she was too short. A broad black-vested belly and chest loomed up, blocking her way. She must get through to Taviri. Sweating, she jabbed fiercely with her fist. It was like hitting stone, he did not move at all, but the huge lungs let out right over her head a prodigious noise, a bellow. She cowered. Then she understood that the bellow had not been at her. Others were shouting. The speaker had said something, something fine about taxes or shadows. Thrilled, she joined the shouting—"Yes! Yes!" —and shoving on, came out easily into the open expanse of the Regimental Drill Field in Parheo. Overhead the evening sky lay deep and colorless, and all around her nodded the tall weeds with dry, white, close-floreted heads. She had never known what they were called. The flowers nodded above her head, swaying in the wind that always blew across the fields in the dusk. She ran among them, and they whipped lithe aside and stood up again swaying, silent. Taviri stood among the tall weeds in his good suit, the dark grey one that made him look like a professor or a play-actor, harshly elegant. He did not look happy, but he was laughing, and saying something to her. The sound of his voice made her cry, and she reached out to catch hold of his hand, but she did not stop, quite. She could not stop. "Oh, Taviri," she said, "it's just on there!" The queer sweet smell of the white weeds was heavy as she went on. There were thorns, tangles underfoot, there were slopes, pits. She feared to fall, to fall, she stopped.

Sun, bright morning-glare, straight in the eyes, relentless. She had forgotten to pull the blind last night. She turned her back on the sun, but the right side wasn't comfortable. No use. Day. She sighed twice, sat up, got her legs over the edge of the bed, and sat hunched in her nightdress looking down at her feet.

The toes, compressed by a lifetime of cheap shoes, were almost square where they touched each other, and bulged out above in corns; the nails were discolored and shapeless. Between the knob-like anklebones ran fine, dry wrinkles. The brief little plain at the base of the toes had kept its delicacy, but the skin was the color of mud, and knotted veins crossed the instep. Disgusting. Sad, depressing. Mean. Pitiful. She tried on all the words, and they all fit, like hideous little hats. Hideous: yes, that one too. To look at oneself and find it hideous, what a job! But then, when she hadn't been hideous, had she sat around and stared at herself like this? Not much! A proper body's not an object, not an implement, not a belonging to be admired, it's just you, yourself. Only when it's no longer you, but yours, a thing owned, do you worry about it—Is it in good shape? Will it do? Will it last?

"Who cares?" said Laia fiercely, and stood up.

It made her giddy to stand up suddenly. She had to put out

her hand to the bed-table, for she dreaded falling. At that she thought of reaching out to Taviri, in the dream.

What had he said? She could not remember. She was not sure if she had even touched his hand. She frowned, trying to force memory. It had been so long since she had dreamed about Taviri; and now not even to remember what he had said!

It was gone, it was gone. She stood there hunched in her nightdress, frowning, one hand on the bed-table. How long was it since she had thought of him—let alone dreamed of him—even thought of him, as "Taviri"? How long since she had said his name?

Asieo said. When Asieo and I were in prison in the North. Before I met Asieo. Asieo's theory of reciprocity. Oh yes, she talked about him, talked about him too much no doubt, maundered, dragged him in. But as "Asieo," the last name, the public man. The private man was gone, utterly gone. There were so few left who had even known him. They had all used to be in jail. One laughed about it in those days, all the friends in all the jails. But they weren't even there, these days. They were in the prison cemeteries. Or in the common graves.

"Oh, oh my dear," Laia said out loud, and she sank down onto the bed again because she could not stand up under the remembrance of those first weeks in the Fort, in the cell, those first weeks of the nine years in the Fort in Drio, in the cell, those first weeks after they told her that Asieo had been killed in the fighting in Capitol Square and had been buried with the Fourteen Hundred in the lime-ditches behind Oring Gate. In the cell. Her hands fell into the old position on her lap, the left clenched and locked inside the grip of the right, the right thumb working back and forth a little pressing and rubbing on the knuckle of the left first finger. Hours, days, nights. She had thought of them all, each one, each one of the Fourteen Hundred, how they lay, how the quicklime worked on the flesh, how the bones touched in the burning dark. Who touched him? How did the slender bones of the hand lie now? Hours, years.

"Taviri, I have never forgotten you!" she whispered, and the stupidity of it brought her back to morning light and the rumpled bed. Of course she hadn't forgotten him. These things go without saying between husband and wife. There were her ugly old feet flat on the floor again, just as before. She had got nowhere at all, she had gone in a circle. She stood up with a grunt of effort and disapproval, and went to the closet for her dressing gown.

The young people went about the halls of the House in becoming immodesty, but she was too old for that. She didn't want to spoil some young man's breakfast with the sight of her. Besides, they had grown up in the principle of freedom of dress and sex and all the rest, and she hadn't. All she had done was invent it. It's not the same.

Like speaking of Asieo as "my husband." They winced. The word she should use as a good Odonian, of course, was "partner." But why the hell did she have to be a good Odonian?

She shuffled down the hall to the bathrooms. Mairo was there, washing her hair in a lavatory. Laia looked at the long, sleek, wet hank with admiration. She got out of the House so seldom now that she didn't know when she had last seen a respectably shaven scalp, but still the sight of a full head of hair gave her pleasure, vigorous pleasure. How many times had she been jeered at, *Longhair, Longhair*, had her hair pulled by policemen or young toughs, had her hair shaved off down to the scalp by a grinning soldier at each new prison? And then had grown it all over again, through the fuzz, to the frizz, to the curls, to the mane. . . . In the old days. For God's love, couldn't she think of anything today but the old days?

Dressed, her bed made, she went down to commons. It was a good breakfast, but she had never got her appetite back since the damned stroke. She drank two cups of herb tea, but couldn't finish the piece of fruit she had taken. How she had craved fruit as a child badly enough to steal it; and in the Fort—oh, for God's love stop it! She smiled and replied to the greetings and friendly inquiries of the other breakfasters and big Aevi who was serving the counter this morning. It was he who had tempted her with the peach, "Look at this, I've been saving it for you," and how could she refuse? Anyway she had always loved fruit, and never got enough; once when she was six or seven she had stolen a piece off a vendor's cart in River Street. But it was hard to eat when everyone was talking so excitedly. There was news from Thu, real news. She was inclined to discount it at first, being wary of enthusiasms, but after she had read the article in the paper, and read between the lines of it, she thought, with a strange kind of certainty, deep but cold, Why, this is it; it has come. And in Thu, not here. Thu will break before this country does; the Revolution will first prevail there. As if that mattered! There will be no more nations. And yet it did matter somehow, it made her a little cold and sad—envious, in fact. Of all the infinite stupidities. She did not join in the talk much, and soon got up to go back to her room, feeling sorry for herself. She could not share their excitement. She was out of it, really out of it. It's not easy, she said to herself in justification, laboriously climbing the stairs, to accept being out of it when you've been in it, in the center of it, for fifty years. Oh, for God's love. Whining!

She got the stairs and the self-pity behind her, entering her room. It was a good room, and it was good to be by herself. It was a great relief. Even if it wasn't strictly fair. Some of the kids in the attics were living five to a room no bigger than this. There were always more people wanting to live in an Odonian House than could be properly accommodated. She had this big room all to herself only because she was an old woman who had had a stroke. And maybe because she was Odo. If she hadn't been Odo, but merely the old woman with a stroke, would she have had it? Very likely. After all, who the hell wanted to room with a drooling old woman? But it was hard to be sure. Favoritism, elitism, leader-worship, they crept back and cropped out everywhere. But she had never hoped to see them eradicated in her lifetime, in one generation; only Time works the great changes. Meanwhile this was a nice, large, sunny room, proper for a drooling old woman who had started a world revolution.

Her secretary would be coming in an hour to help her despatch the day's work. She shuffled over to the desk, a beautiful, big piece, a present from the Nio Cabinetmakers' Syndicate because somebody had heard her remark once that the only piece of furniture she had ever really longed for was a desk with drawers and enough room on top . . . damn, the top was practically covered with papers with notes clipped to them, mostly in Noi's small clear handwriting: Urgent.— Northern Provinces.—Consult w/R. T.?

Her own handwriting had never been the same since Asieo's death. It was odd, when you thought about it. After all, within five years after his death she had written the whole *Analogy*. And there were those letters, which the tall guard with the watery grey eyes, what was his name, never mind, had smuggled out of the Fort for her for two years. *The Prison Letters* they called them now, there were a dozen different editions of them. All that stuff, the letters which people kept telling her were so full of "spiritual strength"—which probably meant she had been lying herself blue in the face when she wrote them, trying to keep her spirits up—and the *Analogy* which was certainly the solidest intellectual work she had ever done, all of that had been written in the Fort in Drio, in the cell, after Asieo's death. One had to do something, and in the Fort they let one have paper and pens. . . . But it had all been written in the hasty, scribbling hand which she had never felt was hers, not her own like the round, black scrollings of the manuscript of *Society Without Government*, forty-five years old. Taviri had taken not only her body's and her heart's desire to the quicklime with him, but even her good clear handwriting.

But he had left her the Revolution.

How brave of you to go on, to work, to write, in prison, after such a defeat for the Movement, after your partner's death, people had used to say. Damn fools. What else had there been to do? Bravery, courage—what was courage? She had never figured it out. Not fearing, some said. Fearing yet going on, others said. But what could one do but go on? Had one any real choice, ever?

To die was merely to go on in another direction.

If you wanted to come home you had to keep going on, that was what she meant when she wrote "True journey is return," but it had never been more than an intuition, and she was farther than ever now from being able to rationalize it. She bent down, too suddenly, so that she grunted a little at the creak in her bones, and began to root in a bottom drawer of the desk. Her hand came on an age-softened folder and drew it out, recognizing it by touch before sight confirmed: the manuscript of *Syndical Organization in Revolutionary Transition*. He had printed the title on the folder and written his name under it, Taviri Odo Asieo, IX 741. There was an elegant handwriting, every letter well-formed, bold, and fluent. But he had preferred to use a voiceprinter. The manuscript was all in voiceprint, and high quality too, hesitancies adjusted and idiosyncrasies of speech normalized. You couldn't see there how he had said "o" deep in his throat as they did on the North Coast. There was nothing of him there but his mind. She had nothing of him at all except his name written on the folder. She hadn't kept his letters, it was sentimental to keep letters. Besides, she never kept anything. She couldn't think of anything that she had ever owned for more than a few years, except this ramshackle old body, of course, and she was stuck with that. . . .

Dualizing again. "She" and "it." Age and illness made one dualist, made one escapist; the mind insisted, *It's not me, it's not me*. But it was. Maybe the mystics could detach mind from body, she had always rather wistfully envied them the chance, without hope of emulating them. Escape had never been her game. She had sought for freedom here, now, body and soul.

First self-pity, then self-praise, and here she still sat, for God's love, holding Asieo's name in her hand, why? Didn't she know his name without looking it up? What was wrong with her? She raised the folder to her lips and kissed the handwritten name firmly and squarely, replaced the folder in the back of the bottom drawer, shut the drawer, and straightened up in the chair. Her right hand tingled. She scratched it, and then shook it in the air, spitefully. It had never quite got over the stroke. Neither had her right leg, or right eye, or the right corner of her mouth. They were sluggish, inept, they tingled. They made her feel like a robot with a short circuit.

And time was getting on, Noi would be coming, what had she been doing ever since breakfast?

She got up so hastily that she lurched, and grabbed at the chair-back to make sure she did not fall. She went down the hall to the bathroom and looked in the big mirror there. Her grey knot was loose and droopy, she hadn't done it up well before breakfast. She struggled with it a while. It was hard to keep her arms up in the air. Amai, running in to piss, stopped and said, "Let me do it!" and knotted it up tight and neat in no time, with her round, strong, pretty fingers, smiling and silent. Amai was twenty, less than a third of Laia's age. Her parents had both been members of the Movement, one killed in the insurrection of '60, the other still recruiting in the South Provinces. Amai had grown up in Odonian Houses, born to the Revolution, a true daughter of anarchy. And so quiet and free and beautiful a child, enough to make you cry when you thought: this is what we worked for, this is what we meant, this is it, here she is, alive, the kindly, lovely future.

Laia Asieo Odo's right eye wept several little tears, as she stood between the lavatories and the latrines having her hair done up by the daughter she had not borne; but her left eye, the strong one, did not weep, nor did it know what the right eye did.

She thanked Amai and hurried back to her room. She had

noticed, in the mirror, a stain on her collar. Peach juice, probably. Damned old dribbler. She didn't want Noi to come in and find her with drool on her collar.

As the clean shirt went on over her head, she thought, What's so special about Noi?

She fastened the collar-frogs with her left hand, slowly.

Noi was thirty or so, a slight, muscular fellow with a soft voice and alert dark eyes. That's what was special about Noi. It was that simple. Good old sex. She had never been drawn to a fair man or a fat one, or the tall fellows with big biceps, never, not even when she was fourteen and fell in love with every passing fart. Dark, spare, and fiery, that was the recipe. Taviri, of course. This boy wasn't a patch on Taviri for brains, nor even for looks, but there it was: she didn't want him to see her with dribble on her collar and her hair coming undone.

Her thin, grey hair.

Noi came in, just pausing in the open doorway—my God, she hadn't even shut the door while changing her shirt! She looked at him and saw herself. The old woman.

You could brush your hair and change your shirt, or you could wear last week's shirt and last night's braids, or you could put on cloth of gold and dust your shaven scalp with diamond powder. None of it would make the slightest difference. The old woman would look a little less, or a little more, grotesque.

One keeps oneself neat out of mere decency, mere sanity, awareness of other people.

And finally even that goes, and one dribbles unashamed.

"Good morning," the young man said in his gentle voice.

"Hello, Noi."

No, by God, it was *not* out of mere decency. Decency be

228 | Ursula K. Le Guin

damned. Because the man she had loved, and to whom her
age would not have mattered—because he was dead, must
she pretend she had no sex? Must she suppress the truth,
like a damned puritan authoritarian? Even six months ago,
before the stroke, she had made men look at her and like to
look at her; and now, though she could give no pleasure, by
God she could please herself.

When she was six years old, and Papa's friend Gadeo used
to come by to talk politics with Papa after dinner, she would
put on the gold-colored necklace that Mama had found on a
trash heap and brought home for her. It was so short that it
always got hidden under her collar where nobody could see
it. She liked it that way. She knew she had it on. She sat on the
doorstep and listened to them talk, and knew that she looked
nice for Gadeo. He was dark, with white teeth that flashed.
Sometimes he called her "pretty Laia." "There's my pretty
Laia!" Sixty-six years ago.

"What? My head's dull. I had a terrible night." It was true.
She had slept even less than usual.

"I was asking if you'd seen the papers this morning."

She nodded.

"Pleased about Soinehe?"

Soinehe was the province in Thu which had declared its
secession from the Thuvian State last night.

He was pleased about it. His white teeth flashed in his
dark, alert face. Pretty Laia.

"Yes. And apprehensive."

"I know. But it's the real thing, this time. It's the beginning
of the end of the Government in Thu. They haven't even tried
to order troops into Soinehe, you know. It would merely pro-
voke the soldiers into rebellion sooner, and they know it."

She agreed with him. She herself had felt that certainty. But she could not share his delight. After a lifetime of living on hope because there is nothing but hope, one loses the taste for victory. A real sense of triumph must be preceded by real despair. She had unlearned despair a long time ago. There were no more triumphs. One went on.

"Shall we do those letters today?"

"All right. Which letters?"

"To the people in the North," he said without impatience.

"In the North?"

"Parheo, Oaidun."

She had been born in Parheo, the dirty city on the dirty river. She had not come here to the capital till she was twenty-two and ready to bring the Revolution. Though in those days, before she and the others had thought it through, it had been a very green and puerile revolution. Strikes for better wages, representation for women. Votes and wages—Power and Money, for the love of God! Well, one does learn a little, after all, in fifty years.

But then one must forget it all.

"Start with Oaidun," she said, sitting down in the armchair. Noi was at the desk ready to work. He read out excerpts from the letters she was to answer. She tried to pay attention, and succeeded well enough that she dictated one whole letter and started on another. "Remember that at this stage your brotherhood is vulnerable to the threat of . . . no, to the danger . . . to . . ." She groped till Noi suggested, "The danger of leader-worship?"

"All right. And that nothing is so soon corrupted by power-seeking as altruism. No. And that nothing corrupts altruism—no. O for God's love you know what I'm trying to say,

Noi, you write it. They know it too, it's just the same old stuff, why can't they read my books!"

"Touch," Noi said gently, smiling, citing one of the central Odonian themes.

"All right, but I'm tired of being touched. If you'll write the letter I'll sign it, but I can't be bothered with it this morning." He was looking at her with a little question or concern. She said, irritable, "There is something else I have to do!"

When Noi had gone she sat down at the desk and moved the papers about, pretending to be doing something, because she had been startled, frightened, by the words she had said. She had nothing else to do. She never had had anything else to do. This was her work: her lifework. The speaking tours and the meetings and the streets were out of reach for her now, but she could still write, and that was her work. And anyhow if she had had anything else to do, Noi would have known it; he kept her schedule, and tactfully reminded her of things, like the visit from the foreign students this afternoon.

Oh, damn. She liked the young, and there was always something to learn from a foreigner, but she was tired of new faces, and tired of being on view. She learned from them, but they didn't learn from her; they had learnt all she had to teach long ago, from her books, from the Movement. They just came to look, as if she were the Great Tower in Rodarred, or the Canyon of the Tulaevea. A phenomenon, a monument. They were awed, adoring. She snarled at them: Think your own thoughts!—That's not anarchism, that's mere obscurantism.—You don't think liberty and discipline are incompatible, do you?—They accepted their tongue-lashing meekly as children, gratefully, as if she were some kind of All-Mother, the idol of the Big Sheltering Womb. She! She who had mined the shipyards at Seissero, and had cursed Premier Inoilte to his face in front of a crowd of seven thousand, telling him he would have cut off his own balls and had them bronzed and sold as souvenirs, if he thought there was any profit in it—she who had screeched, and sworn, and kicked policemen, and spat at priests, and pissed in public on the big brass plaque in Capitol Square that said HERE WAS FOUNDED THE SOVEREIGN NATION STATE OF A–IO ETC ETC, pssssssssss to all that! And now she was everybody's grandmama, the dear old lady, the sweet old monument, come worship at the womb. The fire's out, boys, it's safe to come up close.

"No, I won't," Laia said out loud. "I will not." She was not self-conscious about talking to herself, because she always had talked to herself. "Laia's invisible audience," Taviri had used to say, as she went through the room muttering. "You needn't come, I won't be here," she told the invisible audience now. She had just decided what it was she had to do. She had to go out. To go into the streets.

It was inconsiderate to disappoint the foreign students. It was erratic, typically senile. It was unOdonian. Pssssssss to all that. What was the good working for freedom all your life and ending up without any freedom at all? She would go out for a walk.

"*What is an anarchist? One who, choosing, accepts the responsibility of choice.*"

On the way downstairs she decided, scowling, to stay and see the foreign students. But then she would go out.

They were very young students, very earnest: doe-eyed, shaggy, charming creatures from the Western Hemisphere, Benbili and the Kingdom of Mand, the girls in white trousers, the boys in long kilts, warlike and archaic. They spoke of their hopes. "We in Mand are so very far from the Revolution that maybe we are near it," said one of the girls, wistful and smiling: "The Circle of Life!" and she showed the extremes meeting, in the circle of her slender, dark-skinned fingers. Amai and Aevi served them white wine and brown bread, the hospitality of the House. But the visitors, unpresumptuous, all rose to take their leave after barely half an hour. "No, no, no," Laia said, "stay here, talk with Aevi and Amai. It's just that I get stiff sitting down, you see, I have to change about. It has been so good to meet you, will you come back to see me, my little brothers and sisters, soon?" For her heart went out to them, and theirs to her, and she exchanged kisses all round, laughing, delighted by the dark young cheeks, the affectionate eyes, the scented hair, before she shuffled off. She was really a little tired, but to go up and take a nap would be a defeat. She had wanted to go out. She would go out. She had not been alone outdoors since—when? Since winter! before the stroke. No wonder she was getting morbid. It had been a regular jail sentence. Outside, the streets, that's where she lived.

She went quietly out the side door of the House, past the vegetable patch, to the street. The narrow strip of sour city dirt had been beautifully gardened and was producing a fine crop of beans and ceëa, but Laia's eye for farming was unenlightened. Of course it had been clear that anarchist communities, even in the time of transition, must work towards optimal self-support, but how that was to be managed in the way of actual dirt and plants wasn't her business. There were farmers and agronomists for that. Her job was the streets, the noisy, stinking streets of stone, where she had grown up and lived all her life, except for the fifteen years in prison.

She looked up fondly at the façade of the House. That it had been built as a bank gave peculiar satisfaction to its present occupants. They kept their sacks of meal in the bomb-proof money-vault, and aged their cider in kegs in safe deposit boxes. Over the fussy columns that faced the street carved letters still read, "National Investors and Grain Factors Banking Association." The Movement was not strong on names. They had no flag. Slogans came and went as the need did. There was always the Circle of Life to scratch on walls and pavements where Authority would have to see it. But when it came to names they were indifferent, accepting and ignoring whatever they got called, afraid of being pinned down and penned in, unafraid of being absurd. So this best known and second oldest of all the cooperative Houses had no name except The Bank.

It faced on a wide and quiet street, but only a block away began the Temeba, an open market, once famous as a center for black-market psychogenics and teratogenics, now reduced to vegetables, secondhand clothes, and miserable sideshows. Its crapulous vitality was gone, leaving only half-paralyzed alcoholics, addicts, cripples, hucksters, and fifth-rate whores, pawnshops, gambling dens, fortune-tellers, body-sculptors, and cheap hotels. Laia turned to the Temeba as water seeks its level.

She had never feared or despised the city. It was her country. There would not be slums like this, if the Revolution prevailed. But there would be misery. There would always be misery, waste, cruelty. She had never pretended to be changing the human condition, to be Mama taking tragedy away from the children so they won't hurt themselves. Anything but. So long as people were free to choose, if they chose to drink flybane and live in sewers, it was their business. Just so long as it wasn't the business of Business, the source of profit and the means of power for other people. She had felt all that before she knew anything; before she wrote the first pamphlet, before she left Parheo, before she knew what "capital" meant, before she'd been farther than River Street where she played rolltaggie kneeling on scabby knees on the pavement with the other six-year-olds, she had known it: that she, and the other kids, and her parents, and their parents, and the drunks and whores and all of River Street, were at the bottom of something—were the foundation, the reality, the source. But will you drag civilization down into the mud? cried the shocked decent people, later on, and she had tried for years to explain to them that if all you had was mud, then if you were God you made it into human beings, and if you were human you tried to make it into houses where human beings could live. But nobody who thought he was better than mud would understand. Now, water seeking its level, mud to mud, Laia shuffled through the foul, noisy street, and all the ugly weakness of her old age was at home. The sleepy whores, their lacquered hair-arrangements dilapidated and askew, the one-eyed woman wearily yelling her vegetables to sell, the half-wit beggar slapping flies, these were her country-women. They looked like her, they were all sad, disgusting, mean, pitiful, hideous. They were her sisters, her own people.

She did not feel very well. It had been a long time since she had walked so far, four or five blocks, by herself, in the noise and push and striking summer heat of the streets. She had wanted to get to Koly Park, the triangle of scruffy grass at the end of the Temeba, and sit there for a while with the other old men and women who always sat there, to see what

it was like to sit there and be old; but it was too far. If she
didn't turn back now, she might get a dizzy spell, and she had
a dread of falling down, falling down and having to lie there
and look up at the people come to stare at the old woman in
a fit. She turned and started home, frowning with effort and
self-disgust. She could feel her face very red, and a swimming feeling came and went in her ears. It got a bit much,
she was really afraid she might keel over. She saw a doorstep
in the shade and made for it, let herself down cautiously, sat,
sighed.

Nearby was a fruit-seller, sitting silent behind his dusty,
withered stock. People went by. Nobody bought from him.
Nobody looked at her. Odo, who was Odo? Famous revolutionary, author of *Community*, *The Analogy*, etc. etc. She,
who was she? An old woman with grey hair and a red face
sitting on a dirty doorstep in a slum, muttering to herself.

True? Was that she? Certainly it was what anybody passing
her saw. But was it she, herself, any more than the famous
revolutionary, etc., was? No. It was not. But who was she,
then?

The one who loved Taviri.

Yes. True enough. But not enough. That was gone; he had
been dead so long.

"Who am I?" Laia muttered to her invisible audience, and
they knew the answer and told it to her with one voice. She
was the little girl with scabby knees, sitting on the doorstep
staring down through the dirty golden haze of River Street in
the heat of late summer, the six-year-old, the sixteen-year-
old, the fierce, cross, dream-ridden girl, untouched, un-
touchable. She was herself. Indeed she had been the tireless
worker and thinker, but a blood clot in a vein had taken that

woman away from her. Indeed she had been the lover, the swimmer in the midst of life, but Taviri, dying, had taken that woman away with him. There was nothing left, really, but the foundation. She had come home; she had never left home. "True voyage is return." Dust and mud and a doorstep in the slums. And beyond, at the far end of the street, the field full of tall dry weeds blowing in the wind as night came.

"Laia! What are you doing here? Are you all right?"

One of the people from the House, of course, a nice woman, a bit fanatical and always talking. Laia could not remember her name though she had known her for years. She let herself be taken home, the woman talking all the way. In the big cool common room (once occupied by tellers counting money behind polished counters supervised by armed guards) Laia sat down in a chair. She was unable just as yet to face climbing the stairs, though she would have liked to be alone. The woman kept on talking, and other excited people came in. It appeared that a demonstration was being planned. Events in Thu were moving so fast that the mood here had caught fire, and something must be done. Day after tomorrow, no, tomorrow, there was to be a march, a big one, from Old Town to Capitol Square—the old route. "Another Ninth Month Uprising," said a young man, fiery and laughing, glancing at Laia. He had not even been born at the time of the Ninth Month Uprising, it was all history to him. Now he wanted to make some history of his own. The room had filled up. A general meeting would be held here, tomorrow, at eight in the morning. "You must talk, Laia."

"Tomorrow? Oh, I won't be here tomorrow," she said brusquely. Whoever had asked her smiled, another one laughed, though Amai glanced round at her with a puzzled look. They went on talking and shouting. The Revolution. What on earth had made her say that? What a thing to say on the eve of the Revolution, even if it was true.

She waited her time, managed to get up and, for all her clumsiness, to slip away unnoticed among the people busy with their planning and excitement. She got to the hall, to the stairs, and began to climb them one by one. "The general strike," a voice, two voices, ten voices were saying in the room below, behind her. "The general strike," Laia muttered, resting for a moment on the landing. Above, ahead, in her room, what awaited her? The private stroke. That was mildly funny. She started up the second flight of stairs, one by one, one leg at a time, like a small child. She was dizzy, but she was no longer afraid to fall. On ahead, on there, the dry white flowers nodded and whispered in the open fields of evening. Seventy-two years and she had never had time to learn what they were called.

1974

ELEANOR ARNASON

The Warlord of Saturn's Moons

HERE I AM, a silver-haired maiden lady of thirty-five, a feeder of stray cats, a window-ledge gardener, well on my way to the African violet and antimacassar stage. I can see myself at fifty, fat and a little crazy, making cucumber sandwiches for tea, and I view my future with mixed feelings. Whatever became of my childhood ambitions: joining the space patrol; winning a gold medal at the olympics; climbing Mount Everest alone in my bathing suit, sustained only by my indomitable will and strange psychic arts learned from Hindu mystics? The saddest words of tongue or pen are something-or-other that might have been, I think. I light up a cigar and settle down to write another chapter of *The Warlord of Saturn's Moons*. A filthy habit you say, though I'm not sure if you're referring to smoking cigars or writing science fiction. True, I reply, but both activities are pleasurable, and we maiden ladies lead lives that are notoriously short on pleasure.

So back I go to the domes of Titan and my red-headed heroine deathraying down the warlord's minions. Ah, the smell of burning flesh, the spectacle of blackened bodies collapsing. Even on paper it gets a lot of hostility out of you, so that your nights aren't troubled by dreams of murder. Terribly unrestful, those midnight slaughters and waking shaking in the darkness, your hands still feeling pressure from grabbing the victim or fighting off the murderer.

Another escape! In a power-sledge, my heroine races across Titan's methane snow, and I go and make myself tea. There's a paper on the kitchen table, waiting to tell me all about yesterday's arsons, rapes and bloody murders. Quickly I stuff it into the garbage pail. Outside, the sky is hazy. Another high-pollution day, I think. I can see incinerator smoke rising from the apartment building across the street, which means there's no air alert yet. Unless, of course, they're breaking the law over there. I fling open a cabinet and survey the array of teas. Earl Grey? I ponder, or Assam? Gunpowder? Jasmine? Gen Mai Cha? Or possibly a herb tea: sassafras, mint, Irish moss or mu. Deciding on Assam, I put water on, then go back to write an exciting chase through the icy Titanian mountains. A pursuer's sledge goes over a precipice and, as my heroine hears his long shriek on her radio, my tea kettle starts shrieking. I hurry into the kitchen. Now I go through the tea-making ceremony: pouring boiling water into the pot, sloshing the water around and pouring it out, measuring the tea in, pouring more boiling water on top of the tea. All the while my mind is with my heroine, smiling grimly as she pilots the power-sledge between bare cliffs. Above her in the dark sky is the huge crescent of Saturn, a shining white line slashing across it—the famous Rings. While the tea steeps, I wipe off a counter and wash a couple of mugs. I resist a sudden impulse to pull the newspaper out from among the used tea leaves and orange peelings. I already know what's in it. The Detroit murder count will exceed 1,000 again this year; the war in Thailand is going strong; most of Europe is out on strike. I'm far better off on Titan with my heroine, who is better able to deal with her problems than I am to deal with mine. A deadly shot, she has also learned strange psychic arts from Hindu mystics, which give her great strength, endurance, mental alertness and a naturally pleasant body odor. I wipe my hands and look at them, noticing the bitten fingernails, the torn cuticles. My heroine's long, slender, strong hands have two-inch nails filed to a point and covered with a plastic paint that makes them virtually unbreakable. When necessary, she uses them as claws. Her cuticles, of course, are in perfect condition.

I pour myself a cup of tea and return to the story. Now my heroine is heading for the mountain hideout where her partner waits: a tall, thin, dour fellow with one shining steel prosthetic hand. She doesn't know his name and she suspects he himself may have forgotten it. He insists on being called 409, his number on the prison asteroid from which he has escaped. She drives as quickly as she dares, thinking of his long face, burned almost black by years of strong radiation on Mars and in space, so the white webbing of scars on its right side shows up clearly. His eyes are grey, so pale they seem almost colorless. As I write about 409, I find myself stirred by the same passion that stirs my heroine. I begin to feel uneasy, so I stop and drink some tea. I can see I'm going to have trouble with 409. It's never wise to get too involved with one's characters. Besides, I'm not his type. I imagine the way he'd look at me, indifference evident on his dark, scarred face. I could, of course, kill him off. My heroine would then spend the rest of the story avenging him, though she'd never get to the real murderer—me. But this solution, while popular among writers, is unfair.

I go into the kitchen, extract a carrot from a bunch in the icebox, clean it and eat it. After that, I write the heroine's reunion with 409. Neither of them is demonstrative. They greet each other with apparent indifference and retire to bed. I skip the next scene. How can I watch that red-headed hussy in bed with the man I'm beginning to love? I continue the story at the moment when their alarm bell rings, and they awake to find the warlord's rocket planes have landed all around their hideout. A desperate situation! 409 suggests that he make a run for it in their rocket plane. While the warlord's minions pursue him, my heroine can sneak away in the power-sledge. The plan has little chance of success, but they can think of none better. They bid farewell to one another, and my heroine goes to wait in the sledge for the signal telling her 409 has taken off. As she waits, smoking a cigar, she thinks of what little she knows about 409. He was a fighter pilot in the war against the Martian colony and was shot down and captured. While in prison something happened to him that he either can't remember or refuses to talk about, and, when the war ended and he was released, he became a criminal. As for herself, she had been an ordinary sharpshooter and student of Hindu mysticism, a follower of Swami Bluestone of the Brooklyn Vedic Temple and Rifle Range. Then she discovered by accident the warlord's plot to overthrow the government of Titan, the only one of Saturn's satellites not under his control. With her information about the plot, the government may still be saved. She has to get to Titan City with the microfilm dot!

The alarm bell rings, and she feels the ground shake as 409's plane takes off. Unfortunately I'm writing the story from my heroine's point of view. I want to describe 409 blasting off, the warlord's rocket planes taking off after him, chasing him as he flies through the narrow, twisting valleys, the planes' rockets flaring red in the valley shadows and missiles exploding into yellow fireballs. All through this, of course, 409's scarred face remains tranquil and his hands move quickly and surely over the plane's controls. His steel prosthetic hand gleams in the dim light from the dials. But I can't put this in the story, since my heroine sees none of it as she slides off in the opposite direction, down a narrow trail hidden by overhanging cliffs.

I am beginning to feel tense, I don't know why. Possibly 409's dilemma is disturbing me. He's certainly in danger. In any case, my tea is cold. I turn on the radio, hoping for some relaxing rock music and go to get more tea. But it's twenty to the hour, time for the news, and I get the week-end body count: two men found dead in suspected westside dope house, naked body of woman dragged out of Detroit River. I hurry back and switch to a country music station. On it, someone's singing about how he intends to leave the big city and go back down south. As I go back into the kitchen, I think:

> Carry me back to Titan.
> That's where I want to be.
> I want to repose
> On the methane snows
> At the edge of a frozen sea.

I pour out the old tea and refill the cup with tea that's hot.

The radio begins to make that awful beepity-beep-beepity sound that warns you the news is coming up. I switch back to the rock station, where the news is now over. I'm safe for an-other fifty-five minutes, unless there's a special news flash to announce a five-car pile-up or an especially ghastly murder.

The plan works! For my heroine, at least. She doesn't know

yet if 409 got away. She speeds off unpursued. The power-sledge's heating system doesn't quite keep her warm, and the landscape around her is forbidding: bare cliffs and narrow valleys full of methane snow, overhead the dark blue sky. Saturn has set, and the tiny sun is rising, though she can't see it yet. On the high mountains the ice fields begin to glitter with its light. On she races, remembering how she met 409 in the slums of The Cup on Ganymede, as she fled the warlord's assassins. She remembers being cornered with no hope of escape. Then behind the two assassins a tall figure appeared and the shining steel hand smashed down on the back of one assassin's head. As the other assassin turned, he got the hand across his face. A moment or two more, and both the assassins were on the ground, unconscious. Then she saw 409's twisted grin for the first time and his colorless eyes appraising her.

There I go, I think, getting all heated up over 409. The radio is beginning to bother me, so I shut it off and re-light my cigar. I find myself wishing that men like 409 really existed. Increasingly in recent years, I've found real men boring. Is it possible, as some scientists argue, that the Y chromosome produces an inferior human being? There certainly seem to be far fewer interesting men than interesting women. But theories arguing that one kind of human being is naturally inferior make me anxious. I feel my throat muscles tightening and the familiar tense, numb feeling spreading across my face and my upper back. Quickly I return to my story.

Now out on the snowy plain, my heroine can see the transparent domes of Titan City ahead of her, shining in the pale sunlight. Inside the domes the famous pastel towers rise, their windows reflecting the sun. Her power-sledge speeds down the road, through the drifts that half cover it. Snow sprays up on either side of the sledge, so my heroine has trouble seeing to the left and right. As a result, it's some time before she sees the power-sledges coming up behind her on the right. At the same moment that she looks over and sees them, their sleek silver bodies shining in the sunlight and snow-sprays shooting up around them, her radio begins to go beep-beep-beep. She flicks it on. The voice of Janos Black, the warlord's chief agent on Titan, harsh and slurred by a thick Martian accent, tells her the bad news: 409's plane has been shot down. He ejected before it crashed. Even now the warlord's men are going after the ejection capsule, which is high on a cliff, wedged between a rock spire and the cliff wall. Janos offers her a trade: 409 for the microdot. But Janos may well be lying; 409 may have gotten away or else been blown up. She feels a sudden constriction of her throat at the thought of 409 dead. She flicks off the radio and pushes the power-sledge up to top speed. She realizes as she does so that 409 is unlikely to fare well if Janos gets ahold of him. Janos' wife and children died of thirst after the great Martian network of pipelines was blown apart by Earther bombs, and Janos knows that 409 was a pilot in the Earther expeditionary force.

I write another exciting chase, this one across the snowy plain toward the pink, green, blue and yellow towers of Titan City. The warlord's power-sledges are gaining. Their rockets hit all around my heroine's sledge, and fire and black smoke erupt out of the snow. Swearing in a low monotone, she swings the sledge back and forth in a zig-zag evasive pattern.

I stop to puff on my cigar and discover it's gone out again. My tea is cold. But the story's beginning at last to interest me. I keep on writing.

As my heroine approaches the entrance to Titan City, she's still a short distance ahead of her pursuers. Her radio beeps. It's Janos Black again. He tells her his men have gotten to the ejection capsule and are lowering it down the cliff. Any minute now, they'll have it down where they can open it and get 409 out.

Ignoring Janos, she concentrates on slowing her sledge and bringing it through the city's outer gate into the airlock. A moment or two later, she's safe. But what about 409?

Frankly, I don't know. I stand and stretch, decide to take a bath, and go to turn the water on. The air pollution must be worse than I originally thought. I have the dopey feeling I get on the days when the pollution is really bad. I look out the window. Dark grey smoke is still coming out of the chimneys across the street. Maybe I should call the Air Control number (dial AIR-CARE) and complain. But it takes a peculiar kind of person to keep on being public-spirited after it becomes obvious it's futile. I decide to put off calling Air Control and water my plants instead. Every bit of oxygen helps, I think. I check the bathtub—it's not yet half-full—and go back to writing. After a couple of transitional paragraphs, my heroine finds herself in the antechamber to the Titan Council's meeting room. There is a man there, standing with his back to her. He's tall and slender, and his long hair is a shade between blond and grey. He turns and she recognizes the pale, delicate-looking face. This is Michael Stelladoro, the warlord of Saturn's moons. His eyes, she notices, are as blue as cornflowers and he has a delightful smile. He congratulates her on escaping his power-sledges, then tells her that his men have gotten 409 out of the ejection capsule. He is still alive and as far as they can determine uninjured. They have given

409 a shot of Sophamine. At this my heroine gasps with horror. Sophamine, she knows, is an extremely powerful tranquilizer used to control schizophrenia. One dose is enough to make most people dependent on it, and withdrawal takes the form of a nightmarish psychotic fugue. The warlord smiles his delightful smile and turns on the radio he has clipped to his belt. A moment later my heroine hears 409's voice telling her that he has in fact been captured. He sounds calm and completely uninterested in his situation. That, she knows, is the Sophamine. It hasn't affected his perception of reality. He knows where he is and what is likely to happen to him, but he simply doesn't care. When the Sophamine wears off, all the suppressed emotions will well up, so intense that the only way he'll be able to deal with them will be to go insane, temporarily at least.

The warlord tells her he regrets having to use the Sophamine, but he was certain that 409 would refuse to talk unless he was either drugged or tortured, and there simply wasn't enough time to torture him.

"You fiend!" my heroine cries.

The warlord smiles again, as delightfully as before, and says if she gives the microdot to the Titan Council, he will turn 409 over to Janos Black, who will attempt to avenge on him all the atrocities committed by the Earthers on Mars.

What can she do? As she wonders, the door to the meeting room opens, and she is asked to come in. For a moment, she thinks of asking the Titanians to arrest the warlord. Almost as if he's read her mind, he tells her there's no point in asking the Titanians to arrest him. He has diplomatic immunity and a warfleet waiting for him to return.

She turns to go into the meeting room. "I'll tell Janos the good news," the warlord says softly and turns his radio on.

She hesitates, then thinks, a man this evil must be stopped, no matter what the cost. She goes into the meeting room.

I remember the bath water, leap up and run into the bathroom. The tub is brim-full and about to overflow. I turn off the tap, let out some of the water, and start to undress. After I climb into the tub, I wonder how I'm going to get 409 out of the mess he's in. Something will occur to me. I grab the bar of soap floating past my right knee.

After bathing, I put on a pink and silver muumuu and make a fresh pot of tea. Cleanliness is next to godliness, I think as I sit down to write.

My heroine tells her story to the Titan Council and produces the microdot. On it is the warlord's plan for taking over the government of Titan and a list of all the Titanian officials he has subverted. The president of the council thanks her kindly and tells her that they already have a copy of the microdot, obtained for them by an agent of theirs who has infiltrated the warlord's organization. "Oh no! Oh no!" my heroine cries. Startled, the president asks her what's wrong. She explains that she has sacrificed her partner, her love to bring them the information they already had. "Rest easy," the president says. "Our agent is none other than Janos Black. He won't harm 409."

Thinking of Janos' family dying of thirst in an isolated settlement, my heroine feels none too sure of this. But there's nothing left for her to do except hope.

After that, I describe her waiting in Titan City for news of 409, wandering restlessly through the famous gardens, barely noticing the beds of Martian sandflowers, the blossoming magnolia trees, the pools full of enormous silver carp. Since the warlord now knows that the Titan Council knows about his schemes, the council moves quickly to arrest the officials he's subverted. The newscasts are full of scandalous revelations, and the warlord leaves Titan for his home base on Tethys, another one of Saturn's moons. My heroine pays no attention to the newscasts or to the excited conversations going on all around her. She thinks of the trip she and 409 made from Ganymede and Titan in a stolen moon-hopper, remembering 409's hands on the ship's controls, the way he moved in zero-G, his colorless eyes and his infrequent, twisted smile. Cornball, I think, but leave the passage in. I enjoy thinking about 409 as much as my heroine does.

After two days, Janos Black arrives in a police plane. 409 is with him. Janos comes to see my heroine to bring her the news of their arrival. He's a tall man with a broad chest and spindly arms and legs. His face is ruddy and Slavic, and his hair is prematurely white. He tells her that he kept 409 prisoner in the warlord's secret headquarters in the Titanian mountains till the Titanian police moved in and arrested everybody.

"Then he's all right," she cries joyfully.

Janos shakes his head.

"Why not?"

"The Sophamine," Janos explains. "When it wore off, he got hit with the full force of all his repressed feelings, especially, I think, the feelings he had about the war on Mars. Think of all that anger and terror and horror and guilt flooding into his conscious mind. He tried to kill himself. We stopped him, and he almost killed a couple of us in the process. By we I mean myself and the warlord's men; this happened before the police moved in. We had to give him another shot of Sophamine. He's still full of the stuff. From what I've heard, the doctors want to keep giving it to him. They think the first shot of Sophamine he got destroyed his old system of dealing with his more dangerous emotions, which are now overwhelming him. The doctors say on Sophamine he can function more or less normally. Off it, they think he'll be permanently insane."

"You planned this!" she cries.

Janos shakes his head. "The warlord gave the order, miss. I only obeyed it. But I didn't mind this time. I didn't mind."

I stop to drink some tea. Then I write the final scene in the chapter: my heroine's meeting with 409. He's waiting for her in a room at the Titan City Hospital. The room is dark. He sits by the window looking out at the tall towers blazing with light and at the dome above them, which reflects the towers' light so it's impossible to look through it at the sky. She can see his dark shape and the red tip of the cigar he smokes.

"Do you mind if I turn on the lights?" she asks.

"No."

She finds the button and presses it. The ceiling begins to glow. She looks at 409. He lounges in his chair, his feet up on a table. She realizes it's the first time she's seen him look really relaxed. Before this, he's always seemed tense, even when asleep.

"How are you?" she asks.

"Fine." His voice sounds tranquil and indifferent.

She can't think of anything to say. He looks at her, his dark, scarred face expressionless. Finally he says, "Don't let it bother you. I feel fine." He pauses. She still can't think of anything to say. He continues. "The pigs don't want me for anything here on Titan. I think I'll be able to stay."

"What're you going to do here?"

"Work, I guess. The doctors say I can hold down a job if I keep taking Sophamine." He draws on the cigar, so the tip glows red, then blows out the smoke. He's looking away from her at the towers outside the window. She begins weeping. He looks back at her. "I'm all right. Believe me, I feel fine."

But she can't stop weeping.

Enough for today, I think and put down my pencil. Tomorrow, I'll figure out a way to get 409 off Sophamine. Where there's life there's hope and so forth, I tell myself.

1974

MARTA RANDALL

A Scarab in the City of Time

I SKULK IN a forgotten alley while they scurry by outside, searching for me. Whippety-whip, they dive around corners with unaccustomed haste, and they have all donned worried faces for the occasion. Even the robo-cops look worried, and look well; were there stones in this City they would turn them all. But they won't find me, not me, no. When their programmed darkness falls I move from the alley, slyly insert myself in their streets and avenues, slink through the park to the City Offices and scrawl "I am a scarab in the City of Time" over the windows of the mayor's office. I use a spray of heat-sensitive liquid crystals; my graffito will be pretty tomorrow as the wind and fake sunlight shift it through the spectrum. Then I sneak to an outlying residential section where I've not been before, eluding robo-cops on my way, and steal food from an unlocked house for my night's meals. I wouldn't steal from citizens if I could help it, but my thumbprint isn't registered, isn't legal tender in the City of Time. So I burgle and the Association of Merchants grows rich because of me, as locks and bars appear on doors and windows throughout the City. I'm good for the economy of the City of Time, I am.

I'm a sociologist. I'm not supposed to be doing any of this.

When morning comes they cluster before the City Offices, gesticulating, muttering, shifting, frightened. I watch them from a tree in the park, am tempted to mingle with them, sip the sweet nectar of their dismay. No, no, not yet. I remain hidden as the mayor appears on the steps of the building, glares at my beautiful sign. Workers are trying to remove it, but there's a bonding agent in my paint and the colors shift mockingly under their clumsy hands. The mayor reassures the people, calming them with the dignity of her silver hair and smooth hands, and they begin to disperse. I'm tired. The pseudo-sun is far too bright today, a faint wind rustles the leaves around me. When noon comes I slip from my perch, move easily under the eaves and edges of bushes to the Repairs Center, sneak into a storage room and curl down on a pile of cables to sleep.

♦

The City is hard on the eyes, from the outside. Its hemisphere rises from a lush plain, catches the light of the sun and reflects it back harshly at the resurrected earth. Time has silted soil high around the City, but it's probable that the City doesn't know, or care to know. When we returned to colonize Terra we tried to make contact with the City, sent waves of everything we could manage at the impervious dome, received nothing in reply. Years passed and we built our own cities, clean and open to the fresh winds; sailed our ships and floated through the skies, tilled the soil, farmed the seas. Occasionally threw more junk at the City and argued about it. Some held that the City was dead, a gigantic mausoleum; some that it was inhabited by inbred freaks and monsters; some that it was merely the same City our ancestors had left behind as they fled from a poisoned planet. But no one knew, until I dug down beyond the City's deepest foundations, through the bedrock and up into the City. And I can't get out again.

◆

I awaken at nightfall, as the dome of the City turns dark and the stars come on, and spend some time on the roof of the Repairs Center watching the sky and plotting new mischief. Those stars, those stars—no one has seen the original of these dome-printed constellations in two thousand years, yet here they shine in mimicry of the true sky. I tighten the straps of my pack, slip from the building, through the dim streets. The robo-cops hunt for me while the good citizens of the City sleep. And the bad citizens? There are none in the City of Time, none except me, me, and I only by default. Tiers of buildings loom over my head, tapering to the arch of the dome; cascades of plants spill over the walls and display fragrant, flagrant blossoms; most of the doors are locked, the windows closed tight, the citizenry unquiet in their quiet beds. I move to the museum and inside, pad softly through the dark to the echoing Hall of Animals. Hundreds, thousands of them here, some preserved carcasses, some simply statues of those beasts that were extinct by the time the City locked its dome against the poisoned world. I holograph each exhibit carefully, setting the receptors with delicacy, with art, and when I am finished I move through the hall and append notes in liquid script to the signboards: "This animal survives, outside." "This animal is now twice as big and looks like an elephant (see Exhibit 4659)." "This animal now flies." "This animal now breathes air." And, in huge block letters on the face of the museum, "HERE THERE BE DRAGONS." As I finish, the street explodes into a commotion of light and noise, scores of robo-cops and citizens pour from the cross streets and buildings. Have I tripped an alarm? Possibly, probably, someone has monkeyed with the wiring, created an alarm in this uneventful City. The scarab is the mother of invention. Someone sees me clinging to the face of the museum and sets up a cry in counterpoint to the larger one. In my initial surprise I almost drop the paint, then finish the last swing of the "S" before swinging myself down to the roof of the portico, scamper along the protruding tops of the columns and slither down to an open window. I run through the museum, not stopping to stuff the paint into my pack, up one shaft and down another, followed by the hue and cry behind me. I halt for a bare moment to pop the cube from a holojector and stuff another in its place, flick on the machine, and when I am two corridors away I hear the howling populace come to a sudden halt as they face the new projection. And so they should. I took it just before invading their sealed City, setting my receptors about the rim of the hills surrounding the plain on which the City sits. They are seeing their City from the wrong side, from Out, and as it is now. Perhaps they do not know what it is, but the surprise of its presence gives me time to flee through another corridor, out into a dawn-lit empty street and away.

♦

"When meeting a strange animal, stay quiet until you know where the teeth are," they had told me; when I entered the belly of the City of Time I remembered, moved through shadows. Watched from vantage points as the citizens lived their lives before me, whispered notes into my 'corder, took holographs, invaded their library at night with my screens and read their journals and books, lists and agglomerations. Snuck into their City Offices and recorded their records and records of records until my cubes were filled and most of my food gone, and then I tried to go home. But the robo-techs had found and filled my miniature hell-mouth, sealed it over and sealed my digging tools in it. I searched the City for another way home, delved in corners and edges and ragged remnants, and found nothing. Not a crack nor a leak, door nor window. Nothing. How large a City is, when you search for one small scarab-hole. Nothing. I looked about me at the strange, pale people, I opened my ears to the archaic rhythms of their speech, I sniffed the ancient odors of their air and I wept, homesick, from the tops of trees in the park by the City Offices. When they came looking for me I fled. Stole my food from unlocked houses, stole my sleep in small snatches in small places, lived miserably, yearning for the fresh sweet scents of home. Until it came to me that the only way I could go home was if everyone went home, if the City grated open its rusted doors and let the clean air blow in. I considered this, lurking in odd nooks and corners. I couldn't walk into the mayor's office and say, "Hey, listen, lady. The world's all fresh and clean and lovely outside, and it's time to take a walk in sunlight." People who say that are heretics. They dispose of them. It says so in their books, it is recorded in the records of their courts, their preachers bellow it from the pulpits of their temples. I don't want to die, I don't want to be a martyr. I simply want to go home again, to my children, my husband, the stones and rafters of my home, the voices of my students. So I pound in the night on the gates of the City, and hope that those behind me will hear.

◆

I'm hungry. No food on tonight's expedition, just some water I poured into my wetpouch on the run, from a fountain by the Wheel of Fate. The streets around the Repairs Center are swarming with people up and about, in full hue and cry, and I search for a new place. Here, a church, deserted and dim. I scuttle inside, up to the lofts, through undisturbed dust beneath the eaves, and curl myself into a tight ball behind a filthy window. Feed my hungry belly on nightmares and wait for another dusk. Sleep. Sleep.

Dirty windows? Are their purifiers breaking down, their life supports whimpering to a halt after all this time? Dust?

How pale these people are! Fair pink skins and light brown or yellow hair, light eyes; they look like illustrations from a history book. When they locked themselves up in their unhatched egg there were still races in the world, people simplistically divided into preposterous colors; the people of the City were "white" ones, fair of skin, straight of nose and hair, lords of the globe for a time until they grew frightened and hid. The rest of humanity poured out into the galaxy and soon the ridiculous distinctions were lost, for in space and on new worlds people are people are people, valued for their simple humanity amid environments alien beyond description. The books of the City tell of the battles fought, of the expulsion of the black vermin and yellow lice. If I showed my brown face and epicanthic eyes, my bush of light brown hair, they would stopper my mouth with death before I had a chance to speak. I peer at them from the grimed church window, shake my head, tiptoe to the vestry to steal bread and wine from sacramental silver.

How long does it take for a two-thousand-year-old egg to rot?

They hold a service below me for the expulsion of the demon. A wise conclusion: I obviously could not have come from Out, and I am not one of them. They've checked themselves, most carefully; they are, each of them, finger-printed, foot-printed, voice-printed, retina-printed, lip-printed, brainwave-printed, holographed, measured and metered from the moment of their metered births. They're all present and accounted for, and so I am a demon, a ghost amok in the City of Time. I make a note to add that to the sign on the City Offices, and watch the archaic stars appear. Stars. Floating through ancient skies.

When the prank comes to me it is so obvious, so clear, so simple that I laugh aloud, and the congregation below me freezes in fear. I laugh again, pure joy, and hide in a forgotten closet until they stop looking and flee superstitiously from the building. I follow them out, across the City to the vault of controls. I've picked the locks here before and I do it again now, slip inside, lock the door behind me and consider the panels on the wall. Here, and here, linked to this, and here the main nexus, here the central time control. Then I sit and open my mind to memories, recall the clearest, purest night of resurrected Terra I have seen, and I program the skies of the City of Time, jumping their heavens two thousand years forward in the space of half an hour. I add to the moon the smudge of Jump I, I put our latest comet in the sky. What else? Of course, the weather satellites, all five in stately, if not entirely accurate, orbit through the heavens. The computer is not programmed to let me add a starship, or I would do that too. There. There must be stargazers in the City of Time, people who will look above them and see my altered cosmos, will wonder, speculate, go take a look. They will. They *must*. I lock the door behind me and go to write graffiti on the walls of the static City.

Why has their birthrate declined? The City was built to accommodate twice as many as it now encloses—such an empty City now!

Someone finally noticed the report from the robo-tech that found and sealed my way home, and someone else decided that the hole might have some connection with the haunting of their sealed City. A large group of them has come down to inspect it, while I inspect them. Hope springs eternal, yes, and perhaps one of them will come to the right conclusion. But no, they inspect the sealed hole, they argue at great length about it, stamping their feet on the plasteel floor. Perhaps they think that some small animal with laser teeth has sawed its way around their citadel, or that some anomalous tremor has produced this round aperture with fused sides. Whatever, whatever; they decide finally that the hell-mouth couldn't possibly have been made from the outside; no one lives out there, no one could live out there. They are very certain. After a while they leave and I emerge, howl in rage, kick at the floors and walls, tear at the impervious sides of the machines. The echoes of my disappointment rampage through the vault, activate some electronic curiosity in the robo-techs, and they come to investigate. But I am long gone, following the course of my despair up into the nub of the City.

◆

They argue about it now. I listen to the mayor berate the police system over my unapprehended state, yet there is hesitation in her voice. I hear my pranks and myself denounced from pulpits while the congregation sits oddly silent. Young ones at the schools explode with oratory, wave their urgent hands skyward. I listen, strain my ears, want to rush to them yelling, "Yes, yes, you are almost right! Come, show me the doors, I'll take you Out into clarity! Come!" But I remain hidden, eager, awake, hope boiling within me. Come, hurry, let me go home again!

◆

They still argue, endlessly. I am impatient. It's harvest time Out, the schools and shops are closed and the population pours forth to reap and celebrate. Home! Home! I program their night skies to blink at them, I paint pictures on fountain lips of harvests under round moons, of large cats prowling the yards of houses, calling to be fed and stroked; of giant lilies floating in the calm air of forests. Home! I consider poisoning their water, rerouting their waste system, flooding their streets, giving them twenty-hour nights and two-minute days. I could do it all, easily, from the depths of the service cores, from the corners of the control rooms, but I refrain. The City is unbearable enough to me by itself, without my self-made catastrophes. Home! Jora will be seven by now, Karleen twelve, my corn ripens on the hill and my students wait in classrooms, Petrel stalks the hillside and awaits my return. Home! I huddle in a corner of the park, weeping, until the universe shrinks to accommodate only my soul pain and nothing more. Then, angered, I waken the rusting voice of the call system above the City Offices and bellow through the streets, "For God's sake, walk into the light! The sun shines Out, there are trees and birds and water sweet as spring! Come Out! Come Out and home again!"

◆

They're opening the door. They found it, buried in a forgotten service area, behind piles of wire and cable, guarded by an ancient robo-cop. I watch, amazed, through the shards of plasti-glass in an abandoned storage room, my fingers at my mouth, teeth to nails, reverting to primitivism as the young people overpower the robo-cop by the airlock. They do it quite simply. Five of them lunge at the robot, grab, twist the paneled head until it pops off and rolls down the alley, trailing multicolored wires. The body, relieved of its burden, wanders in a melancholy way down the blind alley and stands bleeping aimlessly at the end of it, uncertain of where to turn. The young ones ignore the distressed machine, turn their attention to the great wheels and plates of the airlock door. Have they . . . yes, they've brought meters, and one of them applies the leads to a small, unobtrusive control box, reads the meter, shakes her head, shakes the meter, tries again, shrugs. More uncertainty, more discussion, then the robot-slayers grasp the great wheel of the door and strain at it. Two others join in, the last one watches uneasily at the entrance to the alley. Why didn't they completely dismantle the robo-cop? Where's the transmitter in the damned thing, anyway? It's likely, possible, probable, certain that the mutilated beast is sending silent, roaring distress signals throughout the City, calling cops and more cops, bringing them rushing to the door to freedom. I watch the young ones as they wrench and twist at the wheel, frightened, excited, defiant, sweaty, the age of my students. The wheel groans, turns, suddenly spins free, spilling the young ones over the polymer pavement. Quickly then, yes, they gather at the door, pry it open slowly, swinging it on its ancient hinges. Hurry! Hurry! From my higher vantage point I can see scurries in the distance, fast approaching, hurry! And the door stands open, they cluster at its mouth, waver, enter one after another. My God, the door's closing! Of course, an airlock, of course. I scramble from my perch, tear through the empty storage center, down to the alley. My pack falls to the floor behind me, my torn tunic catches on something and tears completely from me but I can't stop, mustn't, run, *run*, watching in agony as the door closes, closes, closes and suddenly I am inside, braking the force of my flight on their soft bodies, slumping against the far wall, panting, while they stand gaping at me. The door swings shut, clicks into place. Safe. Safe.

I catch my breath, gesture toward the next door. "Out," I gasp. "S'okay, clean, open."

But they're frightened of me, hair, skin, eyes, semi-nakedness. They huddle together, shivering slightly. I force the beating of my heart down, take a deep breath, tell them of my journey, my trials, my homesickness. Do they believe me? They cluster together, wide-eyed, silent. I've not bathed properly in five months, my hair bushes in lumps around my sun-starved face, my eyes are rimmed with weariness. Why should they believe this horrific apparition? I shrug, reach for the great wheel, yank. It does not budge to my pulling. I grasp it more tightly, desperately, pull again, sob, and then there are two hands, four, ten, sixteen pulling at the wheel

with me. It groans, shivers, turns ponderously, clicks free.
Together we pry the great door open.

And, over the piled dirt of centuries, the sunlight pours in.

1975

KATHLEEN M. SIDNEY

The Anthropologist

"**W**HERE ARE you going?" his sister asked.

"Home."

He awoke, huddled among blue-grey bodies. For warmth? On a planet where no one was ever cold?

He woke up with a question. If nothing else, he was an anthropologist.

If nothing else.

"Why are we huddled here?" he asked them aloud. No one so much as opened an eye. They were used to him. They had always been used to him. From the first day he had stepped into their circle, one E-year ago, not one of them had shown the slightest spark of curiosity concerning him. Or anything else. Was nothing new to them? And nothing old? Half his time was up, and he knew no more about them now than when he began.

Gradually they woke up, stretching, an almost human gesture. And Robert spoke to them aloud, as a man lost in the wilderness for a year might speak to the trees. Pointless questions, to fill in the terrible quiet.

"Where are you going?" his sister asked.

"Out to play."

"They laughed at you."

"Mommy said that's only because I'm so different. They'll get used to me."

And they laughed at him. He was too young to know that it was fear. If he was ridiculed, then he was ridiculous. And gradually they did grow used to him. He had learned the secret of success. He became their pet, a puppy dog who could talk and do tricks for them. If there is one thing stronger than the need for self-respect, it is loneliness. But he was spared one agony: he made a poor scapegoat. They could not easily project their fears about their own human weaknesses onto a beast with three heads and nine legs.

"Mommy, where did I come from?"

His mother was a biologist, a scientist, impatient with lies.

"Remember how I told you about the planets and the suns?"

"Yes."

"Well, you came from another planet, called Epsilon Geminorum V. It's far away from here. Across the stars."

Robert pictured the stars, and the darkness between them.

"Your parents gave you to Earth. Along with two others. I think so that we could raise you as our own children and come to understand them better through you."

"I don't remember that."

"You weren't born yet, really, you were inside an egg."

The laughers had told him he was hatched from an egg. He had thought they were making it up.

"Was Susie hatched, too?"

"In a way. From an egg inside my stomach."

"Didn't I come from a stomach, too?"

"Yes. Your egg was inside a stomach, first, then it was outside. And then you were born."

"But why was I hatched outside?"

"Because that's the way people are born on your planet. It's as good a way as any."

"Did they look like me?"

"Who?"

"My Mom and Dad."

"Yes. But we adopted you, and so we're your parents."

"What happened to the other eggs?"

"Those babies died, Robby. Because we didn't understand that they needed love, just like human children. And they were raised in a sterile laboratory environment until it was too late."

"But I didn't die."

"Because we had taken you home with us. Because we love you."

He hugged her tight. Afraid to let go. Afraid he would die. But she hugged him back, and after a while he relaxed.

"You know what I'm going to be when I grow up?" Susie asked.

"What?"

"A scientist, like Mommy. Do you know what kind?"

"A mad scientist."

They wrestled on the floor, laughing.

"What are you going to be, Robby?"

He was on his way out of the house with Susie when his mother called him back.

"Robby, stay inside this morning. There's someone coming to see you."

He knew what that phrase meant. "It's another test," he told his sister.

"Mommy, can't he come? We're building a tree fort."

"Later, honey, this afternoon."

"Now, Mom, just for a little while?"

"Susie," their mother said warningly.

"Well, he's not a guinea pig." And his sister made a hasty exit.

With Susan gone, and his mother and father working in the cellar lab, Robert had the house to himself. He wandered into his parents' bedroom and, on an impulse, closed the door behind him. He crouched in the center of his father's bed. Who would come to test him today? Dr. Jamison again? Robert had once overheard the man say that tricephs might be less intelligent than human beings. And despite his parents' indignant replies, Robert knew that it was true. He had no doubt that he was inferior to the human race.

The closet door was open. He looked at his father's suits, his mother's dresses. He climbed up on the dresser, and looked at his own twelve-holed garment in the mirror. A "trunk suit," his mother had called it. Yet she had told him that he was almost human biologically. He breathed the same air and ate most of the same foods. His skin was a little thicker than theirs, and heavily pigmented blue-grey, but his blood was red. Yet three heads rose, immobile, from a short stubby trunk. And each possessed one eye and one ear, placed so that he could see and hear in any direction without turning. One head had a functional nose and mouth; on the other two these were rudimentary. And nine legs were spread around him like a spider's, and each possessed a three-pronged hand. Robert studied himself in the mirror, silently asking a question as old as the human race.

"Robert, where are you?" his father called. "Rob, come on. Dr. Jamison will be here any minute." He paused outside the bedroom, mumbling to himself, "Where is the little monster?" and left.

Fifteen minutes later he returned, running toward the sound of objects breaking. The room was a shambles. And scattered in a circle, as if they had been caught up in and tossed from a fan, were all the suits from the closet. A hat was on one of Robert's heads, and one of his long arms was stretched through a shirtsleeve.

Robert saw his father standing quite still at the door, and he began a high-pitched whistling. It was as close as he could come to human crying. His father sat down on the bed and gathered him up in his lap. His mother came into the room, then left again. When she returned, she sat down beside them. The whistling gradually eased and stopped. But for a long time no one moved or spoke.

Finally his father turned to his mother and asked, very softly, "Did you call Dr. Jamison?"

His mother nodded. "He'll put it off. Robby won't have to answer any questions today."

When he was seventeen, he had to choose whether to join the expedition, or to go east with his family, where Susan would start college. She wanted him to join her. They had always been close, but their intimacy had grown during the teen years, when sibling rivalry gave way to very similar views on life, death, and the meaning of the universe. They had asked the same questions, and found the same tentative answers, until their thoughts were so intertwined, they found it impossible to remember which of them had first proposed an idea. But even if the college would consider accepting him as a student, he felt sure he would fail the entrance examinations.

"Where are you going?" his sister asked.

"Home."

"No. Not until you come back."

"To what? A freak show?"

"I'll be waiting."

Robert was reading in the ship's lounge when the argument broke out between Dr. Johnson, an anthropologist, and Dr. Panzer, a biologist.

". . . you don't seem to understand. We're clay. Culture is our mold."

"Then how come we aren't all alike?"

"Because no two of us have precisely the same experiences. But almost all our experiences are within the bounds of our culture. We learn to see the universe according to the preconceptions of our culture. And so we're blind to the truly alien."

Robert looked at his hands in awe.

Blind.

"You're going to what?" Dr. Layton was aghast.

"I'm going to study anthropology."

"Are you joking?"

"It will take us two years to reach Epsilon. The ship's library is extensive on the subject, and I haven't anything better to do with my time."

"Nothing better than to wreck the experiment?"

"It won't do any harm, it should help if I—"

"What do you think we need, another damned scientist? There's already twenty of us on board. And for thirty-two years the best of us have made next to no headway in understanding these creatures. What we need is a triceph who can bridge the gap subjectively. And you're it."

It.

Robert studied anthropology.

He read the reports carefully for the hundredth time. When Layton had said that next to nothing was known about the tricephs, he hadn't been exaggerating. At first, the planet had been rated A for settlement. It was an Eden, with no dangerous animals. All species were herbivores, and most had plenty to eat. Their birth rate was low. The temperature was mild over most of the planet's surface. There was some evidence that conditions had once been harsher, and that the evolution of animal life had passed through a carnivorous stage.

Exploration is a slow process under the best of conditions, and it wasn't until the second year that the team had occasion to kill and dissect a triceph. They uncovered one large and two small brains, heavily interconnected with neural pathways. It appeared that they might have discovered the first sentient aliens. The problem was proving it.

The tricephs were extremely shy of humans. Those captured died almost immediately of unknown causes. However, robosensors proved effective, and a close observation was maintained. The tricephs did not use tools. They wandered in packs of twenty to thirty, with no home base and apparently no territorial limits. They never fought. They had no visible or audible means of communication. Yet they were able to work together in building structures made of vines and grass. The purpose of these structures was a mystery.

They were not used as shelters, nor for raising food. No two structures were exactly alike. Each took approximately six hours to build. Each pack built one structure a day and immediately abandoned it to rot. There were no pack leaders, and none of the members appeared to have any particular tasks that they habitually performed. Yet the building went smoothly and efficiently.

It was noted that none of the tricephs seemed to use any one hand in preference to the other eight. Robert thought long about this. He himself had been taught to write with the hand to the right of his primary head. He was beginning to realize that the nature of intelligence was many-faceted and little understood. A seed of hope had been planted within him eight months before, in the ship's lounge. And now it was taking root.

The tricephs were hermaphroditic and mated once a year (approximately fourteen and a third Earth months). Each paired with only one other individual, and the pairing lasted little longer than a day. Only about ten percent of the matings resulted in offspring. Pregnancy lasted five months, resulting in one egg, which the parent carried in its pouch until it hatched six months later. It took seven months for the young triceph to graduate from the pouch, after which all the elders cared for all the young indiscriminately. Fifteen years later, it reached physical maturity. The life-span was as yet unknown, but there was some indication that it might average around seventy of our years. For all its observations, the team was unable to find absolute proof that triceph sentience existed. If it was proven that the tricephs were sentient, the government would forbid colonization of the planet.

Almost fifteen years after the tricephs were discovered, three of their eggs appeared outside the main entrance to the base. Dr. Edward Simpson was the first to leave that morning, and it was he who discovered the eggs. They had been placed in a huddle directly in front of the entrance, and covered with grass. The eggs were warm, and could not have been there long. The land around the base was flat and had been cleared for half a mile. There was not a triceph in sight.

Robert entered the elevator at C, and Dr. Layton at D. Coincidence had placed them alone together for the first time in a year. The silence was loud. A mutual hatred permeated the air, almost stifling them in the small compartment. As they stepped out into the lounge, Layton admitted to an awareness of Robert's presence.

"So how's our three-headed blue anthropologist?"

"Doing quite well, thank you."

"Is that a touch of pride I hear? Well, I guess you have some right to it. In only one year's time, you've managed to destroy the lifework of at least thirty people."

"I haven't ruined your experiment, I've changed it."

"Oh, really? I'd like to hear the new hypothesis."

"Triceph intelligence is equal to, but different from human intelligence."

"That's two hypotheses."

"All right."

"And a good scientist phrases his hypotheses in the negative. It aids objectivity."

"But you want me to be subjective."

"A subjective triceph. Not a subjective human."

Oddly, they were both taken aback by his remark, and they stared at each other in silence. Finally Layton spoke, and Robert was surprised to hear a note of pleading in his voice.

"Don't you understand how important this is? Do you realize the time and the money that has gone into it? The government won't wait indefinitely. If this experiment fails, the project will be abandoned, and the best we can hope is that they will leave the planet uncolonized. Look, Robert, after all this is over, there will be plenty of time for you to study whatever you want."

"You don't understand, Layton. There isn't going to be any 'after this is over' for me. I'm going home."

They were at a picnic and Robert thought the mood was unusually dismal. Then he realized why. The world was a deep blue-grey. It was dawn, and everyone was cold. Later, perhaps, when the sun came out, they would become warm and happy.

"Mom, I'm hungry."

She gave the sandwich to Dr. Layton, and he held it up for Robert. "Speak, Robby, speak."

Somewhere in the distance, a dog barked. And they could hear children laughing.

Robert reached out a human hand and took the sandwich.

"Mom, I'm cold. Can't we go home?"

"You go, Robby, we want to stay here."

Robert stood, and Susie grinned up at him. "We can hardly see you against the sky."

Robert woke up, shaking. As usual when he had had this dream, he lay awake for some time, listening to the sounds of the ship. Until, gradually, sleep overtook his fear.

Earth, Robert thought, and knew that he was wrong. He had seen the green vegetation and the blue sky in the videos, but he had never expected it to feel so familiar.

"What do you think of it?" Layton asked.

"Like home." The words escaped him before he realized what he had said.

"Yes, well, it will seem even more that way, once you get used to it." The scientist had completely misunderstood him.

Robert entered the forest on a practice run. Now, for the first time, he actually felt that he was on another planet. In motion, he could not forget the tug of the slightly stronger gravity. And on closer scrutiny, the vegetation had an alien shape. Even the veins of the leaves stretched in multiples of three. But leaves they were, green and functioning like the vegetation of Earth. A horizontal forest, Robert thought. Although it reached up for the sun, everything seemed interconnected aboveground. He rarely saw the earth, even in the fields; it was covered with a blanket of vegetation. And in the forest, he could travel on any one of several levels of limbs. He felt awkward at first, yet he found that he was leaving his human companions far behind. With a little practice he would move like a native.

"Are you ready, Robert?" Dr. Layton smiled, a poor attempt at good will.

"Yes."

"We'll fly you over."

"No, I'll walk."

"It's a long way."

"For you, maybe. I was made for these woods."

"Yes, you were. You'll blend in fine."

"Are you sure you won't forget which triceph I am?"

"Don't worry about that. And there'll be a robosensor on you at all times."

"I forgot."

"That's good. Forget as much as you can. Become one of them."

"I might forget altogether, and fail to keep our appointment."

"I'll see you in six months."

"Maybe."

"Robert, have you ever heard of Jamison's theory?"

"I know both Jamison and his theory very well."

"That's right, he worked with you for a while, didn't he?"

"He tested me, if that's what you mean. His theory has it that triceph intelligence has deteriorated, since the conditions on this planet no longer require it for survival. This accounts for their apparent lack of speech and curiosity. And their emotions have become shallow for the same reason. Aggressiveness, in particular, is pointless when all needs are met with little effort, and there are no enemies. Their unexplainable behavior represents half-remembered activities, perhaps, by now, instincts, passed on from generation to generation, and carried out without understanding or reason. Oh yes, and I'm explained as a sort of superintelligent monkey, appearing brighter than I am, because I've been brought up among humans and have learned their habits. My existence suggests that we're capable of learning, but the almost mindless existence of the tricephs suggests that we're no longer capable of originating ideas."

"You're out to disprove that, aren't you?"

"Yes."

"As a scientist?"

"As an anthropologist."

"Yes, you are an anthropologist. Without a degree, but I think you've studied enough to warrant the title." It occurred to Robert that Layton was a chess player. "What would you say is the most important thing an anthropologist must learn?"

The answer was unavoidable. "Objectivity."

"Exactly."

"Impossible."

"In a pure sense. But if we're aware of our biases, we can allow for them."

"All right. I'm aware of my bias, Layton. Are you aware of yours?"

"What are you talking about?"

"Jamison's theory."

"You're wrong."

"Am I?" Robert turned to go.

"Wait a minute, damn you. All I ask is that you refrain from projecting into these creatures an intelligence they may not possess."

"If I don't possess the intelligence, I can't very well project it into them, can I? And if I do, then so do they."

"You can see in them traits you have learned, but which are inherently human."

"What makes you believe I think so much of humankind that I would want tricephs to be the same? No, it's not similarity I'm looking for, it's difference."

"Difference, or superiority?"

"Superiority is a value, and as such, is relative to a given culture."

"What if their intelligence is very similar to ours, Robert, but lower? Will you spend the next two years trying to hide the truth, from us, and from yourself?"

The pattern never varied. They arose and moved on, searching for food. It wasn't difficult to find. And then they began another structure.

"Today is a special day," Robert informed them. "Today is our first anniversary." And today he would once more report to Layton that he had failed to achieve any insight into the triceph culture. The one theory he had offered, a year ago, was beginning to seem no more than a child's dream. Someone handed him a vine to add to the structure. "No, I can't today. I have to report to Layton."

"Mommy, can't he come? We're building a tree fort."

Tree forts are my specialty, you know. It's the one area in which I excel.

Was that the essence of triceph intelligence?

"Someone is coming to see you."

A Dr. Jamison, no doubt.

A high-pitched whistling sound penetrated a forest that was too green, and a sky too blue to seem truly alien. The tricephs moved back and watched impassively, as one day's structure was utterly demolished.

Exhausted, Robert moved away from the wreckage and squatted, panting. He became aware of the sheer childishness of his act. For the first time in months, he remembered the robosensor, and his shame deepened.

The tricephs sat facing him, as if immobilized by the unpredictable.

The unpredictable.

Robert arose, excited.

"Layton," he called to the robosensor, "I'm conducting an experiment. I'm going to put our meeting off a week."

Next day the tricephs built another structure. And Robert destroyed it. Methodically, this time, but quickly and completely. And next day they built again.

At the end of the week Robert kept his appointment with Layton. As he had expected, the scientist was against his interference with the pack. But since he had no alternative except to pull Robert out of the experiment altogether, he reluctantly agreed.

At the end of a month the procedure had not varied. Robert destroyed the structures at various stages of their development. The tricephs waited until he was finished and began again, leaving Robert with the old questions. Did they lack the emotion of frustration, the intelligence to solve the problem, or the experience of problem-solving? He began to suspect that they simply did not care.

That night he dreamed once more of the picnic. And this time he awoke with a loneliness greater than any he had experienced before. "Am I homesick?" he asked them. And the silence was his answer. The irony was too much for him. "Damn all of you," he shouted. "Can't you give me anything of my own?"

Robert followed the pack to a place where three rivers met. There they began another structure. He sat on the bank and watched. He had ceased to destroy their work, but he felt reluctant to help them again. Around midday another pack arrived. In his time with the pack, they had passed other tricephs, but no group had remained near any other. Today, however, the new pack joined in the building of the structure. A third pack arrived around midafternoon, and joined with the others in the building. According to the observers' records, three packs would leave tomorrow, but only after so thorough an interchange of members that they could no longer be identified as the same packs. And by tomorrow morning, the mating would begin. Robert felt no desire to take part in triceph sexual intercourse, and there seemed little likelihood of his being forced into the act. Nevertheless, he watched from a little farther back that day, and that night he slept outside the huddle. His dreams took on a new quality, but when he awoke, he forgot them. In the morning the pack divided into three, roughly the same in number. A process of choice seemed to be involved, and the goal appeared to be exchange and equalization. Yet their movements lacked the hesitation human beings associate with decision. In order to do his part, he chose the smallest pack and followed it along the river. By midmorning they were working on a structure. But the work force was greatly diminished; the mating was well under way. Robert watched from the other side of the river. This seemed to him the final alienation.

That night he lay awake, trying to concentrate on the simple intensity of the sky. Tomorrow he was quitting. He would return to Earth, where, if he could not be happy, at least he had a family to help fill his emptiness.

A creature appeared against the stars. As ugly as Robert, but no more so, it stared down at him, waiting. And as suddenly as that, a desire filled Robert, more intense and more delightful than anything he had known before.

In the morning the triceph left, taking with it the blindness of ecstasy. Robert opened his eyes and was overcome with self-loathing. He could not forgive himself for having mated with an animal.

The tricephs moved on down the river in search of food. Robert watched them go, his skin crawling with a new revulsion. When they were out of sight, he turned and left the river.

Robert lowered his heavy body into the pond and half-floated in a deep peace. He would lay an egg soon, and carry it in his pouch. What had his mother said? It was as good a way as any to be born. He wondered idly about a question he had once asked her. Why, since he was of two sexes, had he been given a man's name? His mother had tried to pass over the question lightly, saying that they had flipped a coin. But Susan had said it was because mankind defined a person according to sex, and men were more respected than women. His mother had said nothing, but her expression was an answer, and Robert began to see the world from Susan's perspective. She was right. And he realized now that their home had been made a refuge from the rest of the world. Here neither sex nor bodily shape defined one's personality or role. But ultimately the world beyond the home dictated their lives, and where the rest of his family could blend in, he had stood out, an alien.

Robert felt his belly. It held the raw material for a thinking, feeling being. Today he was due to meet Layton. He had little idea where this pond was in relation to the meeting place, and no intention of finding out. The robosensor had followed him, but he had destroyed it soon after leaving the pack. He would keep no more appointments with any race. He was growing something, and it was his own.

He heard them coming, and since few creatures on this planet moved in groups, he assumed it was a passing pack of tricephs. Out of idle curiosity he climbed higher among the tangles of the forest to watch unobserved. His revulsion had worn away with time and the hatching of his child, but he would not meet them. When the group came into sight, Robert clutched impulsively at his baby in its pouch. Five human beings were moving in his direction, following a ro-botracker. Robert recognized Layton and Johnson, but was surprised to find that he had already forgotten the names of the other three.

They had picked up his trail, and it was inevitable that they would find him. Rather than be discovered like an animal in hiding, Robert climbed down and approached them. He tried to greet them as he might a casual acquaintance on a city street. Layton spoke softly, as if to a madman. "It's all right, Robert, the experiment is over. You don't have to stay here any longer."

"I told you once before, I'm never going back."

Layton's eyes fastened on the bulge in Robert's pouch. "All right," he said quietly, "but will you stay the night with us?"

"No."

"We won't force you to come back with us. I give you my word."

"But you would like to talk me into it."

"What harm is talk? We've lost a great deal on this experi-ment, can't you allow us that much?"

"All right. But only for tonight." Robert wished he felt certain of that.

They made camp. There were no enemies on this planet, and a sleeping bag would have provided more than enough warmth. Yet the humans lit a heat lamp and set out a robowatch. They were of Earth, and so lacked faith. It had taken Robert a long time to get used to the darkness. And now he found the light, once again, oddly comforting.

After supper Layton sat down next to him. "So, Robert, how have you been?" It had begun.

"Healthy, happy and wise."

"Flippancy is often a cover."

"Of what, insanity?"

"I didn't say that."

"But you would like to prove it."

Layton spoke softly. "Why would I want to do that, Robert?"

"Because then you could obtain legal authority to send me back to Earth. Leaving my baby in your custody."

Layton was silent for a moment. When he spoke, it was as if to a child. "Robert, you don't have the legal rights of a human being."

Robert was stunned. Once a little boy had looked into a mirror. Had he forgotten, even here, in the depths of the Epsilon forest?

"The Alien Act provides the only law that pertains to you. And it states simply that the citizens of Earth may neither colonize nor exploit a planet inhabited by sentient aliens. It was enacted soon after our discovery of tricephs, and will last, I suspect, only as long as we can hope to learn something from our first efforts to understand an alien race."

"If I have no legal rights, why did you allow me to study anthropology?"

"If I had forbidden you to do so, would you have helped us at all?"

Robert tried to regain his composure. "Well, in any case, I'm not going back."

"Haven't you been lonely?"

"I'm not quite alone." Robert looked down at his pouch, stifling an impulse to show off his baby to Layton.

"It's newly hatched, isn't it? Hardly old enough to talk to. Haven't you missed the pack at all?"

"I could hardly converse with the pack. And I miss no one."

"You're lying, Robert, you were never a hermit."

"I won't be alone forever."

"I see. Your offspring is to become your companion, and to hell with the rest of the universe. Is that it?"

"Something like that."

"You're going to die a good twenty years before it does. What is it going to do then, wander around all by itself? Have you ever thought about how lonely *it* might become?"

"What would you suggest?"

"I don't think we were wrong, Robert, in our assumption that this was the way to bridge the gap. We only made one mistake. You might say that we started the bridge, but we never completed it. I think it requires another generation. A triceph raised among its own kind, but with a parent who was raised among humanity."

To bridge the gap, Robert thought, but what of the bridge?

"Isn't this better, Robert, than to leave your offspring utterly alone after your death?"

The robowatch was designed not to alarm the members of the camp against themselves. With legs made for a peculiar forest, Robert left the camp in silence. He had a decision to make, and it would be made beyond the control of humankind.

A few hours later he fell asleep by the riverbank. Like their flesh counterparts, the robotrackers could be misled by water and a confusion of scents.

When Robert awoke, Layton was standing over him. "Running out on us again?"

"How can I be running out on you? I owe you nothing."

The man had evidently come on alone, but leaving a trail, no doubt, for others to follow.

"How did you find me?"

"By robotracker. It's a little more sophisticated than the kind you're used to."

"And you only wanted to talk."

"After all the years and money put into this experiment, did you really think we would give up on the whim of a creature?"

"Is that the imperial 'we'?"

"Robert, it wouldn't be as effective, but if we have to, we'll conduct this experiment without you. If you're willing to help, you'll have the opportunity to guide the development of your offspring; if you aren't, we take over that function. The choice is yours."

"That's very considerate of you."

"More considerate than you've been of us."

"This child is mine, Layton, and no one is going to take it from me." He wondered if the man realized the intensity of his feeling.

"Cooperate, Robert, and you can keep your child. But fight

us and you'll lose. Fighting is a human prerogative, it's not in the nature of your species."

"Like speech, curiosity, intelligence, and aggressiveness?"

"That's ri—"

Robert leaped at the man. He had forgotten how heavy the child made him, and he fell short. But Layton was stunned by the inconceivable, and Robert had time to leap again. With arms to spare, he pinned him down, grabbed a rock, and knocked him unconscious. He hoped he had done no serious damage, but would not have stayed in any case. The robocontrol was in Layton's pocket; Robert brought in the sensor and destroyed it. Then he left the river.

That day he concentrated on covering his trail, circling back often to be sure no person or device was following him. He passed the place where three rivers met. There was no sign of the packs, other than the remains of a decaying structure. That night he slept in a perch well above the ground. He awoke before dawn and made his plan. The packs moved slowly. He had only to go back to the place where the rivers met, and follow their trail of decayed structures. He could cover their twelve months' journey in a day. And then? He felt incapable of thinking beyond that. But he knew he would have to see them once more before he made his decision. "We'll see," he told his child.

As he awaited the dawn, his mind moved restlessly across the past day. Layton had been wrong. He had been aggressive, and therefore tricephs had that potential. But he had scored below average on the intelligence tests. Of course, there was as yet no indication of where he stood in relation to other tricephs; he could be a retardate or a genius. Layton had been wrong, and Jamison had been wrong. Might not the tests also have been wrong? He knew enough psychology, now, to guess how his own attitude could have influenced them. And what of feeling? Could a human feel more deeply than he, and not go insane?

Dawn touched the sky with its first cold light.

"Where are you going, Robert?" Susan asked.

For the first time since he had left the pack, he became aware of the full weight of his loneliness. He thought of the camp and its warm light, and of the home of his parents. Where was Susan now? Was she really waiting? For what, a creature who could only be a burden in her life? He dismissed the thought. And his loneliness deepened. Finally he had to admit to the irony of the truth. However much he hated Layton, he needed humankind. His baby moved, and Robert hugged his pouch, whispering softly, "When you look in the mirror, what will you see?" He pictured two suns, and the emptiness between them.

It was late the following night before he found the pack. A few tricephs awoke and moved over, leaving room for him to join the group. Exhausted, he took his place, and the creatures huddling around him made him feel warm and safe. Like the pouch? He fell asleep. And he was in a blue-grey sea, drowning. He opened his eyes. It was dawn. He stepped out of the group, and as he did so, the triceph next to him opened its eyes. It didn't move in, as they usually did when someone left, to close in the warmth. It seemed to him that the triceph was waiting. Robert looked away, dreading his decision. How far was the base camp? Three days? Was Layton badly hurt? Robert suspected that the same laws which could not protect him, could execute him. He looked back at the huddle. The gap was still open. Dawn, he thought, is the color of loneliness. With a strange feeling, deeper and more painful than anything he had ever experienced before, Robert removed his baby from himself and placed it in the open space. Without a moment's hesitation, the triceph picked it up and placed it in its own empty pouch. Already his child seemed indistinguishable from the others.

As Robert left, he turned frequently to look back at the pack. But no one was watching him.

1975

GAYLE N. NETZER

Hey, Lilith!

NOT HAVING much else to do lately, I've been reading a lot of science fiction. Which is probably why I'm not surprised when, all of a sudden, I find myself in the middle of this ruined city. Science fiction is like that, you know—awful things happen and practically everybody comes to a sticky end, but the main characters just carry on, cool and collected. Of course, very few of them are middle-aged females. And that's what makes this story different.

Anyway, here I am, perched calmly on a chunk of concrete when this weird-looking woman appears out of nowhere.

"Hello!" she chirps.

I like to think I don't look it, but just the same, I'm pushing fifty. This dame is even older—stringy neck, wrinkles, the whole bit. Bright black eyes, though. They make me a bit uncomfortable the way they look me over, so my hello back is chilly. It doesn't faze her.

"Are you by yourself?"

What else have I been since I got my divorce? I don't bother to answer. So she plunks herself down beside me and says brightly that her name is Lilith.

Lilith? "Oh, yes! Wasn't that Adam's first wife? The one there was all that nasty talk about after he married Eve?"

"I'm afraid so," she winces. "Of course, that was a long time ago! Now, why I stopped by was, some of us ladies have been getting together . . ."

"And why the hell would I be interested in that?" I interrupt.

The old broad looks sadly at me. "Well, just give me a call when you're ready," she says, fading back into the landscape.

I settle back on my chunk of concrete and fume. What does she mean, ready? And this business of being Lilith! Although, if she really is, a sci-fi story would be the place to show up. To calm myself, I speculate about the funny colored sky and the zig-zaggy skyline. What happened this time, I wonder? A few minutes later, the Professor trots up briskly, so I ask him.

He's a little out of breath, but he tells me anyway. "Just the usual," he says cheerfully. "Earthquakes, tidal waves, giant insects! Oh, yes, and a few H-bombs! Did away with practically everybody, of course. That's why I'm in such a hurry. I have to find a beautiful girl so I can start rebuilding civilization!"

I bridle a little. "A beautiful girl? Why do you need a beautiful girl?"

The professor stands very straight. "Rebuilding civilization is *very* hard work!" he informs me, pulling in his stomach and puffing out his chest. "I'm gonna need lots of coffee and sandwiches. To say nothing of after-hours recreation. That's strictly for the benefit of the human race, of course!" He eyes me challengingly.

I eye him back. Receding hairline, bags under his eyes, a bit of a paunch. "You and I must be about the same age," I muse. "How about me?"

Dignity goes down the drain. "You!" he squalls. "*You're* middle-aged!"

So, what else is new? I go on from there. "I'm real healthy, got a good twenty years left in me!" I coax. "Besides, you and I have a lot in common, same generation and all!"

That really does it. The Professor's face turns magenta. "Buzz off, sister!" he snarls. "Don't need any more letters typed, or phone numbers looked up! Got *important* things on my mind now!" Off he stomps, snorting with outrage.

The baggy seat of his pants is still joggling in the distance when I hear somebody whistling happily. I look around, and here's this young guy. Flopping gracefully at my feet, he dazzles me with a lovely set of teeth.

"And what do you have on *your* mind?" If I sound a bit snappish, it's because I am. It doesn't bother him any.

"Oh I'm just tagging along after the Professor!" He says brightly, "That beautiful girl's liable to show up any time, and I want to be where the action is!"

"Are you planning on taking her away from him?" I enquire, perking up a bit.

He looks at me reproachfully. "Of course not! No, I'm just going to give the old boy a hand with civilization. And eventually another beautiful girl will come along. Or the Professor's oldest daughter will reach puberty. Either way I can't lose!"

The snappish feeling returns. However, there he is, right in front of me, so, not having anything else to do, I look him over. Nice vee of hairy chest. Interesting bulge in the appropriate place.

"Look," I say, thoughtfully, "as long as you have to wait a while anyway, maybe you and me . . ."

He sits up and stares. Then he starts to grin. The grin turns into a guffaw. He gets to his feet and rocks back and forth.

"You and me?" he gasps. "You've got to be putting me on!" Shaking with laughter, he staggers off after the Professor.

I watch until he is out of sight, too. That pretty well uses up the stock characters, I reflect. Except maybe for a devoted young married couple, or a doddering retainer or two. Some bad guys, about to get their just deserts. And a few kindly aliens. I heave a sigh. Then I get slowly to my feet. It takes a couple of tries, but finally it comes out:

"HEY, LILITH!"

1976

RACCOONA SHELDON

The Screwfly Solution

THE YOUNG man sitting at 2° N, 75° W sent a casually venomous glance up at the nonfunctional shoofly *ventilador* and went on reading his letter. He was sweating heavily, stripped to his shorts in the hotbox of what passed for a hotel room in Cuyapán.

> How do other wives *do* it? I stay busy-busy with the Ann Arbor grant review programs and the seminar, saying brightly "Oh yes, Alan is in Colombia setting up a biological pest control program, isn't it wonderful?" But inside I imagine you being surrounded by nineteen-year-old raven-haired cooing beauties, every one panting with social dedication and filthy rich. And forty inches of bosom busting out of her delicate lingerie. I even figured it in centimeters, that's 101.6 centimeters of busting. Oh, darling, darling, do what you want only *come home safe.*

Alan grinned fondly, briefly imagining the only body he longed for. His girl, his magic Anne. Then he got up to open the window another cautious notch. A long pale mournful face looked in—a goat. The room opened on the goatpen, the stench was vile. Air, anyway. He picked up the letter.

Everything is just about as you left it, except that the Peedsville horror seems to be getting worse. They're calling it the Sons of Adam cult now. Why can't they *do* something, even if it is a religion? The Red Cross has set up a refugee camp in Ashton, Georgia. Imagine, refugees in the U.S.A. I heard two little girls were carried out all slashed up. Oh, Alan.

Which reminds me, Barney came over with a wad of clippings he wants me to send you. I'm putting them in a separate envelope; I know what happens to very fat letters in foreign POs. He says, in case you don't get them, what do the following have in common? Peedsville, São Paulo, Phoenix, San Diego, Shanghai, New Delhi, Tripoli, Brisbane, Johannesburg and Lubbock, Texas. He says the hint is, remember where the Intertropical Convergence Zone is now. That makes no sense to me, maybe it will to your superior ecological brain. All I could see about the clippings was that they were fairly horrible accounts of murders or massacres of women. The worst was the New Delhi one, about "rafts of female corpses" in the river. The funniest (!) was the Texas Army officer who shot his wife, three daughters and his aunt, because God told him to clean the place up.

Barney's such an old dear, he's coming over Sunday to help me take off the downspout and see what's blocking it. He's dancing on air right now, since you left his spruce budworm-moth antipheromone program finally paid off. You know he tested over 2,000 compounds? Well, it seems that good old 2,097 *really* works. When I asked him what it does he just giggles,

you know how shy he is with women. Anyway, it seems
that a one-shot spray program will save the forests,
without harming a single other thing. Birds and people
can eat it all day, he says.

Well sweetheart, that's all the news except Amy
goes back to Chicago to school Sunday. The place
will be a tomb, I'll miss her frightfully in spite of her
being at the stage where I'm her worst enemy. The
sullen sexy subteens, Angie says. Amy sends love to
her Daddy. I send you my whole heart, all that words
can't say.

Your Anne

Alan put the letter safely in his notefile and glanced over the
rest of the thin packet of mail, refusing to let himself dream
of home and Anne. Barney's "fat envelope" wasn't there. He
threw himself on the rumpled bed, yanking off the lightcord
a minute before the town generator went off for the night. In
the darkness the list of places Barney had mentioned spread
themselves around a misty globe that turned, troublingly,
briefly in his mind. Something . . .

But then the memory of the hideously parasitized children
he had worked with at the clinic that day took possession
of his thoughts. He set himself to considering the data he
must collect. *Look for the vulnerable link in the behavioral
chain*—how often Barney—Dr. Barnhard Braithwaite—had
pounded it into his skull. Where was it, where? In the morning he would start work on bigger canefly cages . . .

At that moment, five thousand miles North, Anne was
writing:

Oh, darling, darling, your first three letters are here, they all came together. I *knew* you were writing. Forget what I said about swarthy heiresses, that was all a joke. My darling I know, I know . . . us. Those dreadful canefly larvae, those poor little kids. If you weren't my husband I'd think you were a saint or something. (I do anyway.)

I have your letters pinned up all over the house, makes it a lot less lonely. No real news here except things feel kind of quiet and spooky. Barney and I got the downspout out, it was full of a big rotted hoard of squirrel-nuts. They must have been dropping them down the top, I'll put a wire over it. (Don't worry, I'll use a ladder this time.)

Barney's in an odd, grim mood. He's taking this Sons of Adam thing very seriously, it seems he's going to be on the investigation committee if that ever gets off the ground. The weird part is that nobody seems to be doing anything, as if it's just too big. Selina Peters has been printing some acid comments, like When one man kills his wife you call it murder, but when enough do it we call it a lifestyle. I think it's spreading, but nobody knows because the media have been asked to down-play it. Barney says it's being viewed as a form of contagious hysteria. He insisted I send you this ghastly interview, printed on thin paper. It's *not* going to be published, of course. The quietness is worse, though, it's like something terrible was going on just out of sight. After reading Barney's thing I called up Pauline in San Diego to make sure she was all right. She sounded funny, as if she wasn't saying everything

. . . my own sister. Just after she said things were great she suddenly asked if she could come and stay here awhile next month. I said come right away, but she wants to sell her house first. I wish she'd hurry.

Oh, the diesel car is okay now, it just needed its filter changed. I had to go out to Springfield to get one but Eddie installed it for only $2.50. He's going to bankrupt his garage.

In case you didn't guess, those places of Barney's are all about latitude 30° N or S—the horse latitudes. When I said not exactly, he said remember the equatorial convergence zone shifts in winter, and to add in Libya, Osaka, and a place I forget—wait, Alice Springs, Australia. What has this to do with anything, I asked. He said, "Nothing—I hope." I leave it to you, great brains like Barney can be weird.

Oh my dearest, here's all of me to all of you. Your letters make life possible. But don't feel you *have* to, I can tell how tired you must be. Just know we're together, always everywhere.

Your Anne

Oh PS I had to open this to put Barney's thing in, it wasn't the secret police. Here it is. All love again. A.

In the goat-infested room where Alan read this, rain was drumming on the roof. He put the letter to his nose to catch the faint perfume once more, and folded it away. Then he pulled out the yellow flimsy Barney had sent and began to read, frowning.

PEEDSVILLE CULT/SONS OF ADAM SPECIAL. Statement by driver Sgt. Willard Mews, Globe Fork, Ark. We hit the roadblock about 80 miles west of Jacksonville. Major John Heinz of Ashton was expecting us, he gave us an escort of two riot vehicles headed by Capt. T. Parr. Major Heinz appeared shocked to see that the NIH medical team included two women doctors. He warned us in the strongest terms of the danger. So Dr. Patsy Putnam (Urbana, Ill.), the psychologist, decided to stay behind at the Army cordon. But Dr. Elaine Fay (Clinton, N.J.) insisted on going with us, saying she was the epi-something (epidemiologist).

We drove behind one of the riot cars at 30 mph for about an hour without seeing anything unusual. There were two big signs saying "SONS OF ADAM—LIBERATED ZONE." We passed some small pecan packing plants and a citrus processing plant. The men there looked at us but did not do anything un-usual. I didn't see any children or women of course. Just outside Peedsville we stopped at a big barrier made of oil drums in front of a large citrus warehouse. This area is old, sort of a shantytown and trailer park. The new part of town with the shopping center and developments is about a mile further on. A warehouse worker with a shotgun came out and told us to wait for the Mayor. I don't think he saw Dr. Elaine Fay then, she was sitting sort of bent down in back.

Mayor Blount drove up in a police cruiser and our chief, Dr. Premack, explained our mission from the

Surgeon General. Dr. Premack was very careful not to make any remarks insulting to the Mayor's religion. Mayor Blount agreed to let the party go on into Peedsville to take samples of the soil and water and so on and talk to the doctor who lives there. The mayor was about 6′ 2″, weight maybe 230 or 240, tanned, with grayish hair. He was smiling and chuckling in a friendly manner.

Then he looked inside the car and saw Dr. Elaine Fay and he blew up. He started yelling we had to all get the hell back. But Dr. Premack managed to talk to him and cool him down and finally the Mayor said Dr. Fay should go into the warehouse office and stay there with the door closed. I had to stay there too and see she didn't come out, and one of the Mayor's men would drive the party.

So the medical people and the Mayor and one of the riot vehicles went on into Peedsville and I took Dr. Fay back into the warehouse office and sat down. It was real hot and stuffy. Dr. Fay opened a window, but when I heard her trying to talk to an old man outside I told her she couldn't do that and closed the window. The old man went away. Then she wanted to talk to me but I told her I did not feel like conversing. I felt it was real wrong, her being there.

So then she started looking through the office files and reading papers there. I told her that was a bad idea, she shouldn't do that. She said the government expected her to investigate. She showed me a booklet or magazine they had there, it was called

Man Listens To God by Reverend McIllhenny. They had a carton full in the office. I started reading it and Dr. Fay said she wanted to wash her hands. So I took her back along a kind of enclosed hallway beside the conveyor to where the toilet was. There were no doors or windows so I went back. After awhile she called out that there was a cot back there, she was going to lie down. I figured that was all right because of the no windows, also I was glad to be rid of her company.

When I got to reading the book it was very intriguing. It was very deep thinking about how man is now on trial with God and if we fulfill our duty God will bless us with a real new life on Earth. The signs and portents show it. It wasn't like, you know, Sunday school stuff. It was deep.

After awhile I heard some music and saw the soldiers from the other riot car were across the street by the gas tanks, sitting in the shade of some trees and kidding with the workers from the plant. One of them was playing a guitar, not electric, just plain. It looked so peaceful.

Then Mayor Blount drove up alone in the cruiser and came in. When he saw I was reading the book he smiled at me sort of fatherly, but he looked tense. He asked me where Dr. Fay was and I told him she was lying down in back. He said that was okay. Then he kind of sighed and went back down the hall, closing the door behind him. I sat and listened to the guitar man, trying to hear what he was singing. I felt really hungry, my lunch was in Dr. Premack's car.

After awhile the door opened and Mayor Blount came back in. He looked terrible, his clothes were messed up and he had bloody scrape marks on his face. He didn't say anything, he just looked at me hard and fierce, like he might have been disoriented. I saw his zipper was open and there was blood on his clothing and also on his (private parts).

I didn't feel frightened, I felt something important had happened. I tried to get him to sit down. But he motioned me to follow him back down the hall, to where Dr. Fay was. "You must see," he said. He went into the toilet and I went into a kind of little room there, where the cot was. The light was fairly good, reflected off the tin roof from where the walls stopped. I saw Dr. Fay lying on the cot in a peaceful appearance. She was lying straight, her clothing was to some extent different but her legs were together. I was glad to see that. Her blouse was pulled up and I saw there was a cut or incision on her abdomen. The blood was coming out there, or it had been coming out there, like a mouth. It wasn't moving at this time. Also her throat was cut open.

I returned to the office. Mayor Blount was sitting down, looking very tired. He had cleaned himself off. He said, "I did it for you. Do you understand?"

He seemed like my father, I can't say it better than that. I realized he was under a terrible strain, he had taken a lot on himself for me. He went on to explain how Dr. Fay was very dangerous, she was what they call a cripto-female (crypto?), the most dangerous kind. He had exposed her and purified the situation.

He was very straightforward, I didn't feel confused at all, I knew he had done what was right.

We discussed the book, how man must purify himself and show God a clean world. He said some people raise the question of how can man reproduce without women but such people miss the point. The point is that as long as man depends on the old filthy animal way God won't help him. When man gets rid of his animal part which is woman, this is the signal God is awaiting. Then God will reveal the new true clean way, maybe angels will come bringing new souls, or maybe we will live forever, but it is not our place to speculate, only to obey. He said some men here had seen an Angel of the Lord. This was very deep, it seemed like it echoed inside me, I felt it was an inspiration.

Then the medical party drove up and I told Dr. Premack that Dr. Fay had been taken care of and sent away, and I got in the car to drive them out of the Liberated Zone. However, four of the six soldiers from the roadblock refused to leave. Capt. Parr tried to argue them out of it but finally agreed they could stay to guard the oil-drum barrier.

I would have liked to stay too the place was so peaceful but they needed me to drive the car. If I had known there would be all this hassle I never would have done them the favor. I am not crazy and I have not done anything wrong and my lawyer will get me out. That is all I have to say.

In Cuyapán the hot afternoon rain had temporarily ceased. As Alan's fingers let go of Sgt. Willard Mews's wretched document he caught sight of pencil-scrawled words in the margin. Barney's spider hand. He squinted.

Man's religion and metaphysics are the voices of his glands. Schönweiser, 1878.

Who the devil Schönweiser was Alan didn't know, but he knew what Barney was conveying. This murderous crackpot religion of McWhosis was a symptom, not a cause. Barney believed something was physically affecting the Peedsville men, generating psychosis, and a local religious demagog had sprung up to "explain" it.

Well, maybe. But cause or effect, Alan thought only of one thing: eight hundred miles from Peedsville to Ann Arbor. Anne should be safe. She *had* to be.

He threw himself on the lumpy cot, his mind going back exultantly to his work. At the cost of a million bites and cane-cuts he was pretty sure he'd found the weak link in the cane-fly cycle. The male mass-mating behavior, the comparative scarcity of ovulant females. It would be the screwfly solution all over again with the sexes reversed. Concentrate the pheromone, release sterilized females. Luckily the breeding populations were comparatively isolated. In a couple of seasons they ought to have it. Have to let them go on spraying poison meanwhile, of course; damn pity, it was slaughtering everything and getting in the water, and the caneflies had evolved to immunity anyway. But in a couple of seasons, maybe three, they could drop the canefly populations below reproductive viability. No more tormented human bodies with those stinking larvae in the nasal passages and brain. . . . He drifted off for a nap, grinning.

Up north, Anne was biting her lip in shame and pain.

Sweetheart, I shouldn't admit it but your wife is ~~scared~~ a bit jittery. Just female nerves or something, nothing to worry about. Everything is normal up here. It's so eerily normal, nothing in the papers, nothing anywhere except what I hear through Barney and Lillian. But Pauline's phone won't answer out in San Diego; the fifth day some strange man yelled at me and banged the phone down. Maybe she's sold her house—but why wouldn't she call?

Lillian's on some kind of Save-the-Women committee, like we were an endangered species, ha-ha—you know Lillian. It seems the Red Cross has started setting up camps. But she says, after the first rush, only a trickle are coming out of what they call "the affected areas." Not many children, either, even little boys. And they have some air-photos around Lubbock showing what look like mass graves. Oh, Alan . . . so far it seems to be mostly spreading west, but something's happening in St. Louis, they're cut off. So many places seem to have just vanished from the news, I had a nightmare that there isn't a woman left alive down there. And nobody's *doing* anything. They talked about spraying with tranquillizers for awhile and then that died out. What could it do? Somebody at the U.N. has proposed a convention on—you won't believe this—*femicide*. It sounds like a deodorant spray.

Excuse me honey, I seem to be a little hysterical. George Searles came back from Georgia talking about

God's Will—Searles the life-long atheist. Alan, something crazy is happening.

But there are no facts. Nothing. The Surgeon General issued a report on the bodies of the Rahway Rip-Breast Team—I guess I didn't tell you about that. Anyway, they could find no pathology. Milton Baines wrote a letter saying in the present state of the art we can't distinguish the brain of a saint from a psychopathic killer, so how could they expect to find what they don't know how to look for?

Well, enough of these jitters. It'll be all over by the time you get back, just history. Everything's fine here, I fixed the car's muffler again. And Amy's coming home for the vacations, *that'll* get my mind off faraway problems.

Oh, something amusing to end with—Angie told me what Barney's enzyme does to the spruce budworm. It seems it blocks the male from turning around after he connects with the female, so he mates with her *head* instead. Like clockwork with a cog missing. There're going to be some pretty puzzled female spruceworms. Now why couldn't Barney tell me that? He really is such a sweet shy old dear. He's given me some stuff to put in, as usual. I didn't read it.

Now don't worry my darling everything's fine.

I love you, I love you so.

Always, all ways your Anne

Two weeks later in Cuyapán when Barney's enclosures slid out of the envelope, Alan didn't read them either. He stuffed them into the pocket of his bush-jacket with a shaking hand and started bundling his notes together on the rickety table, with a scrawled note to Sister Dominique on top. *Anne, Anne my darling.* The hell with the canefly, the hell with everything except that tremor in his fearless girl's firm handwriting. The hell with being five thousand miles away from his woman, his child, while some deadly madness raged. He crammed his meager belongings into his duffel. If he hurried he could catch the bus through to Bogotá and maybe make the Miami flight.

In Miami he found the planes north jammed. He failed a quick standby; six hours to wait. Time to call Anne. When the call got through some difficulty he was unprepared for the rush of joy and relief that burst along the wires.

"Thank God—I can't believe it—Oh, Alan, my darling, are you really—I can't believe—"

He found he was repeating too, and all mixed up with the canefly data. They were both laughing hysterically when he finally hung up.

Six hours. He settled in a frayed plastic chair opposite *Aerolineas Argentinas,* his mind half back at the clinic, half on the throngs moving by him. Something was oddly different here, he perceived presently. Where was the decorative fauna he usually enjoyed in Miami, the parade of young girls in crotch-tight pastel jeans? The flounces, boots, wild hats and hairdos and startling expanses of newly-tanned skin, the brilliant fabrics barely confining the bob of breasts and buttocks? Not here—but wait; looking closely, he glimpsed two young faces hidden under unbecoming parkas, their bodies draped in bulky nondescript skirts. In fact, all down the long vista he could see the same thing: hooded ponchos, heaped-on clothes and baggy pants, dull colors. A new style? No, he thought not. It seemed to him their movements suggested furtiveness, timidity. And they moved in groups. He watched a lone girl struggle to catch up with others ahead of her, apparently strangers. They accepted her wordlessly.

They're frightened, he thought. Afraid of attracting notice. Even that gray-haired matron in a pantsuit resolutely leading a flock of kids was glancing around nervously.

And at the Argentine desk opposite he saw another odd thing: two lines had a big sign over them, *Mujeres*. Women. They were crowded with the shapeless forms and very quiet.

The men seemed to be behaving normally; hurrying, lounging, griping and joking in the lines as they kicked their luggage along. But Alan felt an undercurrent of tension, like an irritant in the air. Outside the line of storefronts behind him a few isolated men seemed to be handing out tracts. An airport attendant spoke to the nearest man; he merely shrugged and moved a few doors down.

To distract himself Alan picked up a *Miami Herald* from the next seat. It was surprisingly thin. The international news occupied him for awhile; he had seen none for weeks. It too had a strange empty quality, even the bad news seemed to have dried up. The African war which had been going on seemed to be over, or went unreported. A trade summit-meeting was haggling over grain and steel prices. He found himself at the obituary pages, columns of close-set type dominated by the photo of an unknown defunct ex-senator. Then his eye fell on two announcements at the bottom of the page. One was too flowery for quick comprehension, but the other stated in bold plain type:

THE FORSETTE FUNERAL HOME REGRETFULLY
ANNOUNCES IT WILL NO LONGER ACCEPT
FEMALE CADAVERS

Slowly he folded the paper, staring at it numbly. On the back was an item headed *Navigational Hazard Warning*, in the shipping news. Without really taking it in, he read:

> *AP/Nassau*: The excursion liner *Carib Swallow* reached port under tow today after striking an obstruction in the Gulf Stream off Cape Hatteras. The obstruction was identified as part of a commercial trawler's seine floated by female corpses. This confirms reports from Florida and the Gulf of the use of such seines, some of them over a mile in length. Similar reports coming from the Pacific coast and as far away as Japan indicate a growing hazard to coastwise shipping.

Alan flung the thing into the trash receptacle and sat rubbing his forehead and eyes. Thank God he had followed his impulse to come home. He felt totally disoriented, as though he had landed by error on another planet. Four and a half hours more to wait. . . . At length he recalled the stuff from Barney he had thrust in his pocket, and pulled it out and smoothed it.

The top item, however, seemed to be from Anne, or at least the Ann Arbor News. Dr. Lillian Dash, together with several hundred other members of her organization, had been arrested for demonstrating without a permit in front of the White House. They seemed to have started a fire in an oil drum, which was considered particularly heinous. A number of women's groups had participated, the total struck Alan as more like thousands than hundreds. Extraordinary security precautions were being taken, despite the fact that the President was out of town at the time.

The next item had to be Barney's, if Alan could recognize the old man's acerbic humor.

> *UP/Vatican City 19 June.* Pope John IV today intimated that he does not plan to comment officially on the so-called Pauline Purification cults advocating the elimination of women as a means of justifying man to God. A spokesman emphasized that the Church takes no position on these cults but repudiates any doctrine involving a "challenge" to or from God to reveal His further plans for man.
>
> Cardinal Fazzoli, spokesman for the European Pauline movement, reaffirmed his view that the Scriptures define woman as merely a temporary companion and instrument of Man. Women, he states, are nowhere defined as human, but merely as a transitional expedient or state. "The time of transition to full humanity is at hand," he concluded.

The next item appeared to be a thin-paper xerox from a recent issue of *Science*:

SUMMARY REPORT OF THE AD HOC
EMERGENCY COMMITTEE ON FEMICIDE
The recent world-wide though localized outbreaks of femicide appear to represent a recurrence of similar outbreaks by some group or sect which are not

uncommon in world history in times of psychic stress. In this case the root cause is undoubtedly the speed of social and technological change, augmented by population pressure, and the spread and scope are aggravated by instantaneous world communications, thus exposing more susceptible persons. It is not viewed as a medical or epidemiological problem; no physical pathology has been found. Rather it is more akin to the various manias which swept Europe in the 17th century, e.g., the Dancing Manias, and like them, should run its course and disappear. The chiliastic cults which have sprung up around the affected areas appear to be unrelated, having in common only the idea that a new means of human reproduction will be revealed as a result of the "purifying" elimination of women.

We recommend that (1) inflammatory and sensational reporting be suspended; (2) refugee centers be set up and maintained for women escapees from the focal areas; (3) containment of affected areas by military cordon be continued and enforced; and (4) after a cooling-down period and the subsidence of the mania, qualified mental health teams and appropriate professional personnel go in to undertake rehabilitation.

SUMMARY OF THE MINORITY
REPORT OF THE AD HOC COMMITTEE

The nine members signing this report agree that there is no evidence for epidemiological contagion of femicide in the strict sense. *However*, the geographical relation of the focal areas of outbreak strongly suggest that they cannot be dismissed as purely psychosocial phenomena. The initial outbreaks have occurred around the globe near the 30th parallel, the area of principal atmospheric downflow of upper winds coming from the Intertropical Convergence Zone. An agent or condition in the upper equatorial atmosphere would thus be expected to reach ground level along the 30th parallel, with certain seasonal variations. One principal variation is that the downflow moves north over the East Asian continent during the late winter months, and these areas south of it (Arabia, Western India, parts of North Africa) have in fact been free of outbreaks until recently, when the downflow zone has moved south. A similar downflow occurs in the Southern Hemisphere, and outbreaks have been reported along the 30th parallel running through Pretoria and Alice Springs, Australia. (Information from Argentina is currently unavailable.)

This geographical correlation cannot be dismissed, and it is therefore urged that an intensified search for a physical cause be instituted. It is also urgently recommended that the rate of spread from known focal points be correlated with wind conditions. A watch for similar outbreaks along the secondary down-welling zones at 60° north and south should be kept.

(signed for the minority)
Barnhard Braithwaite

Alan grinned reminiscently at his old friend's name, which seemed to restore normalcy and stability to the world. It looked as if Barney was onto something, too, despite the prevalence of horses' asses. He frowned, puzzling it out.

Then his face slowly changed as he thought how it would be, going home to Anne. In a few short hours his arms would be around her, the tall, secretly beautiful body that had come to obsess him. Theirs had been a late-blooming love. They'd married, he supposed now, out of friendship, even out of friends' pressure. Everyone said they were made for each other, he big and chunky and blond, she willowy brunette; both shy, highly controlled, cerebral types. For the first few years the friendship had held, but sex hadn't been all that much. Conventional necessity. Politely reassuring each other, privately—he could say it now—disappointing.

But then, when Amy was a toddler, something had happened. A miraculous inner portal of sensuality had slowly opened to them, a liberation into their own secret unsuspected heaven of fully physical bliss . . . Jesus, but it had been a wrench when the Colombia thing had come up. Only their absolute sureness of each other had made him take it. And now, to be about to have her again, trebly desirable from the spice of separation—feeling-seeing-hearing-smelling-grasping. He shifted in his seat to conceal his body's excitement, half mesmerized by fantasy.

And Amy would be there, too; he grinned at the memory of that prepubescent little body plastered against him. She was going to be a handful, all right. His manhood understood Amy a lot better than her mother did; no cerebral phase for Amy . . . But Anne, his exquisite shy one, with whom he'd found the way into the almost unendurable transports of the flesh . . . First the conventional greeting, he thought; the news, the unspoken, savored, mounting excitement behind their eyes; the light touches; then the seeking of their own room, the falling clothes, the caresses, gentle at first—the flesh, the *nakedness*—the delicate teasing, the grasp, the first thrust—

—A terrible alarm-bell went off in his head. Exploded from his dream, he stared around, then finally down at his hands. *What was he doing with his open clasp-knife in his fist?*

Stunned, he felt for the last shreds of his fantasy, and realized that the tactile images had not been of caresses, but of a frail neck strangling in his fist, the thrust had been the Plunge of a blade seeking vitals. In his arms, legs, phantasms of striking and trampling bones cracking. And Amy—

Oh God, Oh God—

Not sex, bloodlust.

That was what he had been dreaming. The sex was there, but it was driving some engine of death.

Numbly he put the knife away, thinking only over and over, it's got me. It's got me. Whatever it is, it's got me. *I can't go home.*

After an unknown time he got up and made his way to the United counter to turn in his ticket. The line was long. As he waited, his mind cleared a little. What could he do, here in Miami? Wouldn't it be better to get back to Ann Arbor and turn himself in to Barney? Barney could help him, if anyone could. Yes, that was best. But first he had to warn Anne.

The connection took even longer this time. When Anne finally answered he found himself blurting unintelligibly, it took awhile to make her understand he wasn't talking about a plane delay.

"I tell you, I've caught it. Listen, Anne, for God's sake. If I should come to the house don't let me come near you. I mean it. I mean it. I'm going to the lab, but I might lose control and try to get to you. Is Barney there?"

"Yes, but darling—"

"Listen. Maybe he can fix me, maybe this'll wear off. But I'm not safe, Anne, Anne, I'd kill you, can you understand? Get a—get a weapon. I'll try not to come to the house. But if I do, don't let me get near you. Or Amy. It's a sickness, it's real. Treat me—treat me like a fucking wild animal. Anne, say you understand, say you'll do it."

They were both crying when he hung up.

He went shaking back to sit and wait. After a time his head seemed to clear a little more. *Doctor, try to think.* The first thing he thought of was to take the loathsome knife and throw it down a trash-slot. As he did so he realized there was one more piece of Barney's material in his pocket. He uncrumpled it; it seemed to be a clipping from *Nature*.

At the top was Barney's scrawl: "Only guy making sense. U.K. infected now, Oslo, Copenhagen out of communication. Damfools still won't listen. Stay put."

COMMUNICATION FROM PROFESSOR IAN MacINTYRE, GLASGOW UNIV.

A potential difficulty for our species has always been implicit in the close linkage between the behavioural expression of aggression/predation and sexual reproduction in the male. This close linkage involves (a) many of the same neuromuscular pathways which are utilized both in predatory and sexual pursuit, grasping, mounting, etc., and (b) similar states of adrenergic arousal which are activated in both. The same linkage is seen in the males of many other species; in some, the expression of aggression and copulation alternate or even coexist, an all-too-familiar example being the common house cat. Males of many species bite, claw, bruise, tread or otherwise assault receptive females during the act of intercourse; indeed, in some species the male attack is necessary for female ovulation to occur.

In many if not all species it is the aggressive behaviour which appears first, and then changes to copulatory behaviour when the appropriate signal is presented (*e.g.*, the three-tined stickleback and the European robin). Lacking the inhibiting signal, the male's fighting response continues and the female is attacked or driven off.

It seems therefore appropriate to speculate that the present crisis might be caused by some substance, perhaps at the viral or enzymatic level, which effects a failure of the switching or triggering function in the higher primates. (Note: Zoo gorillas and chimpanzees have recently been observed to attack or destroy their mates; rhesus not.) Such a dysfunction could be expressed by the failure of mating behaviour to modify or supervene over the aggressive/predatory response; *i.e.*, sexual stimulation would produce attack only, the stimulation discharging itself through the destruction of the stimulating object.

In this connection it might be noted that exactly this condition is a commonplace of male functional pathology, in those cases where murder occurs as a response to and apparent completion of, sexual desire.

It should be emphasized that the aggressions/copulation linkage discussed here is specific to the male; the female response (*e.g.*, lordotic reflex) being of a different nature.

Alan sat holding the crumpled sheet a long time; the dry, stilted Scottish phrases seemed to help clear his head, despite the sense of brooding tension all around him. Well, if pollution or whatever had produced some substance, it could presumably be countered, filtered, neutralized. Very very carefully, he let himself consider his life with Anne, his sexuality. Yes; much of their loveplay could be viewed as genitalized, sexually-gentled savagery. Play-predation . . . He turned his mind quickly away. Some writer's phrase occurred to him: "The panic element in all sex." Who? Fritz Leiber? The violation of social distance, maybe; another threatening element. Whatever, it's our weak link, he thought. Our vulnerability . . . The dreadful feeling of *rightness* he had experienced when he found himself knife in hand, fantasizing violence, came back to him. As though it was the right, the only way. Was that what Barney's budworms felt when they mated with their females wrong-end-to?

At long length, he became aware of body need and sought a toilet. The place was empty, except for what he took to be a heap of clothes blocking the door of the far stall. Then he saw the red-brown pool in which it lay, and the bluish mounds of bare, thin buttocks. He backed out, not breathing, and fled into the nearest crowd, knowing he was not the first to have done so.

Of course. Any sexual drive. Boys, men, too.

At the next washroom he watched to see men enter and leave normally before he ventured in.

Afterward he returned to sit, waiting, repeating over and over to himself: *Go to the lab. Don't go home. Go straight to the lab.* Three more hours; he sat numbly at 26° N, 81° W, breathing, breathing . . .

Dear diary. Big scene tonite, Daddy came home!!! Only he acted so funny, he had the taxi wait and just held onto the doorway, he wouldn't touch me or let us come near him. (I mean funny weird, not funny Ha-ha.) He said, I have something to tell you, this is getting worse not better. I'm going to sleep in the lab but I want you to get out, Anne, Anne, I can't trust myself any more. First thing in the morning you both get on the plane for Martha's and stay there. So I thought he had to be joking, I mean with the dance next week and Aunt Martha lives in Whitehorse where there's nothing nothing nothing. So I was yelling and Mother was yelling and Daddy was groaning, Go now! And then he started crying. Crying!!! So I realized, wow, this is serious, and I started to go over to him but Mother yanked me back and then I saw she had this big KNIFE!!! And she shoved me in back of her and started crying too Oh Alan, Oh Alan, like she was insane. So I said, Daddy, I'll never leave you, it felt like the perfect thing to say. And it was thrilling, he looked at me real sad and deep like I was a grown-up while Mother was treating me like I was a mere infant as usual. But Mother ruined it raving Alan the child is mad, darling go. So he ran out the door yelling Be gone, Take the car, Get out before I come back.

Oh I forgot to say I was wearing what but my gooby green with my curltites still on, wouldn't you know of all the shitty luck, how could I have known such a beautiful scene was ahead we never

*know life's cruel whimsy. And mother is dragging
out suitcases yelling Pack your things hurry! So
she's going I guess but I am not repeat not going
to spend the fall sitting in Aunt Martha's grain silo
and lose the dance and all my summer credits. And
Daddy was trying to* communicate *with us, right?
I think their relationship is obsolete. So when she
goes upstairs I am splitting, I am going to go over
to the lab and see Daddy.*

*Oh PS Diane tore my yellow jeans she promised
me I could use her pink ones Ha-ha that'll be the
day.*

I ripped that page out of Amy's diary when I heard the squad
car coming. I never opened her diary before but when I found
she'd gone I looked. . . . Oh, my darling little girl. She went to
him, my little girl, my poor little fool child. Maybe if I'd taken
time to explain, maybe—

Excuse me, Barney. The stuff is wearing off, the shots they
gave me. I didn't feel anything. I mean, I knew somebody's
daughter went to see her father and he killed her. And cut his
throat. But it didn't mean anything.

Alan's note, they gave me that but then they took it away.
Why did they have to do that? His last handwriting, the last
words he wrote before his hand picked up the, before he—

I remember it. "*Sudden and light as that, the bonds gave.
And we learned of finalities besides the grave. The bonds of
our humanity have given, we are finished. I love—*"

I'm all right, Barney, really. Who wrote that, Robert Frost?
The bonds gave. . . . Oh, he said, tell Barney: *The terrible
rightness.* What does that mean?

You can't answer that, Barney dear. I'm just writing this to stay sane, I'll put it in your hidey-hole. Thank you, thank you Barney dear. Even as blurry as I was, I knew it was you. All the time you were cutting off my hair and rubbing dirt on my face, I knew it was right because it was you. Barney I never thought of you as those horrible words you said. You were always Dear Barney.

By the time the stuff wore off I had done everything you said, the gas, the groceries. Now I'm here in your cabin. With those clothes you made me put on I guess I do look like a boy, the gas man called me "Mister."

I still can't really realize, I have to stop myself from rushing back. But you saved my life, I know that. The first trip in I got a paper, I saw where they bombed the Apostle Islands refuge. And it had about those three women stealing the Air Force plane and bombing Dallas, too. Of course they shot them down, over the Gulf. Isn't it strange how we do nothing? Just get killed by ones and twos. Or more, now they've started on the refuges. . . . Like hypnotized rabbits. We're a toothless race.

Do you know I never said "we" meaning women before? "We" was always me and Alan, and Amy of course. Being killed selectively encourages group identification. . . . You see how sane-headed I am.

But I still can't really realize.

My first trip in was for salt and kerosene. I went to that little Red Deer store and got my stuff from the old man in the back, as you told me—you see, I remembered! He called me "Boy," but I think maybe he suspects. He knows I'm staying at your cabin.

Anyway, some men and boys came in the front. They were

all so *normal*, laughing and kidding. I just couldn't believe, Barney. In fact I started to go out past them when I heard one of them say "Heinz saw an angel." An *angel*. So I stopped and listened. They said it was big and sparkly. Coming to see if man is carrying out God's will, one of them said. And he said, Moosenee is now a liberated zone, and all up by Hudson Bay. I turned and got out the back, fast. The old man had heard them too. He said to me quietly, I'll miss the kids.

Hudson Bay, Barney, that means it's coming from the north too, doesn't it? That must be about 60°.

But I have to go back once again, to get some fishhooks. I can't live on bread. Last week I found a deer some poacher had killed, just the head and legs. I made a stew. It was a doe. Her eyes; I wonder if mine look like that now.

I went to get the fishhooks today. It was bad, I can't ever go back. There were some men in front again, but they were different. Mean and tense. No boys. And there was a new sign out in front, I couldn't see it; maybe it says Liberated Zone too.

The old man gave me the hooks quick and whispered to me, "Boy, them woods'll be full of hunters next week." I almost ran out.

About a mile down the road a blue pickup started to chase me. I guess he wasn't from around there, I ran the VW into a logging draw and he roared on by. After a long while I drove out and came on back, but I left the car about a mile from here and hiked in. It's surprising how hard it is to pile enough brush to hide a yellow VW.

Barney, I can't stay here. I'm eating perch raw so nobody will see my smoke, but those hunters will be coming through.

I'm going to move my sleeping bag out to the swamp by that big rock, I don't think many people go there.

Since the last lines I moved out. It feels safer. Oh, Barney, how did this *happen*?

Fast, that's how. Six months ago I was Dr. Anne Alstein. Now I'm a widow and bereaved mother, dirty and hungry, squatting in a swamp in mortal fear. Funny if I'm the last woman left alive on Earth. I guess the last one around here, anyway. Maybe some holed out in the Himalayas, or sneaking through the wreck of New York City. How can we last?

We can't.

And I can't survive the winter here, Barney. It gets to 40° below. I'd have to have a fire, they'd see the smoke. Even if I worked my way south, the woods end in a couple hundred miles. I'd be potted like a duck. No. No use. Maybe somebody is trying something somewhere, but it won't reach here in time . . . and what do I have to live for?

No. I'll just make a good end, say up on that rock where I can see the stars. After I go back and leave this for you. I'll wait to see the beautiful color in the trees one last time.

I know what I'll scratch for an epitaph.

HERE LIES THE SECOND MEANEST

PRIMATE ON EARTH.

Good-bye, dearest dearest Barney.

I guess nobody will ever read this, unless I get the nerve and energy to take it to Barney's. Probably I won't. Leave it in a Baggie, I have one here; maybe Barney will come and look. I'm up on the big rock now. The moon is going to rise soon, I'll do it then. Mosquitoes, be patient. You'll have all you want.

The thing I have to write down is that I saw an angel too. This morning. It was big and sparkly, like the man said; like a Christmas tree without the tree. But I knew it was real because the frogs stopped croaking and two bluejays gave alarm calls. That's important; it was *really there.*

I watched it, sitting under my rock. It didn't move much. It sort of bent over and picked up something, leaves or twigs, I couldn't see. Then it did something with them around its middle, like putting them into an invisible sample-pocket.

Let me repeat—it was *there.* Barney, if you're reading this, THERE ARE THINGS HERE. And I think they've done whatever it is to us. Made us kill ourselves off.

Why? Well, it's a nice place, if it wasn't for people. How do you get rid of people? Bombs, death-rays—all very primitive. Leave a big mess. Destroy everything, craters, radioactivity, ruin the place.

This way there's no muss, no fuss. Just like what we did to the screwfly. Pinpoint the weak link, wait a bit while we do it for them. Only a few bones around; make good fertilizer.

Barney dear, good-bye. I saw it. It was there.

But it wasn't an angel.

I think I saw a real-estate agent.

1977

ELINOR BUSBY

Time to Kill

SHE HAD to escape the crowd. Picking up her skirts Heidi ran through dusty streets. Her sandals fell off and stones hurt her feet, but dodging around corners she managed to elude them and get to the time machine and shut the door, flip the levers and shimmer away to where she belonged.

The crowd hated her. They had a right to hate her; she had committed a murder, a willful, premeditated murder of a person who had done no wrong. But that wasn't the reason they hated her. They had not discovered the body she had left crumpled in a dark corner behind the temple.

The crowd hated her because—"Witch! Witch!"—she heard their cries.

She was wrong. Noticeably wrong. She had done so much research, tried hard to be authentic, had even learned to weave so that her clothes would be right. It hadn't worked. Even her Hebrew, so painstakingly learned, was too formal and incorrectly pronounced. Worst of all were her attitudes. She didn't know how to hold her body or even how to look at people properly.

It was a miracle they had let her exist in their time long enough to accomplish her mission. She wished they hadn't. "No, no," she thought. "I did the right thing. I *have* to have done the right thing."

She was surprised that she was still alive. It was a suicide mission, changing the past to alter the future, and she a part

322 | Elinor Busby

of that future, of the smog, population pressure, resource depletion and sense of impending doom. She had forced the Changeover; why was she still alive to remember what she had rather not?

"Lyle," said Heidi, "what part of the past do you think they intend to change?"

"It's a Top Secret project. Are you sure we're private enough?"

They were sitting in a park, no one very near.

"What's to bug? A blade of grass?"

"There are always lip readers—more every year with noise pollution increasing. If we hold our heads quite close together and look directly at each other, it should be all right?"

"Kiss, kiss," said Heidi, drily. They both grinned. They were friends, not lovers.

"The idea, of course, is to change the past to improve the present. If it's successful many of us will never have been born."

"Lyle, why do you like to tell me what I already know?"

"I like to, that's all. Do you really mind?"

She laughed. "It wouldn't do me much good. Where do you think they will put Changeover?"

"As close to present as they can and still have it do any good at all. They want to eliminate as few people as possible, just enough to give the survivors a chance, a viable planet."

"That's dumb! They should put Changeover far enough back to make it a really nice world."

"I agree—but you and I are low on the totem pole. They won't ask our advice. Dr. Halvorson wants Changeover about twenty years ago, just after the end of the Vietnam war. He says that's a good time because a lot of people were concerned about ecology, and would accept a better automobile engine, less polluting, not run on gasoline, and so forth."

"Hah! Detroit had less than no desire to retool and had a stranglehold on Congress."

"Well—that's what Dr. Yamagata says, too. His idea is that Changeover should be run back to before World War I. He wants Henry Ford gently hinted into developing some better type of vehicle."

"Him? He was as independent as a hog on ice. I *think* I see him taking a hint from a Time Traveller."

"Where would *you* put it, Heidi?"

"I'd like something really drastic. I wish we could go back to ancient Greek and Roman times, and Vikings and Druids, when people worshipped goddesses and gods, trees and fountains. People were close to the Mother Earth, a part of Mother Nature. The world went wrong when we lost the Female Principle—choked out by God the Father and God the Son."

"Blaming everything on us fellows, are you?" said Lyle, grinning. "Not that I can claim to be either God the Father or God the Son.

"But I think maybe you're right."

Heidi and Lyle talked many times after that, and became increasingly convinced that elimination of Christianity would save the world.

"It was St. Paul," said Lyle. "Christ himself did no real harm. St. Paul invented all that 'better to marry than to burn' stuff. He transferred the puritanical aspects of Judaism into Christianity, when Jesus had been happy to associate with publicans and whores, and had said 'let he among you who is without sin cast the first stone.'"

"And it was St. Paul who brought Christianity out of Palestine into Rome. To save the world from Christianity, all we have to do is eliminate Paul."

"I don't agree," said Heidi. "I think you're right that St. Paul was responsible for the anti-life interpretation of Christ's teachings, but if it hadn't been he, perhaps it would have been someone else. The only way to be sure is to kill Jesus."

"I always *liked* Jesus," said Lyle.

"Well, yes," said Heidi. "But killing him is the only way to be sure of preventing Christianity."

"Then *you* do it," said Lyle.

Heidi laughed. "Lyle, no way would anyone expect you to do something as decisive as killing."

Heidi, with Lyle's help, made her plans and preparations. The machine was completed, and while the factions of Dr. Halvorson and Dr. Yamagata were still arguing about Changeover times and methods, Heidi and Lyle moved.

Heidi, with Lyle standing guard, slipped into the time machine and set the controls, both geographic and chronologic. She was at the temple when Jesus, twelve years old, arrived to question the rabbis. She had thought that would be the easiest time—smart ass kid—making his elders look stupid.

It was not an easy time. A young boy, radiant in early puberty, with brilliant dark eyes that seemed to look through her, examine her darkest secrets and accept them all.

She talked to him just long enough to establish his identity. She knew he was God and she loved him with all her heart. Then she stuck the knife into his chest.

She was back. Lyle was still there, standing guard. Of course. She had returned at essentially the same time she left.

"Did you really go back? Are you sure the controls were set right?"

She nodded. The doors to the laboratory were being battered. The energy drain had been noted. In their last moments of freedom, Heidi and Lyle ran to the window and looked out. Too many people, too much smog. No changes of any kind were evident.

"You blew it," said Lyle. "Your Female Principle is as suppressed as ever. You didn't do a thing to stop Mithraism."

1977

M. LUCIE CHIN

The Best Is Yet to Be

CATHERINE MADE a somber appraisal of the face for the hundredth time since bringing it home from the hospital. Deep-set grey eyes with a slight droop to the corners, what she had labeled "basic basset hound." A longish nose. High cheekbones over a squared-off jaw. The mouth had to be the best element. It undulated in a pleasingly sensuous line, ending in a slightly upward emphasis which almost balanced the eyes. Even when she laughed those eyes set the mood of her face. They were the stongest, if not exactly the best, feature. She had almost forgotten. No, she *had* forgotten.

The rest of the body didn't matter much. Whatever small annoyances she experienced after each homecoming could be adjusted to quickly enough, and one's weight could be dealt with. She wasn't too particular about that sort of thing. It was the face that counted.

What's in a face?

Nothing, if fashion is all that concerns you. But Catherine had always identified with faces, particularly the eyes. If the mind was the seat of reason, the face was clearly the gateway to the personality.

She considered the reflection in the mirror, elbows on the dressing table, fingers laced together, thumbs supporting her chin, the mouth hidden behind a low mountain range of knuckles which peaked just below her nose. She and her image mesmerized each other in the dim light of the table lamp. The thin grey-white tendrils of smoke from her forgotten cigarette drifted upward before the eyes, locked in contact with themselves. Sobriety seemed inherent in the structure of the face. She had become accustomed to a more pliable expressiveness. The eyes dictated too much. The state of mind with which she regarded herself was evidence enough of that.

The aroma of cigarette smoke was becoming rank. It intruded upon her attention and she looked down. She had lit it when she had sat to comb her hair and had only taken one long pull. Already over half its length was a frail, cantilevered thing of dull white fluff-and-nothing clinging together for lack of anything better to do. She unclasped her hands and gently tapped the tabletop watching the ash collapse into the ashtray. The butt fell back onto the dressing table and she picked it up, took another drag and stubbed it out. It had been years since she had quit smoking but since coming home from the hospital this last time she had begun again without really noticing. Harvard had noticed, but then it was his business to look for such things.

"Maybe I'll get a face lift," she said to the reflection, half aloud. "Like so."

With the middle finger of each hand Catherine pushed upward at her temples. The eyebrows winged out and the droopy corners disappeared giving her eyes a startled Egyptian sort of look. She turned her head silently from side to side. The effect was somewhat exotic.

"If I have to live with you I may as well like it."

But Catherine knew Harvard would never agree. He would strenuously oppose anything which might threaten the fragile balance of her situation and unnecessary surgery would most definitely head the list. If nothing else, he had his reputation to protect. How would posterity view the man who let Catherine van Dyck die? Unfortunately, history had no choices and neither did he. It was too bad he refused to believe it.

He had a vested interest in "Catherine the Great." She was a family heirloom of sorts. He had inherited her from his father who had inherited her from the generation before and once more again.

But she could feel the difference this time. Even as she left the bedroom and reached too high for the doorknob she was sure. She would take this body to the grave . . . or it would take her, depending on how you looked at it. Oddly, in spite of all the operations and all the frantic searches over the years of her life, the sureness of it did not bother her. She felt it was what she had been waiting for. A time for everything and everything in its time, she thought.

On the landing was a young woman, in her late twenties, blonde, hazel-eyed, and average in height. A look of anticipation was knit into her brows. "Kitty?" she said in a quiet voice.

Catherine broke into a smile, throwing her head back in a soundless laugh and waltzed a long dark shadow about the upstairs hall in the amber glow of the afternoon sun, which gushed through the windows. With outstretched arms and a smug serenity she whirled to a stop in front of the young woman.

"Sara! Well, how do I look?"

She made two more slow, regal turns while Sara observed carefully.

"About twice your height and half your age."

"My dear," Catherine said in an indulgent voice, as she swept an arm around Sara's shoulders, "there isn't a functioning human body on the face of the earth that is half my age."

She reached for the banister, missed, reached again. "And I only gained eight inches."

"It must be strange seeing the world from 5′ 10″ after so long at 5′ 2″."

"It isn't like I haven't been here before, or very nearly. Actually 5′ 2″ took a lot more getting used to, and I only had it for 28 years . . . but then you weren't around the last time. I must say this is a pleasantly novel experience. I haven't been able to look you in the eye since you were twelve." And she smiled and squeezed Sara's shoulders.

Sara looked at her and hung her head. "I don't know if I can get used to it, Aunt Kitty."

"What did you expect?"

"I don't know. It's been six months since I saw you and then you were my father's age. Now you are younger than I am."

"Correction, six months ago I *looked* your father's age. In point of fact I am old enough to be his great-grandmother . . . and you know what that makes you." Catherine was using the mock-stern lecture voice she found most appropriate at such times as it became necessary to remind people of who she was. She was well pleased with the vocal range of this body. Though it was only 25 years old it responded perfectly to all the nuances of voice she liked to employ. Her own enduring self-concept had always been contralto. The 5′ 2″ personage had been annoyingly soprano.

"Don't let it bother you, dear, you'll get used to it. If I can get used to it anyone can."

"But it's more important for me to come to terms with this than for most others. One of these days the responsibility will be mine and I—"

"Believe me, this time next year you won't remember what the former Cat van Dyck looked like without making an effort." They reached the downstairs hall, windowless and dusklike in the light of one antique wall lamp. "I don't know why your father likes this place so dark. It is downright morbid." She hunched up her shoulders a bit resting her gaze on Sara. "Don't you find that a bit curious for a man dedicated to the preservation of a life?"

"I guess I never paid much attention to this place."

"I have found myself thinking about a lot of things lately, peripheral things really, but at one time they seemed to be a very vital thing . . . for me anyhow . . . Lately I feel like a walking mausoleum. I'm not even a freak anymore—" she gave an odd smile which was at once smug and humorless "—I'm an institution."

Sara had been watching her closely, appraisingly. "You are one of the finest human beings I have ever known, Aunt Kitty. You have been my best friend since I was old enough to know one adult from another. And even after I knew how special you really were I never had to relate to it till now."

"I have always had to."

"All the more reason for you to remember your humanity. Since the preservation of that life you spoke of is obviously not the perpetuation of any particular body there must be something else worth keeping alive. Call it anything you want, but the person you have continued to be all this time is inexorably bound up with its own humanness. *That* is important. This seems like a hell of a time for you to forget it."

"I don't forget."

Remembering what she and her father had talked about shortly after her arrival, Sara tilted her head and looked at Catherine sideways. But Catherine had not sounded totally serious. The voice was unfamiliar but the tone it employed was light, slightly facetious. Catherine had always preferred to play devil's advocate whenever she found the opportunity. Was she playing now?

"Where is your father?" Catherine said.

"In the parlor with Chris."

"Then why are we standing here, while your husband twiddles his thumbs and your father bores him to death with the details of his latest triumph?"

Sara smiled and followed her across the room. "Oh, Aunt Kitty, you know Chris is fascinated with my father."

"God only knows why, the man only has one subject he is willing to talk about. And that's another thing . . . this 'Aunt Kitty' business. I was only a courtesy aunt anyway. I think, considering our apparent respective ages, it would prove less awkward if you dropped the aunt."

"If that's what you want, I'll do my best," Sara said.

"Just consider it another part of the Harvard family legacy," Catherine said, opening the doors into the parlor.

The room was brightly lit, with a fire dancing frantically in the heavy mantled fireplace. It was bracketed by two floral-print couches which faced each other over a low coffee table on which stood a massive bouquet of flowers.

Dr. John B. Harvard II stood to the left of the fireplace, harassing the condemned wood with a poker. He was of average height, a little more than average in weight, on the thin edge of sixty and handsome as all the Harvard men had been since the first John, Catherine's John, the one who had started all this. Across from him, seated on the right hand couch, was a younger man of about thirty, taller and leaner, darkly good looking with bright green eyes and a quick, equally bright smile. Christian and Sara Kent had been married about five years and Catherine liked him immensely.

Harvard heard the door and straightened at the side of the hearth.

"Ah, here we are!" he beamed.

Chris turned and rose from his seat, his right hand extended, a smile washing his face.

"Kitty . . ." He had intended to say something like "How are you" or, perhaps, "It's wonderful to see you again" or maybe both. But he found he could not get beyond the one word. The smile did not exactly fade, but it transformed itself into an almost cliched expression of wonder. He stood mutely, letting his eyes find their own way from her head to the hem of her long, well-fitted gown, up to the short, precisely shaped cap of auburn hair, down again, finally anchoring themselves on her face.

"Close your mouth, Christian, you look ridiculous," Catherine said. She did a quick two-step and a spin, laughing. "The Cat has once again landed on her feet," she announced to the ceiling, arms outstretched.

"Very theatrical," Harvard said, no longer smiling. "I suggest you save that for the press and behave yourself in the meantime."

"Go to hell," Catherine replied, seating herself on the couch opposite the one Chris was once again occupying. She leaned forward and picked up the nearest glass. "What's this?"

"Scotch," Harvard said, "and you're not having any."

Catherine was ignoring him.

"I used to like scotch," she said, setting the ice into a circling chase in the topaz liquid. The rim of the glass escaped her lips by a hair's breadth and John Harvard set the drink on the mantle and glared at her.

"I don't know what's gotten into you lately."

Sara didn't know either. She was worried. There were things Catherine had never been able to do. Strenuous exercise had always been considered risky, though some kinds of exercise were essential. Infections of all types were guarded against obsessively, her diet and medications were carefully scrutinized, her physical condition religiously checked at closely spaced intervals. Sara had never known her to smoke or drink, assuming she understood how it could interfere with the body's resistance to all kinds of things. But it was more than that. She had never heard Catherine swear before and though she had always had a firm will where her own interests were concerned, she had never known her to be deliberately obstinate. She watched and filed things away for future reference.

"Don't be an ass," Catherine said, leaning back against the upholstered garden paths. "*Nothing* has gotten into me . . . it is what *I* have gotten into."

"Cute."

"I wish you'd do your homework. Your father and grandfather kept copious notes on the situation."

Harvard grunted.

"What situation?" Sara asked.

"Let's face it, no one's psyche is perfect. No matter how well prepared you may be, the experience of suddenly finding yourself thirty or forty years younger than you were can't fail to make you somewhat euphoric. The personality invariably adjusts itself to the perceived age of the body." She shrugged and smiled, "You just can't help it."

"Euphoric is hardly the word I would use to describe your recent behavior," Harvard said sternly.

"How about snotty?" she said turning to him.

"It fits."

"I thought you'd like it."

"I don't, not at all. Now you listen to me," he had the greatest urge to add "young lady" but he caught himself and pointed a finger instead. "I don't care what you think about this time around. I have listened to you, and you have not said one word I can attribute to anything but gut feelings on your part . . . and you know what I think about that kind of thing. Crap! Show me something I can test, measure—"

"You won't live that long," Catherine said coolly and Sara and Chris looked startled.

"I still have another 35 years left according to statistics. With your track record we could well have another go around before I have to pass the problem over to Sara."

"Don't hold your breath."

"Oh, Cat," he grumbled in exasperation.

"Yes!" she said sitting suddenly erect. Her face was stone-like. Not anger, or defiance, but the most solid sincerity Sara had ever seen; and Catherine's new face reflected it superbly. It was amazing how well she was able to know its power in so short a time. "Yes!" her voice was as sober as her face, "and I am in my ninth life."

"And I don't want to hear any more about *that*, either!" Harvard said, replacing the poker with a clank.

Chris was looking embarrassed. He was also looking at his watch and clearing his throat.

"If we don't get going soon we are going to be late for dinner," he said quietly.

"Saved by the bell," Catherine said, relaxing back against the couch.

"Good heavens!" Harvard grabbed up his coat as he hastened toward the door, eyes checking and double-checking his own watch. "I will bring the car around. Meet me at the front door." And he was gone.

"Aunt—" Sara caught herself and began again. "Kitty, was that really necessary?"

"No, but your father is such a bloody stubborn man. His father and his grandfather used to listen to me at least. He can be so sanctimonious sometimes it's sickening. I live inside this body and I have a far better feel for what goes on in here than anyone is willing to believe . . . even you, I dare say." And she got up and walked out.

"Kitty!" Sara caught her just beyond the door. "I just don't want to see you two fighting. You're like a part of the family. You *are* a part of it. You know how much you mean to all of us. But especially to Dad."

Catherine relented a bit with a deep sigh.

"I know. He can't mean me anything but the best he knows how, which is a great deal. And I am grateful. You can't imagine *how* grateful. But I know a thing which he refuses to accept, and it's frustrating . . . infuriating! Besides, my current mode of behavior is not without historical precedent. If he could see that and place it in its proper perspective it would make things a great deal easier for him."

Catherine reached into the closet too high for the coat and

missed. She shoved both hands into the draping of her skirt and glared at the ceiling for a moment. Then she stared into the closet an instant and slowly, deliberately reached for the coat again.

"Gotcha!"

Chris stood behind her, concerned.

"Catherine, are you alright?"

She laughed and handed him the coat, which he helped her into.

"Yes, I'm fine, I'm better than I have been in ages. It's just a little orientation problem. Your wife was right when she said it must be strange looking at the world from 5′ 10″ after so long at 5′ 2″.

"One's perspective of the world is purely a thing of the mind," she said tapping her temple lightly with a lacquered nail. "The body has no memory of itself. One therefore relates to what one knows of the world through experience. For the last 28 years I have experienced coat hangers as things which must be reached *up* for.

"It is a common problem for brain transplant patients who are not always lucky enough to find themselves hosted by a body of the same relative dimensions as the old one."

The horn sounded on the driveway and they moved quickly out the door.

Catherine, with an occasional assist from John Harvard, continued to outline the trials and tribulations of adjusting to a new body. Chris was fascinated. Sara listened and nodded occasionally and kept mental notes.

The experience was like unexpectedly finding yourself in a whole new world. The body has its rhythms, its own special feel, which may escape notice by the conscious mind but do not elude the subconscious. It is an alien environment as potent as the ones surrounding the colonies on the moon or the research stations on Mars and must be adjusted to in much the same way. Assess everything, particularly that which the mind finds most disturbing, and assimilate it . . . consciously at first, later attempting to cope with things on a more reflexive level. Some people are not capable of accomplishing it. The psychological obstacles are, perhaps, too formidable or sometimes too subtle. In spite of careful screening and the medical team's painstaking efforts to find a compatible host body, the end result is not always what the patient may have anticipated. Recipients are no longer allowed to see the donor body before the event. The psychological after-effects of such meetings as did occur in the early days were devastating. *Most* people preferred not to know. Still, the suicide rate among those deemed suitable was far higher than most concerned individuals felt was within reason.

Catherine was supremely adaptable. Of the eight bodies which had hosted her brain since the death of her original one 185 years before, some had lasted far longer than others but none had failed her immediately. The first was the shortest, five years; the second had been twelve, but the third, that had lasted for 37 years. After that some were better and some not as good, but one thing they all had in common; no matter how long the association, eventually they all moved to evict their tenant.

That in itself was not unusual. Though the rate of permanent acceptance was quite high now, there was still a significant number of initial rejections. Some of these patients were not capable of surviving a second operation, but of those that did, the vast majority never rejected again. Aside from Catherine, there was only one other known survivor of a third transplant. He had died of natural causes several years before and the autopsy had shown that he and his host were still fully integrated. But Catherine van Dyck was unique. Not only had she survived eight such transplants, she was the oldest living human being in the world, still active in mind and fluid in character, without a trace of senility or the psychosis which plagued the lives of the less fortunate of her sort. Counting the original 25 years of her life before the chain of surgery which bound her to the Harvard medical monarch, she was 210 and sometimes, privately, she felt every day of it.

She was unique in another respect too. She was the first. The first human, that is, to come through the operation cognizant, functional, and alive more than two weeks later. She was a living legend (Harvard kept saying it was the best kind). The world at large seemed to consider her immortal and sometime around the date of her fourth transplant (her fifth life as she preferred to put it) she had been dubbed by some unknown member of the press as Catherine the Great and it had stuck. She had lived through roughly four generations and each one had felt compelled to contribute a biography or two to the myth growing in her wake. They were factually pretty accurate and all quite nearly the same.

They were also all wrong. When the time came she would leave them the story and dare them to believe it. They would probably prefer the myth. Myths are comfortable and pliable and entertaining and not filled with the dreams of the walking dead whose lives she shared through the use of their bodies. It was not a horror. It was an obligation she felt to the gift of the donor . . . that a person may still live as long as they are remembered. Catherine preserved all of them within her.

She sought out as much as she could learn about each of the unknowns who had given her their blessing in the form of their bodies and tried to incorporate into her life at least one of the goals they had striven for. It was a private thing. She had never told anyone, but she swore that in the end, as long as she was remembered, they would be. They were wrong about other things too. Things she had forgotten over all the years. Things which were strangely bidden to mind lately. Things she would not forget again.

She thought about a great deal of this as John Harvard's car sensed its way to the destination he had punched into the dash panel and she sat in the back, chatting and playing cards over the small, retractable table with her three companions. She thought about it, but she talked about the initial shock of waking up to a new beginning in a hospital bed, of doing weeks of double takes when you faced a stranger in the mirror, of reaching too high for some things or too low for others, of going shopping and trying to squeeze into something three sizes too small, learning to modulate a new voice, bouts with the psychiatrists and physical therapists, and getting used to the looks on the faces of your friends when they don't recognize you—all the things the average brain transplant patient is likely to have to go through. But not the things that were hers and hers alone.

The dinner party was a press conference in disguise. Out of disguise, it was the sort of thing the influential people in the business of fund raising did to court the favors of the sort of money which found benefit events tacky. Money in general was never discussed, but all the right people were nestled together in a warm and nurturing environment with good food and fine wine and things were allowed to develop naturally. Lluella Harvard was imbued with an absolute genius for gathering the manna of the rich for the benefit of her various projects. Thus she was the principal fund raiser for, among other things, the Novak Memorial Hospital which was sometimes referred to as the court of Catherine the Great. She was also John Harvard's former wife.

Lluella Harvard was like a natural force, compelling and potentially devastating. She could be no more ignored than the tide, nor could she be contained or controlled any more successfully. But she was far from arbitrary. She carried on her life with an elegant calculation firmly bound to her vested interests. What benefited Lluella benefited a great many things.

There was no animosity in the separation of one of the world's more notable couples. After 29 years of marriage, they had simply had no time for each other any longer. They were both too thoroughly bound up in their own purposeful directions and pursuing them independently seemed finally the best course. After 8 years of separation they were still cordial and friendly, which is about as much as they had been for a fair part of the marriage.

Lluella was as close to Catherine as anyone had been over the years till Sara came along. Lluella had recognized very early that there was something quite special between Cat and her little daughter. Catherine she found to be somewhat more enigmatic than most people, but how can one really expect to be able to read someone who has lived *so* long, and in such a way. She knew Catherine kept her own counsel far more intimately than John Harvard was willing to recognize. He knew her reactions and reflexes and attitudes and opinions far better than anyone (with the exception of Sara) but he did not look for anything behind what she was willing to admit to. Plumbing the depths was Lluella's talent and though she had recognized their existence she had never cared to intrude.

She watched the driveway now, feeling unnaturally fidgety. They were late and she could not restrain herself from looking for the car. It was unlike John. He was almost legendary in his promptness. Catherine, on the other hand, could be having problems. Lluella worried that Catherine might not really have been up to this quite yet after all. But this was an important evening and Cat would be well aware of it. She would probably not have declined the invitation unless there were serious complications. Catherine was hardly a martyr but she had a strong sense of responsibility, along with a certain degree of the theatrical. Her image was carefully tended.

Lluella realized, however, that the fidgets were not purely due to the lack of punctuality. In the first year of her marriage she had watched her husband's craft transform a stately, matriarchal being of slightly Wagnerian dimensions and formidable presence, visually in her late sixties, into a petite, bright-eyed cherub of 30. They were suddenly, disconcertingly, contemporaries. If the knowledge of Catherine the Great in the fullness and power of her maturity was a cogent experience for the mind, this other aspect was subtly awesome.

When the car crunched to a stop on the drive, she felt as though she had suddenly come awake and opened the door to greet them herself. Sara and Chris were the first up the steps, giving her a hug and kiss each and John was making pleasantry at her from somewhere behind them. Then he stepped up, took her hand, and planted a kiss on her cheek. When he stepped aside there was a stranger at the foot of the stairs.

Lluella felt the touch of awe once again.

"Cat?"

"Hello, Lluella," an unfamiliar voice said.

"It suits you," she said and felt it was true.

"I'm more than satisfied," Catherine said smiling as she climbed the stairs. "A point here or there that I might want to alter, but nothing of significance."

"Forget it," Harvard grumbled, and Lluella looked from him to Cat and back again trying to weigh the tone of his voice and the look of defiance which flashed into her eyes.

"Who do we have inside?" he asked.

Lluella began to recite the guest list but he amended his request asking for the representatives of the press his former wife would not have neglected to include.

"Thomas Hooker . . ."

Harvard looked sour.

"You may not like the man—"

"He's an idiot."

"—but he represents the best medical journal in the country."

"I didn't ask you to throw him out," he said holding up his hands. "Who else?"

"Walter Dale, Francois Soufflot—"

"Ah, you've gone international."

She shot him a wifely look and finished, "—and Adella Chambers."

Harvard turned to Catherine soberly. "Watch out for that one."

"I'm hardly a novice at this," Catherine answered, archness in her voice.

"Just watch what you say. I don't want any of this nonsense cropping up in the wrong places. And this is the first wrong place."

He began to turn but Lluella caught him with a look.

"Are you two at war?"

Harvard cleared his throat.

"If so I want you to bottle it up and cork it tight right here. There are to be no skirmishes in my dining room. Is that perfectly clear? And I mean both of you!"

"It's alright mother, really," Sara said. "They are both rational adults. I hardly think they would be that foolish."

"They have been that foolish already," Lluella said. "They let *me* see it. I don't want anyone else to."

"It has nothing to do with John," Catherine said, "except at the point where he refuses to accept what I have said to him. *He* is the one who insists upon making an issue of it."

Harvard was standing with arms folded, looking stern.

"Allow me to acquaint you with what she is capable of saying this evening, so you'll recognize it in time to head it off—if necessary," he emphasized in Catherine's direction.

"Cat has arbitrarily come to the conclusion that this is the last go-around for her. Her favorite phrase these days is 'the cat is in her ninth life.' This is her last body she tells me . . . no more."

"That sounds disturbingly suicidal, Cat," Lluella said.

Catherine turned and looked silently out across the lawn. Lluella felt rebuffed. She had never known Catherine to be deliberately rude.

"If she intends to do herself in," Harvard continued, "it

won't be a quiet dignified departure. She's begun smoking, drinking when I can't catch her; the other day she took the car out, all alone I might add, and went swimming at the beach, and she has a whole new vocabulary to go with her new face. She also has an attitude problem these days."

"Which is directly related to your own, doctor," Catherine said turning slowly. "It's *my* business. It's my life, and I know what I know. I'm not going to *kill* myself, I'm going to *live* my life. I can and I will . . . *this* time . . . . and when I'm done there will be no need to go on to another. Excuse me," and she passed into the house.

Lluella realized she looked startled, standing there wide-eyed with her hand covering her mouth like that. Sara looked much the same only a little less dramatic with her hands in her pockets. Chris was frowning and John glowered darkly.

"Since leaving the hospital she seems to have developed this death wish," he said somberly. "It galls me, it really does. That she would throw away all the work that has been dedicated to her existence over the years, all the research done in her name, all the refinement of techniques developed to make each new phase of her life better, fuller, healthier. I'm not discounting the benefits that have accrued to mankind in general, but she has been for so long the motivation, the inspiration, the most truly compelling factor in all this—to chuck it all now—it seems downright ungrateful. Look at the years she has been given."

"Perhaps those years are becoming too much," Chris said.

"No," he shook his head, "she's clear as a bell. She's basically unencumbered by the burdens of old age."

"I was thinking more in terms of just plain being tired," Chris said.

Harvard gave a short chuckle. "She suddenly seems to have far more energy than is good for her. And that is what's so puzzling. This sudden lust for life seems at odds with her refusal even to consider another transplant operation."

"Well, look at it this way," Chris said, trying to move things toward the door. "It is only a few months since the last operation. Apparently she has taken well to the new body, she feels good, better than she has in several lives, and she *is* a little euphoric. But 20 years from now . . ."

"I hope so," Harvard said and turned to go in.

But Lluella was not so sure. Look deeper, John, she thought; there is more to this. She wasn't sure what but she knew it was there. The woman at the bottom of the stairs had not simply looked like a stranger, she was one.

Down in the large, pastel-lit livingroom, Catherine was making the rounds introducing herself to everyone, acquaintances and strangers alike. Lithe, tall, and attractive, she was supremely self-possessed and charming.

Sara and Chris were immediately swallowed up by a small knot of family friends. Lluella stood beside her ex-husband and watched Catherine move about the room, a smile sparkling across her face, a few inaudible words passed to someone who either looked pleased or startled. Lluella searched Cat's eyes for some clue, some hint of the secrets that eyes sometimes tease one with while the words speak of other things. But Catherine was playing a role just now and was not ready to give up anything. John was watching too but Lluella knew his signals would be different. She wished she knew what she was thinking so she could tell him to be alert to something he would normally not search out, but she could not get a firm hold on the ideas.

Half a dozen mechanical servers drifted gracefully through the assembled guests, offering up chilled champagne and *hors d'oeuvres*. As one of the sleek silver and pink gadgets floated by, tidbit-laden and tempting, Catherine helped herself and took up a glass of champagne with which she toasted the man she was speaking to.

Harvard muttered something and moved to relieve her of the glass but Lluella caught his arm. "Why bother?"

"But she *knows* better than that!"

"Precisely. So what's the point? She can't lose, John. If you start a scene she may not tear you to pieces, but Chambers certainly will. Besides," she removed her hand, "I think she knows exactly what she is doing."

"Whose side are you on?"

"No one's, except maybe my own. In all my life she is the only person besides you who did not play politics with me. I respect her. She is also the only person I can't manipulate in some way. Oh, don't look so surprised, of course I know I do that! I have to admit I find Cat more than a little awesome, especially when I look at that young, near-child of a body and think of the mind inside. Who am I to presume to dictate *anything* to her?"

"Well *I* am her doctor!"

"And that's *all* you are. Has it ever occurred to you that maybe the family has been playing God with that woman for too long?"

Harvard looked at Lluella intensely for a moment. Then his gaze slowly began to turn introspective and finally turned away. "Not till now," he said quietly.

"Leave her be, John. She knows what she is about. She must. If the experience of life counts for anything, and we obviously believe it does or we would not work so hard to prolong hers, then what can we possibly have to say to her that she doesn't already know?"

"Not a goddamn blessed thing," he muttered as a pink and silver server waltzed within reach and Harvard scooped up two glasses, handing one to Lluella. The rims chimed delicately above the hum of conversation and as Lluella sipped hers, Harvard turned to look across the room, caught Catherine's eye and raised his glass to her. She responded in kind and as he tasted the chill of his own he was at least reassured somewhat by the fact that she had not smiled at him.

Chris was the only member of the family who did not feel the need to scrutinize Catherine carefully at dinner. She was mercurial; exuberant at one moment and serenely serious at the next, politely fielding questions and thoroughly honest in her responses. But she volunteered nothing. She was herself searching for something. She examined the assembly as carefully and thoroughly as the Harvard clan observed her.

In the livingroom once again she was immediately laid siege to by the Hooker-Dale-Soufflot-Chambers contingent. Adella Chambers was by far the most irrepressible and, though she was noted for astute judgements and an admirable lack of bias, Catherine found her totally impossible to like. It was eventually all she could do to remain civil. Though none of the others offended her overtly, she was struck by the uniform quality of their questions, or rather the lack of quality. Trivia. She felt her ire rising and let it. Chambers seemed to take notice but did not change her tack. Catherine did not care. She was earnest if somewhat cool in her answers, a departure from the pleasant though occasionally grandiose image the world had come to form of her. Catherine watched Chambers take careful note of the two cigarettes and the brandy and did not laugh at the occasional bit of humor Hooker would employ to try to lighten the mood. Finally, when Adella Chambers asked the only question of the evening with any potential, Catherine saw a place to sow the first seed.

"And what grand project does Cat van Dyck have planned for this reincarnation?"

Catherine leaned back against the sofa and saw John Harvard standing silent and sober behind Walter Dale. He would say nothing and Catherine returned her gaze to Miss Chambers's face and spoke in quiet deliberation which matched perfectly the expression on her face.

"I'm thinking of becoming a lawyer."

A ripple of laughter from Hooker-Dale-Soufflot. "That's a formidable undertaking. Whatever for?"

"Because I *am* a lawyer. It's what I was in the first life and it is what Kate Wall was."

Chambers arched an eyebrow and smiled indulgently. "Really? And who in the world is Kate Wall?"

Slowly Catherine slid her right arm from the back of the couch and extended it before her, fingers spread, palm almost touching the journalist's nose. She held it there rigidly till the hand began to tremble with the effort she forced into it. Then she slowly drew back, balling it into a fist which she laid in her lap. She had the woman's eyes the instant her hand moved and she held them with the powerful force of her own. Chambers glared back in defiance at the affront to her dignity. But Catherine assailed her with all the awful honesty she could pack into a look and Adella Chambers retreated with a shudder. She looked down at her pad and wrote nothing. The others were silent and bewildered.

"I see," Chambers said at last, trying to shake herself back to life. "That is a noble aim. I hope you are up to it. Tell me, are you still planning to attend the opening of the ballet season in—"

"I have a question for you," Catherine said bluntly, her face carved of alabaster.

"Of course."

"What does the world *expect* of me?"

Chambers seemed satisfyingly flustered.

"Why . . . nothing."

Catherine nodded slowly. "That, unfortunately, is what I thought." And she stood and walked away.

They all turned to watch her leave and in the next instant her seat on the sofa was filled with the smiling person of John Harvard. Chambers looked at him, confusion still clouding her eyes.

"A little insight can be a devastating thing, can't it young lady?"

It was Hooker who responded. "I thought no one was supposed to know who their donors were."

"They aren't. But I have a suspicion she always does, somehow."

Adella Chambers was watching Catherine's back withdrawing across the room.

"How does she stay sane?" she murmured. "I could never—"

"She isn't Catherine the Great for nothing."

"Is she serious about this lawyer business?" Dale asked.

"I hope not," Harvard said, "but—who knows."

"I hope she is," said Adella Chambers folding her pad and rising to go.

"Adella!" Dale said. "You're not leaving! The night is still young."

"It has suddenly gotten very old for me. Besides, I have something important to do at home. I have half a dozen biographies to burn."

She walked away to another chorus of chuckles and in short order the English language was abandoned and the conversation continued in "Medicalese."

Catherine sat in Lluella's powder room and communed with her image in the mirror for the hundred and first time.

"Too bad," she said to herself. "They just aren't ready." She stared at her own eyes in silence for another minute, then intoned in a low voice:

> *"The time has come," the Walrus said,*
> *"To speak of many things;*
> *Of shoes and ships and sealing wax*
> *And cabbages and Kings . . .*

but *not*," she said jabbing the right index finger at the one which rushed forth to meet it at the glass, "why the sea is Boiling Hot! and Certainly not what you had on your mind to tell them. *So* . . . you lose. You lose . . . I lose . . . we lose."

She placed the palms of both hands on the mirror parenthesizing the face.

"So make the best of it," the mouth in the mirror reflected in reverse.

Catherine shook her head slowly, looking down at her cigarette and continuing to ignore it. "Asses." Then back to her reflection with a little half smile. "So what else is new?"

When she got tired of waiting for the image in the mirror to answer she crushed out the butt and left the dressing room.

Chris was waiting for her, leaning against the wall smiling beautifully. In one hand he held a bottle of champagne and in the other a bouquet of tulip glasses. He held the trio up before his face and studied them a second.

"They aren't the right shape I suppose, but they are all I could swipe from the pantry and I doubt that the wine will care." He smiled again. "Madam desires the pleasure of your company on the veranda. Shall we?" he said, offering his arm.

"Why not," she said, but she took the bottle from his hand instead and led the way.

Partially roofed and flagstone floored, the veranda embraced two sides of the huge old house. At the back it was open and balcony-like, though it was on the ground floor, for the lawn sloped away close beyond it at a spectacular angle. The lake, far below and kilometers away, caught the light the moon gave up and glowed in the distance, ringed by a bodyguard of low hills black with forest. It was one of the few such views left and Catherine knew it well. Three generations of Harvards had owned this land. She felt they were survivors together but during the day it was apparent where encroachment was beginning. Within a few years, she thought . . . but didn't finish it. This too was one more of the signs which marked the way for her.

Two torches flickered softly in the light breeze. Chris set the glasses on the table where Sara sat and proceeded to open the bottle. The cork was launched to the moon and the glasses filled before anyone said anything.

"To what?" Catherine asked.

"Let's see," Chris said, seating himself across from Sara.

"How about law school?" Sara said, glass uplifted.

"Or prudence, maybe?" Catherine said. "I saw you, lurking over by the fireplace."

"My wife doesn't lurk," Chris said. "She's more elegant than that."

"True."

"Are you serious? About law school I mean?"

"Yes."

"It's a lot of work, Kitty. Do you honestly think you are up to it?"

"Yes."

"I can't argue with you about it," he said, "but I'm sure there is someone else who will."

"Oh, I have no doubt about that. But it is something I have to do."

"If nothing else, it made a smashing impact with the press," Sara said. "Adella Chambers may never be the same. You hit her with rather a low blow."

"I hope she gets home and dreams about it all night . . . and for a long time after! It rolled off all the others like water off ducks, but with her I think I sank a barb. If it plagues her long enough maybe she will begin to understand there are more important things in heaven and earth than whether I open the ballet season or what I had for dinner the night the bandages came off. If she can see where I am coming from then maybe she will eventually be of some use to me."

"Use," Sara said.

"Yes, use. I have something to say but they are obviously

not ready to hear it. Even my doctor does not believe me. And he, of all people, should want to."

"And exactly where, to use the archaic vernacular, *are* you coming from?" Chris asked.

"From a place very far away. From a place that died over 180 years ago. From where I call myself Cat and think myself Catherine, and know why. From across a void which has felt like eternity on the dark side of the moon. From all the lonely corners of the places my mind goes to when I'm alone in my bed. From all the people I have tried to be because I was no longer myself, and they were simply no longer."

"To where?" Sara said. "Back to the beginning?"

"To where I left off."

"What makes you think you can recapture that?"

"The fact that I have."

"How?"

"You and your father need to learn to trust a little more in instinct."

"*Some*thing must tell you."

"I think Kitty knows herself well enough to determine what she is and is not capable of," Chris said. He felt chilly but it was nothing his jacket could remedy. He wanted to change the subject.

"Maybe you should have gone to Med School, babe," Sara said to him. "Kitty might prefer someone who believes in her every intuition just because she is unique."

"I'm unique alright. Has it ever occurred to you that I am the world's most persistent failure? I am uniquely suited to successive brain transplants and yet I have been uniquely plagued by successive rejections. It has become a game, called keep Catherine alive. So I'm continually supplied with new bodies, new leases on life. Is that success?"

"Why not," Sara said. "Look how long you have been here. They must be doing something right."

"Ah, but therein lies the fallacy. You miss the point as everyone does. If the transplant rejects, does that not constitute a failure? I'm not saying whose. It isn't a matter of blame. We have forgotten what we started out to do.

"So we succeed in keeping the Cat alive. Wonderful! But was that ever the point? There is no one left alive who remembers the original intention but me. What about the motivation?"

"My great, great-grandfather loved you. He wanted you to live forever."

"*No!*" Catherine pounced on the word. "Never! No one lives forever. The *universe* won't last forever. All John wanted was to live out his life with me . . . for me to live out mine with him. The first operation was a gamble. The second was desperation. By the third the game had begun. But he never planned the relay race we have run since he passed my care along to Paul. That third operation was a changing of the guard. And all the generations of Harvards that have followed have faithfully passed the baton, but somewhere along the way they lost sight of the finish line. And I sit like a human vulture waiting for the death of a brain to leave an otherwise healthy body for me to consume and pass off.

"*Why?* Because it has always been a *medical* problem, something that surgery could fix, over and over. They all got caught in it, that need to keep *fixing*. They forgot the incentive and so did I, till the last few weeks."

She turned to the rail and looked out across the valley, to

the moonglow crisp and cold and diamond bright on the lake below. Neither Chris nor Sara could find words. Spellbound by the intensity of the voice and the gnawing hint of the rightness of the point of view, they stayed mute and waited to be led where she would have them go. They felt the presence of her logic but could not yet see its shape.

The angle of Catherine's gently torchlit-moonlit face presenting itself to Sara was quiet in its expression, far away, as though seeing back through the whole measure of her time. She seemed to have forgotten they were there. But when she spoke again, to the moon and the night, her voice was low and soft and perfect:

> Grow old along with me,
> The best is yet to be,
> The last of life for which the first was made.

"Elizabeth Browning," Sara said.

"And John Harvard . . . the first one. It was all he wanted. All *we* ever wanted. Just to grow old together. He couldn't stand the thought that he, almost 20 years my senior, might outlive me, and he found he had the power to keep me with him, and I let him. I had nothing to lose. We never expected the fourth life to last so long, but the state-of-the-art was improving and I had a good donor.

"So John grew older and passed beyond our little dream . . ."

"And you stayed young," Sara said, feeling lost now on the dark side of her moon.

"If you *believe that* you are hopeless, just like the rest of them," she said with a newly alert coolness in her voice. Then in a simpering, mocking sneer, "Catherine is ageless."

"Bullshit! I'm over two hundred years old and I've hit middle age as often as I have 30." She turned and gestured in the air with her hand. "Five times I have been through menopause. Believe me, once is enough!"

Sara felt a quick trickle of a smile and submerged the urge to giggle. Once again she wondered if Catherine was playing games. What she said was, "Dad says you have a death wish. I really can't tell. Do you?"

"Maybe. I do not have a wish to continue *ad infinitum*. If that qualifies, then so be it. But it is a moot point. There will be no more operations."

"Then I have to agree with Doc," Chris said. "It sounds like a death wish. The next time you reject—"

"I won't."

"How can you be so sure?" Sara said.

"After all this time how can I not be sure?"

"Do you really believe this nine lives business?"

"Oh, I don't know. It is just one of a whole ream of things I can not quite ignore, but it is unquestionably the least important. Your father finds it a convenient point of protest, that's all. He has the family affliction, and if this night doesn't purge *you* of it then I shall quit trying and quietly keep my peace.

"It is an out and out perversity, but over all these generations the Harvard family's reputation has been based on the unattainable. Your father has achieved what none of the others could do. Yet he sees as he has been conditioned to in this one narrow area. All their failures have brought the project success and his own success he can not see as anything but the ultimate failure, so he refuses to believe it."

She was suddenly adamant, almost angry.

"I will not be forced to consent to transplant! And they can not take me from this body if it does not first move to give me up!

"I *will* die! In my own good time and however nature dictates. I am here to stay this time." Her eyes were dark and intense and her voice was passionate. "My life has been given back to me . . . exactly where I left it. She died within hours of the age at which I died the first time. Our dates of birth are the same, our chosen professions are the same, height, weight, coloring . . ." Catherine was fishing in her evening bag as she spoke. Sara watched her withdraw a folded envelope and reached for it when Catherine handed it to her.

"I brought that for the press but found the time not to be right. I was going to show it to your father but he does not want to know any more than the rest of them. But you have to, both of you. We are going to be walking this road together and you must not only know where it leads but where it comes from."

In the envelope was a sheet of paper with two parallel lists under the names of Catherine and her latest donor. It expanded upon the similarities between the two women in extensive detail, and the comparison was uncannily striking. But what caught and held Sara was the photograph; old and cracked and brittle, fading in color, it held its image in an ancient grip. Sara handed the paper to Chris and took the photograph to the illumination of a torch.

"I wasn't sure I still had it," Catherine said. "It took me a long time to find it. That is your great, great-grandfather."

"Yes, I know. I think I must have seen a thousand pictures of him in all kinds of places."

"After the operation, when he was suddenly a genius and I was a miracle the whole world wanted to see us, to know about us. Pictures, interviews, stories, books . . . rumors. But before that, when he was only brilliant and I was a new lawyer with a fresh, crisp degree, considering becoming the stepmother of his 18 year old son . . . who cared?

"Paul took that . . . six weeks before the first operation. I had just turned 25.

"Sara do you understand me?"

But Sara had nothing to say. She was staring at the young woman standing close beside the older man. A man she had seen in the family album and in her history and medical books. A man who had passed much of his looks down to the male heirs of his family but who remained distinct and always recognizable. Yes, she had seen that face before, often. And the woman she had seen too, but only once. She searched the somber eyes below the straight, full cascade of faded auburn bangs, looking for a sign, an assurance which she found in flesh and blood in Catherine when she raised her head and fixed upon the living face. Chris stood by his wife, peering over her shoulder. Sara's eyes trod the road from face to photo and back several times before Catherine caught and held them with her own. They *were* her own. They always had been. And Sara could not deny it, though she tried.

"I have the thread again," Catherine said in a quiet voice. "And the knot is tied. It will not come undone again. I have a life to finish."

Chris looked at the ancient picture and wondered about all the things that can happen to a life in transit . . . from light to light . . . on the dark side of the moon.

And Sara nodded and knew it was *right* . . . even if it wasn't true.

1978

JOAN D. VINGE

View from a Height

S ATURDAY, THE 7TH

I WANT TO know why those pages were missing! How am
I supposed to keep up with my research if they leave out
pages—?

(*Long sighing noise.*)

Listen to yourself, Emmylou: You're listening to the sound
of fear. It was an oversight, you know that. Nobody did it to
you on purpose. Relax, you're getting Fortnight Fever. Tomorrow you'll get the pages, and an apology too, if Harvey
Weems knows what's good for him.

But still, five whole pages; and the table of contents. How
could you miss *five* pages? And the table of contents.

How do I know there hasn't been a coup? The Northwest's
finally taken over completely, and they're censoring the
media—And like the Man without a Country, everything they
send me from now on is going to have holes cut in it.

In *Science*?

Or maybe Weems has decided to drive me insane—?

Oh, my God . . . it would be a short trip. Look at me. I don't
have any fingernails left.

("*Arrwk. Hello, beautiful. Hello? Hello?*")

("Ozymandias! Get out of my hair, you devil." *Laughter.*
"Polly want a cracker? Here . . . gently! That's a boy.")

It's beautiful when he flies. I never get tired of watching
him, or looking at him, even after twenty years. Twenty

360

years. . . . What did the *psittacidae* do, to win the right to wear a rainbow as their plumage? Although the way we've hunted them for it, you could say it was a mixed blessing. Like some other things.

Twenty years. How strange it sounds to hear those words, and know they're true. There are gray hairs when I look in the mirror. Wrinkles starting. And Weems is bald! Bald as an egg, and all squinty behind his spectacles. How did we get that way, without noticing it? Time is both longer and shorter than you think, and usually all at once.

Twelve days is a long time to wait for somebody to return your call. Twenty years is a long time gone. But I feel somehow as though it was only last week that I left home. I keep the circuits clean, going over them and over them, showing those mental home movies until I could almost step across, sometimes, into that other reality. But then I always look down, and there's that tremendous abyss full of space and time, and I realize I can't, again. You can't go home again.

Especially when you're almost one thousand astronomical units out in space. Almost there, the first rung of the ladder. Next Thursday is the day. Oh, that bottle of champagne that's been waiting for so long. Oh, the parallax view! I have the equal of the best astronomical equipment in all of near-Earth space at my command, and a view of the universe that no one has ever had before; and using them has made me the only astrophysicist ever to win a PhD in deep space. Talk about your field work.

Strange to think that if the Forward Observatory had massed less than its thousand-plus tons, I would have been replaced by a machine. But because the installation is so large, I in my infinite human flexibility, even with my infinite human appetite, become the most efficient legal tender. And the farther out I get the more important my own ability to judge what happens, and respond to it, becomes. The first—and maybe the last—manned interstellar probe, on a one-way journey into infinity . . . into a universe unobscured by our own system's gases and dust . . . equipped with eyes that see everything from gamma to ultra-long wavelengths, and ears that listen to the music of the spheres.

And Emmylou Stewart, the captive audience. Adrift on a star . . . if you hold with the idea that all the bits of inert junk drifting through space, no matter how small, have star potential. Dark stars, with brilliance in their secret hearts, only kept back from letting it shine by Fate, which denied them the critical mass to reach their kindling point.

Speak of kindling: the laser beam just arrived to give me my daily boost, moving me a little faster, so I'll reach a little deeper into the universe. Blue sky at bedtime; I always was a night person. I'm sure they didn't design the solar sail to filter light like the sky . . . but I'm glad it happened to work out that way. Sky-blue was always my passion—the color, texture, fluid purity of it. This color isn't exactly right; but it doesn't matter, because I can't remember how any more. This sky is a sun-catcher. A big blue parasol. But so was the original, from where I used to stand. The sky is a blue parasol . . . did anyone ever say that before, I wonder? If anyone knows, speak up—

Is anyone even listening. Will anyone ever be?

("Who cares, anyway? Come on, Ozzie—climb aboard. Let's drop down to the observation porch while I do my meditation, and try to remember what days were like.")

Weems, damn it, I want satisfaction!

SUNDAY, THE 8TH

That idiot. That intolerable moron—how could he do that to me? After all this time, wouldn't you think he'd know me better than that? To keep me waiting for twelve days, wondering and afraid: twelve days of all the possible stupid paranoias I could weave with my idle hands and mind, making myself miserable, asking for trouble—

And then giving it to me. God, he must be some kind of sadist! If I could only reach him, and hurt him the way I've hurt these past hours—

Except that I know the news wasn't his fault, and that he didn't mean to hurt me . . . and so I can't even ease my pain by projecting it onto him.

I don't know what I would have done if his image hadn't been six days stale when it got here. What would I have done, if he'd been in earshot when I was listening; what would I have said? Maybe no more than I did say.

What can you say, when you realize you've thrown your whole life away?

He sat there behind his faded blotter, twiddling his pen, picking up his souvenir moon rocks and laying them down— looking for all the world like a man with a time bomb in his desk drawer—and said, "Now don't worry, Emmylou. There's no problem . . ." Went on saying it, one way or another, for five minutes; until I was shouting, "What's *wrong*, damn it?"

"I thought you'd never even notice the few pages . . ." with that sidling smile of his. And while I'm muttering, "I may have been in solitary confinement for twenty years, Harvey, but it hasn't turned my brain to mush," he said.

"So maybe I'd better explain, first—" and the look on his

face; oh, the look on his face. "There's been a biomed break-through. If you were here on Earth, you . . . well, your body's immune responses could be . . . made normal . . ." And then he looked down, as though he could really see the look on my own face.

Made normal. Made normal. It's all I can hear. I was born with no natural immunities. No defense against disease. No help for it. No. *No, no, no*; that's all I ever heard, all my life on Earth. Through the plastic walls of my sealed room; through the helmet of my sealed suit. . . . And now it's all changed. They could cure me. But I can't go home. I knew this could happen; I knew it had to happen someday. But I chose to ignore that fact, and now it's too late to do anything about it.

Then why can't I forget that I could have been f-free. . . .

. . . I didn't answer Weems today. Screw Weems. There's nothing to say. Nothing at all.

I'm so tired.

MONDAY, THE 9TH

Couldn't sleep. It kept playing over and over in my mind. . . . Finally took some pills. Slept all day, feel like hell. Stupid. And it didn't go away. It was waiting for me, still waiting, when I woke up.

It isn't fair—!

I don't feel like talking about it.

TUESDAY, THE 10TH

Tuesday, already. I haven't done a thing for two days. I haven't even started to check out the relay beacon, and that damn thing has to be dropped off this week. I don't have any strength; I can't seem to move, I just sit. But I have to get back to work. Have to . . .

Instead I read the printout of the article today. Hoping I'd find a flaw! If that isn't the greatest irony of my entire life. For two decades I prayed that somebody would find a cure for me. And for two more decades I didn't care. Am I going to spend the next two decades hating it, now that it's been found?

No . . . hating myself. I could have been free, they could have cured me; if only I'd stayed on Earth. If only I'd been patient. But now it's too late . . . by twenty *years*.

I want to go home. I want to go home. . . . But you can't go home again. Did I really say that, so blithely, so recently? *You* can't: You, Emmylou Stewart. You are in prison, just like you have always have been in prison.

It's all come back to me so strongly. Why me? Why must I be the ultimate victim— In all my life I've never smelled the sea wind, or plucked berries from a bush and eaten them, right there! Or felt my parents' kisses against my skin, or a man's body. . . . Because to me they were all deadly things.

I remember when I was a little girl, and we still lived in Victoria—I was just three or four, just at the brink of under-standing that I was the only prisoner in my world. I remember watching my father sit polishing his shoes in the morning, before he left for the museum. And me smiling, so deviously, "Daddy . . . I'll help you do that, if you let me come out—"

And he came to the wall of my bubble and put his arms into the hugging gloves, and said, so gently, "No." And then he began to cry. And I began to cry too, because I didn't know why I'd made him unhappy. . . .

And all the children at school, with their "spaceman" jokes, pointing at the freak; all the years of insensitive people asking the same stupid questions every time I tried to go out anywhere . . . worst of all, the ones who weren't stupid, or insensitive. Like Jeffrey . . . no, I will not think about Jeffrey! I couldn't let myself think about him then. I could never afford to get close to a man, because I'd never be able to touch him. . . .

And now it's too late. Was I controlling my fate, when I volunteered for this one-way trip? Or was I just running away from a life where I was always helpless; helpless to escape the things I hated, helpless to embrace the things I loved.

I pretended this was different, and important . . . but was that really what I believed? No! I just wanted to crawl into a hole I couldn't get out of, because I was so afraid.

So afraid that one day I would unseal my plastic walls, or take off my helmet and my suit; walk out freely to breathe the air, or wade in a stream, or touch flesh against flesh . . . and die of it.

So now I've walled myself into this hermetically sealed tomb for a living death. A perfectly sterile environment, in which my body will not even decay when I die. Never having really lived, I shall never really die, dust to dust. A perfectly sterile environment; in every sense of the word.

I often stand looking at my body in the mirror after I take a shower. Hazel eyes, brown hair in thick waves with hardly any gray . . . and a good figure; not exactly stacked, but not unattractive. And no one has ever seen it that way but me. Last night I had the Dream again . . . I haven't had it for such a long time . . . this time I was sitting on a carved wooden beast in the park beside the Provincial Museum in Victoria; but not as a child in my suit. As a college girl, in white shorts and a bright cotton shirt, feeling the sun on my shoulders, and—Jeffrey's arms around my waist. . . . We stroll along the bayside hand in hand, under the Victorian lamp posts with their bright hanging flower-baskets, and everything I do is fresh and spontaneous and full of the moment. But always, always, just when he holds me in his arms at last, just as I'm about to . . . I wake up.

When we die, do we wake out of reality at last, and all our dreams come true? When I die . . . I will be carried on and on into the timeless depths of uncharted space in this computerized tomb, unmourned and unremembered. In time all the atmosphere will seep away; and my fair corpse, lying like Snow White's in inviolate sleep, will be sucked dry of moisture, until it is nothing but a mummified parchment of shriveled leather and bulging bones. . . .

("*Hello? Hello, baby? Good night. Yes, no, maybe. . . . Awk. Food time!*")

("Oh, Ozymandias! Yes, yes, I know . . . I haven't fed you, I'm sorry. I know, I know . . .")

(*Clinks and rattles.*)

Why am I so selfish? Just because I can't eat, I expect him to fast, too. . . . No. I just forgot.

He doesn't understand, but he knows something's wrong; he climbs the lamp pole like some tripodal bem, using both feet and his beak, and stares at me with that glass-beady bird's eye, stares and stares and mumbles things. Like a lunatic! Until I can hardly stand not to shut him in a cupboard, or something. But then he sidles along my shoulder and kisses me—such a tender caress against my cheek, with that hooked prehensile beak that could crush a walnut like a grape—to let me know that he's worried, and he cares. And I stroke his feathers to thank him, and tell him that it's all right . . . but it's not. And he knows it.

Does he ever resent his life? Would he, if he could? Stolen away from his own kind, raised in a sterile bubble to be a caged bird for a caged human. . . .

I'm only a bird in a gilded cage. I want to go home.

WEDNESDAY, THE 11TH

Why am I keeping this journal? Do I really believe that sometime some alien being will find this, or some starship from Earth's glorious future will catch up to me . . . glorious future, hell. Stupid, selfish, short-sighted fools. They ripped the guts out of the space program after they sent me away, no one will ever follow me now. I'll be lucky if they don't declare me dead and forget about me.

As if anyone would care what a woman all alone on a lumbering space probe thought about day after day for decades, anyway. What monstrous conceit.

I did lubricate the bearings on the big scope today. I did that much. I did it so that I could turn it back toward Earth . . . toward the sun . . . toward the whole damn system. Because I can't even see it, all crammed into the space of two moon diameters, even Pluto; and too dim and small and far away below me for my naked eyes, anyway. Even the sun is no more than a gaudy star that doesn't even make me squint. So I looked for them with the scope. . . .

Isn't it funny how when you're a child you see all those drawings and models of the solar system with big, lumpy planets and golden wakes streaming around the sun. Somehow you never get over expecting it to look that way in person. And here I am, one thousand astronomical units north of the solar pole, gazing down from a great height . . . and it doesn't look that way at all. It doesn't look like anything; even through the scope. One great blot of light, and all the pale tiny diamond chips of planets and moons around it, barely distinguishable from half a hundred undistinguished stars trapped in the same arc of blackness. So meaningless, so insignificant . . . so disappointing.

Five hours I spent, today, listening to my journal, looking back and trying to find—something, I don't know, something I suddenly don't have anymore.

I had it at the start. I was disgusting; Pollyanna Grad-student skipping and singing through the rooms of my very own observatory. It seemed like heaven, and a lifetime spent in it couldn't possibly be long enough for all that I was going to accomplish, and discover. I'd never be bored, no, not me. . . .

And there was so much to learn about the potential of this place, before I got out to where it supposedly would matter, and there would be new things to turn my wonderful extended senses toward . . . while I could still communicate easily with my dear mentor Dr. Weems, and the world. (Who'd ever have thought, when the lecherous old goat was my thesis advisor at Harvard, and making jokes to his other grad students about "the lengths some women will go to to protect their virginity," that we would have to spend a lifetime together.)

There was Ozymandias's first word . . . and my first birthday in space, and my first anniversary . . . and my doctoral degree at last, printed out by the computer with scrolls made of little x's and taped up on the wall.

Then day and night and day and night, beating me black and blue with blue and black . . . my fifth anniversary, my eighth, my decade. I crossed the magnetopause, to become truly the first voyager in interstellar space . . . but by then there was no one left to *talk* to anymore, to really share the experience with. Even the radio and television broadcasts drifting out from Earth were diffuse and rare; there were fewer and fewer contacts with the reality outside. The plodding routines, the stupifying boredom—until sometimes I stood screaming down the halls just for something new; listening to the echoes that no one else would ever hear, and pretending they'd come to call; trying so hard to believe there was something to hear that wasn't *my* voice, *my* echo, or Ozymandias making a mockery of it.

("*Hello, beautiful. That's a crock. Hello, hello?*")

("Ozymandias, get *away* from me—")

But always I had that underlying belief in my mission: that I was here for a purpose, for more than my own selfish reasons, or NASA's (or whatever the hell they call it now), but for Humanity, and Science. Through meditation I learned the real value of inner silence, and thought that by creating an inner peace I had reached equilibrium with the outer silences. I thought that meditation had disciplined me, I was in touch with my self and with the soul of the cosmos. . . . But I haven't been able to meditate since—it happened. The inner silence fills up with my own anger screaming at me, until I can't remember what peace sounds like.

And what have I really discovered, so far? Almost nothing. Nothing worth wasting my analysis or all my fine theories—or my freedom—on. Space is even emptier than anyone dreamed, you could count on both hands the bits of cold dust or worldlet I've passed in all this time, lost souls falling helplessly through near-perfect vacuum . . . all of us together. With my absurdly long astronomical tape-measure I have fixed precisely the distance to NGC 2419 and a few other features, and from that made new estimates about a few more distant ones. But I have not detected a miniature black hole insatiably vacuuming up the vacuum; I have not pierced the invisible clouds that shroud the ultra-long wavelengths like fog; I have not discovered that life exists beyond the Earth in even the most tentative way. Looking back at the solar system I see nothing to show definitively that we even exist, anymore. All I hear anymore when I scan is electromagnetic noise, no coherent thought. Only Weems every twelfth night, like the last man alive. . . . Christ, I still haven't answered him.

Why bother? Let him sweat. Why bother with any of it. Why waste my precious time.

Oh, my precious time. . . . Half a lifetime left that could have been mine, on Earth.

Twenty years—I came through them all all right. I thought I was safe. And after twenty years, my facade of discipline and self-control falls apart at a touch. What a self-deluded hypocrite I've been. Do you know that I said the sky was like a blue parasol eighteen years ago? And probably said it again fifteen years ago, and ten, and five—

Tomorrow I pass 1000 AUs.

THURSDAY, THE 12TH

I burned out the scope. I burned out the scope. I left it pointing toward the Earth, and when the laser came on for the night it shone right down the scope's throat and burned it out. I'm so ashamed. . . . Did I do it on purpose, subconsciously?

("*Goodnight starlight. Arrk. Good night. Good . . .*")

("Damn it, I want to hear another human voice—!")

(*Echoing*, "*voice, voice, voice voice . . .*")

When I found out what I'd done I ran away. I ran and ran through the halls. . . . But I only ran in a circle: This observatory, my prison, myself . . . I can't escape. I'll always come back in the end, to this green-walled room with its desk and its terminals, its cupboards crammed with a hundred thousand dozens of everything, toilet paper and magnetic tape and oxygen tanks. . . . And I can tell you exactly how many steps it is to my bedroom or how long it took me to crochet the afghan on the bed . . . how long I've sat in the dark and silence, setting up an exposure program or listening for the feeble pulse of a radio galaxy two billion light-years away. There will never be anything different, or anything more.

When I finally came back here, there was a message waiting. Weems, grinning out at me half-bombed from the screen—"Congratulations," he cried, "on this historic occasion! Emmylou, we're having a little celebration here at the lab; mind if we join you in yours, one thousand astronomical units from home—?" I've never seen him drunk. They really must have meant to do something nice for me, planning it all six days ahead. . . .

To celebrate I shouted obscenities I didn't even know I knew at him, until my voice was broken and my throat was raw.

Then I sat at my desk for a long time with my jackknife lying open in my hand. Not wanting to die—I've always been too afraid of death for that—but wanting to hurt myself. I wanted to make a fresh hurt, to take my attention off the terrible thing that is sucking me into myself like an imploding star. Or maybe just to punish myself, I don't know. But I considered the possibility of actually cutting myself quite calmly; while some separate part of me looked on in horror. I even pressed the knife against my flesh . . . and then I stopped and put it away. It hurts too much.

I can't go on like this. I have duties, obligations, and I can't face them. What would I do without the emergency automechs? . . . But it's the rest of my life, and they can't go on doing my job for me forever—

Later.

I just had a visitor. Strange as that sounds. Stranger yet—it was Donald Duck. I picked up half of a children's cartoon show today, the first coherent piece of nondirectional, unbeamed television broadcast I've recorded in months. And I don't think I've ever been happier to see anyone in my life. What a nice surprise, so glad you could drop by. . . . Ozymandias loves him; he hangs upside down from his swing under the cabinet with a cracker in one foot, cackling away and saying, "Give us a kiss, *smack-smack-smack*". . . We watched it three times. I even smiled, for a while; until I remembered myself. It helps. Maybe I'll watch it again until bedtime.

FRIDAY, THE 13TH

Friday the Thirteenth. Amusing. Poor Friday the Thirteenth, what did it ever do to deserve its reputation? Even if it had any power to make my life miserable, it couldn't hold a candle to the rest of this week. It seems like an eternity since last weekend.

I repaired the scope today; replaced the burnt-out parts. Had to suit up and go outside for part of the work . . . I haven't done any outside maintenance for quite a while. Odd how both exhilarating and terrifying it always is when I first step out of the airlock, utterly alone, into space. You're entirely on your own, so far away from any possibility of help, so far away from anything at all. And at that moment you doubt yourself, suddenly, terribly . . . just for a moment.

But then you drag your umbilical out behind you and clank along the hull in your magnetized boots that feel so reassuringly like lead ballast. You turn on the lights and look for the trouble, find it and get to work; it doesn't bother you anymore. . . . When your life seems to have torn loose and be drifting free, it creates a kind of sea anchor to work with your hands; whether it's doing some mindless routine chore or the most intricate of repairs.

There was a moment of panic, when I actually saw charred wires and melted metal, when I imagined the damage was so bad that I couldn't repair it again. It looked so final, so—masterful. I clung there by my feet and whimpered and clenched my hands inside my gloves, like a great shining baby, for a while. But then I pulled myself down and began to pry here and unscrew there and twist a component free . . . and little by little I replaced everything. One step at a time; the way we get through life.

By the time I'd finished I felt quite calm, for the first time in days; the thing that's been trying to choke me to death this past week seemed to falter a little at my demonstration of competence. I've been breathing easier since then; but I still don't have much strength. I used up all I had just overcoming my own inertia.

But I shut off the lights and hiked around the hull for a while, afterwards—I couldn't face going back inside just then: Looking at the black convex dish of the solar sail I'm embedded in, up at the radio antenna's smaller dish occluding stars as the observatory's cylinder wheels endlessly at the hub of the spinning parasol. . . .

That made me dizzy, and so I looked out into the starfields that lie on every side. Even with my own poor, unaugmented senses there's so much more to see out here, unimpeded by atmosphere or dust, undominated by any sun's glare. The brilliance of the Milky Way, the depths of star and nebula and farthest galaxy breathlessly suspended . . . as I am. The realization that I'm lost for eternity in an uncharted sea.

Strangely, although that thought aroused a very powerful emotion when it struck me, it wasn't a negative one at all: It was from another scale of values entirely; like the universe itself. It was as if the universe itself stretched out its finger to touch me. And in touching me, singling me out, it only heightened my awareness of my own insignificance.

That was somehow very comforting. When you confront the absolute indifference of magnitudes and vistas so overwhelming, the swollen ego of your self-important suffering is diminished. . . .

And I remembered one of the things that was always so important to me about space—that here *any*one has to put on a spacesuit before they step outside. We're all aliens, no one better equipped to survive than another. I am as normal as anyone else, out here.

I must hold onto that thought.

SATURDAY, THE 14TH

There is a reason for my being here. There is a reason.

I was able to meditate earlier today. Not in the old way, the usual way, by emptying my mind. Rather by letting the questions fill up the space, not fighting them; letting them merge with my memories of all that's gone before. I put on music, that great mnemonic stimulator; letting the images that each tape evoked free-associate and interact.

And in the end I could believe again that my being here was the result of a free choice. No one forced me into this. My motives for volunteering were entirely my own. And I was given this position because NASA believed that I was more likely to be successful in it than anyone else they could have chosen.

It doesn't matter that some of my motives happened to be unresolved fear or wanting to escape from things I couldn't cope with. It really doesn't matter. Sometimes retreat is the only alternative to destruction, and only a madman can't recognize the truth of that. Only a madman. . . . Is there anyone "sane" on Earth who isn't secretly a fugitive from something unbearable somewhere in their life? And yet they function normally.

If they ran, they ran toward something, too, not just away. And so did I. I had already chosen a career as an astrophysicist before I ever dreamed of being a part of this project. I could have become a medical researcher instead, worked on my own to find a cure for my condition. I could have grown up hating the whole idea of space and "spacemen," stumbling through life in my damned ugly sterile suit. . . .

But I remember when I was six years old, the first time I saw a film of suited astronauts at work in space . . . they looked just like me! And no one was laughing. How could I help but love space, then?

(And how could I help but love Jeffrey, with his night-black hair, and his blue flightsuit with the starry patch on the shoulder. Poor Jeffrey, poor Jeffrey, who never even realized his own dream of space before they cut the program out from under him. . . . I will not talk about Jeffrey. I will not.)

Yes, I could have stayed on Earth, and waited for a cure! I knew even then there would have to be one, someday. It was both easier and harder to choose space, instead of staying.

And I think the thing that really decided me was that those people had faith enough in me and my abilities to believe that I could run this observatory and my own life smoothly for as long as I lived. Billions of dollars and a thousand tons of equipment resting on me; like Atlas holding up his world.

Even Atlas tried to get rid of his burden; because no matter how vital his function was, the responsibility was still a burden to him. But he took his burden back again too, didn't he; for better or worse. . . .

I worked today. I worked my butt off getting caught up on a week's worth of data processing and maintenance, and I'm still not finished. Discovered while I was at it that Ozymandias had used those missing five pages just like the daily news: crapped all over them. My sentiments exactly! I laughed and laughed.

I think I may live.

SUNDAY, THE 15TH

The clouds have parted.

That's not rhetorical—among my fresh processed data

is a series of photo reconstructions in the ultra-long wave-lengths. And there's a gap in the obscuring gas up ahead of me, a break in the clouds that extends thirty or forty light-years. Maybe fifty! Fantastic. What a view. What a view I have from here of everything, with my infinitely extended vision: of the way ahead, of the passing scene—or looking back to-ward Earth.

Looking back. I'll never stop looking back, and wishing it could have been different. That at least there could have been two of me, one to be here, one who could have been normal, back on Earth; so that I wouldn't have to be forever torn in two by regrets—

("*Hello. What's up, doc? Avast!*")

("Hey, watch it! If you drink, don't fly.")

Damn bird. . . . If I'm getting maudlin, it's because I had a party today. Drank a whole bottle of champagne. Yes, I had *the* party . . . we did, Ozymandias and I. Our private 1000 AU celebration. Better late than never, I guess. At least we did have something concrete to celebrate—the photos. And if the celebration wasn't quite as merry as it could have been, still I guess it will probably seem like it was when I look back on it from the next one, at 2000 AUs. They'll be coming faster now, the celebrations. I may even live to celebrate 8000. What the hell, I'll shoot for 10,000—

After we finished the champagne . . . Ozymandias thinks '98 was a great year, thank God he can't drink as fast as I can . . . I put on my Strauss waltzes, and the *Barcarolle*: Oh, the Berliner Philharmonic; their touch is what a lover's kiss must be. I threw the view outside onto the big screen, a ballroom of stars, and danced with my shadow. And part of the time I wasn't dancing above the abyss in a jumpsuit and headphones, but waltzing in yards of satin and lace across a ball-room floor in 19th century Vienna. What I wouldn't give to be *there* for a moment out of time. Not for a lifetime, or even a year, but just for an evening; just for one waltz.

Another thing I shall never do. There are so many things we can't do, any of us, for whatever the reasons—time, talent, life's callous whims. We're all on a one-way trip into infinity. If we're lucky we're given some life's work we care about, or some person. Or both, if we're very lucky.

And I do have Weems. Sometimes I see us like an old married couple, who have grown to a tolerant understanding over the years. We've never been soul mates, God knows, but we're comfortable with each others' silences. . . .

I guess it's about time I answered him.

1978

CYNTHIA FELICE

No One Said Forever

CAROL STOOD on the balcony of the rented mountain home staring out over the dry meadow to the bus stop beyond. Squinting to see through harsh reflections, she watched people with yellow hard hats leaving the roadside. The aluminum bus flashed only a few seconds more, then was in mountain shadow as it sped toward the foothills. Carol could see that most of the passengers had walked to the juniper-lined parking lot provided by Consolidated Mines. One man separated from the others and struck out across the meadow on foot. Twenty steps into the meadow and he was lost in heat waves, a dancing apparition of a man floating over gold.

Carol turned and went into the house, drawing the drapes over the balcony window to cut out direct sunlight. The air coolers were blowing through the vents in the house, making it cool by comparison to the out-of-doors, but still too warm for comfort. Mike had forgotten to turn on the cooling system as he left that morning. It was chilly before sunrise when he got up and he forgot to ensure that it would be cool for her when she awakened in the sun-baked bedroom. But the house was the right temperature for him when he returned in the mid-afternoon. Carol always remembered to turn on the blowers before she left for Denver. Mike took for granted the conditions and circumstances that made his life comfortable, discarding burdens as easily as rubbish. He grasped impressions, absorbed ideas, sorted them with ease and never lost a moment of sleep over indecision. Carol had not slept for the past two nights. And today she'd forgotten the blowers until she returned home early and found it hot.

She greeted Mike at the kitchen door with open arms and a smile.

"Hey, Carol," he said, surprised but happy. "Off early today?" He tossed his hard hat to a cushioned chair and ran his hand through his sweaty hair. His sun-browned arms circled her enthusiastically as day-old whiskers scratched her cheek and pricked her lips.

Mike's smile faded at Carol's lack of response and he gathered her closer. "What's wrong, Carol?" he whispered.

Carol's answer was slow in coming. "I've been transferred, Mike."

"What!" He released her abruptly, brushed the hard hat from the chair and sank angrily onto the cushion. He shook his head with disgust as he muttered a string of oaths. Then there was a choked sound of involuntary regret and fury. "Consolidated has let me transfer twice in two years to keep up with your transfers. I can't get another without losing seniority."

Carol opened the refrigerator and pulled out a can of Coors, set it on the table in front of Mike and sat down opposite him. The oaths, the loudness of his voice had nothing to do with her. When Mike vented anger, Mike did it here and now. No nerves, no ulcers for him. Still, Carol was extremely uncomfortable when he did. Mike sensed it now, took a few long gulps to cool himself and shook his head again.

"We're going to have to put up with this one, Carol," he said more moderately. "I don't see any other way . . . unless you can get out of it?" He looked up from the beer can, brows raised in query.

"No." Carol shifted uncomfortably in the chair. "I can't get out of it. That's the nature of the job, I knew it when I took it."

He shrugged and something useless fell away from him. (Herself?) "Well, then, we'll just have to make do with long weekends and vacations for a while. How long is the assignment?"

Carol hesitated. "Looks like two years minimum."

"Minimum!" Mike whistled. "It's going to be an expensive two years: two households . . . plane fares . . ."

"No, we won't have that to worry about," Carol said with a temporary external calm. She envied Mike's ability to decide so easily, to throw off pressure before he was even aware of its distorting effects. She didn't focus on the apparition she'd glimpsed from the corner of her eye. Then, unable to resist, Carol looked askance and saw herself, wide-eyed and trembling, staring at Mike. Carol frowned.

"What?" Mike finished the beer in two more swallows.

"I'm going to Antarctica . . . wintering over."

"Antarctica!" The can crushed easily; Mike's rage was rising again. "Damn Capitol Computer . . . they're inhuman! I can't go with you even if I want to and I sure as hell can't afford weekend visits!"

Carol knew his words were clipped by anger but she had heard each as if enunciated in the long, pausing voice of a stadium speaker. When, in utter frustration, he stamped out of the kitchen to the stairs in the hall, there was only the space of a heartbeat to measure the time. Yet in that measure she saw veins popping in his forehead, the glint in his narrow eyes, felt the breath of his passing envelop her, swirling along her skin and scalp. The floor seemed to vibrate with every maddeningly slow step.

"And they ask a hell of a lot from their employees, too!" he shouted over his shoulders. "If I were you I'd tell them to shove it!" Pause . . . eternity passed . . . Gently: "Carol?"

Carol's stomach flip-flopped as slowly as an iced fish. "I can't, Mike. There's no one else who isn't already on project they can send. Besides, it's a good assignment for me . . . one I ought to jump for. Hallerud's not going. It will be *my* project once Dr. Lincoln leaves Byrd Station." Carol followed Mike to the stairs; he was on the landing above—why had it taken so long for him to get there?—shirt off, pants unbuckled, ready for the shower. Time refused to accelerate when Carol wanted it to. This scene should be finished. It was eating out her heart.

"Promotion?" Mike said.

Rage was gone from him. She tried to ignore its lingering effects on her stomach. "Implied, but not firm. It'll come." That kind of confidence she had.

"Good for you, Carol," he said, almost sincerely. "So, you didn't even try to dodge it?"

"Not too hard," she admitted.

Mike stood quietly, grimacing with just a hint of comprehension. "Okay, babe, I understand. Look, I've some time coming. We'll take a vacation . . . fly to Acapulco, spend a week or two." He looked at her. "How long before you leave?"

"I'm sorry, Mike. They've given me the rest of the week off to get ready. I leave Sunday."

"S u n d a y !   T h i s   i s . . ."

Another voice, her own, close by: "It's all right, Mike." Frantic notes, clearly her own: "I can't go through with it, I knew I couldn't." Shame, relief: "I'll call and tell them to find someone else." Carol knew the words were on her tongue, but. . . . She saw the one who had spoken, herself, stepping away from the stairs, hurrying to the kitchen phone. The listener at the top of the stairs sighed. He glanced toward the kitchen, nodded, satisfied. Carol blinked.

". . . i s   T h u r s d a y   a l r e a d y !"   Mike ran the rest of the way up the stairs to the bathroom. Doors slammed and shower faucets were wrenched.

The other Mike was still nodding with satisfaction as he turned to the bedroom. Carol wondered why Mike had not bumped him off the stairs when he ran past. She glanced toward the kitchen; a sunshaft filled with blue dust motes where her phone was cradled. The other Carol would be standing on the patio composing a refusal. Carol went to hear her, knowing it would be poorly done, terribly lame. But the patio was empty. "I don't need to know what she . . . I . . . would say." She clutched her elbows. "I never said forever," Carol whispered. She was on the defensive without being aware of how she'd come there.

The sky was gold above the mountains. Suspended pink-orange clouds were shading the patio an hour before shade was due. Danny wolfed the steak dinner like the appreciative cub he was, hardly noticing his parents' lack of appetite. He managed the day's news between mouthfuls and was off to the meadow to play in the lingering daylight.

"We should have told him," Mike said, interrupting the peace of the evening.

Carol felt an unreasonable twinge of fear. "Tomorrow is soon enough. You and I need to . . . to talk things over."

"Like what? Absence makes the heart grow fonder? Or . . ."

"No. Like will you keep the house or move up to the mining camp? Shall I arrange for storage of my things or will you do that so we can spend the next few days together?" She was determined not to let him twist the knife that already had her guts in turmoil.

"I'll take care of all that," he said sourly.

"Then you're going to give up the house?" She felt vaguely disappointed.

"No sense in keeping a big place like this for Danny and me alone. I've plenty of seniority to get a nice place in camp."

"Schools are better down here," she pointed out.

"So, I'll lead a protest to improve the quality of education. It will give me something to do."

Carol's breath shortened in anticipation. "That sounds like you plan to wait for me." She suppressed cynical laughter and bit her cheek waiting for his answer.

Mike sighed as he looked out over the meadow. "I don't know . . . yes—you know damn well I will."

How do I know? Words are easy. No one is forever. Discard: irrational.

"Will you get leave?" He was musing aloud, considering chimerical hopes along with reality.

"No chance. I'm wintering over. I may get a week in New Zealand next summer . . . that'd be winter for you."

"Maybe we should have gotten married. Then they'd pay our fare or send you home to visit us." Mike's tone was bitter, his face dark with the stark brilliance of hindsight.

Carol laughed flippantly. "They know they're minimizing

excess baggage by choosing a single person." Then suddenly it didn't seem so amusing. "My mother had to do that, you know." *Everything changed. Discard: irrelevant.*

Mike stared at her a moment. "You mean her leaving you?"

Carol shrugged. "I don't blame her. She had no choice and I adjusted. Children always do." *Do they? Don't they?*

The black elm by the balcony swayed with the first touch of evening breeze; each branch moved differently, each had the same origin, each branched from the same trunk but somehow each swayed individually. The tiny uppermost branches seemed fragile. Carol was unsure if they'd been wise to sprout from the sturdy trunk and seek the sun on their own. But the heavy limbs near the base of the tree hardly stirred, content, perhaps, over the years with their decision. Carol wanted to be strong, as were the oldest limbs, or better yet, as the trunk of the tree. But she felt as strained as the uppermost twig, brittle . . . *No!*

She shook her head. Mike was watching Danny pick himself out of the tall grass where a friend's none-too-gentle tag had dumped him. "Danny will be fine," Carol said softly.

Mike didn't look at Carol. "By the time you get back, he'll be as tired of batching as I will."

"It's such a long time," she said doubtfully.

Mike seemed surprised. "I just assumed . . ."

"You always do."

"You don't want to make a commitment, do you?"

"Two years is a long time . . ."

"Christ, Carol, you know I'm not asking for a vow of chastity, but we've got eight good years invested together that I'd like to double. Two years isn't forever." He slammed his coffee cup down.

Carol frowned. "I'd like to come back to you, but . . ." *I never said forever, you never said forever. No one says forever!*

"But," he prodded impatiently.

"Two years is a long time," she said helplessly.

"All right! No commitment . . . and if I'm busy when you get back, I'm sure you'll understand."

No. I won't understand, but two years is a long time.

Mike lit a cigarette and walked to the edge of the patio. Agitated, he puffed heavily. Mountain zephyrs wafted the smoke away as quickly as he produced it, but his own aura was enough to fog the whole patio. He ground out the cigarette with his heel and crossed his arms. "Is the pay good?" he finally asked.

"Astronomical. And no living expenses, either." She wanted to sound proud but instead it came out as if by way of explanation.

"Why do they need you at Byrd Station?"

He'd sounded genuinely interested. "You know I can't discuss my work," Carol said unhappily. Mike looked at her sharply and she turned away to avoid his gaze, mopping up some spilled coffee with a napkin.

"I thought there wasn't supposed to be any classified work on Antarctica."

"There isn't." She put the wet napkin in the ashtray.

"But?"

Even with her back turned Carol felt the restraint Mike was exercising. He didn't like pulling answers from her. He expected—and deserved, she reminded herself—openness and honesty. "Technically I won't be breaking the treaty. I'll be observing the auroras and working in the Space Disturbance Forecast network."

"But you'll be making other observations too? Applying research from your last project?"

"Mike!" she whined. She turned, made an exasperated gesture.

"I'm not being nosy about your damn top-secret work! I'm concerned about your well-being," Mike said angrily. "You'll be thousands of miles from aid. People get killed in outposts! There are crevasses and blizzards and maybe some Russians who won't like what you're doing."

"People get killed detonating explosives too," Carol said evenly.

"I don't have camps full of Russians around to screw up my charges. There's a difference!" Carol's brow had furrowed and her chin was set defiantly. "Okay, okay, I'll knock it off." He realized that she'd related as much as she could and that further baiting would be futile. "I learned what I wanted to know anyway. Lots of compensation to keep an employee happy on a supposedly peaceful international project. It must be important."

"It is."

"What the hell am I worrying about," he said. "You can outfox any damn Russian anyhow." He laughed nervously as he kicked a stone off the patio. His gaze met Carol's. "I'm going to miss you," he said, mistaking the fear in her eyes for tenderness and longing. Or had he glimpsed the other Carol? The one beside her who wanted to stay?

"You'll get over it, Mike . . ." She wasn't able to say more. Mike didn't seem to realize that it was an unfinished sentence.

"That's your experience, Carol, not mine. You've been separated from your loved ones so many times . . . two fathers, your mother, Frank . . ."

"I've learned to accept it," she said quietly. "At least this

time it is I who will leave. It's not me being left behind." She
felt a perverse comfort in that thought.

"Frank?"

"Even Frank. He didn't have to go on that last mission. His
job was to train the men, not lead them."

"But you *have* to go?"

"Oh, Mike," Carol said unhappily. "Are we going to start
that again?"

"No," he replied quickly. "Look, I'm going to call Consolidated and get the rest of the week off. Saturday we'll get you
packed and we'll all fly to San Francisco together."

"There's little to pack." Carol fell silent. "Mike, this is so
hard."

"Did you think being on the other side of the fence would
make it easy?"

"Of course not. It's just that up to now we've managed our
lives so well. Perhaps I never expected luck to desert me."
The audacity of the lie struck her: She'd always expected to
be discarded again.

Mike shrugged and she stifled a sob in response to his casual gesture. She barely heard him over the screams of pain
filling her mind.

"Let's face it," he was saying. "We've been offered pro-
motions because the companies know we're willing to relo-
cate and because it's cheaper to move a single person than
a household. Which of us would have agreed to subjugate
his job to the other's? Mine would have been the logical one
financially . . ."

"And mine would be, traditionally," she finished for him.
"Some people feel it's a wholesome approach. My grandmother did it that way. My mother . . ."

"It works fine for cab drivers and interior decorators. They can work anywhere. I can't and you can't. It's as simple as that."

Carol hesitated, afraid to pursue memories of what her mother had done . . . as simply as that. "It seemed as if you were having regrets."

"Why? Because I was angry? I'm still angry. I don't like it at all, but I don't see a choice open to us . . . unless you want to turn it down."

Carols looked at him: one impatient, the other slow.

"My grandmother was right . . ." said slow Carol.

Impatient Carol stared, watched slow Carol receive a rewarding smile from her Mike. She longed for a smile for herself. She knew she could have the kisses the other Mike was giving that Carol—that slow, reprehensible Carol! Who was she? She certainly looked and felt better than Carol did right now. Or was it only Mike who looked so contented? Carol eyed Carol and Mike as they walked hand in hand into the meadow, fading there, too far removed from her own reality. *That Carol is a fool . . . a happy fool.*

"I won't turn it down!" *I'm no fool.*

Mike nodded slowly. "I can accept that, Carol, but I don't see why you don't want to come back." He was studying her from across the patio.

"There's always been some woman around you. You're good-looking, you have a sympathetic ear and charisma that won't stop. You've never lacked for company. I don't think it's practicable to make vows we might be forced to break."

Mike laughed. "I'm worried that you might die down there and you're concerned about me getting laid once in a while."

Carol flushed. "I'm not immune either."

"I don't care about your sex life. You know I'll never even

ask. I just don't want this to be the end for us. I'm not ready
to settle for that. I want to know you're coming back!"

"Mike, if you insist on pursuing this topic, we're going to
have a lousy weekend," she said coldly.

"Then be prepared for the lousiest weekend of your life
because I'm not going to let it all end here and now, clean and
simple. Hell no! Forget it! You can't get off that easy!"

Mike was right. It was the worst measured period of time
she'd ever spent in her life. A weekend she'd never forget.
She never could, she never tried. Too many tender moments;
speeding away from her like autumn leaves in a maelstrom.
Too many dramatic confrontations, laggards in realtime,
with the reprehensible Carol clinging to her Mike a thousand unrestrained times while Carol deliberately regarded
her. The endless details: packing, papers, tickets. Mike's
relentless pressure (slow Carol yielding). Danny's stricken
face when he came to realize that separation was imminent.
Carol's own memories of exactly the same anguish so many
times before. Acceptance that it was happening again.

And then they were sitting in the San Francisco terminal.
The few personal items she deemed irreplaceable by company issue were already checked. The weekend was gone. A
finality hung over her.

While Carol and Mike sipped coffee purchased from a
dispenser, Danny roamed the terminal. The boy seemed
to have a healthy excitement . . . he was looking forward to
watching the jet take off. His disappointment had faded; he
rallied quickly to the prospect of moving up to the mining
camp with his father: new home, new school, new friends . . .
he'd apparently decided it was fair compensation for losing

a mother. Mike's influence, Carol decided; Mike's genes. She was sincerely glad for her small son . . . and envious. Sturdy as a tree trunk.

Mike reached across the small table where they were sitting and took her hand in his. "Carol, come back to me."

"I can't confine myself to a commitment like that," she said, trying to keep the snap out of her voice. (Slow Carol was melting again.) Carol closed her eyes in disgust.

"I don't want to confine you. But dammit, don't deny eight years of love."

Carol rubbed a tired eye with her free hand, looked at him curiously through the other. He was holding her hand with an urgency she'd never suspected he could possess at the finale. "I'm not denying it," she said tiredly.

The loudspeaker in the terminal began to make an announcement. Mike talked over it. "You are! You don't believe I wouldn't endanger what we've had while you're gone."

Carol shook her head. "We each have an independent existence, Mike." Slow Carol was staring at her. Carol was too tired even to snarl at the woman.

Mike was disgusted. "I never said we didn't."

"You made it clear that you wanted me to turn this project down."

"It was a legitimate alternative that needed to be explored."

"It wasn't to me." (Slow Carol listened carefully.)

"I understand that. But you needed to know how I felt."

"You were explicit, as I recall," she said with memories of the emotion-charged weekend running through her mind.

"We're digressing," Mike said impatiently. "It's got nothing to do with the project. It's you and me. I'm telling you I value what we've had enough to know I won't jeopardize it while you're gone. Two years *is* a long time, but it isn't forever."

(Slow Carol frowned.)

"It's hard to visualize you without a woman in your life," she said, without bitterness.

"I can't either, but I also know I'll be right here to meet you when you come back. Why is that so hard to accept?"

Carol felt dizzy, frightened and elated. *Why indeed?* she asked herself. *Because it's never happened before?* "It could destroy us," she said thoughtfully. "It could change us," she protested.

"We're strong enough to risk it."

"I'm afraid . . ." Carol *who?* admitted that.

"I know, Carol." Mike squeezed her hand and let it go, waiting for her to answer. His eyes searched the terminal, found Danny standing at the drinking fountain across the concourse. Carol followed his gaze. "You won't drop out of his life. You endured that yourself too many times to do it to him." Mike looked back at Carol, who still watched her son. Her head was nodding now. Mike bit his lip angrily. "I didn't mean to say that. I only meant . . ."

"I know what you meant. You've been extremely careful not to use Danny as a lever. I appreciate that, but you're right. I can't abandon him. I've come to expect it for myself, but I can't do it to him."

Mike frowned. He was uncertain of her meaning. "But you can do it to me?" he finally ventured to ask.

"No, not to you either." Deep-rooted raptures of expectation were building to almost painful intensity. "It is *me* doing this . . . not you, Frank or my parents. It's me who's leaving. I *can* come back!" She waited for the inner voice to denounce her words. It was blissfully silent.

(Slow Carol smiled, then was gone.)

Carol smiled. *A risk is involved, perhaps....* She looked at Mike's self-satisfied grin. Perhaps not. Goodbye wasn't going to mean forever; not to Carol and not if she didn't want it that way.

1978

C. J. CHERRYH

Cassandra

F*IRES.*

They grew unbearable here.

Alis felt for the door of the flat and knew that it would be solid. She could feel the cool metal of the knob amid the flames . . . saw the shadow-stairs through the roiling smoke outside, clearly enough to feel her way down them, convincing her senses that they would bear her weight.

Crazy Alis. She made no haste. The fires burned steadily. She passed through them, descended the insubstantial steps to the solid ground—she could not abide the elevator, that closed space with the shadow-floor, that plummeted down and down; she made the ground floor, averted her eyes from the red, heatless flames.

A ghost said good morning to her . . . old man Willis, thin and transparent against the leaping flames. She blinked, bade it good morning in return—did not miss old Willis' shake of the head as she opened the door and left. Noon traffic passed, heedless of the flames, the hulks that blazed in the street, the tumbling brick.

The apartment caved in—black bricks falling into the inferno. Hell amid the green, ghostly trees. Old Willis fled, burning, fell—turned to jerking, blackened flesh—died, daily. Alis no longer cried, hardly flinched. She ignored the horror spilling about her, forced her way through crumbling brick that held no substance, past busy ghosts that could not be troubled in their haste.

Kingsley's Cafe stood, whole, more so than the rest. It was refuge for the afternoon, a feeling of safety. She pushed open the door, heard the tinkle of a lost bell. Shadowy patrons looked, whispered.

Crazy Alis.

The whispers troubled her. She avoided their eyes and their presence, settled in a booth in the corner that bore only traces of the fire.

WAR, the headline in the vender said in heavy type. She shivered, looked up into Sam Kingsley's wraithlike face.

"Coffee," she said. "Ham sandwich." It was constantly the same. She varied not even the order. Mad Alis. Her affliction supported her. A check came each month, since the hospital had turned her out. Weekly she returned to the clinic, to doctors who now faded like the others. The building burned about them. Smoke rolled down the blue, antiseptic halls. Last week a patient ran—burning—

A rattle of china. Sam set the coffee on the table, came back shortly and brought the sandwich. She bent her head and ate, transparent food on half-broken china, a cracked, fire-smudged cup with a transparent handle. She ate, hungry enough to overcome the horror that had become ordinary. A hundred times seen, the most terrible sights lost their power over her: she no longer cried at shadows. She talked to ghosts and touched them, ate the food that somehow stilled the ache in her belly, wore the same too-large black sweater and worn blue shirt and grey slacks because they were all she had that seemed solid. Nightly she washed them and dried them and put them on the next day, letting others hang in the closet. They were the only solid ones.

She did not tell the doctors these things. A lifetime in and out of hospitals had made her wary of confidences. She knew what to say. Her half-vision let her smile at ghost-faces, cannily manipulate their charts and cards, sitting in the ruins that had begun to smolder by late afternoon. A blackened corpse lay in the hall. She did not flinch when she smiled good-naturedly at the doctor.

They gave her medicines. The medicines stopped the dreams, the siren screams, the running steps in the night past her apartment. They let her sleep in the ghostly bed, high above ruin, with the flames crackling and the voices screaming. She did not speak of these things. Years in hospitals had taught her. She complained only of nightmares, and restlessness, and they let her have more of the red pills.

WAR, the headline blazoned.

The cup rattled and trembled against the saucer as she picked it up. She swallowed the last bit of bread and washed it down with coffee, tried not to look beyond the broken front window, where twisted metal hulks smoked on the street. She stayed, as she did each day, and Sam grudgingly refilled her cup, that she would nurse as far as she could and then order another one. She lifted it, savoring the feel of it, stopping the trembling of her hands.

The bell jingled faintly. A man closed the door, settled at the counter.

Whole, clear in her eyes. She stared at him, startled, heart pounding. He ordered coffee, moved to buy a paper from the vender, settled again and let the coffee grow cold while he read the news. She had a view only of his back while he read, scuffed brown leather coat, brown hair a little over his collar. At last he drank the cooled coffee all at one draught, shoved money onto the counter and left the paper lying, headlines turned face down.

A young face, flesh and bone among the ghosts. He ignored them all and went for the door.

Alis thrust herself from her booth.

"Hey!" Sam called at her.

She rummaged in her purse as the bell jingled, flung a bill onto the counter, heedless that it was a five. Fear was coppery in her mouth; he was gone. She fled the cafe, edged around debris without thinking of it, saw his back disappearing among the ghosts.

She ran, shouldering them, braving the flames—cried out as debris showered painlessly on her, and kept running.

Ghosts turned and stared, shocked—*he* did likewise, and she ran to him, stunned to see the same shock on his face, regarding her.

"What is it?" he asked.

She blinked, dazed to realize he saw her no differently than the others. She could not answer. In irritation he started walking again, and she followed. Tears slid down her face, her breath hard in her throat. People stared. He noticed her presence and walked the faster, through debris, through fires. A wall began to fall and she cried out despite herself.

He jerked about. The dust and the soot rose up as a cloud behind him. His face was distraught and angry. He stared at her as the others did. Mothers drew children away from the scene. A band of youths stared, cold-eyed and laughing.

"Wait," she said. He opened his mouth as if he would curse

her; she flinched, and the tears were cold in the heatless wind of the fires. His face twisted in an embarrassed pity. He thrust a hand into his pocket and began to pull out money, hastily, tried to give it to her. She shook her head furiously, trying to stop the tears—stared upward, flinching, as another building fell into flames.

"What's wrong?" he asked her. "What's wrong with you?"

"Please," she said. He looked about at the staring ghosts, then began to walk slowly. She walked with him, nerving herself not to cry out at the ruin, the pale moving figures that wandered through burned shells of buildings, the twisted corpses in the street, where traffic moved.

"What's your name?" he asked. She told him. He gazed at her from time to time as they walked, a frown creasing his brow. He had a face well-worn for youth, a tiny scar beside the mouth. He looked older than she. She felt uncomfortable in the way his eyes traveled over her: she decided to accept it—to bear with anything that gave her this one solid presence. Against every inclination she reached her hand into the bend of his arm, tightened her fingers on the worn leather. He accepted it.

And after a time he slid his arm behind her and about her waist, and they walked like lovers.

WAR, the headline at the newsstand cried.

He started to turn into a street by Tenn's Hardware. She balked at what she saw there. He paused when he felt it, faced her with his back to the fires of that burning.

"Don't go," she said.

"Where do you want to go?"

She shrugged helplessly, indicated the main street, the other direction.

He talked to her then, as he might talk to a child, humoring her fear. It was pity. Some treated her that way. She recognized it, and took even that.

His name was Jim. He had come into the city yesterday, hitched rides. He was looking for work. He knew no one in the city. She listened to his rambling awkwardness, reading through it. When he was done, she stared at him still, and saw his face contract in dismay at her.

"I'm not crazy," she told him, which was a lie, that everyone in Sudbury would have known, only *he* would not, knowing no one. His face was true and solid, and the tiny scar by the mouth made it hard when he was thinking; at another time she would have been terrified of him. Now she was terrified of losing him amid the ghosts.

"It's the war," he said.

She nodded, trying to look at him and not at the fires. His fingers touched her arm, gently. "It's the war," he said again. "It's all crazy. Everyone's crazy."

And then he put his hand on her shoulder and turned her back the other way, toward the park, where green leaves waved over black, skeletal limbs. They walked along the lake, and for the first time in a long time she drew breath and felt a whole, sane presence beside her.

They bought corn, and sat on the grass by the lake, and flung it to the spectral swans. Wraiths of passersby were few, only enough to keep a feeling of occupancy about the place— old people, mostly, tottering about the deliberate tranquillity of their routine despite the headlines.

"Do you see them," she ventured to ask him finally, "all thin and grey?"

He did not understand, did not take her literally, only shrugged. Warily, she abandoned that questioning at once. She rose to her feet and stared at the horizon, where the smoke bannered on the wind.

"Buy you supper?" he asked.

She turned, prepared for this, and managed a shy, desperate smile. "Yes," she said, knowing what else he reckoned to buy with that—willing, and hating herself, and desperately afraid that he would walk away, tonight, tomorrow. She did not know men. She had no idea what she could say or do to prevent his leaving, only that he would when someday he realized her madness.

Even her parents had not been able to bear with that—visited her only at first in the hospitals, and then only on holidays, and then not at all. She did not know where they were.

There was a neighbor boy who drowned. She had said he would. She had cried for it. All the town said it was she who pushed him.

Crazy Alis.

Fantasizes, the doctors said. Not dangerous.

They let her out. There were special schools, state schools. And from time to time—hospitals.

Tranquilizers.

She had left the red pills at home. The realization brought sweat to her palms. They gave sleep. They stopped the dreams. She clamped her lips against the panic and made up her mind that she would not need them—not while she was not alone. She slipped her hand into his arm and walked with him, secure and strange, up the steps from the park to the streets.

And stopped.

The fires were out.

Ghost-buildings rose above their jagged and windowless shells. Wraiths moved through masses of debris, almost obscured at times. He tugged her on, but her step faltered, made him look at her strangely and put his arm about her.

"You're shivering," he said. "Cold?"

She shook her head, tried to smile. The fires were out. She tried to take it for a good omen. The nightmare was over. She looked up into his solid, concerned face, and her smile almost became a wild laugh.

"I'm hungry," she said.

They lingered long over a dinner in Graben's—he in his battered jacket, she in her sweater that hung at the tails and elbows: the spectral patrons were in far better clothes, and stared at them, and they were set in a corner nearest the door, where they would be less visible. There was cracked crystal and broken china on insubstantial tables, and the stars winked coldly in gaping ruin above the wan glittering of the broken chandeliers.

Ruins, cold, peaceful ruin.

Alis looked about her calmly. One could live in ruins, only so the fires were gone.

And there was Jim, who smiled at her without any touch of pity, only a wild, fey desperation that she understood—who spent more than he could afford in Graben's, the inside of which she had never hoped to see—and told her—predictably—that she was beautiful. Others had said it. Vaguely she resented such triteness from him, from him whom she had decided to trust. She smiled sadly, when he said it, and gave it up for a frown and, fearful of offending him with her melancholies, made it a smile again.

Crazy Alis. He would learn and leave tonight if she were not careful. She tried to put on gaiety, tried to laugh.

And then the music stopped in the restaurant, and the noise of the other diners went dead, and the speaker was giving an inane announcement.

Shelters . . . shelters . . . shelters.

Screams broke out. Chairs overturned.

Alis went limp in her chair, felt Jim's cold, solid hand tugging at hers, saw his frightened face mouthing her name as he took her up into his arms, pulled her with him, started running.

The cold air outside hit her, shocked her into sight of the ruins again, wraith figures pelting toward that chaos where the fires had been worst.

And she knew.

"No!" she cried, pulling at his arm. "No!" she insisted, and bodies half-seen buffeted them in a rush to destruction. He yielded to her sudden certainty, gripped her hand and fled with her against the crowds as the sirens wailed madness through the night—fled with her as she ran her sighted way through the ruin.

And into Kingsley's, where cafe tables stood abandoned with food still on them, doors ajar, chairs overturned. Back they went into the kitchens and down and down into the cellar, the dark, the cold safety from the flames.

No others found them there. At last the earth shook, too deep for sound. The sirens ceased and did not come on again.

They lay in the dark and clutched each other and shivered, and above them for hours raged the sound of fire, smoke sometimes drifting in to sting their eyes and noses. There was the distant crash of brick, rumblings that shook the ground, that came near, but never touched their refuge.

And in the morning, with the scent of fire still in the air, they crept up into the murky daylight.

The ruins were still and hushed. The ghost-buildings were solid now, mere shells. The wraiths were gone. It was the fires themselves that were strange, some true, some not, playing above dark, cold brick, and most were fading.

Jim swore softly, over and over again, and wept.

When she looked at him she was dry-eyed, for she had done her crying already.

And she listened as he began to talk about food, about leaving the city, the two of them. "All right," she said.

Then clamped her lips, shut her eyes against what she saw in his face. When she opened them it was still true, the sudden transparency, the wash of blood. She trembled, and he shook at her, his ghost-face distraught.

"What's wrong?" he asked. "What's wrong?"

She could not tell him, would not. She remembered the boy who had drowned, remembered the other ghosts. Of a sudden she tore from his hands and ran, dodging the maze of debris that, this morning, was solid.

"Alis!" he cried and came after her.

"No!" she cried suddenly, turning, seeing the unstable wall, the cascading brick. She started back and stopped, unable to force herself. She held out her hands to warn him back, saw them solid.

The brick rumbled, fell. Dust came up, thick for a moment, obscuring everything.

She stood still, hands at her sides, then wiped her sooty

face and turned and started walking, keeping to the center of the dead streets.

Overhead, clouds gathered, heavy with rain.

She wandered at peace now, seeing the rain spot the pavement, not yet feeling it.

In time the rain did fall, and the ruins became chill and cold. She visited the dead lake and the burned trees, the ruin of Graben's, out of which she gathered a string of crystal to wear.

She smiled when, a day later, a looter drove her from her food supply. He had a wraith's look, and she laughed from a place he did not dare to climb and told him so.

And recovered her cache later when it came true, and settled among the ruined shells that held no further threat, no other nightmares, with her crystal necklace and tomorrows that were the same as today.

One could live in ruins, only so the fires were gone.

And the ghosts were all in the past, invisible.

1978

LISA TUTTLE

Wives

A SMELL OF sulfur in the air on a morning when the men had gone, and the wives, in their beds, smiled in their sleep, breathed more easily, and burrowed deeper into dreams.

Jack's wife woke, her eyes open and her little nose flaring, smelling something beneath the sulfur smell. One of those smells she was used to not noticing, when the men were around. But it was all right, now. Wives could do as they pleased, so long as they cleaned up and were back in their proper places when the men returned.

Jack's wife—who was called Susie—got out of bed too quickly and grimaced as the skintight punished her muscles. She caught sight of herself in the mirror over the dressing table: her sharp teeth were bared, and she looked like a wild animal, bound and struggling. She grinned at that, because she could easily free herself.

She cut the skintight apart with scissors, cutting and ripping carelessly. It didn't matter that it was ruined—skintights were plentiful. She had a whole boxful, herself, in the hall closet behind the Christmas decorations. And she didn't have the patience to try soaking it off slowly in a hot bath, as the older wives recommended. So her muscles would be sore and her skintight a tattered rag—she would be free that much sooner.

She looked down at her dead-white body, feeling distaste.

She felt despair at the sight of her small arms, hanging limp, thin and useless in the hollow below her ribs. She tried to flex them but could not make them move. She began to massage them with her primary fingers, and after several minutes the pain began, and she knew they weren't dead yet.

She bathed and massaged her newly uncovered body with oil. She felt terrifyingly free, naked and rather dangerous, with the skintight removed. She sniffed the air again and that familiar scent, musky and alluring, aroused her.

She ran through the house—noticing, in passing, that Jack's pet spider was eating the living room sofa. It was the time for building nests and cocoons, she thought happily, time for laying eggs and planting seeds; the spider was driven by the same force that drove her.

Outside, the dusty ground was hard and cold beneath her bare feet. She felt the dust all over her body, raised by the wind and clinging to her momentary warmth. She was coated in the soft yellow dust by the time she reached the house next-door—the house where the magical scent came from, the house which held a wife in heat, longing for someone to mate with.

Susie tossed her head, shaking the dust out in a little cloud around her head. She stared up at the milky sky and around at all the houses, alien artifacts constructed by men. She saw movement in the window of the house across the street and waved—the figure watching her waved back.

Poor old Maggie, thought Susie. Old, bulging and ugly, unloved, and nobody's wife. She was only housekeeper to two men who were, rather unfortunately Susie thought, in love with each other.

But she didn't want to waste time by thinking of wives and men, or by feeling pity, now. Boldly, like a man, Susie pounded at the door.

It opened. "Ooooh, Susie!"

Susie grinned and looked the startled wife up and down. You'd never know from looking at her that the men were gone and she could relax—this wife, called Doris, was as dolled-up as some eager-to-please newlywed and looked, Susie thought, more like a real woman than any woman had ever looked.

Over her skintight (which was bound more tightly than Susie's had been) Doris wore a low-cut dress, her three breasts carefully bound and positioned to achieve the proper, double-breasted effect. Gaily patterned and textured stockings covered her silicone-injected legs, and she tottered on heels three centimeters high. Her face was carefully painted, and she wore gold bands on neck, wrists and fingers.

Then Susie ignored what she looked like, and her nose told her much more. The smell was so powerful now that she could feel her pouch swelling in lonely response.

Doris must have noticed, for her eyes rolled, seeking some safe view.

"What's the matter?" Susie asked, her voice louder and bolder than it ever was when the men were around. "Didn't your man go off to war with the others? He stay home sick in bed?"

Doris giggled. "Ooooh, I wish he would, sometime! No, he was out of here before it was light."

Off to see his mistress before leaving, Susie thought. She knew that Doris was nervous about being displaced by one of the other wives her man was always fooling around with—

there were always more wives than there were men, and her man had a roving eye.

"Calm down, Doris. Your man can't see you now, you know." She stroked one of Doris' hands. "Why don't you take off that silly dress, and your skintight. I know how constricted you must be feeling. Why not relax with me?"

She saw Doris' face darken with emotion beneath the heavy make-up, and she grasped her hand more tightly when Doris tried to pull away.

"Please don't," Doris said.

"Come on," Susie murmured, caressing Doris' face and feeling the thick paint slide beneath her fingers.

"No, don't . . . please . . . I've tried to control myself, truly I have. But the exercises don't work, and the perfume doesn't cover the smell well enough—he won't even sleep with me when I'm like this. He thinks it's disgusting, and it is. I'm so afraid he'll leave me."

"But he's gone now, Doris. You can let yourself go. You don't have to worry about him when he's not around. It's safe, it's all right, you can do as you please now—we can do anything we like and no one will know." She could feel Doris trembling.

"Doris," she whispered and rubbed her face demandingly against hers.

At that, the other wife gave in, and collapsed in her arms.

Susie helped Doris out of her clothes, tearing at them with hands and teeth, throwing shoes and jewelry high into the air and festooning the yard with rags of dress, stockings and undergarment.

But when Doris, too, was naked, Susie suddenly felt shy

and a little frightened. It would be wrong to mate here in the settlement built by men, wrong and dangerous. They must go somewhere else, somewhere they could be something other than wives for a little while, and follow their own natures without reproach.

They went to a place of stone on the far northern edge of the human settlement. It was a very old place, although whether it had been built by the wives in the distant time before they were wives or whether it was natural, neither Susie nor Doris could say. They both felt that it was a holy place, and it seemed right to mate there, in the shadow of one of the huge, black, standing stones.

It was a feast, an orgy of life after a season of death. They found pleasure in exploring the bodies which seemed so similar to men's, but which they knew to be miraculously different, each from the other, in scent, texture, and taste. They forgot that they had ever been creatures known as wives. They lost their names and forgot the language of men as they lay entwined.

There were no skintights imprisoning their bodies now, barring them from sensation, freedom and pleasure, and they were partners, not strangers, as they explored and exulted in their flesh. This was no mockery of the sexual act—brutishly painful and brief as it was with the men—but the true act in all its meaning.

They were still joined at sundown, and it was not until long after the three moons began their nightly waltz through the clouds that the two lovers fell asleep at last.

"In three months," Susie said dreamily, "we can. . . ."

"In three months we won't do anything."

"Why not? If the men are away. . . ."

"I'm hungry," Doris said. She wrapped her primary arms around herself. "And I'm cold, and I ache all over. Let's go back."

"Stay here with me, Doris. Let's plan."

"There's nothing to plan."

"But in three months we must get together and fertilize it."

"Are you crazy? Who would carry it then? One of us would have to go without a skintight, and do you think either of our husbands would let us slop around for four months without a skintight? And then when it's born how could we hide it? Men don't have babies, and they don't want anyone else to. Men kill babies, just as they kill all their enemies."

Susie knew that what Doris was saying was true, but she was reluctant to give up her new dream. "Still, we might be able to keep it hidden," she said. "It's not so hard to hide things from a man. . . ."

"Don't be so stupid," Doris said scornfully. Susie noticed that she still had smears of make-up on her face. Some smears had transferred themselves to Susie in the night. They looked like bruises or bloody wounds. "Come back with me now," Doris said, her voice gentle again. "Forget this, about the baby. The old ways are gone—we're wives now, and we don't have a place in our lives for babies."

"But someday the war may end," Susie said. "And the men will all go back to Earth and leave us here."

"If that happens," Doris said, "then we would make new lives for ourselves. Perhaps we would have babies again."

"If it's not too late then," Susie said. "If it ever happens." She stared past Doris at the horizon.

"Come back with me."

Susie shook her head. "I have to think. You go. I'll be all right."

She realized when Doris had gone that she, too, was tired, hungry and sore, but she was not sorry she had remained in the place of stone. She needed to stay awhile longer in one of the old places, away from the distractions of the settlement. She felt that she was on the verge of remembering something very important.

A large, dust-colored lizard crawled out of a hole in the side of a fallen rock, and Susie rolled over and clapped her hands on it. But it wriggled out of her clutches like air or water or the wind-blown dust and disappeared somewhere. Susie felt a sharp pang of disappointment along with her hunger—she had a sudden memory of how that lizard would have tasted, how the skin of its throat would have felt, tearing between her teeth. She licked her dry lips and sat up. In the old days, she thought, I caught many such lizards. But the old days were gone, and with them the old knowledge and the old abilities.

I'm not what I used to be, she thought. I'm something else, now—a "wife," created by man in the image of something I have never seen, something called "woman."

She thought about going back to her house in the settlement and of wrapping herself in a new skintight and then selecting the proper dress and shoes to make a good impression on the returning Jack; she thought about painting her face and putting rings on her fingers. She thought about burning and boiling good food to turn it into the unappetizing messes Jack favored and about killing the wide-eyed "coffee fish" to get the oil to make the mildly addictive drink the men called "coffee." She thought about watching Jack, and listening to him, always alert for what he might want, what he might ask,

what he might do. Trying to anticipate him, to earn his praise
and avoid his blows and harsh words. She thought about letting him "screw" her and about the ugly jewelry and noisome
perfumes he brought her.

Susie began to cry, and the dust drank her tears as they
fell. She didn't understand how this had all begun, how or
why she had become a wife, but she could bear it no longer.

She wanted to be what she had been born to be—but she
could not remember what that was. She only knew that she
would be Susie no longer. She would be no man's wife.

"I remembered my name this morning," Susie said with quiet
triumph. She looked around the room. Doris was staring
down at her hands, twisting in her lap. Maggie looked half-
asleep, and the other two wives—Susie didn't remember their
names; she had simply gathered them up when she found
them on the street—looked both bored and nervous.

"Don't you see?" Susie persisted. "If I could remember
that, I'm sure I can remember other things in time. All of us
can."

Maggie opened her eyes all the way. "And what would that
do," she asked, "except make us discontented and restless,
as you are?"

"What *good* . . . why, if we all began to remember, we could
live our lives again—our *own* lives. We wouldn't have to be
wives, we could be . . . ourselves."

"Could we," said Maggie sourly. "And do you think the men
would watch us go? Do you think they'd let us walk out of
their houses and out of their lives without stopping us? Don't
you—you who talk about remembering—don't you remember how it was when the men came? Don't you remember

the slaughter? Don't you remember just who became wives, and why? We, the survivors, became wives because the men wouldn't kill their wives, not if we kept them happy and believing we weren't the enemy. If we try to leave or change, they'll kill us like they've killed almost everything else in the world."

The others were silent, but Susie suspected they were letting Maggie speak for them.

"But we'll die," she said. "We'll die like this, as wives. We've lost our identities, but we can have them back. We can have our world back, and our lives, if we only take them. We're dying as a race and as a world, now. Being a wife is a living death, just a postponement of the end, that's all."

"Yes," said Maggie, irony hanging heavily from the word. "So?"

"So why do we have to let them do this to us? We can hide—we can run far away from the settlement and hide. Or, if we have to, we can fight back."

"That's not our way," said Maggie.

"Then what *is* our way?" Susie demanded. "Is it our way to let ourselves be destroyed? They've already killed our culture and our past—we have no 'way' anymore—we can't claim we do. All we are now is imitations, creatures molded by the men. And when the men leave—*if* the men leave—it will be the end for us. We'll have nothing left, and it will be too late to try to remember who we were."

"It's already too late," Maggie said. Susie was suddenly impressed by the way she spoke and held herself, and wondered if Maggie, this elderly and unloved wife she once had pitied, had once been a leader of her people.

"Can you remember why we did not hide or fight before?" Maggie asked. "Can you remember why we decided that the best thing for us was to change our ways, to do what you are now asking us to undo?"

Susie shook her head.

"Then go and try to remember. Remember that we made a choice when the men came, and now we must live with that choice. Remember that there was a good reason for what we did, a reason of survival. It is too late to change again. The old way is not waiting for our return, it is dead. Our world has been changed, and we could not stop it. The past is dead, but that is as it should be. We have new lives now. Forget your restlessness and go home. Be a good wife to Jack—he loves you in his way. Go home and be thankful for that."

"I can't," she said. She looked around the room, noticing how the eyes of the others fell before hers. So few of them had wanted to listen to her, so few had dared venture out of their homes. Susie looked at Maggie as she spoke, meaning her words for all the wives. "They're killing us slowly," she said. "But we'll be just as dead in the end. I would rather die fighting, and take some of them with me."

"You may be ready to die now, but the rest of us are not," Maggie said. "But if you fought them, you would get not only your own death, but the deaths of all of us. If they see you snarling and violent, they will wake up and turn new eyes on the rest of us and see us not as their loving wives but as beasts, strangers, dangerous wild animals to be destroyed. They forget that we are different from them now; they are willing to forget and let us live as long as we keep them comfortable and act as wives should act."

"I can't fight them alone, I know that," Susie said. "But if you'll all join with me, we have a chance. We could take them by surprise, we could use their weapons against them. Why not? They don't expect a fight from us—we could win. Some of us would die, of course, but many of us would survive. More than that—we'd have our own lives, our own world, back again."

"You think your arguments are new," said Maggie. There was a trace of impatience in her usually calm voice. "But I can remember the old days, even if you can't. I remember what happened when the men first came, and I know what would happen if we angered them. Even if we managed somehow to kill all the men here, more men would come in their ships from the sky. And they would come to kill us for daring to fight them. Perhaps they'd simply drop fire on us, this time being sure to burn out all of us and all life on our world. Do you seriously ask us to bring about this certain destruction?"

Susie stared at her, feeling dim memories stir in response to her words. Fire from the sky, the burning, the killing. . . . But she couldn't be certain she remembered, and she would rather risk destruction than go back to playing wife again.

"We could hide," she said, pleading. "We could run away and hide in the wilderness. The men might think we had died—they'd forget about us soon, I'm certain. Even if they looked for us at first, we could hide. It's our world, and we know it as they don't. Soon we could live again as we used to, and forget the men."

"Stop this dreaming," Maggie said. "We can never live the way we used to—the old ways are gone, the old world is gone, and even your memories are gone, that's obvious. The only way we know how to live now is with the men, as their wives.

Everything else is gone. We'd die of hunger and exposure if the men didn't track us down and kill us first."

"I may have forgotten the old ways, but you haven't. You could teach us."

"I remember enough to know what is gone, to know that we can't go back. Believe me. Think about it, Susie. Try—"

"Don't call me that!"

Her shout echoed in the silence. No one spoke. Susie felt the last of her hope drain out of her as she looked at them. They did not feel what she felt, and she would not be able to convince them. In silence, still, she left them, and went back to her own house.

She waited for them there, for them to come and kill her.

She knew that they would come; she knew she had to die. It was as Maggie had said: one renegade endangered them all. If one wife turned on one man, all the wives would be made to suffer. The look of love on their faces would change to a look of hatred, and the slaughter would begin again.

Susie felt no desire to try to escape, to hide from the other wives as she had suggested they all hide from the men. She had no wish to live alone; for good or ill, she was a part of her people, and she did not wish to endanger them nor to break away from them.

When they came, they came together, all the wives of the settlement, coming to act in concert so none should bear the guilt alone. They did not hate Susie, nor did she hate them, but the deadly work had to be done.

Susie walked outside, into their midst. To make it easier for them—to act with them, in a sense—Susie offered not the slightest resistance. She presented the weakest parts of her body to their hands and teeth, that her death should come more quickly. And as she died, feeling her body pressed, pounded and torn by the other wives, Susie did not mind the pain. She felt herself a part of them all, and she died content.

After her death, one of the extra wives took on Susie's name and moved into her house. She got rid of the spider's gigantic egg-case first thing—Jack might like his football-sized pet, but he wouldn't be pleased by the hundreds of pebble-sized babies that would come spilling out of the egg-case in a few months. Then she began to clean in earnest: a man deserved a clean house to come home to.

When, a few days later, the men returned from their fighting, Susie's man Jack found a spotless house, filled with the smells of his favorite foods cooking, and a smiling, sexily dressed wife.

"Would you like some dinner, dear?" she asked.

"Put it on hold," he said, grinning wolfishly. "Right now I'll take a cup of hot coffee—in bed—with you on the side."

She fluttered her false eyelashes and moved a little closer, so he could put his arm around her if he liked.

"Three tits and the best coffee in the universe," he said with satisfaction, squeezing one of the bound lumps of flesh on her chest. "With this to come home to, it kind of makes the whole war-thing worthwhile."

1979

CONNIE WILLIS

Daisy, in the Sun

NONE OF the others were any help. Daisy's brother, when she knelt beside him on the kitchen floor and said, "Do you remember when we lived at Grandma's house, just the three of us, nobody else?" looked at her blankly over the pages of his book, his face closed and uninterested. "What is your book about?" she asked kindly. "Is it about the sun? You always used to read your books out loud to me at Grandma's. All about the sun."

He stood up and went to the windows of the kitchen and looked out at the snow, tracing patterns on the dry window. The book, when Daisy looked at it, was about something else altogether.

"It didn't always snow like this at home, did it?" Daisy would ask her grandmother. "It couldn't have snowed all the time, not even in Canada, could it?"

It was the train this time, not the kitchen, but her grandmother went on measuring for the curtains as if she didn't notice. "How can the trains run if it snows all the time?" Her grandmother didn't answer her. She went on measuring the wide curved train windows with her long yellow tape measure. She wrote the measurements on little slips of paper, and they drifted from her pockets like the snow outside, without sound.

Daisy waited until it was the kitchen again. The red cafe curtains hung streaked and limp across the bottom half of

419

the square windows. "The sun faded the curtains, didn't it?" she asked slyly, but her grandmother would not be tricked. She measured and wrote and dropped the measurements like ash around her.

Daisy looked from her grandmother to the rest of them, shambling up and down the length of her grandmother's kitchen. She would not ask them. Talking to them would be like admitting they belonged here, muddling clumsily around the room, bumping into each other.

Daisy stood up. "It *was* the sun that faded them," she said. "I remember," and went into her room and shut the door.

The room was always her own room, no matter what happened outside. It stayed the same, yellow ruffled muslin on the bed, yellow priscillas at the window. She had refused to let her mother put blinds up in her room. She remembered that quite clearly. She had stayed in her room the whole day with her door barricaded. But she could not remember why her mother had wanted to put them up or what had happened afterward.

Daisy sat down cross-legged in the middle of the bed, hugging the yellow ruffled pillow from her bed against her chest. Her mother constantly reminded her that a young lady sat with her legs together. "You're fifteen, Daisy. You're a young lady whether you like it or not."

Why could she remember things like that and not how they had gotten here and where her mother was and why it snowed all the time yet was never cold? She hugged the pillow tightly against her and tried, tried to remember.

It was like pushing against something, something both yielding and unyielding. It was herself, trying to push her breasts flat against her chest after her mother had told her she was growing up, that she would need to wear a bra. She had tried to push through to the little girl she had been before, but even though she pressed them into herself with the flats of her hands, they were still there. A barrier, impossible to get through.

Daisy clutched at the yielding pillow, her eyes squeezed shut. "Grandma came in," she said out loud, reaching for the one memory she could get to, "Grandma came in and said . . ."

She was looking at one of her brother's books. She had been holding it, looking at it, one of her brother's books about the sun, and as the door opened he reached out and took it away from her. He was angry—about the book? Her grandmother came in, looking hot and excited, and he took the book away from her. Her grandmother said, "They got the material in. I bought enough for all the windows." She had a sack full of folded cloth, red-and-white gingham. "I bought almost the whole bolt," her grandmother said. She was flushed. "Isn't it pretty?" Daisy reached out to touch the thin pretty cloth. And . . . Daisy clutched at the pillow, wrinkling the ruffled edge. She had reached out to touch the thin pretty cloth and then . . .

It was no use. She could not get any farther. She had never been able to get any farther. Sometimes she sat on her bed for days. Sometimes she started at the end and worked back through the memory and it was still the same. She could not remember anymore on either side. Only the book and her grandmother coming in and reaching out her hand.

Daisy opened her eyes. She put the pillow back on the bed

and uncrossed her legs and took a deep breath. She was going to have to ask the others. There was nothing else to do.

She stood a minute by the door before she opened it, wondering which of the places it would be. It was her mother's living room, the walls a cool blue and the windows covered with venetian blinds. Her brother sat on the gray-blue carpet reading. Her grandmother had taken down one of the blinds. She was measuring the tall window. Outside the snow fell.

The strangers moved up and down on the blue carpet. Sometimes Daisy thought she recognized them, that they were friends of her parents or people she had seen at school, but she could not be sure. They did not speak to each other in their endless, patient wanderings. They did not even seem to see each other. Sometimes, passing down the long aisle of the train or circling her grandmother's kitchen or pacing the blue living room, they bumped into each other. They did not stop and say excuse me. They bumped into each other as if they did not know they did it, and moved on. They collided without sound or feeling, and each time they did they seemed less and less like people Daisy knew and more and more like strangers. She looked at them anxiously, trying to recognize them so she could ask them.

The young man had come in from outside. Daisy was sure of it, though there was no draft of cold air to convince her, no snow for the young man to shrug from his hair and shoulders. He moved with easy direction through the others, and they looked up at him as he passed. He sat down on the blue couch and smiled at Daisy's brother. Her brother looked up from his book and smiled back. He has come in from outside, Daisy thought. He will know.

She sat down near him, on the end of the couch, her arms

crossed in front of her. "Has something happened to the sun?" she asked him in a whisper.

He looked up. His face was as young as hers, tanned and smiling. Daisy felt, far down, a little quiver of fear, a faint alien feeling like that which had signaled the coming of her first period. She stood up and backed away from him, only a step, and nearly collided with one of the strangers.

"Well, hello," the boy said. "If it isn't little Daisy!"

Her hands knotted into fists. She did not see how she could not have recognized him before—the easy confidence, the casual smile. He would not help her. He knew, of course he knew, he had always known everything, but he wouldn't tell her. He would laugh at her. She must not let him laugh at her.

"Hi, Ron," she was going to say, but the last consonant drifted away into uncertainty. She had never been sure what his name was.

He laughed. "What makes you think something's happened to the sun, Daisy-Daisy?" He had his arm over the back of the couch. "Sit down and tell me all about it." If she sat down next to him he could easily put his arm around her.

"Has something happened to the sun?" she repeated, more loudly, from where she stood. "It never shines anymore."

"Are you sure?" he said, and laughed again. He was looking at her breasts. She crossed her arms in front of her.

"Has it?" she said stubbornly, like a child.

"What do you think?"

"I think maybe everybody was wrong about the sun." She stopped, surprised at what she had said, at what she was remembering now. Then she went on, forgetting to keep her arms in front of her, listening to what she said next. "They all thought it was going to blow up. They said it would swallow the whole earth up. But maybe it didn't. Maybe it just burned out, like a match or something, and it doesn't shine anymore and that's why it snows all the time and—"

"Cold," Ron said.

"What?"

"Cold," he said. "Wouldn't it be cold if that had happened?"

"What?" she said stupidly.

"Daisy," he said, and smiled at her. She reeled a little. The tugging of fear was farther down and more definite.

"Oh," she said, and ran, veering, around the others milling up and down, up and down, into her own room. She slammed the door behind her and lay down on the bed, holding her stomach and remembering.

Her father had called them all together in the living room. Her mother perched on the edge of the blue couch, already looking frightened. Her brother had brought a book in with him, but he stared blindly at the page.

It was cold in the living room. Daisy moved into the one patch of sunlight, and waited. She had already been frightened for a year. And in a minute, she thought, I'm going to hear something that will make me more afraid.

She felt a sudden stunning hatred of her parents, able to pull her in out of the sun and into darkness, able to make her frightened just by talking to her. She had been sitting on the porch today. That other day she had been lying in the sun in her old yellow bathing suit when her mother called her in.

"You're a big girl now," her mother had said once they were in her room. She was looking at the outgrown yellow suit that was tight across the chest and pulled up on the legs. "There are things you need to know."

Daisy's heart had begun to pound. "I wanted to tell you so you wouldn't hear a lot of rumors." She had had a booklet with her, pink and white and terrifying. "I want you to read this, Daisy. You're changing, even though you may not notice it. Your breasts are developing and soon you'll be starting your period. That means . . ."

Daisy knew what it meant. The girls at school had told her. Darkness and blood. Boys wanting to touch her breasts, wanting to penetrate her darkness. And then more blood.

"No," Daisy said. "No. I don't want to."

"I know it seems frightening to you now, but someday soon you'll meet a nice boy and then you'll understand—"

No, I won't. Never. I know what boys do to you.

"Five years from now you won't feel this way, Daisy. You'll see—"

Not in five years. Not in a hundred. No.

"I won't have breasts," Daisy shouted, and threw the pillow off her bed at her mother. "I won't have a period. I won't let it happen. No!"

Her mother had looked at her pityingly. "Why, Daisy, it's already started." She had put her arms around her. "There's nothing to be afraid of, honey."

Daisy had been afraid ever since. And now she would be more afraid, as soon as her father spoke.

"I wanted to tell you all together," her father said, "so you would not hear some other way. I wanted you to know what is really happening and not just rumors." He paused and took a ragged breath. They even started their speeches alike.

"I think you should hear it from me," her father said. "The sun is going to go nova."

Her mother gasped, a long, easy intake of breath like a

sigh, the last easy breath her mother would take. Her brother closed his book. "Is that all?" Daisy thought, surprised.

"The sun has used up all the hydrogen in its core. It's starting to burn itself up, and when it does, it will expand and . . ." he stumbled over the word.

"It's going to swallow us up," her brother said. "I read it in a book. The sun will just explode, all the way out to Mars. It'll swallow up Mercury and Venus and Earth and Mars and we'll all be dead."

Her father nodded. "Yes," he said, as if he was relieved that the worst was out.

"No," her mother said. And Daisy thought, "This is nothing. Nothing." Her mother's talks were worse than this. Blood and darkness.

"There have been changes in the sun," her father said. "There have been more solar storms, too many. And the sun is releasing unusual bursts of neutrinos. Those are signs that it will—"

"How long?" her mother asked.

"A year. Five years at the most. They don't know."

"We have to stop it!" Daisy's mother shrieked, and Daisy looked up from her place in the sun, amazed at her mother's fear.

"There's nothing we can do," her father said. "It's already started."

"I won't let it," her mother said. "Not my children. I won't let it happen. Not to my Daisy. She's always loved the sun."

At her mother's words, Daisy remembered something. An old photograph her mother had written on, scrawling across the bottom of the picture in white ink. The picture was herself as a toddler in a yellow sunsuit, concave little girl's chest and pooching toddler's stomach. Bucket and shovel and toes dug into the hot sand, squinting up into the sunlight. And her mother's writing across the bottom, "Daisy, in the sun."

Her father had taken her mother's hand and was holding it. He had put his arm around her brother's shoulders. Their heads were ducked, prepared for a blow, as if they thought a bomb was going to fall on them.

Daisy thought, "All of us, in a year or maybe five, surely five at the most, all of us children again, warm and happy, in the sun." She could not make herself be afraid.

It was the train again. The strangers moved up and down the long aisle of the dining car, knocking against each other randomly. Her grandmother measured the little window in the door at the end of the car. She did not look out the little window at the ashen snow. Daisy could not see her brother.

Ron was sitting at one of the tables that were covered with the heavy worn white damask of trains. The vase and dull silver on the table were heavy so they would not fall off with the movement of the train. Ron leaned back in his chair and looked out the window at the snow.

Daisy sat down across the table from him. Her heart was beating painfully in her chest. "Hi," she said. She was afraid to add his name for fear the word would trail away as it had before and he would know how frightened she was.

He turned and smiled at her. "Hello, Daisy-Daisy," he said.

She hated him with the same sudden intensity she had felt for her parents, hated him for his ability to make her afraid. "What are you doing here?" she asked.

He turned slightly in the seat and grinned at her.

"You don't belong here," she said belligerently. "I went to

Canada to live with my grandmother." Her eyes widened. She had not known that before she said it. "I didn't even know you. You worked in the grocery store when we lived in California." She was suddenly overwhelmed by what she was saying. "You don't belong here," she murmured.

"Maybe it's all a dream, Daisy."

She looked at him, still angry, her chest heaving with the shock of remembering. "What?"

"I said, maybe you're just dreaming all this." He put his elbows on the table and leaned toward her. "You always had the most incredible dreams, Daisy-Daisy."

She shook her head. "Not like this. They weren't like this. I always had good dreams." The memory was coming now, faster this time, a throbbing in her side where the pink and white book said her ovaries were. She was not sure she could make it to her room. She stood up, clutching at the white tablecloth. "They weren't like this." She stumbled through the milling people toward her room.

"Oh, and Daisy," Ron said. She stopped, her hand on the door of her room, the memory almost there. "You're still cold."

"What?" she said blankly.

"Still cold. You're getting warmer, though."

She wanted to ask him what he meant, but the memory was upon her. She shut the door behind her, breathing heavily, and groped for the bed.

All her family had had nightmares. The three of them sat at breakfast with drawn, tired faces, their eyes looking bruised. The lead-backed curtains for the kitchen hadn't come yet, so they had to eat breakfast in the living room where they could close the venetian blinds. Her mother and father sat on the blue couch with their knees against the crowded coffee table. Daisy and her brother sat on the floor.

Her mother said, staring at the closed blinds, "I dreamed I was full of holes, tiny little holes, like dotted swiss."

"Now, Evelyn," her father said.

Her brother said, "I dreamed the house was on fire and the fire trucks came and put it out, but then the fire trucks caught on fire and the firemen and the trees and—"

"That's enough," her father said. "Eat your breakfast." To his wife he said gently, "Neutrinos pass through all of us all the time. They pass right through the earth. They're completely harmless. They don't make holes at all. It's nothing, Evelyn. Don't worry about the neutrinos. They can't hurt you."

"Daisy, you had a dotted swiss dress once, didn't you?" her mother said, still looking at the blinds. "It was yellow. All those little dots, like holes."

"May I be excused?" her brother asked, holding a book with a photo of the sun on the cover.

Her father nodded and her brother went outside, already reading. "Wear your hat!" Daisy's mother said, her voice rising perilously on the last word. She watched him until he was out of the room, then she turned and looked at Daisy with her bruised eyes. "You had a nightmare too, didn't you, Daisy?"

Daisy shook her head, looking down at her bowl of cereal. She had been looking out between the venetian blinds before breakfast, looking out at the forbidden sun. The stiff plastic blinds had caught open, and now there was a little triangle of sunlight on Daisy's bowl of cereal. She and her mother were both looking at it. Daisy put her hand over the light.

430 | Connie Willis

"Did you have a nice dream, then, Daisy, or don't you remember?" She sounded accusing.

"I remember," Daisy said, watching the sunlight on her
hand. She had dreamed of a bear. A massive golden bear with
shining fur. Daisy was playing ball with the bear. She had
in her two hands a little blue-green ball. The bear reached
out lazily with his wide golden arm and swatted the blue ball
out of Daisy's hands and away. The wide, gentle sweep of his
great paw was the most beautiful thing she had ever seen.
Daisy smiled to herself at the memory of it.

"Tell me your dream, Daisy," her mother said.

"All right," Daisy said angrily. "It was about a big yellow
bear and a little blue ball that he swatted." She swung her
arm toward her mother.

Her mother winced.

"Swatted us all to kingdom come, Mother!" she shouted
and flung herself out of the dark living room into the bright
morning sun.

"Wear your hat," her mother called after her, and this time
the last word rose almost to a scream.

Daisy stood against the door for a long time, watching him.
He was talking to her grandmother. She had put down her
yellow tape measure with the black coal numbers and was
nodding and smiling at what he said. After a very long time
he reached out his hand and covered hers, patting it kindly.

Her grandmother stood up slowly and went to the window,
where the faded red curtains did not shut out the snow, but
she did not look at the curtains. She stood and looked out at
the snow, smiling faintly and without anxiety.

Daisy edged her way through the crowd in the kitchen,

frowning, and sat down across from Ron. His hands still rested flat on the red linoleum-topped table. Daisy put her hands on the table, too, almost touching his. She turned them palm up, in a gesture of helplessness.

"It isn't a dream, is it?" she asked him.

His fingers were almost touching hers. "What makes you think I'd know? I don't belong here, remember? I work in a grocery store, remember?"

"You know everything," she said simply.

"Not everything."

The cramp hit her. Her hands, still palm up, shook a little and then groped for the metal edge of the red table as she tried to straighten up.

"Warmer all the time, Daisy-Daisy," he said.

She did not make it to her room. She leaned helplessly against the door and watched her grandmother, measuring and writing and dropping the little slips of paper around her. And remembered.

Her mother did not even know him. She had seen him at the grocery store. Her mother, who never went out, who wore sunglasses and long-sleeved shirts and a sunhat, even inside the darkened blue living room—her mother had met him at the grocery store and brought him home. She had taken off her hat and her ridiculous gardening gloves and gone to the grocery store to find him. It must have taken incredible courage.

"He said he'd seen you at school and wanted to ask you out himself, but he was afraid I'd say you were too young, isn't that right, Ron?" Her mother spoke in a rapid, nervous voice. Daisy was not sure whether she had said Ron or Rob or Rod.

"So I said, why don't you just come on home with me right now and meet her? There's no time like the present, I say. Isn't that right, Ron?"

He was not embarrassed by her at all. "Would you like to go get a coke, Daisy? I've got my car here."

"Of course she wants to go. Don't you, Daisy?"

No. She wished the sun would reach out lazily, the great golden bear, and swat them all away. Right now.

"Daisy," her mother said, hastily brushing at her hair with her fingers. "There's so little time left. I wanted you to have—" *Darkness and blood. You wanted me to be as frightened as you are. Well, I'm not, Mother. It's too late. We're almost there now.*

But when she went outside with him, she saw his convertible parked at the curb, and she felt the first faint flutter of fear. It had the top down. She looked up at his tanned, easily smiling face, and thought, "He isn't afraid."

"Where do you want to go, Daisy?" he asked. He had his bare arm across the back of the seat. He could easily move it from there to around her shoulders. Daisy sat against the door, her arms wrapped around her chest.

"I'd like to go for a ride. With the top down. I love the sun," she said to frighten him, to see the same expression she could see on her mother's face when Daisy told her lies about the dreams.

"Me, too," he said. "It sounds like you don't believe all that garbage they feed us about the sun, either. It's a lot of scare talk, that's all. You don't see me getting skin cancer, do you?" He moved his golden-tanned arm lazily around her shoulder to show her. "A lot of people getting hysterical for nothing. My physics teacher says the sun could emit neutrinos at the present rate for five thousand years before the sun would collapse. All this stuff about the aurora borealis. Geez, you'd think these people had never seen a solar flare before. There's nothing to be afraid of, Daisy-Daisy."

He moved his arm dangerously close to her breast.

"Do you have nightmares?" she asked him, desperate to frighten him.

"No. All my dreams are about you." His fingers traced a pattern, casually, easily on her blouse. "What do you dream about?"

She thought she would frighten him like she frightened her mother. Her dreams always seemed so beautiful, but when she began to tell them to her mother, her mother's eyes became wide and dark with fear. And then Daisy would change the dream, make it sound worse than it was, ruin its beauty to make it frighten her mother.

"I dreamed I was rolling a golden hoop. It was hot. It burned my hand whenever I touched it. I was wearing earrings, little golden hoops in my ears that spun like the hoop when I ran. And a golden bracelet." She watched his face as she told him, to see the fear. He traced the pattern aimlessly with his finger, closer and closer to the nipple of her breast.

"I rolled the hoop down a hill and it started rolling faster and faster. I couldn't keep up with it. It rolled on by itself, like a wheel, a golden wheel, rolling over everything."

She had forgotten her purpose. She had told the dream as she remembered it, with the little secret smile at the memory. His hand had closed over her breast and rested there, warm as the sun on her face.

He looked as if he didn't know it was there. "Boy, my psych teacher would have a ball with that one! Who would think a kid like you could have a sexy dream like that? Wow! Talk about Freudian! My psych teacher says—"

"You think you know everything, don't you?" Daisy said.

His fingers traced the nipple through her thin blouse, tracing a burning circle, a tiny burning hoop.

"Not quite," he said, and bent close to her face. Darkness and blood. "I don't know quite how to take you."

She wrenched free of his face, free of his arm. "You won't take me at all. Not ever. You'll be dead. We'll all be dead in the sun," she said, and flung herself out of the convertible and back into the darkened house.

Daisy lay doubled up on the bed for a long time after the memory was gone. She would not talk to him anymore. She could not remember anything without him, but she did not care. It was all a dream anyway. What did it matter? She hugged her arms to her.

It was not a dream. It was worse than a dream. She sat very straight on the edge of the bed, her head up and her arms at her side, her feet together on the floor, the way a young lady was supposed to sit. When she stood up, there was no hesitation in her manner. She walked straight to the door and opened it. She did not stop to see what room it was. She did not even glance at the strangers milling up and down. She went straight to Ron and put her hand on his shoulder.

"This is hell, isn't it?"

He turned, and there was something like hope on his face. "Why, Daisy!" he said, and took her hands and pulled her down to sit beside him. It was the train. Their folded hands rested on the white damask tablecloth. She looked at the hands. There was no use trying to pull away.

Her voice did not shake. "I was very unkind to my mother. I used to tell her my dreams just to make her frightened. I used to go out without a hat, just because it scared her so much. She couldn't help it. She was so afraid the sun would explode." She stopped and looked at her hands. "I think it did explode and everybody died, like my father said. I think . . . I should have lied to her about the dreams. I should have told her I dreamed about boys, about growing up, about things that didn't frighten her. I could have made up nightmares like my brother did."

"Daisy," he said. "I'm afraid confessions aren't quite in my line. I don't—"

"She killed herself," Daisy said. "She sent us to my grand-mother's in Canada and then she killed herself. And so I think that if we are all dead, then I went to hell. That's what hell is, isn't it? Coming face to face with what you're most afraid of."

"Or what you love. Oh, Daisy," he said, holding her fingers tightly, "Whatever made you think that this was hell?"

In her surprise, she looked straight into his eyes. "Because there isn't any sun," she said.

His eyes burned her, burned her. She felt blindly for the white-covered table, but the room had changed. She could not find it. He pulled her down beside him on the blue couch. With him still clinging to her hands, still holding onto her, she remembered.

They were being sent away, to protect them from the sun. Daisy was just as glad to go. Her mother was angry with her all the time. She forced Daisy to tell her her dreams, every morning at breakfast in the dark living room. Her mother had put blackout curtains up over the blinds so that no light got in at all, and in the blue twilight not even the little summer slants of light from the blinds fell on her mother's frightened face.

There was nobody on the beaches. Her mother would not let her go out, even to the grocery store, without a hat and sunglasses. She would not let them fly to Canada. She was afraid of magnetic storms. They sometimes interrupted the radio signals from the towers. Her mother was afraid the plane would crash.

She sent them on the train, kissing them goodbye at the train station, for the moment oblivious to the long dusty streaks of light from the vaulted train-station windows. Her brother went ahead of them out to the platform, and her mother pulled Daisy suddenly into a dark shadowed corner. "What I told you before, about your period, that won't happen now. The radiation—I called the doctor and he said not to worry. It's happening to everyone."

Again Daisy felt the faint pull of fear. Her period had started months ago, dark and bloody as she had imagined. She had not told anyone. "I won't worry," she said.

"Oh, my Daisy," her mother said suddenly. "My Daisy in the sun," and seemed to shrink back into the darkness. But as they pulled out of the station, she came out into the direct sun and waved goodbye to them.

It was wonderful on the train. The few passengers stayed in their cabins with the shades drawn. There were no shades in the dining room, no people to tell Daisy to get out of the sunlight. She sat in the deserted dining car and looked out the wide windows. The train flew through forests, then branch forests of spindly pines and aspens. The sun flickered in on Daisy—sun and then shadows and then sun, running across her face. She and her brother ordered an orgy of milkshakes and desserts and nobody said anything to them.

Her brother read his books about the sun out loud to her. "Do you know what it's like in the middle of the sun?" he asked her. *Yes. You stand with a bucket and a shovel and your bare toes digging into the sand, a child again, not afraid, squinting up into the yellow light.*

"No," she said.

"Atoms can't even hold together in the middle of the sun. It's so crowded they bump into each other all the time, bump bump bump, like that, and their electrons fly off and run around free. Sometimes when there's a collision, it lets off an X-ray that goes *whoosh*, all the way out at the speed of light, like a ball in a pinball machine. *Bing-bang-bing*, all the way to the surface."

"Why do you read those books anyway? To scare yourself?"

"No. To scare Mom." That was a daring piece of honesty, suitable not even for the freedom of Grandma's, suitable only for the train. She smiled at him.

"You're not even scared, are you?"

She felt obliged to answer him with equal honesty. "No," she said, "not at all."

"Why not?"

Because it won't hurt. Because I won't remember afterwards. Because I'll stand in the sun with my bucket and shovel and look up and not be frightened. "I don't know," Daisy said. "I'm just not."

"I am. I dream about burning all the time. I think about how much it hurts when I burn my finger and then I dream about it hurting like that all over forever." He had been lying to their mother about his dreams, too.

"It won't be like that," Daisy said. "We won't even know it's happened. We won't remember a thing."

"When the sun goes nova, it'll start using itself up. The core will start filling up with atomic ash, and that'll make the sun start using up all its own fuel. Do you know it's pitch dark in the middle of the sun? See, the radiations are X-rays, and they're too short to see. They're invisible. Pitch dark and ashes falling around you. Can you imagine that?"

"It doesn't matter." They were passing a meadow and Daisy's face was full in the sun. "We won't be there. We'll be dead. We won't remember anything."

Daisy had not realized how relieved she would be to see her grandmother, narrow face sunburned, arms bare. She was not even wearing a hat. "Daisy, dear, you're growing up," she said. She did not make it sound like a death sentence. "And David, you still have your nose in a book, I see."

It was nearly dark when they got to her little house. "What's that?" David asked, standing on the porch.

Her grandmother's voice did not rise dangerously at all. "The aurora borealis. I tell you, we've had some shows up here lately. It's like the Fourth of July."

Daisy had not realized how hungry she had been to hear someone who was not afraid. She looked up. Great red curtains of light billowed almost to the zenith, fluttering in some solar wind. "It's beautiful," Daisy whispered, but her grandmother was holding the door open for her to go in, and so happy was she to see the clear light in her grandmother's eyes, she followed her into the little kitchen with its red linoleum table and the red curtains hanging at the windows.

"It is so nice to have company," her grandmother said,

climbing onto a chair. "Daisy, hold this end, will you?" She dangled the long end of a yellow plastic ribbon down to Daisy. Daisy took it, looking anxiously at her grandmother. "What are you doing?" she asked.

"Measuring for new curtains, dear," she said, reaching into her pocket for a slip of paper and a pencil. "What's the length, Daisy?"

"Why do you need new curtains?" Daisy asked. "These look fine to me."

"They don't keep the sun out," her grandmother said. Her eyes had gone coal-black with fear. Her voice was rising with every word. "We have to have new curtains, Daisy, and there's no cloth. Not in the whole town, Daisy. Can you imagine that? We had to send to Ottawa. They bought up all the cloth in town. Can you imagine that, Daisy?"

"Yes," Daisy said, and wished she could be afraid.

Ron still held her hands tightly. She looked steadily at him. "Warmer, Daisy," he said. "Almost here."

"Yes," she said.

He untwined their fingers and rose from the couch. He walked through the crowd in the blue living room and went out the door into the snow. She did not try to go to her room. She watched them all, the strangers in their endless, random movement, her brother walking while he read, her grandmother standing on a chair, and the memory came quite easily and without pain.

"You wanta see something?" her brother asked.

Daisy was looking out the window. All day long the lights

had been flickering, even though it was calm and silent outside. Their grandmother had gone to town to see if the fabric for the curtains had come in. Daisy did not answer him.

He shoved the book in front of her face. "That's a prominence," he said. The pictures were in black and white, like old-fashioned snapshots, only under them instead of her mother's scrawled white ink it said, "High Altitude Observatory, Boulder, Colorado."

"That's an eruption of hot gas hundreds of thousands of feet high."

"No," Daisy said, taking the book into her own lap. "That's my golden hoop. I saw it in my dream."

She turned the page.

David leaned over her shoulder and pointed. "That was the big eruption in 1946 when it first started to go wrong only they didn't know it yet. It weighed a billion tons. The gas went out a million miles."

Daisy held the book like a snapshot of a loved one.

"It just went, *bash*, and knocked all this gas out into space. There were all kinds of—"

"It's my golden bear," she said. The great paw of flame reached lazily out from the sun's black surface in the picture, the wild silky paw of flaming gas.

"This is the stuff you've been dreaming?" her brother asked. "This is the stuff you've been telling me about?" His voice went higher and higher. "I thought you said the dreams were nice."

"They were," Daisy said.

He pulled the book away from her and flipped angrily through the pages to a colored diagram on a black ground. It showed a glowing red ball with concentric circles drawn inside it. "There," he said, shoving it at Daisy. "That's what's going to happen to us." He jabbed angrily at one of the circles inside the red ball. "That's us. That's us! Inside the sun! Dream about that, why don't you?"

He slammed the book shut.

"But we'll all be dead, so it won't matter," Daisy said. "It won't hurt. We won't remember anything."

"That's what you think! You think you know everything. Well, you don't know what anything is. I read a book about it and you know what it said? They don't know what memory is. They think maybe it isn't even in the brain cells. That it's in the atoms somewhere and even if we're blown apart that memory stays. What if we do get burned by the sun and we still remember? What if we go on burning and burning and remembering and remembering forever?"

Daisy said quietly, "He wouldn't do that. He wouldn't hurt us." There had been no fear as she stood digging her toes into the sand and looking up at him, only wonder. "He—"

"You're crazy!" her brother shouted. "You know that? You're crazy. You talk about him like he's your boyfriend or something! It's the sun, the wonderful sun who's going to kill us all!" He yanked the book away from her. He was crying.

"I'm sorry," Daisy was about to say, but their grandmother came in just then, hatless, with her hair blowing around her thin sunburned face.

"They got the material in," she said jubilantly. "I bought enough for all the windows." She spilled out two sacks of red gingham. It billowed out across the table like the northern lights, red over red. "I thought it would never get here."

Daisy reached out to touch it.

She waited for him, sitting at the white-damask table of the dining car. He hesitated at the door, standing framed by the snow of ash behind him, and then came gaily in, singing.

"Daisy, Daisy, give me your theory do," he sang. He carried in his arms a bolt of red cloth. It billowed out from the bolt as he handed it to her grandmother—she standing on the chair, transfixed by joy, the pieces of paper, the yellow tape measure fallen from her forever.

Daisy came and stood in front of him.

"Daisy, Daisy," he said gaily. "Tell me—"

She put her hand on his chest. "No theory," she said. "I know."

"Everything, Daisy?" He smiled the easy, lopsided smile, and she thought sadly that even knowing she would not be able to see him as he was, but only as the boy who had worked at the grocery store, the boy who had known everything.

"No, but I think I know." She held her hand firmly against his chest, over the flaming hoop of his breast. "I don't think we are people anymore. I don't know what we are—atoms stripped of our electrons maybe, colliding endlessly against each other in the center of the sun while it burns itself to ash in the endless snowstorm at its heart."

He gave her no clue. His smile was still confident, easy. "What about me, Daisy?" he asked.

"I think you are my golden bear, my flaming hoop, I think you are Ra, with no end to your name at all, Ra who knows everything."

"And who are you?"

"I am Daisy, who loved the sun."

He did not smile, did not change his mocking expression.

But his tanned hand closed over hers, still pushing against his chest.

"What will I be now, an X-ray zigzagging all the way to the surface till I turn into light? Where will you take me after you have taken me? To Saturn, where the sun shines on the cold rings till they melt into happiness? Is that where you shine now, on Saturn? Will you take me there? Or will we stand forever like this, me with my bucket and shovel, squinting up at you?"

Slowly, he gave her hand back to her. "Where do you want to go, Daisy?"

Her grandmother still stood on the chair, holding the cloth as if it were a benediction. Daisy reached out and touched the cloth, as she had in the moment when the sun went nova. She smiled up at her grandmother. "It's beautiful," she said. "I'm so glad it's come."

She bent suddenly to the window and pulled the faded curtains aside, as if she thought because she knew she might be granted some sort of vision, might see for some small moment the little girl that was herself—with her little girl's chest and toddler's stomach—might see herself as she really was: Daisy, in the sun. But all she could see was the endless snow.

Her brother was reading on the blue couch in her mother's living room. She stood over him, watching him read. "I'm afraid now," Daisy said, but it wasn't her brother's face that looked back at her.

"All right, then," Daisy thought. "None of them are any help. It doesn't matter. I have come face to face with what I fear and what I love and they are the same thing."

"All right, then," Daisy said, and turned back to Ron. "I'd

like to go for a ride. With the top down." She stopped and squinted up at him. "I love the sun," she said.

When he put his arm around her shoulder, she did not move away. His hand closed on her breast and he bent down to kiss her.

1979

BIOGRAPHICAL NOTES

Eleanor Arnason (b. December 28, 1942) was born Eleanor Atwood Arnason in New York City to H. Harvard Arnason, an art historian, and Elizabeth (Yard) Arnason, a social worker; her father grew up in a community of Icelandic immigrants in Canada, and her mother among American missionaries in western China. She traveled widely with her parents as a young child, living in Chicago, London, Paris, Washington, D.C., and Honolulu. At age seven, she moved into Idea House #2, a house-design project built by the Walker Art Center in Minneapolis, of which her father became director in 1951. She spent eleven years there, during which time she became one of three teenage editors of the fanzine *All Mimsy.* Arnason went on to attend Swarthmore College, from which she earned a bachelor's degree in Art History in 1964, and the University of Minnesota. Leaving graduate school in 1967, she worked as an office clerk in Brooklyn and Detroit for seven years before returning to the Twin Cities, where she took a variety of jobs to support herself while she pursued a literary career. "I never wanted to be a housewife, a mother, or anything that was allowed to women in those days: a secretary, a teacher or a nurse," she later recalled; "I wanted to be a writer, a space cadet and someone who changed the world for the better."

Arnason published her first SF story, "A Clear Day in the Motor City," in 1973, and her most recent, "Laki," in 2021;

her story collections include *Ordinary People* (2005), *Mammoths of the Great Plains* (2010), *Big Mama Stories* (2013), *Hidden Folk* (2014), and *Hwarhath Stories: Transgressive Tales by Aliens* (2016). She has also written eight novels, her first, *The Sword Smith*, in 1978 and her most recent, *Tomb of the Fathers*, in 2010. Over the years, she has received scores of nominations for the Hugo, Nebula, Locus, and Otherwise (formerly known as the James Tiptree, Jr.) Awards, and counts among her wins the 1991 inaugural Tiptree Award for Gender-bending Science Fiction, the 1992 Mythopoeic Fantasy Award for Adult Literature, the 1999 HOMer Novelette Award, and the 2000 Gaylactic Spectrum Award for Short Fiction. She now lives in St. Paul, Minnesota, with her companion Patrick Arden Wood, and blogs about SF, politics, economics, art, and birdwatching.

Elinor Busby (b. September 30, 1924) was born Elinor Doub in Tacoma, Washington, the third of four daughters of Frances Sprague (Darling) Doub, a homemaker, and Walter Doub, an insurance broker. In school, she wrote poetry and took an interest in archaeology and the social sciences. She attended the University of Washington, working part-time as a secretary for the University Arboretum Foundation. In 1953, she joined the Seattle science fiction fan organization The Nameless Ones, meeting her husband, club president and future SF writer F. M. "Buz" Busby, through the group. They married in 1954 and later had a daughter, Michelle.

Busby made her initial contributions to SF as a publisher, editor, and writer of fanzines, including *Fendenzien* (1957), *Polarity* (1957), *Fapulous* (1959), and *Salud* (1960). In 1958, she began a collaboration with Burnett R. Toskey, Wally

Weber, and her husband on *Cry of the Nameless*, editing the letters column; in 1960, she shared the Hugo Award for Best Fanzine for their second issue, becoming the first woman to receive the prestigious award. In 1963 she served as Guest of Honor at Westercon 16, in San Francisco.

Busby became an author in her own right in 1977, at the age of fifty-three, with the publication in *Amazing Stories* of "Time to Kill," featured in this anthology, followed by the weird SF story "The Night of the Red, Red Moon" in Jessica Amanda Salmonson's 1983 *Tales by Moonlight* anthology. She has since written two Regency romance novels and several young adult fantasy books. In 2013, at CorFlu 30 in Portland, Oregon, she received the Fan Activity Achievement Award for Lifetime Achievement.

C. J. Cherryh (b. September 1, 1942) was born Carolyn Janice Cherry in St. Louis, Missouri, and raised in Lawton, Oklahoma; she began publishing as "C. J. Cherryh" in 1976 at the suggestion of her first editor, Donald A. Wollheim, who thought "Cherry" sounded like the surname of a romance novelist, and who preferred the androgynous "C. J." The daughter of Basil L. Cherry, a field representative for the Social Security Administration, and Lois (Vandeventer) Cherry, a housewife, Cherryh was inspired to write as a child after the cancellation of her favorite TV show, *Flash Gordon*—though only her brother, David, ever read these early stories. In high school, Cherryh excelled in Latin, winning a national scholarship to pursue classical studies in college. She graduated from the University of Oklahoma, Norman, in 1964 with a B.A. in Latin, then earned an M.A. in classics from Johns Hopkins University in 1965, subsequently teaching Latin and ancient history in Oklahoma City's public school system.

While teaching, Cherryh began writing fiction more seriously, though she initially had little success with publishing. However, in 1976, she signed a three-book contract with DAW Books; the contract was worth a year of her salary, which allowed her to quit teaching and focus on writing full-time. Cherryh has since written more than eighty novels and short story compilations. Her longest series are set in her Alliance-Union and Foreigner universes, though she has also published four stand-alone novels and many essays, some of them collected in *The Use of Archaeology in Worldbuilding* (1978) and *Linguistic Sexism in SF and Fantasy* (1980). She won her first award in 1977—the John W. Campbell Award for Best New Writer—which was followed by her first Hugo in 1979, when "Cassandra" (featured in this volume) was voted Best Short Story. In 1989, her novel *Cyteen* collected Hugo, Locus, and SF Chronicle awards. Over the course of her career, Cherryh has won three Hugos, one Locus, and one Nebula Award; more recently, she earned the 2020 Prometheus Award for Best Libertarian SF Novel and the 2021 Robert A. Heinlein Award. In 2001, the Fort Bend Astronomy Club officially named asteroid 2001 FE9 "77185 Cherryh" in her honor.

Cherryh is a longtime resident of Spokane, Washington, where she lives with fellow SF writer Jane Fancher; the two were domestic partners for almost three decades before legally marrying in 2014. At the age of sixty-one, Cherryh took up figure skating, and from there began to compete in local competitions with her wife. She maintains a personal blog, "Wave Without a Shore," and continues to write fiction.

M. Lucie Chin (b. May 5, 1947) was born Mary Lucie Choate, the first of three children of Robert and Helen (LeMaster) Choate, in Alameda, California. Her mother was a school-teacher; her father, who held music degrees from Cornell, Northeastern, and Stanford, later moved the family from California to Newton, Massachusetts, where he became dean of the School of Fine Arts at Boston University. After graduating from Newton High School, Chin attended Boston University, earning a Bachelor of Fine Arts in Painting. She married and by the mid-1970s had moved to New York City, where she worked as an illustrator, freelance graphic artist, dollmaker, photographer, and theater professional. In 1979 she began to study fencing, and in 1988 (by which point she had divorced), she became fight choreographer and fencing master for the Kings County Shakespeare Company. Chin has since worked on over thirty of the company's produc-tions, in roles including fencing instruction, set design and construction, and weapons and costume construction.

Against the backdrop of her enduring theater career, Chin's foray into SF was comparatively brief. Two of her short stories, "The Best Is Yet to Be" and "The Heirs of Joseph Penn," appeared in the January and September 1978 editions of *Galileo*; a sequel to the latter, "The Legacy of Joseph Penn," followed in May 1979. With "Dragon . . . Ghost" (*Ares*, March 1980), she published the first of several fantasy stories—including "Lan Lung" (1981), "Ku Mei Li: A Chinese Ghost Story" (1981), "The Snow Fairy" (1985), and "Catmagic" (1987)—influenced by Chinese mythology. Chin considered this mythos to be "rich in traditions and ideas almost analogous to Western thinking, but . . . one or two small steps to the side." Her first and only novel, *The Fairy of Ku-She* (1988), was named a Locus Award finalist. Chin now lives in Brooklyn, where she continues to support local theater productions and volunteers at the Wyckoff House Museum.

Miriam Allen deFord (August 21, 1888–February 22, 1975) was born in Philadelphia, the oldest child of Moïse deFord and Frances (Allen) deFord. Both of deFord's parents were doctors, her mother a gynecologist at a time when few women were represented in that profession. At fourteen, with her mother's encouragement, she volunteered at suffragette headquarters in Philadelphia, later marching in suffrage parades across the Northeast and soapboxing on behalf of the cause.

After graduating from Temple University in 1911, deFord moved to Boston, where she became a staff writer at *Associated Advertising* magazine. In 1914, she met poet, lecturer, and "philosophical anarchist" Armistead Collier, whom she married the following year, moving to San Diego. Divorcing Collier in 1921, she married her second husband, socialist and science writer Maynard Shipley. After a short stint as one of California's first female insurance claims adjusters, deFord was hired as a staff correspondent for the Federal Press, a daily news service for the American labor press. She helped Shipley organize the Science League of America, which advocated for science-based education and the separation of church and state during the anti-evolution crusades of the 1920s. During these years she met labor leader Harry Bridge and Socialist Party of America presidential candidate Eugene Debs, and corresponded extensively with Charles Fort, pioneering explorer of "Fortean" scientific anomalies.

After the death of her husband in 1934, she moved into a suite of the Ambassador Hotel in San Francisco, where she lived for the rest of her life.

DeFord began writing fiction at an early age; her first publication appeared when she was twelve years old and over the next few decades she placed her poetry and stories in venues including *Scribners, Birth Control Review,* and *Harper's.* She published her first story of genre interest in 1924 but did not write genre fiction with any regularity until the 1940s, when fellow mystery author Anthony Boucher, the first editor of *The Magazine of Fantasy and Science Fiction,* began soliciting SF stories from authors outside the field. DeFord appreciated that science fiction allowed her to engage political themes: many of her stories from the 1950s explore the most pressing issues of the day, including the nuclear war and cultural alienation. In the 1960s, the self-described "born feminist" joined other New Wave and feminist authors in experimenting with science fiction as a vehicle for exploring the relations of science, society, and sex. As deFord herself put it, while mystery fiction typically dealt with gender issues only insofar as it allowed for "the woman [to be just as likely] an active criminal or murderer as a man," science fiction, with its emphasis on using other worlds and alien creatures as a funhouse mirror to our own society, allowed her to deal at length with themes including "matrimony, reproduction, and sex."

Over the course of her SF career, deFord published close to eighty stories. Many of these were reprinted in her collections *Xenogenesis* (1969) and *Elsewhere, Elsewhen, Elsehow* (1971). She also edited the original anthology *Space, Time, and Crime* (1964), a collection of science fiction stories with mystery elements. In this period, deFord also continued to write mysteries, weird fiction, and true crime books; several of her stories were adapted for television, including Rod Serling's *Night Gallery*, and in 1961 she won the Edgar Award from the Mystery Writers of America for *The Overbury Affair*. An active member of the Mystery Writers of America, the Rationalist Press Association, and the Authors Guild, as well as a board member of the Science Fiction Writers of America, deFord continued writing "six to eighteen hours a day" on her 1935 Royal typewriter until her death in 1975. The deFord story featured in this anthology, "A Way Out," was published when the author was eighty-five.

Cynthia Felice (b. October 12, 1942) was born Cynthia Lindgren in Chicago, Illinois, the younger of two daughters of Erik Axel Lindgren, a Swedish immigrant who served in the navy during World War II, and Mildred Lindgren. After graduating from North Park Academy High School, she studied the liberal arts at North Park University. In 1961 she married Robert Felice, with whom she had two boys, Erik and Bobby. Felice has worked, over the years, as a motel owner, sales engineer for capital equipment in the electronics field, and manager of configuration control departments for major corporations; her 1984 paper "The Future Is Now for Automating Document Control: A Case History for the User" was named Outstanding Paper by the Society for Technical Communication.

In a 2008 interview Felice recalled that she became certain she wanted to be a writer in high school, because a pen in her hand and full pages brought her happiness; her mother disapproved of such a career, so she wrote in secret until she moved away from home. She cofounded the Colorado Springs Writers Workshop in 1972 and in 1976 attended the Clarion Writers Workshop; and she published her first SF story, "Longshanks," in *Galileo*. Her first novel, *Godsfire*, appeared in 1978, as did "No One Said Forever," featured in this anthology. She went on to write three novels with Connie Willis—*Water Witch* (1982), *Light Raid* (1989), and *Promised Land* (1997)—along with solo efforts *The Sunbound* (1981), *Eclipses* (1983), *Downtime* (1985), *Double Nocturne* (1986), *The Khan's Persuasion* (1991), and *Iceman* (1991). Now widowed, she lives in Colorado Springs, Colorado; her hobbies include astronomy, gardening, mountaineering, river rafting, and horseback riding.

Sonya Dorman Hess (June 4, 1924–February 14, 2005), born Sonya Gloria Hess in New York City, was raised by foster parents on a farm in West Newbury, Massachusetts, after her mother, a dancer and model, died when Hess was an infant. Unable to afford more than a year of agricultural college, she worked as a stable hand, maid, fish canner, riding instructor, and tuna boat cook while giving herself an education, reading widely in world literature. After a brief first marriage in 1945–46, she married Jack Dorman, an engineer, in 1950, and had a daughter, Sherri, in 1959. Moving from Stony Point, New York, to West Mystic and then New London, Connecticut, during the 1970s, the family bred Akitas and other dogs and exhibited at dog shows.

Hess published approximately two dozen science fiction stories from 1961 to 1980, gathering three of these as a young adult novel, *Planet Patrol*, in 1978; she also published fiction in *The Saturday Evening Post*, *Redbook*, and other mainstream magazines. Hess's stories were particularly associated with science fiction's New Wave. Her experimental novel "Onyx" was rejected by publishers in 1971, but her collected *Poems* appeared in 1970, followed by *Palace of Earth* (1984), *Constellations of the Inner Eye* (1991), *Carrying What You Love* (1996), and other volumes of poetry. She moved to Taos, New Mexico, after her divorce in 1986, publishing once again under her maiden name, and died there at eighty. Hess's recognition from the science fiction community includes a 1978 Science Fiction Poetry Association Rhysling Award for "The Corruption of Metals," and a 1995 James Tiptree, Jr., retroactive award for "When I Was Miss Dow" (1963).

Ursula K. Le Guin (October 21, 1929–January 22, 2018), born Ursula Kroeber in Berkeley, California, was the daughter of Theodora (Kracaw) Kroeber, an anthropology student and, later, a writer, and Alfred Kroeber, head of the University of California anthropology department; she had three older brothers and stepbrothers with whom she spent summers on the family's small ranch in the Napa Valley. At ten or eleven she submitted one of her early literary productions to *Astounding Science Fiction*, of which she was a devoted reader.

Graduating from Berkeley High School in 1947, Le Guin attended Radcliffe College and then Columbia University, from which she earned a master's degree in Renaissance French and Italian Language and Literature in 1952. The following year, on the way to France as a Fulbright scholar to pursue her doctorate, she met fellow Fulbright recipient Charles Alfred Le Guin, and they married in Paris. Returning to the U.S., both began teaching, first at Mercer University in Macon, Georgia (he in the history department, she in French), then at the University of Idaho. Settling permanently in Portland, Oregon, they raised three children, Elisabeth (b. 1957), Caroline (b. 1959), and Theo (b. 1964).

Le Guin's first published works—"Folksong from the Montayna Province" (*Prairie Poet*, Fall 1959) and "An die Musik" (*Western Humanities Review*, Summer 1961)—began her series set in the fictional European nation of Orsinia, later expanded with the story collection *Orsinian Tales* (1976) and the novel *Malafrena* (1979). She began to appear in genre magazines with the time-travel story "April in Paris," in the September 1962 *Fantastic Stories of the Imagination*, and published her first science fiction novel, *Rocannon's World*, in 1966.

Le Guin's subsequent works include the multiple-award-winning novels *The Left Hand of Darkness* (1969), *The Lathe of Heaven* (1971), *The Dispossessed: An Ambiguous Utopia* (1974), and *Tehanu: The Last Book of Earthsea* (1990); story collections *The Wind's Twelve Quarters* (1975), *The Compass Rose* (1982), *Changing Planes* (2003), and others; and collections of essays and poetry. In 1993, with Brian Attebery, she edited *The Norton Book of Science Fiction: North American Science Fiction, 1960–1990*. Le Guin's accomplishments have long been recognized by her peers: in 1975 she was named the sixth Gandalf Grand Master of Fantasy; in 1989 the Science Fiction Research Association granted her a Pilgrim Award for Lifetime Achievement; in 2001 she was inducted into the Science Fiction Hall of Fame; and in 2003 she became the Science Fiction and Fantasy Writers of America's twentieth Grand Master. Elected to the American Academy of Arts and Letters in 2017, before her death in Portland Le Guin was revising and adding new material to her 1985 novel *Always Coming Home*, for a new edition in the Library of America series.

Vonda N. McIntyre (August 28, 1948–April 1, 2019) was born Vonda Neel McIntyre in Louisville, Kentucky, the elder of two daughters of Harrell Neel McIntyre and Vonda B. (Keith) McIntyre, a former member of the Women's Army Corps. She spent her early childhood on the East Coast and in the Netherlands before her family settled in Bellevue, Washington, when she was twelve years old. As a child, McIntyre was a self-described "horse freak" who kept her retired horse on the grounds currently occupied by Microsoft. She grew up reading and watching science fiction and wrote screenplays based on her favorite TV shows. At Sammamish High School, she became an author and editor for her high school magazine. McIntyre received her B.S. (with honors) in Biology at the University of Washington in 1970 and began graduate study in genetics that same year, but soon left academia to write full-time.

McIntyre became involved with the professional science fiction community during her final years at the University of Washington: she sold her first story, "Breaking Point," to *Venture Science Fiction* in 1969; attended the Clarion Science Fiction Writers' Workshop in 1970; and then, with founder Robin Scott Wilson's blessing, established the Clarion West Writers Workshop in Seattle in 1971. McIntyre won her first Nebula Award in 1973 for "Of Mist, and Grass, and Sand," featured in this anthology. That story became the opening of her Hugo and Nebula Award–winning novel, *Dreamsnake* (1978). A self-described second-wave feminist who credited her success to women SF writers including Kate Wilhelm, Joanna Russ, and Ursula K. Le Guin (whom she affectionately called "Buntho"), McIntyre was instrumental in the publication of the first all-female science fiction anthologies: she connected Pamela Sargent with the company that published Sargent's *Women of Wonder* anthology in 1975, and in 1976, with Susan Janice Anderson, coedited her own anthology, *Aurora: Beyond Equality*.

Over the course of her career, McIntyre published sixteen novels (including several *Star Trek* novels), over three dozen short stories, and numerous essays. Her stories have been translated into many different languages. From 1974 to 2016, she received thirty-five nominations and five major prizes for her fiction, including three Nebulas, one Hugo, and one Locus Award. In 2008, she cofounded Book View Café, a publishing cooperative for fantasy and science fiction authors. Among her many accomplishments, McIntyre was also a gifted crafter of beaded and crocheted sea creatures, many of which were given to graduates of Clarion West and others of which have been exhibited in major galleries.

McIntyre died at home in Seattle of pancreatic cancer, surrounded by friends in 2019; she completed an as yet unpublished novel, *Curve of the World*, in her final months. In 2022, her novel *The Moon and the Sun* (1997) was adapted for film as *The King's Daughter*.

Gayle N. Netzer (July 14, 1917–March 5, 2001) was born Gayle Noreen Tiller in Whitefish, Montana, the third child of iceman William Tiller and his wife, Mabel Evelyn (Foot) Tiller. She graduated from Helena High School, where she was a member of the Latin club, in 1935, and later from

Montana State University. In 1941 she married Emmanuel M. Netzer in Drummond, Montana, with whom she went on to have three children. Following the couple's divorce in 1967, Netzer joined the Big Sky Country Chapter of Parents Without Partners Inc., hosting events for the organization. She became a frequent contributor to the "Reader's Alley" section of the Helena *Independent Record*, arguing in one letter: "little girls today are growing up with the knowledge that they are not just females, but people. That's something it took my generation the better part of a lifetime to find out. Courage, ladies, courage!"

In the 1970s, Netzer became active in science fiction fandom, helping to found the Helena Science Fiction Club (the only woman in the club's original group of seven members). In 1979, the club supported its first fan convention, MosCon, in Moscow, Idaho. Around these years, she published two short stories in feminist fanzines. The first, "Hey, Lilith!," appeared in *The Witch and the Chameleon* in 1976 and is reprinted in this volume. The second, "Dear God," appeared in *Aurora* in the winter of 1983–84. She died in Missoula, Montana.

Doris Piserchia (October 11, 1928–September 15, 2021) was born Doris Elaine Summers in Fairmont, West Virginia, where her mother, Viola (Critchfield) Summers, raised eight other children, and where her father, Dewey Summers, worked as a foreman in a glass factory. She discovered science fiction at age eleven and read "tons" of it, preferring Clifford Simak, George O. Smith, Theodore Sturgeon, and A. E. van Vogt. At East Fairmont High, from which she graduated in 1946, she served as staff editor for the school newspaper, *Yellow Jacket*, and played basketball for the Hornets. Working as a lifeguard to pay her tuition, Piserchia went on to earn a teaching degree in Physical Education in 1950 from Fairmont State College; she also swam competitively and qualified for the Olympics in diving at this time.

Unable to bear "the thought of living the rest of my life in Fairmont," she chose to enlist in the navy, attaining the rank of lieutenant. In 1953 she married Joseph Piserchia, then an army major, who grew up in Jersey City, New Jersey, after emigrating from Italy. The next year, the couple moved to San Francisco and Piserchia left the navy to have her daughter, Linda, followed by three sons and another daughter (in 1957, 1958, 1961, and 1962, respectively), as the family moved to military posts in Fort Knox, Tennessee; Frankfurt, Germany; Salt Lake City, Utah; and finally Tinton Falls, New Jersey (among other places). From 1963 to 1965 Piserchia took graduate courses in educational psychology at the University of Utah and began to write speculative fiction, publishing her first story, the humorous "Rocket to Gehenna," in *Fantastic* in September 1966. She published another fifteen stories from 1972 to 1976, all while dealing with the health challenges of a husband who returned from Vietnam with a "wrecked heart." As she noted in the introduction to one of her stories, "I live in a madhouse and my nerves are shot," but writing provided her with a much needed "lifeline."

Piserchia also published more than a dozen SF novels, beginning with *Mister Justice* in 1973 and including *Star Rider* (1974), *A Billion Days of Earth* (1976), *Earthchild* (1977), *Spaceling* (1978), *The Spinner* (1980), *The Fluger* (1980), *Doomtime* (1981), *Earth in Twilight* (1981), *The Dimensioneers* (1982), and *The Deadly Sky* (1983); *Blood*

Country (1981) and *I, Zombie* (1982) appeared under a male pseudonym, Curt Selby. In 1985, her first daughter died of a brain tumor, and the couple took on the task of adopting and raising their granddaughter, then three years old; "looking back on it now," Piserchia later recalled, "I realize I should have gotten some extensive grief therapy. My energy seemed to slip away, along with will and ambition." Toward the end of her life, after the death of her husband in 1997, Piserchia spoke out in the press against nuclear waste disposal at the nearby Oyster Creek power station. She died at ninety-two surrounded by children, grandchildren, and a great-granddaughter. She earned a Locus nomination for Best Novel for *Star Rider*, and her fiction has been translated into German, French, Dutch, Italian, and Croatian. At least one of her stories—"The Residents of Kingston," originally scheduled for publication in Harlan Ellison's *Last Dangerous Visions*—remains unpublished.

Marta Randall (b. April 26, 1948) was born Marta Dolores Randall in Mexico City to Richard Baleme Randall, a California teacher, and Nelly (Amador y Spat) Randall, a native of Yucatán. At the age of two she moved with her parents to Berkeley, California, where she was raised with her two siblings, Richard and Margaret; she attended Berkeley High School. Marrying Robert H. Bergstresser in 1966, she had a son, Richard, and worked her way through college, graduating from San Francisco State University in 1970. Three years later, Randall and Bergstresser divorced. From 1968 to 2013, she built a career as a legal assistant and paralegal (with a six-year detour in the 1980s as a freelance writer for a video-game developer). She had a daughter, Kaitlin, in 1985, with Christopher E. Conley, to whom she was married from 1983 to 2012.

Growing up, Randall was entranced by adventure stories: "I wasn't going to be the one stuck at home baking cookies, I was going to be the one balancing on the raft in the lashing seas, gripping the mast with one hand while the other held on to the cookies somebody else had baked." She published her first SF story, "Smack Run," as Marta Bergstresser in 1973—the only time she published with this name; her *Collected Stories* appeared in 2007, and she continues to add to this body of work. Beginning with *A City in the North* (1976), *Islands* (1976), and *Journey* (1978), she has published nine novels, most recently *Mapping Winter* (2019) and *The River South* (2019).

In 1980 and 1981 Randall coedited two volumes in the *New Dimensions* anthology series with Robert Silverberg. She served as vice president of the Science Fiction Writers of America (SFWA, recently renamed the Science Fiction Writers Association), and in 1982 became the group's first female president. Around this time, she also began teaching at the Clarion Writers East and West Workshops, Portland State University, Playwrights Unlimited, the University of California at Berkeley extension program, the Gotham Writers program, and elsewhere. She has been honored with many award nominations, including three Nebula nominations (for the novel *Islands* in 1976, the novella *Dangerous Games* in 1980, and the anthology *New Dimensions 12* in 1981); her fiction has been translated into German, Swedish, and French. She now lives in Hawaii, to which she retired in 2013.

Joanna Russ (February 22, 1937–April 29, 2011), often cited as the author of the landmark feminist SF novel *The Female Man* (1975), was also a prolific reviewer and essayist and published several collections of short fiction, including *Alyx* (1976), *The Zanzibar Cat* (1983), *Extra(ordinary) People* (1984), and *The Hidden Side of the Moon* (1988). Born Joanna Ruth Russ in the Bronx to public school teachers Evarett and Bertha (Zinner) Russ, she demonstrated early aptitude in the sciences (becoming a finalist in the 1953 Westinghouse Science Talent Search for her project "Growth of Certain Fungi Under Colored Light and in Darkness") but turned to literature at Cornell, where she studied with Vladimir Nabokov and published in undergraduate magazines. After college, she attended the Yale School of Drama, earning an MFA in Playwriting in 1960, and began a career as an English professor at Queensborough Community College in New York.

Russ read science fiction as a teenager because it promised a world "where things could be different." She sold her first science fiction story, "Nor Custom Stale," while still in graduate school. In 1963 she married journalist Albert Amateau and then in 1967 divorced him. During this period Russ established herself as a leading voice in science fiction's New Wave, one who embraced the radical politics of her time— especially its feminist variants—and who wove it into her stories accordingly. As she noted in a letter to Susan Koppelman, Russ saw anger as an important part of both politics and art, noting that "from now on, I will not trust anyone who isn't angry." While some members of the SF community were uneasy with Russ's political views, others recognized the innovative nature of her fiction and in 1968 she received a Hugo nomination for her first novel, *Picnic on Paradise*, which follows the adventures of a female mercenary named Alyx.

Teaching subsequently at Cornell, SUNY Binghamton, the University of Colorado at Boulder, and the University of Washington (from which she retired in poor health in the 1990s), Russ published influential feminist literary criticism (including *How to Suppress Women's Writing*, 1983, and *To Write Like a Woman: Essays in Feminism and Science Fiction*, 1995) alongside her fiction. Her story "When It Changed," included in this anathology, won a 1973 Nebula Award; "Souls" received both Hugo and Locus Awards in 1983. In 1995, Russ received retrospective Tiptree Awards (for the best explorations of sex and gender in speculative fiction) for "When It Changed" and *The Female Man*. She died in Tucson after a series of strokes and was posthumously inducted into the Science Fiction and Fantasy Hall of Fame and named a Science Fiction and Fantasy Writers of America Grand Master. Her papers are archived at the University of Oregon.

Pamela Sargent (b. March 20, 1948) was born in Ithaca, New York, to Edward H. Sargent, Jr., and Shirley Richards Sargent. Her parents, both aspiring musicians in their youth, met while attending Cornell University; after graduation, her father served in the U.S. Marine Corps before moving with his wife to Albany, where he became a longtime faculty member at the Albany College for Teachers; Sargent's mother worked for the New York State Education Department until her retirement in 1979. From a young age, Sargent was a voracious reader, consuming everything from

Sherlock Holmes and *Charlotte's Web* to the works of James Michener. Sargent credits astronomer and science fiction author Fred Hoyle's monograph *The Nature of the Universe* for sparking her interest in astronomy and, eventually, for prompting her decision to write science fiction.

Sargent attended the State University of New York, Binghamton, from which she graduated with a B.A. in 1968 and an M.A. in 1970; both degrees were in Philosophy. She began to read science fiction extensively around this time because she was intrigued by the fact that tales about other worlds and times could just as easily center on women as on men. Though Sargent held a variety of odd jobs while in school—including modeling, factory work, and sales—she has been a freelance writer and editor since 1971. Her first short story, "Landed Minority," appeared in the September 1970 issue of *The Magazine of Fantasy and Science Fiction*. "Oasis" (1971), "Julio 204" (1972), "The Other Perceiver" (1972), "Gather Blue Roses" (1972), and "A Sense of Difference" (1972) soon followed.

As she established her literary reputation, Sargent became interested in assembling an anthology of science fiction stories written entirely by women. No such collection had ever been published before: editors continually rebuffed Sargent when approached with the idea, both because they thought she was still too untested an author and because they thought such an anthology would only appeal to a niche audience—if there were even enough good stories to fill such an anthology at all. It was not until fellow SF author Vonda McIntyre leveraged her position with an editor at Vintage Books that the idea was taken seriously: McIntyre contacted Sargent, who was then, finally, able to sell what would become *Women of Wonder* (1975). For the next decade, *Women of Wonder* remained in print and spawned two sequels. Sargent notes that after publishing the anthology, she "would encounter people, mostly but not all women, who had thought there was nothing of interest in [science fiction] for them until they saw *Women of Wonder* in a bookstore or library." Twenty years later, in the mid-1990s, Sargent compiled two more *Women of Wonder* anthologies for Harcourt Brace.

Sargent has earned dozens of Locus, Homer, Nebula, and Otherwise (formerly known as James Tiptree, Jr.) nominations, for both her original stories and her anthologies. Her novelette, *Danny Goes to Mars*, won both the Locus and Nebula Awards in 1993. In 2000, Sargent was honored with the "Service to SFWA" award in 2000 for her work editing three of the SFWA's annual Nebula Awards volumes and for coediting the *SFWA Bulletin* from 1983 to 1991 with her partner George Zebrowski; in 2012, she received the Science Fiction Research Association Award for Lifetime Contributions to Science Fiction and Fantasy Scholarship. Her 1983 novel *Earthseed* continues to appear on recommended reading lists for young adults, and it was optioned by Paramount Studios in 2011. Sargent currently lives in Albany, New York.

Raccoona Sheldon (August 24, 1915–May 19, 1987) was a secondary pseudonym of Alice Bradley Sheldon, most famously known as James Tiptree, Jr. (see Tiptree entry for further biographical detail). Sheldon created this alternate persona nine years after she began publishing as Tiptree. Initially invented out of concern that her real identity as a woman would be exposed, Alice Sheldon quickly came to appreciate how the Raccoona Sheldon persona allowed her to "communicate as a woman at least part of the time" and to "say some things impossible [using] a male persona." Drawing on the skills she developed as an intelligence officer, Sheldon set out to make Raccoona Sheldon a fully realized individual: she rented a post office box and set up a bank account in her name in Wisconsin. As she began to consider retiring the Tiptree persona, Sheldon—as Tiptree—started introducing her "friend," Raccoona Sheldon, to others in the SF community.

Like Tiptree, Raccoona Sheldon was active in both the fan and professional science fiction communities. She submitted artwork and written correspondence to popular, feminist-friendly fanzines, including *Khatru* and *The Witch and the Chameleon*. Raccoona Sheldon's first novelette, *Angel Fix*, appeared in *Worlds of If* in 1974. Over the course of the 1970s, three more Raccoona Sheldon stories appeared in major science fiction outlets, including "The Screwfly Solution" (featured in this anthology), which won the 1977 Nebula Award for Best Novelette and would later be adapted for television.

In 1978 Sheldon revealed her true identity before fans, who were beginning to piece together that identity based on her mother's obituary, could do so for her. The February 1978 issue of *Khatru* featured a James Tiptree, Jr./Alice Sheldon section in which Alice Sheldon proclaimed, "Everything by the [Tiptree] signature was me." She confessed to the creation of the Raccoona Sheldon persona in the same interview, even admitting to "giving her some of Tip's weaker tales to peddle." Sheldon continued to use both writer-personae even after her secret was out. In 1981, she anthologized the works of Raccoona Sheldon in *Out of Everywhere and Other*

Extraordinary Visions. In 1985, she used the pen name one more time, for her short story on abortion rights, "Morality Meat," published in the feminist anthology *Dispatches from the Frontiers of the Female Mind.* In addition to the 1977 Nebula Award, Raccoona Sheldon's stories received multiple Locus, Hugo, and Nebula nominations, and have been translated into German, Finnish, Romanian, and other languages.

Kathleen M. Sidney (b. October 19, 1944) was born Kathleen Marion Sidney in Paterson, New Jersey. Her father, Paul Sidney, worked as a salesman in a jewelry store; he "spent most of his childhood and early adult years wandering around Europe," she later recalled. Her mother, Kathleen (Mulgrue) Sidney, was "raised in an orphanage in Montreal"; the couple already had a son. Sidney received her diploma from Ramapo Regional High School in Franklin Lakes, New Jersey, in 1962. She attended Fairleigh Dickinson University as a day student while living in Oakland, New Jersey, graduating in 1966, and subsequently took advanced classes at Kean College. From 1971 to 1978 she worked as a special education teacher in Paterson.

Sidney—a self-described " frustrated film director"—wrote the screenplay "Image," her earliest known work, in 1970. Around 1974 she became active in the SF community, attending DisCon II, the 32nd World Science Fiction Convention, in Washington, D.C. From 1975 to 1977, she published three pieces of short fiction in some of the most prestigious anthologies of the decade. "The Anthropologist" (1975, featured in this volume) appeared in Damon Knight's *Orbit 17*, "The Teacher" (1976) in Knight's *Orbit 18*, and "The Traders" (1977) in Kate Wilhelm's *Clarion SF*. She published one genre novel, *Michael and the Magic Man*, in 1980, and wrote an unproduced teleplay, "Oasis," in 2005. She currently lives in Flagstaff, Arizona.

Kathleen Sky (b. August 5, 1943) was born Kathleen Ellen McKinney in Alhambra, California, the eldest daughter of Ballard B. McKinney, who worked loading produce and dry goods, and Betty Rosamond (Wade) McKinney; she also has four half siblings from her parents' later marriages. After high school she studied mortuary science and veterinary medicine but is not known to have taken a degree. She married Karl Sky, a Czech immigrant, in Nevada in 1965; though the couple divorced in 1971, she continued to publish as Kathleen Sky.

By her own account, Sky decided to pursue a literary career after watching an episode of the original *Star Trek* television series and realizing she could write "better than that." She published her first story, "One Ordinary Day, with Box," in 1972. That same year, she married fellow SF author Stephen Goldin, whom she met at a fan convention. (They wed in Los Angeles in a medieval-themed ceremony attended by members of the Society of Creative Anachronism, Sky making her wedding dress, a queen's lady's costume, out of taffeta.) With Goldin, she cowrote two SF stories and the popular nonfiction guide *The Business of Being a Writer* (1982), traveling and giving talks in support of the book before divorcing Goldin in 1982.

Along with a half dozen additional stories, Sky published the novels *Birthright* (1975), *Ice Prison* (1976), and *Witchdame* (1985) and two official *Star Trek* novels, *Vulcan!* (1978) and *Death's Angel* (1981). In 1979, she was invited to make a cameo appearance in *Star Trek: The Motion Picture*, appearing as a crew member on the bridge of the *Enterprise*.

James Tiptree, Jr. (August 24, 1915–May 19, 1987) was the primary pseudonym of Alice Bradley Sheldon. Born Alice Hastings Bradley in Chicago, Illinois, to author Mary Hastings Bradley and lawyer and naturalist Herbert Bradley, she was educated at the University of Chicago Laboratory Schools and then at finishing schools in Lausanne, Switzerland, and Tarrytown, New York. As a child, she accompanied her parents on three safari expeditions to Africa, becoming the child-celebrity protagonist and illustrator of her mother's books *Alice in Jungleland* (1927) and *Alice in Elephantland* (1929). In 1934, after a year at Sarah Lawrence, she married Princeton undergraduate William Davey; both attended the University of California at Berkeley and then New York University without taking degrees. An aspiring painter, she exhibited her work at the Art Institute of Chicago and the Corcoran Gallery.

After her divorce in 1941, Tiptree worked as an art critic for the *Chicago Sun* before enlisting in the Women's Army Auxiliary Corps, where she trained as a photo-intelligence analyst and rose to the rank of major. Stationed in Europe in 1945–46, she married fellow intelligence officer Huntington Denton Sheldon. After their return to the United States, the Sheldons ran an ill-fated chicken hatchery before joining the newly minted CIA in 1953, where Tiptree helped expand the agency's photo-intelligence section and later specialized in the analysis of African politics. After completing her undergraduate education at American University in 1959, Tiptree studied psychology at George Washington University, earning her Ph.D. in 1967 and publishing "Preference for Familiar Versus Novel Stimuli as a Function of the Familiarity of the Environment" in the *Journal of Comparative and Physiological Psychology* in 1969.

Tiptree had been interested in science fiction since she was a child; while in high school she traded pulp magazines with her uncle Harry, who first introduced her to them, and by the time she joined the army, her personal collection had grown to over 1,300 issues. She created her famous pseudonym in 1967 when she began submitting her own work to magazines, inspired by a jar of Tiptree marmalade she saw at the supermarket. As her stories began to appear in print and to attract attention—she won the 1974 Hugo Award for "The Girl Who Was Plugged In," the 1974 Nebula Award for "Love Is the Plan the Plan Is Death," and both Hugo and Nebula Awards in 1977 for "Houston, Houston, Do You Read?"—Sheldon withheld details about her identity, offering "Tip" as an increasingly elaborate persona both for publication and in her extensive private correspondence with writers including Philip K. Dick, Harlan Ellison, Ursula K. Le Guin, and Joanna Russ. She also published a handful of items as Raccoona Sheldon, ostensibly one of Tiptree's female friends. Tiptree was publicly exposed as Sheldon early in 1977, prompting good-natured embarrassment among critics who had discerned "something inherently masculine" in Tiptree's prose, and wide discussion of the relationship among reading, writing, and gender. Her friends took the revelation in stride; in the foreword to *Star Songs for Old Primates* Ursula K. Le Guin affectionately labels Tiptree her "Gethenian friend."

Tiptree collected her stories in *Ten Thousand Light-Years from Home* (1973), *Warm Worlds and Otherwise* (1975),

Star Songs of an Old Primate (1978), *Out of the Everywhere, and Other Extraordinary Visions* (1981), *The Starry Rift* (1986), and other volumes; she also published two novels, *Up the Walls of the World* (1978) and *Brightness Falls from the Air* (1985). Under her famous pseudonym, she won three Nebulas, one SF Chronicle, one World Fantasy, and four Seiun awards, and her stories have been translated into a dozen languages, including French, Japanese, and Croatian. At the age of seventy-one, an increasingly ill and depressed Alice Sheldon shot her husband and then herself, completing what many of Sheldon's community believed to be a suicide pact. In 1991 members of WisCon, the world's oldest feminist science fiction convention, created the James Tiptree, Jr. Literary Award to honor work that explores and expands ideas about gender; in 2019, the WisCon Motherboard changed the name of the prize to the Otherwise Award, both in recognition of increasing fan concern about Tiptree's final acts and to honor the BIPOC and LGBTQ+ authors who are—like Tiptree before them—teaching audiences to think of strange new futures for human sex and gender relations.

Lisa Tuttle (b. September 16, 1952) was born Lisa Gracia Tuttle in Houston, Texas, to Robert Elliott Tuttle, Jr., and Elizabeth Jane (Whalen) Tuttle, both of whom were avid readers. When she was nine Tuttle's father gave her his old typewriter, which she used to produce a family newspaper, unfinished novels, short stories, poems, and a few letters to the editor that were published in the *Houston Post*. Tuttle attended Mirabeau B. Lamar High School, where she worked on the school newspaper. Outside school, Tuttle became involved in science fiction fandom and reestablished the Houston Science Fiction Society with the help of her peers, founding, editing, and publishing the club's fanzine, *Mathom*. After high school, Tuttle pursued a bachelor's degree in English and Creative Writing at Syracuse University in New York. During her college years, she was involved with the university's science fiction group and wrote for the fanzine *Tomorrow And. . .* During this period, Tuttle also attended the Clarion Writers Workshop twice: once in New Orleans in the summer of 1970 and then again in Seattle in 1972, where she sold her first short story, "Stranger in the House," to Robin Scott Wilson for the *Clarion II* anthology.

In 1973, Tuttle cofounded the Turkey City Writers Workshop in Austin, Texas, with fellow SF authors Steve Waldrop and Bruce Sterling, among others. She received her degree in 1974 and returned to Texas, where she took a job at a local newspaper, the *Austin American-Statesman*. That same year, Tuttle tied with Spider Robinson for the John W. Campbell/Astounding Award for Best New Writer. In that same period, she dated George R. R. Martin and together they coauthored the award-winning "The Storms of Windhaven" (1976), which would later become the novel *Windhaven* (1981). In 1981, she moved to London, marrying fellow writer Christopher Priest; the two divorced in 1987 and three years later she married editor and writer Colin Murray, with whom she had a daughter, Emily. In 1982, Tuttle became the first and only person to refuse a Nebula nomination (for "The Bone Flute") when she discovered another writer was actively campaigning for votes; when Tuttle won the award but declined to attend the ceremony, the prize was accepted on her behalf by the SFWA.

To date, Tuttle has written eleven novels and over one

hundred short stories in the science fiction, fantasy, and horror genres, resulting in forty nominations and seven prizes, including Locus, Nebula, British Science Fiction, IHG, and Imaginaire awards; her fiction has been translated into French, Dutch, Romanian, and other languages. Additionally, Tuttle has written notable pieces of nonfiction for the *Encyclopedia of Feminism* (1986) and *Heroines: Women Inspired by Women* (1988) while teaching science fiction at London University's City Lit College. She has also edited two horror anthologies, *Skin of the Soul: New Horror Stories by Women* (1990) and *Crossing the Border: Tales of Erotic Ambiguity* (1998), and written children's and young adult books under a variety of pen names, including Laura Waring, Ben M. Baglio, and Lucy Daniels. She was a featured artist in the 1993 television miniseries *New Nightmares* and her stories have been adapted for television series, including *The Hitchhiker*, *Monsters*, and *The Hunger* as well as the 2005 French film *Propriété Commune*. Tuttle currently resides in rural Scotland with her husband, where she writes and reviews science fiction, fantasy, and horror for *The Guardian*. Her latest collection of horror stories, *The Dead Hours of Night,* was published in 2021.

Joan D. Vinge (b. April 2, 1948) was born Joan Carol Dennison in Baltimore, Maryland, to Seymore Dennison, an aircraft engineer, and Carol Erwin, an executive secretary; her mother claimed Erie Indian heritage. When Vinge was eight her father's work moved the family to San Diego, California; she developed an early interest in astronomy when he bought the family a telescope and taught Vinge the names of the constellations. In junior high, she discovered Andre Norton's young adult science fiction, and began writing her own SF as a "secret hobby." She graduated from Hilltop Senior High in 1965 and earned her bachelor's degree in Anthropology from San Diego State University in 1971. In 1972 she married fellow author and mathematics and computer science professor Venor Vinge.

Vinge's first story, "Toy Soldier," appeared in Damon Knight's prestigious *Orbit* series in 1974. She quickly gained a reputation as one of the leading female writers of engineering-oriented or "hard" science fiction: in 1978, her novelette *Eyes of Amber* won a Hugo Award, and her novelette *Fireship* won both Hugo and Analog Awards. Divorcing in 1979, the following year she married SF writer and editor James Frenkel, with whom she had two children, Jessica and Joshua. Her second novel, *The Snow Queen* (1980), received both the Hugo and Locus Awards. Since then, she has published more than a dozen novels (including adaptations of the films *Ladyhawke*, *Mad Max: Beyond Thunderdome*, and *47 Ronin*), a collection of shorter fiction (*Phoenix in the Ashes*, 1985), and many uncollected stories and essays; her works have been widely translated.

In 1998 Vinge taught at the Clarion Writers Workshop at Michigan State University. A 2002 car crash left her with minor brain damage and fibromyalgia, but within five years she regained her ability to write and published a new edition of her book *Psion* while completing her novel *Ladysmith*. Now a proud grandmother, she lives in Green Valley, Arizona.

Kate Wilhelm (June 8, 1928–March 8, 2018), born Kate Gertrude Meredith in Toledo, Ohio, was the fourth child of Jesse and Ann (McDowell) Meredith, both natives of Kentucky; at twelve, she moved with her family to Louisville, where her father worked in a flour mill. Soon after her graduation from Louisville Girls' High School she married Joseph Wilhelm and had two sons, Douglas in 1949 and Richard in 1953. Her first published story, "The Pint-Size Genie," appeared in *Fantastic* in October 1956, and she became a regular contributor to genre magazines thereafter, collecting her stories in *The Mile-Long Spaceship* (1963), *The Downstairs Room and Other Speculative Fiction* (1968), *Abyss* (1971), *The Infinity Box* (1975), *Somerset Dreams and Other Fictions* (1978), *Listen, Listen* (1981), *Children of the Wind* (1989), and *The Angels Sing* (1992).

Divorcing her first husband, in 1963 Wilhelm married fellow writer Damon Knight; together, they raised five children from previous marriages and had a son of their own. As hosts of the Milford Science Fiction Writers' Conference from their home in Milford, Pennsylvania, and later, as cofounders of the Clarion Science Fiction and Fantasy Workshop, they began a tradition of literary mentorship and mutual criticism that has influenced many careers and continues to the present. They both also lectured on speculative fiction at universities around the world.

Wilhelm won Nebula Awards in 1969 (for "The Planners"), 1987 (for "The Girl Who Fell into the Sky"), and 1988 (for "Forever Yours, Anna"); her 1976 novel *Where Late the Sweet Birds Sang* received both Hugo and Locus Awards, and in 2003 she was inducted into the Science Fiction Hall of Fame. Along with speculative fiction she has also published more than a dozen mystery novels, her first, *More Bitter Than Death*, in 1963, and her most recent, cowritten with Richard Wilhelm and featuring her noted detective protagonist Barbara Holloway, *Mirror, Mirror* in 2017. She died in Eugene, Oregon, where she had lived since the 1970s.

Connie Willis (b. December 31, 1945) was born Constance Elaine Trimmer in Denver, Colorado, the daughter of William Trimmer and LaMarlys (Cook) Trimmer. As a child she spent most of her free time reading at the Englewood Public Library; later, with the encouragement of her English teacher at Englewood High School, she joined the Writer's Club and worked as an editor for the school yearbook. After earning the title of "Most Academic" her senior year and receiving her high school diploma in 1963, she attended Colorado State College (now the University of Northern Colorado). In 1967 she graduated with a B.A. in English and Elementary Education, married physicist Courtney Willis, and began her career as a teacher of elementary and middle school.

Willis's first science fiction story, "The Secret of Santa Titicaca" was published by *Worlds of Fantasy* in 1970, but she did not sell another story until "Capra Corn" and "Samaritan" in 1978. She published three stories in 1979: among these was "Daisy, in the Sun," which earned Willis her first of what would come to be many Hugo nominations. In 1982, Willis won a grant from the National Endowment for the Arts, which allowed her to quit teaching and take up writing full-time. Later that same year, she won her first Hugo for the short story "Fire Watch." While Willis is generally opposed to sequel stories (claiming they are "never as good as the first"), "Fire Watch" became the first installment in her *Time Travel* series, a collection of the aforementioned short story as well as the novels *Doomsday Book* (1992), *To Say Nothing of the Dog* (1998), and *Blackout* (2010); all are set in her "Oxford time travel universe" but otherwise contain little overlap in characters and plot. Every work in the series won the Hugo Award in its eligible year.

Willis has won seven Nebula Awards and more Hugo Awards, eleven to date, than any other writer; in 2009 she was inducted into the Science Fiction Hall of Fame, and in 2011 she was named the twenty-eighth Science Fiction Writers of America Grand Master. Her fiction has been translated into at least nine languages. Today, Willis lives in Greeley, Colorado, with her husband, where she continues to write fiction and the occasional essay.

Chelsea Quinn Yarbro (b. September 15, 1942), who goes by "Quinn," was born Karin Field Erickson in Berkeley, California, the elder of two daughters of Lillian (Chatfield) Erickson, a Berkeley art graduate who later worked as an art teacher, and Clarence Erickson, a mapmaker for Rand McNally who went on to open his own cartographic firm. She attended Berkeley High School, where she was active in theater and singing groups, and then San Francisco State, where she studied playwriting. During and after college she acted semi-professionally and managed a children's theater, while also working in the family firm as a demographic cartographer. Around 1962, wanting "a name people would remember" and beginning to imagine a literary career for herself, she took her present name, suggested to her by a favorite aunt.

Yarbro's first published story, "The Posture of Prophecy," appeared in *If* magazine in September 1969; later that year she married Donald Paul Simpson, an artist and science fiction fan (they divorced in 1982). In 1970 she was named secretary of the Science Fiction Writers of America, noting in the press at the time that only 13 percent of the organization's members were women, and that the field was "rife with male chauvinism." Her first novel—*Ogilvie, Tallant & Moon*, a mystery—appeared in 1976, followed the same year by the apocalyptic *Time of the Fourth Horseman*; in 1978 she published *Hôtel Transylvania*, the first in a best-selling series of historical horror novels featuring the vampire Count Saint-Germain, and *False Dawn*, an ecological disaster novel (and sequel to "Frog Pond," included in the present volume). She has so far published eighty novels in different genres—some under pseudonyms including Trystam Kith, Camille Gabor, Vanessa Pryor, and (with Bill Fawcett) Quinn Fawcett—plus seven short fiction collections including *Cautionary Tales* (1978), *Signs & Portents* (1984), and *Apprehensions and Other Delusions* (2003), as well as a series of channeled spiritualist conversations beginning with *Messages from Michael* (1979).

To date, Yarbro's fiction has been translated into over half a dozen languages, including French, Dutch, and Portuguese. She has earned twenty-one award nominations and is a winner of the Lord Ruthven Award (1998), the World Horror Convention Grand Master Award (2003), the International Horror Guild Living Legend Award (2005), the Bram Stoker Award for Lifetime Achievement (2008), and the World Fantasy Award for Lifetime Achievement (2014). She was a founding member of the Horror Writers' Association and its first woman president (1988–90). Yarbro lives in the San Francisco Bay Area. When not busy reading or writing, she enjoys the symphony and opera.

NOTES

In the notes below, the reference numbers denote page and line of this volume (the line count includes headings but not blank lines). Biblical references are keyed to the King James Version.

23.2 *The Funeral*] Wilhelm wrote the following "Afterword" to this story for its appearance in the Harlan Ellison anthology *Again, Dangerous Visions* (1972):

About this story. We are such a godawful preachy nation, always talking about how much we do for the kids, how much we love them, how we spoil them with excessive permissiveness because we can't bear to hurt them or deny them any of life's little joys. We do Orwell proud in our expertise at doubletalk. We live a double standard in so many areas that most of us just don't have the time to listen to our own words and compare them with our actions. I am not interested in imaginary problems in imaginary times; it seems that I am too much involved in this world to create artificial ones where my ingenuity can put things right. So I see this story as the culmination of a lot of isolated items, some big and documented, some small and private. Chicago was one of them, but only one, and not the most important, just the most publicized. What was most revolting about chicago (it will become a general usage word) was the fact that afterward a majority of over 10 to 1 Americans approved the action taken by the police. Let anyone who disbelieves my story mull over that figure.

Just as in a divorce action the cause given might be the marital equivalent of chicago, but the real reasons are small daily injustices, so the generation gap, I think, has been prodded along with small daily doses of adult irresponsibility, until now there does exist a situation that is explosive.

If you, a well dressed and apparently affluent member of the adult community, enter a soda fountain, a hamburger joint, or restaurant, and sit down for service, you'll get it before the group of teen agers who were there first, although you might want only a cup of coffee or a coke and they might order several dollars worth of junk. It is not an economical issue. I've seen a

saleslady turn away from a teen aged girl with her purchase in
her hand, needing only to be paid for, to wait on a middle aged
woman who then took fifteen minutes to make up her mind.
I would have been waited on next, if I had allowed it. When I
insisted that the girl be helped next, the saleslady became surly
and rude. No one can show respect for my advanced age by
showering disrespect on another. Okay, so it's pecking order. If
it turned out that there was equality in most other areas, they
could put up with this sort of thing, but there isn't.

Equality under the law. I joke. I can drive a car with a noisy
muffler, and if I am stopped at all, it is only for a reprimand.
My son gets a ticket for the same thing—in my car. And in the
courts I can have all the legal counsel I can afford, and the state
will provide more if I need help, theoretically. A juvenile is at
the mercy of a judge who probably is as qualified to understand
adolescents as my dear old spinster aunt.

Just as long as the kids accept our standards, we leave them
alone, but let them adopt their own standards, different than
ours, and there is furor. Haircuts, sandals, mini-skirts (before
Jackie and her crowd made them more or less respectable) and
so on. Why can't they be like us, is what the school boards are
really moaning. Cut their hair, wear decent clothes, drink their
gin, smoke their cigarettes, and leave that other stuff alone. We
accept teens and booze and beer. There may be a little bit of
public outcry about a group of thirteen year olds caught at a
beer party, but by the following weekend, it's a dead issue. But
if it's pot! My God, call the FBI!

For sale ads feature houses with three or four bedrooms,
three baths, two car garages, pools, etc. Ask about the schools:
oh, double shift for the present, and the teachers are on strike
right now, but we have the best parking lot available for the
kids' cars. Is this love?

You see a bunch of businessmen at lunch or dinner, getting
louder and louder while an indifferent management smiles. A
group of college boys, or high school kids would get thrown out
in a minute. The VFW can take over a town, "bomb" citizens
from upper floors with bags of god knows what, and the chamber of commerce fights for the privilege of having them again.
Kids get the JD treatment for the same sort of provocation.

Sorry, Harlan, I'm going on too much, could go on for pages.
But this is the sort of data that sociologists deal with, not writers
of fiction. At least not directly. I think this is a demented society, and one of the reasons for the dementia is our everlovin'

refusal to see the reality behind our honeyed words. If we were as good as we talk about being, I'd want stock in harps. It's a whole society of Let's Pretenders, and I wish, oh, how much I wish we'd all just stop.

59.2 *When It Changed*] Russ wrote the following "Afterword" to this story for its appearance in the Harlan Ellison anthology *Again, Dangerous Visions* (1972):

I find it hard to say anything about this story. The first few paragraphs were dictated to me in a thoughtful, reasonable, whispering tone I had never heard before; and once the Daemon had vanished—they always do—I had to finish the thing by myself in a voice not my own.

The premise of the story needs either a book or silence. I'll try to compromise. It seems to me (in the words of the narrator) that sexual equality has not yet been established on Earth and that (in the word of GBS) the only argument that can be made against it is that it has never been tried. I have read SF stories about manless worlds before; they are either full of busty girls in wisps of chiffon who slink about writing with lust (Keith Laumer wrote a charming, funny one called "The War with the Yukks"), or the women have set up a static, beelike society in imitation of some presumed primitive matriarchy. These stories are written by men. Why women who have been alone for generations should "instinctively" turn their sexual desires toward persons of whom they have only intellectual knowledge, or why female people are presumed to have an innate preference for Byzantine rigidity I don't know. "Progress" is one of the sacred cows of SF so perhaps the latter just goes to show that although women can run a society by themselves, *it isn't a good one.* This is flattering to men, I suppose. Of SF attempts to depict real matriarchies ("He will be my concubine for tonight," said the Empress of Zar coldly) it is better not to speak. I remember one very good post-bomb story by an English writer (another static society, with the Magna Mater literally and supernaturally in existence) but on the whole we had better just tiptoe past the subject.

In my story I have used assumptions that seem to me obviously true. One of them is the idea that almost all characterological sex differences we take for granted are in fact learned not innate. I do not see how anyone can walk around with both eyes open and both halves of his/her brain functioning and not realize this. Still, the mythology persists in SF, as elsewhere, that women are naturally gentler than men, that they are naturally less creative than men, or less intelligent, or shrewder, or more cowardly, or more dependent, or more self-centered, or more self-sacrificing, or more materialistic, or shyer, or God knows what, whatever is most convenient at the moment. True, you can make people into anything. There are matrons of fifty so domesticated that any venture away from home is a continual flutter: where's the No Smoking sign, is it on, how do I fasten my seat belt, oh dear can you see the stewardess, she's serving the men first, they always do, isn't it awful. And what's so fascinating about all this was that the strong, competent "male" to whom such a lady in distress turned for help recently was Carol Emshwiller. Wowie, zowie, Mr. Wizard! This flutteriness is not "femininity" (something men are always so anxious women will lose) but pathology.

It's men who get rapturous and yeasty about the wonderful mystery of Woman, lovely Woman (this is getting difficult to write as I keep imagining my reader to be the George-Georgina of old circuses: half-bearded, half-permanent-waved). There are few women who go around actually feeling: Oh, what a fascinating feminine mystery I am. This makes it clear enough, I think which sex (in general) has the higher prestige, the more freedom, the more education, the more money, in Sartre's sense which is subject and which is object. Every role in life has its advantages and disadvantages, of course; a fiery feminist student here at Cornell recently told an audience that a man who acquires a wife acquires a "life-long slave" (fierce look) while the audience justifiably giggled and I wondered how I'd ever been inveigled into speaking on a program with such a lackwit. I also believe, like the villain of my story, that human beings are born with instincts (though fuzzy ones) and that being physically weaker than men and having babies makes a difference. But it makes less and less of a difference now.

Also, the patriarchal society must have considerable survival value. I suspect that it is actually more stable (and more rigid) than the primeval matriarchal societies hypothesized by some anthropologists. I wish somebody knew. To take only one topic: it seems clear that if there is to be a sexual double standard, it must be the one we know and not the opposite; male potency is too biologically precious to repress. A society that made its well-bred men impotent, as Victorian ladies were made frigid, would rapidly become an unpeopled society. Such things ought to be speculated about.

Meanwhile my story. It did not come from this lecture, of course, but vice versa. I had read a very fine SF novel, Ursula Le Guin's *The Left Hand of Darkness*, in which all the characters are humanoid hermaphrodites, and was wondering at the obduracy of the English language, in which everybody is "he" or "she" and "it" is reserved for typewriters. But how can one call a hermaphrodite "he," as Miss Le Guin does? I tried (in my head) changing all the masculine pronouns to feminine ones, and marveled at the difference. And then I wondered why Miss Le Guin's native "hero" is male in *every* important sexual encounter of his life except that with the human male in the book. Weeks later the Daemon suddenly whispered, "Katy drives like a maniac," and I found myself on Whileaway, on a country road at night. I might add (for the benefit of both the bearded and unbearded sides of the reader's cerebrum) that I never write to shock. I consider that as immoral as writing to please. Katharina and Janet are respectable, decent, even conventional people, and if they shock *you*, just think what a copy of *Playboy* or *Cosmopolitan* would do to *them*. Resentment of the opposite sex (*Cosmo* is worse) is something they have yet to learn, thank God.

Which is why I visit Whileaway—although I do not live there because there are no men there. And if you wonder about my sincerity in saying *that*, George-Georgina, I must just give you up as hopeless.

60.14   I.C.] Internal combustion.

92.25   tridimens] Three-dimensional broadcasting (as opposed to the two-dimensional broadcasting associated with television).

102.10–11   birdtail] A cocktail, as misremembered by the alien protagonist.

135.6   Evel Knievel] Robert Craig "Evel" Knievel (1938–2007) was a celebrity stunt performer, best known for his motorcycle jumps.

136.14   flipflop] A type of electronic circuit fundamental to digital computing.

138.2   Big Blue Meanies] See the animated Beatles' movie *Yellow Submarine* (1968), in which the Blue Meanies take over and oppress the peaceful, utopian Pepperland.

138.23   bellevue] A psychiatric hospital (after Bellevue Hospital Center in New York, known historically for its treatment of psychiatric patients).

141.16   houri] A beautiful young virgin woman, possibly of supernatural origin, who accompanies the Muslim faithful in Paradise.

150.1   waldo] A remote manipulator that, through electronic, hydraulic, or mechanical connections, allows a human operator to work a hand-like mechanism and move dangerous materials from a safe distance. The term is used in engineering and is an homage to Robert A. Heinlein's 1942 story "Waldo, Or Magic Incorporated," in which the eponymous main character uses remote devices to manage his space habitat.

154.13   Benelux] A political and economic union that includes Belgium, the Netherlands, and Luxembourg.

155.1   vargueno] Also spelled bargueño, an ornate, drop-front writing cabinet or traveling desk popularized during the Spanish renaissance and often seen in Spanish colonial contexts.

156.24   Van Allen warble?] A Van Allen belt is a zone of energetic charged particles, mostly from solar winds, that are held around a planet by its atmosphere. A Van Allen warble occurs when such a belt interferes with communications broadcasting.

157.11   peri] In Persian mythology and folklore, a spirit descended from evil angels; more commonly figured in modern times as a benevolent genie or fairy.

160.27   Harlow?] Jean Harlow (1911–1937), a Hollywood actress of the 1930s sometimes referred to as the "Blonde Bombshell."

165.12–13   hypergolics] Used in rocket engines, propellant fuels whose components spontaneously ignite when they come into contact.

165.15–16   *Green Mansions . . .* burned Rima alive] See *Green Mansions: A Romance of the Tropical Forest* (1904), a novel by William Henry Hudson in which an explorer falls in love with the teenaged last survivor of a birdlike people living in the jungles of Venezuela. Named Rima, she is eventually killed by Venezuelan natives who believe her to be a witch.

169.9   PPs] "PPs" are, as Tiptree explains a few pages later, pleasure-pain implants. In this story, PPs are used initially to control prisoners and soldiers, but then quickly adapted for commercial entertainment purposes.

177.26   AX90] The Lockheed XF-90 was a prototype fighter-bomber developed for the U.S. Air Force shortly after World War II; Tiptree's "AX90" suggests a world in which the plane went into production.

178.5 Goldsboro AB] Seymour Johnson Air Force Base in Goldsboro, North Carolina, which has been home to both a U.S. Army Air Corps technical training school and a federal prison camp.

181.30 Crotty] Extremely dirty (from the French *croté*).

184.6–7 NIXON UNVEILS PHASE TWO] President Richard Nixon unveiled "Phase Two" of an economic recovery program on October 7, 1971, as was reported in wire-service headlines the following day.

202.3–4 *Whom do you lead . . . farewell?*] From the poem "Kashmiri Song," first collected in 1901 in *The Garden of Kama, and Other Love Lyrics from India* by Laurence Hope, a pseudonym of Violet Nicolson (1865–1904), and set to music the following year by Any Woodforde-Finden (1860–1919). Also known as "Pale Hands I Love," the song became widely popular; Rudolph Valentino recorded a version in 1923.

218.2 *The Day Before the Revolution*] As published in Le Guin's story collection *The Wind's Twelve Quarters* (1975), this story bore a dedication, "In memoriam Paul Goodman, 1911–1972"; Goodman was a public intellectual in the anarchist tradition, most often remembered for his book *Growing Up Absurd* (1960). Le Guin's introduction to her story is reprinted below; "the ones who walked away from Omelas" refers to her philosophical vignette of the same title, published in 1973, in which "those who walk away" are those who refuse to participate in systems of governance that prioritize profit over human need.

> My novel *The Dispossessed* is about a small worldful of people who call themselves Odonians. The name is taken from the founder of their society, Odo, who lived several generations before the time of the novel, and who therefore doesn't get into the action—except implicitly, in that all of the action started with her.
>
> Odonianism is anarchism. Not the bomb-in-the-pocket stuff, which is terrorism, whatever name it tries to dignify itself with; not the social-Darwinist economic "libertarianism" of the far right; but anarchism, as prefigured in early Taoist thought, and expounded by Shelley and Kropotkin, Goldman and Goodman. Anarchism's principal target is the authoritarian State (capitalist or socialist); its principal moral-practical theme is cooperation (solidarity, mutual aid). It is the most idealistic, and to me the most interesting, of all political theories.
>
> To embody it in a novel, which had not been done before, was a long and hard job for me, and absorbed me totally for many months. When it was done I felt lost, exiled—a displaced

person. I was very grateful, therefore, when Odo came out of the shadows and across the gulf of Probability, and wanted a story written, not about the world she made, but about herself.

This story is about one of the ones who walked away from Omelas.

238.5   antimacassar] A piece of cloth placed over the back or arm of a chair to protect it from dirt and grease; Macassar oil was a popular nineteenth-century men's hair tonic. Common in the Victorian era, antimacassars quickly came to be associated with old-fashioned—and just plain old—women in the twentieth century.

251.2   *Scarab*] In ancient Egypt, scarabs symbolized good luck, renewal, rebirth, and transformation.

287.23–24   Lilith . . . married Eve?] A female figure from Mesopotamian and Judaic mythology, usually described as either Adam's first wife and/or the first female demon, who was cast out of Eden for refusing to obey Adam's commands. She was reclaimed as a symbol of female independence and defiance against patriarchy by second-wave feminists.

306.11   seine] A fishing net that hangs in the water with floats at the top and weights at the bottom.

308.11   chiliastic cults] Chiliasm, more commonly known as millennialism, is the belief advanced by a variety of religions that after great strife, there will be a period of peace and plenty on Earth prior to the end of the world and the final judgment of humanity. Historically speaking, such cults often lead to great social unrest.

313.30   lordotic reflex] From the Greek *lordos* ("bent backward"), a bodily posture adopted by female rodents, and some other mammals, to facilitate reproduction.

314.10   "The panic element . . . Leiber?] From Fritz Leiber's review of "Fantasy Books" in the November 1976 issue of *Fantastic*.

316.25–26   *"Sudden and light as that . . . besides the grave."*] See Robert Frost's poem "The Impulse," his 1916 sequence "The Hill Wife."

323.28   'better to marry . . . burn'] See 1 Corinthians 7:9.

324.1–2   'let he among you . . . first stone.'] See John 8:7.

325.11   Mithraism."] A widespread Roman mystery cult or mystery religion (c. first to fourth century C.E.), possibly of pre-Zoroastrian Iranian origin; practiced in underground temples, it was denounced by early Christians and suppressed in increasingly Christian Rome.

350.16–22   *The time has come . . .* Boiling Hot!] See the Lewis Carroll poem "The Walrus and the Carpenter," originally published in *Through the Looking Glass* (1871).

355.13–16   *Grow old along with me . . .* Browning,"] See Robert (not Elizabeth) Browning's dramatic monologue "Rabbi Ben Ezra," first collected in *Dramatis Personae* (1864).

360.17   the Man Without a Country] See Edward Everett Hale's 1863 short story "The Man Without a Country," in which an army officer who denounces his country during a treason trial is sentenced to life imprisonment at sea without a single sight of or news about the United States for the rest of his life.

361.1   *psittacidae*] One of three families of true parrots in the superfamily Psittacoidea.

367.24   bem] Bug-eyed monster.

370.3   magnetopause] The boundary between a magnetosphere and the surrounding plasma. In planetary science, it specifically marks the boundary between a planet's magnetic field and the solar winds.

395.2   *Cassandra*] In Greek mythology, a Trojan priestess who was given the gift of prophecy by Apollo; when she refused to provide sexual favors in return, the god cursed her to always speak the truth but always be disbelieved. Modern feminist genre authors, including Christa Wolf, Marion Zimmer Bradley, and Octavia Butler, have all used the figure of Cassandra as the starting point for characters who show how oppositional female points of view emerge from the patriarchal cultures that try to marginalize or erase them.

442.26   Ra] God of the sun, in ancient Egypt.

SOURCES & ACKNOWLEDGMENTS

This volume presents twenty-three science fiction stories of the 1970s, in approximate chronological order of their first publication. Most of the texts of these stories have been taken from their original magazine or anthology appearances; the texts of Pamela Sargent's "If Ever I Should Leave You" and Ursula K. Le Guin's "The Day Before the Revolution" have been taken from these authors' subsequent story collections, which restore versions of these stories they preferred.

Great efforts have been made to locate all owners of copyrighted material in this book. Any owner who has inadvertently been omitted will gladly be acknowledged in future printings.

Sonya Dorman Hess, "Bitching It," *Quark/2*, ed. Samuel R. Delaney and Marilyn Hacker (New York: Paperback Library, 1971), 137–44. Copyright © 1971, 1998 by Sonya Dorman Hess. Reprinted by permission of the Estate of Sonya Dorman and the Virginia Kidd Agency, Inc.

Chelsea Quinn Yarbro, "Frog Pond," *Galaxy* 31.4 (March 1971): 162–70. Copyright © 1971 by Chelsea Quinn Yarbro. Reprinted by permission of the author and Big Megaphone, Inc.

Kate Wilhelm, "The Funeral," *Again, Dangerous Visions*, ed. Harlan Ellison (Garden City, N.Y.: Doubleday, 1972), 218–41. Copyright © InfinityBox Press, LLC. Reprinted by permission of InfinityBox Press, LLC.

Joanna Russ, "When It Changed," *Again, Dangerous Visions*, ed. Harlan Ellison (Garden City, N.Y.: Doubleday, 1972), 253–60. Copyright © 1972 by Joanna Russ. Reprinted by permission of Diana Finch Literary Agency on behalf of the Russ Estate.

Kathleen Sky, "Lament of the Keeku Bird," *The Alien Condition*, ed. Stephen Goldin (New York: Ballantine, 1973), 1–20.

Miriam Allen deFord, "A Way Out," *The Alien Condition*, ed. Stephen Goldin (New York: Ballantine, 1973), 49–62.

Vonda N. McIntyre, "Of Mist, and Grass, and Sand," *Analog Science Fiction/Science Fact* 92.2 (October 1973): 73–91. Copyright © 1973 the Literary Estate of Vonda N. McIntyre. Reprinted by permission of Clarion West, the Literary Estate of Vonda N. McIntyre.

James Tiptree, Jr., "The Girl Who Was Plugged In," *New Dimensions III*, ed. Robert Silverberg (New York: New American Library, 1973), 51–84. Copyright © 1973 by James Tiptree, Jr., © 2001 by Jeffrey D. Smith. Reprinted in *Her Smoke Rose Up Forever*, reprinted here by permission of the author's estate and Virginia Kidd Literary Agency, Inc.

Pamela Sargent, "If Ever I Should Leave You," *Starshadows* (New York: Ace, 1977), 162–77. First published (with unauthorized alterations) in *Worlds of If* 22.3 (January–February 1974): 113–23. Copyright © 1974 by Universal Publishing and Distributing Corp., copyright © 1977 by the author. Reprinted by permission of Pamela Sargent and her agents, Richard Curtis Associates, Inc.

Doris Piserchia, "Pale Hands," *Orbit 15*, ed. Damon Knight (New York: Harper & Row, 1974), 28–40. Copyright © 1974 by Doris Piserchia. Reprinted by permission of the Estate of Doris Piserchia.

Ursula K. Le Guin, "The Day Before the Revolution," *The Wind's Twelve Quarters* (New York: Harper & Row, 1975), 285–303. First published in *Galaxy* 35.8 (August 1974): 18–30. Copyright © 1974 by Ursula K. Le Guin. Reprinted by permission of Curtis Brown, Ltd.

Eleanor Arnason, "The Warlord of Saturn's Moons," *New Worlds 6*, ed. Charles Platt and Hilary Bailey (New York: Avon, 1974), 109–18. Copyright © 1974 by Eleanor Arnason. Reprinted by permission of the author.

Marta Randall, "A Scarab in the City of Time," *New Dimensions Science Fiction 5*, ed. Robert Silverberg (New York: Harper & Row, 1975), 35–42. Copyright © 1975 by Marta Randall. Reprinted by permission of the author.

Kathleen M. Sidney, "The Anthropologist," *Orbit 17*, ed. Damon Knight (Harper & Row, 1975), 4–23.

Gayle N. Netzer, "Hey, Lilith!" *The Witch and the Chameleon 5/6* (1976): 1–2.

Raccoona Sheldon, "The Screwfly Solution," *Analog Science Fiction/Science Fact* 97.6 (June 1977): 54–59. Copyright © 1977 by Alice B. Sheldon, © 2005 by Jeffrey D. Smith. Used by permission of Jeffrey D. Smith and the Virginia Kidd Agency, Inc.

Elinor Busby, "Time to Kill," *Amazing Stories* 51.1 (October 1977): 89–91. Copyright © 1977 by Elinor Busby. Reprinted by permission of the author and her daughter, Michele Rowley.

M. Lucie Chin, "The Best Is Yet to Be," *Galileo* 1.6 (January 1978): 46–55. Copyright © 1978 by M. Lucie Chin. Reprinted by permission of the author.

Joan D. Vinge, "View from a Height," *Analog Science Fiction/Science Fact* 98.6 (June 1978): 12–28. Copyright © 1978 by Joan D. Vinge. Reprinted by permission of the author and the author's agents, Writers House LLC.

Cynthia Felice, "No One Said Forever," *Millennial Women*, ed. Virginia Kidd (New York: Delacorte Press, 1978), 5–20. Copyright © 1978 by Cynthia Felice. Reprinted by permission of the author.

C. J. Cherryh, "Cassandra," *The Magazine of Fantasy and Science Fiction* 55.4 (October 1978): 41–48. Copyright © 1978 by C. J. Cherryh. Reprinted by permission of the author.

Lisa Tuttle, "Wives," *The Magazine of Fantasy and Science Fiction* 57.6 (December 1979): 6–14. Copyright © 1979 by Lisa Tuttle. Reprinted by permission of the author.

Connie Willis, "Daisy, in the Sun," *Galileo* 2.3 (November 1979): 72–78. Copyright © 1979 by Connie Willis. Reprinted by permission of The Lotts Agency, Ltd.

This
book is set in 10.125
Georgia Pro, a face designed for
digital composition by Matthew Carter
and rendered by Tom Richner in 1993 for
the Microsoft Corporation; it was initially created specifically for use and readability on computer
screens. (The font's name is a reference to a tabloid
headline, "Alien heads found in Georgia.") Adobe Gar-
amond Pro Italic and Alternate Gothic No. 2 are used as
display fonts. The paper is cream-white opaque stock with
an eggshell finish and exceeds the requirements for per-
manence of the American National Standards Institute.

The binding board is covered in Brillianta, a woven rayon
cloth made by Van Heek–Scholco Textielfabrieken,
Holland. Composition by Gopa & Ted2, Inc.
Printing and binding by Sheridan Books,
Inc., in Chelsea, MI. Jacket printing by
Phoenix Color Corp., in Hag-
erstown, MD.